ARKHAM HORROR

It is the height of the Roaring Twenties – a fresh enthusiasm for the arts, science, and exploration of the past have opened doors to a wider world, and beyond…

And yet, a dark shadow grows over the town of Arkham. Alien entities known as Ancient Ones lurk in the emptiness beyond space and time, writhing at the thresholds between worlds.

Occult rituals must be stopped and alien creatures destroyed before the Ancient Ones make our world their ruined dominion.

Only a handful of brave souls with inquisitive minds and the will to act stand against the horrors threatening to tear this world apart.

Will they prevail?

ALSO AVAILABLE

ARKHAM HORROR™

DARK ORIGINS

❧ THE COLLECTED NOVELLAS VOLUME 1 ❧

DAVE GROSS
GRAEME DAVIS
RICHARD LEE BYERS
CHRIS A JACKSON

ACONYTE®

This collection first published by Aconyte Books in 2021

ISBN 978 1 83908 118 7

Ebook ISBN 978 1 83908 119 4

Cover art by Anders Finér

Distributed in North America by Simon & Schuster Inc, New York, USA

Printed in the United States of America

9 8 7 6 5 4 3 2 1

ACONYTE BOOKS

An imprint of Asmodee Entertainment Ltd

Mercury House, Shipstones Business Centre

North Gate, Nottingham NG7 7FN, UK

aconytebooks.com // twitter.com/aconytebooks

CONTENTS

HOUR OF THE HUNTRESS

DAVE GROSS

CHAPTER 1

The whistle's shriek yanked her out of an asylum nightmare. A simultaneous jolt threatened to fling her to the floor before she caught the armrest. For an interminable instant, she wasn't sure whether she was Izzie, locked in an unwanted steam bath, or Jenny, a passenger on a slowing train.

"Last stop!" the conductor called. "Arkham, Massachusetts."

Jenny sat upright. Heart pounding, she measured her breaths to calm herself. "Hold on, Izzie," she muttered. "I'm coming."

Steam washed past the car windows. The brakes squealed, and the engine ceased huffing. The other passengers, all men, had already risen from their seats. In their brown suits and wire-framed cheaters, they looked like bankers returning from Boston appointments.

None had tried striking up a conversation during the journey. Under the circumstances, Jenny considered that a relief. Still, it made her wonder just how rumpled she must appear. As the only woman in the car, she had expected some attention. In Paris, Jenny hadn't been able to walk from her flat to the café without parrying three flirtations and a proposition.

9

Izzie's letters had spilled out of the literary journal as Jenny dozed. The journal lay on her lap, opened to the last page of Hemingway's "Hills Like White Elephants." On the day she left Paris, she'd searched half a dozen shops to see what the editor had done with Ernest's latest. She finally bought a copy at Shakespeare and Company along with a few packages of Gauloises.

As Jenny gathered the fallen pages of Izzie's letters, she glimpsed an unsettling passage:

… prints in the woods. I mean, it was a man in a dark cloak! He was just standing there watching me while those dreadful screams went on and on and…

Jenny folded the letter. It was insane.

Of course, the doctors had said the same of Izzie when they committed her.

After months of visiting her sister in the sanitarium, Jenny had escaped her family's drama to live with their aunt in Paris. Izzie made her own escape much later, with her psychiatrists' tentative approval. Despite her guilt at abandoning Izzie, Jenny wrote to her. After months of wounded silence, Izzie began to respond. Gradually, they became confidantes once more, as they had been as girls. Just as Jenny had begun to think the worst was past, the weird events described in Izzie's recent letters dashed Jenny's hopes.

The train came to a halt. Jenny tucked the last page in with the rest of the letters and shoved the magazine back into her handbag.

When the station agent opened the door, the men rushed out. Jenny called after them, "You fellows really know how to shake a girl's confidence!"

No one looked back. That was fine. When Jenny felt low, a little sass always cheered her, even when it went unappreciated.

The men dashed across the platform to elbow each other at the taxi stand. The sun had set, and the station's electric lights lent their faces an anxious pallor.

"What's gotten into them?" Jenny asked herself. If anyone had cause for haste, it was she. Unfortunately, she had no clear idea where to find the hotel room she'd reserved from Boston. Worse, she had no idea where Izzie was staying in Arkham. The return address had read only "General Delivery."

Jenny stepped down from the train. The gray-haired station agent offered his hand. With the other, he touched the brim of his cap and bowed, cautious of a bad back. "Miss."

Jenny favored him with a smile. Despite her fellow passengers, it appeared courtesy was not quite extinct in Arkham.

A breeze scattered leaves across the platform. Maple red and oak yellow skittered about her feet, along with a crumpled orange handbill. Jenny retrieved the flyer and held it up to the light.

ARKHAM HARVEST FESTIVAL
October 22–30
Independence Square
Parade & Pageant
Harvest King & Queen
Formal Ball
Hay Rides
Harvest Festival Feast
Wholesome Fun for the Whole Family
Volunteers contact the chairwoman, Mrs Winthrop Olmstead

The text was banal enough, but Jenny gasped at the accompanying image. It was a crude depiction of a man's face, rough as though carved into a long-eroded stone. The man's hair and beard appeared braided, but Jenny knew that what seemed like braids in this crude print were willow fronds. She'd seen the same image on a medallion she owned, one she had paid a Marseillais jeweler to duplicate for Izzie. They were two of a kind and – as far as Jenny knew – only two.

Jenny's hand went to her throat, only to touch her traveling pearls. Before she could panic, she remembered she had secured the medallion in her luggage. In one of her letters, Izzie had asked whether she still wore it, so Jenny had brought it along as a lucky charm. Perhaps it had been lucky, for its appearance on the flyer confirmed Izzie was in Arkham.

"I said, come for the festival, miss?" asked the old station agent.

"Oh!" Jenny lost the flyer to a gust of wind. "No, I've come to, ah, visit my sister." She stopped herself from saying "find my sister."

Behind the station agent, a truck pulled away from the taxi stand, luggage heaped in the bed. Jenny recognized her "gBe"-monogrammed luggage pasted with stamps from across Europe, the Near East, and North Africa.

"Is that–?" said Jenny.

"Don't worry, miss. Bill Washington's taking those to the hotel. All you need is a…" There were no more taxis waiting in the queue. The station agent checked his watch and frowned. "I'm sure another will be along any time." He shuffled back to his office.

The man's dubious tone did little to reassure Jenny. She wondered just how long she would have to wait. The only other person remaining on the platform was a strapping young lad in oily coveralls. He'd unloaded a sidecar from the train and was attaching it to a red motorcycle. She couldn't see his face, but he had shoulders to make a rugby player envious. A plume of blue smoke rose above his newsboy cap.

Another gust of wind blew across the platform. Jenny rubbed her arms, wishing she'd worn a sweater. From somewhere in the surrounding dark, she heard a piteous cry. At first it sounded human, but when it came again she decided it must be an animal, perhaps a lamb. Jenny considered what the Harvest Festival feast meant for livestock.

"Good luck escaping the supper table, little fellow."

As the train engine began its slow chuff to depart, the mechanic moved to the motorcycle's other side. Jenny glimpsed a huge wrench clenched in a fist that was all knuckles and sinew. The light in the station agent's office went out. A moment later, so did the lights on the platform.

"Hey, Charley!" the mechanic shouted in a high voice. "I'm working here!"

"Sorry, Lonnie." The platform light came back on. A moment later, Charley emerged from the office, locked the door, and began to walk away.

"Excuse me!" called Jenny. "Where are you going?"

"Sorry, miss. That was the last train, so I'm off duty."

"You don't expect me to wait alone for a taxi, do you?"

The old man said, "Lonnie will keep an eye on you until another taxi comes 'round. Won't you, Lonnie?"

The big wrench rose up from behind the motorcycle and waved assurance.

Jenny didn't like it, but she saw little alternative than to make the sort of fuss she considered beneath her dignity. Besides, it wasn't as though she couldn't take care of herself if this Lonnie proved frisky.

That's what she liked to tell herself, anyway.

Jenny fished the cigarette case out of her handbag and fumbled with the holder. After another gust of wind, she gave up struggling with a light. As she stuffed it all back in her handbag, she noticed a figure standing just beyond the station's far corner.

Cloaked in shadow, the figure looked taller and straighter than Charley. Besides, Jenny had seen the station agent walk off in the opposite direction.

"Who's there?" She left her hand in the bag, hoping a would-be masher would think she had a derringer.

The man stepped forward. There was something strange about the way he moved. Only his shoulder and one leg came into the light. The shadows pooled beneath his coat, and the leg looked crooked. One could almost imagine a hoof where his foot should be.

Jenny recalled the e e cummings poem about spring with its goat-footed balloon man. Unlike the whistling faun in the poem, the figure on the platform remained silent. Lines from Izzie's letter came to mind next: *… it was a* man *in a dark cloak! He was just standing there watching me…* Cold dread oozed down Jenny's spine.

Showing fear only encouraged bad men, so Jenny pushed her bluff. Forming a pistol with her fingers, she pointed the bag at the stranger. "Show yourself."

It was difficult to look menacing without removing the gun that wasn't in her handbag. For a long, cool moment, the figure stood still.

Then he took a step forward.

"I'm warning you," said Jenny. She kept the warble out of her voice, but it stuck in her throat like a pigeon trapped in the chimney.

The stranger took another step.

A hand fell on Jenny's shoulder. She whirled around, and the pigeon escaped. "Aaah!"

A big wrench clattered to the platform floor. Lonnie shrieked back, higher and longer than Jenny. The cigar bounced down the front of the greasy coveralls and sparked on the platform floor. Jenny got her first good look at the mechanic.

Lonnie wasn't a big strapping lad after all. She was a big strapping lass. The revelation did nothing to diminish the threat of her big fist quivering beside her freckled cheek, poised to strike.

"Sorry!" both women shouted.

"I didn't mean to startle you, miss." Lonnie lowered her fist. Her cheeks flushed – whether from excitement or embarrassment, Jenny couldn't tell.

"There's a man," said Jenny. She pointed to where he had been, but there was no one there. "Oh, he's gone."

"Ain't that always the story?" Lonnie retrieved her cigar. As she rose, her lopsided grin exposed a missing eyetooth.

Jenny sighed, tension pouring out of her trembling arms. She flailed for a moment before extricating the "gun" from her handbag. "That kind of story I can handle," she said. "It's just that with this wind and the dark and the breeze and the leaves…"

"Yeah. Spooky." Lonnie looked down at her. The mechanic stood a good six feet tall. Her work shirt fit tight over cannonball biceps. When she grinned, the muscles on her neck stood out. "Listen, I don't mind sticking around, but I don't think there's going to be another cab. You ain't the only one in Arkham's got the heebie-jeebies these days."

"Oh?" said Jenny. "Do tell."

"I guess it's old hat to those from the big city, but in a small town like Arkham, people get shook up when young girls go missing."

Jenny clenched a fist to stifle the shakes. She couldn't tell whether it was fear or rage that made her tremble.

"'Girls', plural?" said Jenny. "How long has this been going on?"

"Since the end of summer, I guess."

Jenny estimated intercontinental postal delivery times. Izzie couldn't have been a victim of the current wave of kidnappings – unless she had been its first victim. She considered lightening the mood by paraphrasing Wilde's adage that losing more than one looks like carelessness. She decided it was not the moment for a joke.

"Listen, Miss…?" said Lonnie.

"Barnes."

"Lonnie Ritter; Ritter's Plumbing and Motor Shop. Wait, I got a card." She dug inside the bib pocket of her overalls and produced a rectangle of dingy paper. She brushed it off with the heel of her hand but passed it to Jenny when it became obvious she was only making it dirtier.

"Say, Lonnie," said Jenny, dropping the card into her bag. "How would you like to earn a fare?"

"Yeah?" Lonnie tapped ash off her cigar and looked Jenny's French dress up and down. "A fancy lady like you isn't afraid to ride in a sidecar?"

"I'll drive the bike myself as long as you tell me the way to the Continental Hotel."

"No way! Papa ordered this rig special. Anybody gets a scratch on the Big Chief, he'd murder 'im. And me, too! Hop in."

Jenny stepped into the sidecar, avoiding the big toolbox Lonnie had set on the floor. Lonnie straddled the bike and pulled down the brim of her cap. "I oughta have goggles," she sighed. "With an aviator's cap, I'd look just like Amelia Earhart."

"Who's she?"

"Who's Amelia Earhart?! Why, she's only the pilot of *The Canary*, which set a new altitude record for women! I shook her hand in Boston."

Jenny directed a pointed glance at Lonnie's heroic arms. "And has Miss Earhart regained the use of that hand?"

"Ha!" Lonnie gripped the handles. She started the engine on the second kick. With a roar, the bike flew off the platform and onto the street. Lonnie spat out her cigar. Jenny held onto her hat.

As they rounded the first corner, the sidecar rose a foot off the ground. "What do you weigh?" yelled Lonnie. "Ninety pounds sopping wet?"

Jenny made an effort to smile as if she'd received a compliment, but she felt her stomach lurch. She gripped the safety bar and hoped it wasn't obvious she was hanging on for dear life.

They drove past several factories and warehouses, dark but for lonely beacons at the guard stations. Black shadows pooled beneath loading docks and water towers. The only building still filled with lighted offices was labeled "Arkham Advertiser" in big white letters. Jenny smelled ink. She heard the hum and clatter of a printing press.

The industrial buildings gave way to residential blocks. Clotheslines crisscrossed the dark alleys between brick tenements. Jenny tried not to imagine they were enormous spider webs. As Lonnie drove past a row of storefronts, the motorcycle headlight raked across a sign reading "Curiositie Shoppe."

"How quaint," said Jenny, but Lonnie didn't hear her over the roar of the Big Chief's engine.

They passed a sign marked "Miskatonic River" and ascended a

raised bridge. To either side, the ripples of dark currents reflected light from the waterfront streetlamps.

South of the river, Lonnie took the next turn a little slower – a courtesy that saved their lives.

A horned figure rose shrieking before them. Lonnie squeezed the brakes so hard the rear wheel rose up along with the sidecar. The rig swung around, forcing Jenny face-to-face with the interloper.

"Blaaaah!" Toothy jaws gaped at Jenny, unleashing a hellish stench.

"What the devil?" bellowed Lonnie.

"Naaaah!" blatted the goat. Its coat was black except for a rusty red patch around one eye and horn. A rope hung from its neck, the frayed end wet with saliva.

Jenny recoiled from the animal's barnyard pong. Its muzzle followed her into the sidecar, dipping down to forage. She rescued her handbag and stepped up onto the seat. The goat nipped at the toes of her Mary Janes. She kicked, not too hard for fear of angering the beast. "Shoo! Get away, you cad!"

Lonnie guffawed. "Is that how you deal with mashers in the city?"

"This isn't exactly the sort I'm used to meeting in Paris."

"Paris? Ooh la la!"

At first, Jenny couldn't tell whether Lonnie's tone was admiring or mocking. One look at the big woman's gap-toothed grin convinced Jenny of her sincerity.

Jenny hopped out of the sidecar. "On second thought, he's not as hairy as a few Frenchmen I've met."

The women stood for a moment, allowing the goat to sniff around in the sidecar while Lonnie recovered from her latest bout of laughter. It was an infectious sound, but Jenny found herself strangely immune. She wondered how close Izzie was. If Jenny called out her name, would she hear?

Jenny looked out at the piers jutting into the river beyond the waterfront street. Her first impression was that they wouldn't have seemed out of place in one of the small towns along the Seine. Then she noted a garish logo on the side of a cartage company and another on the petroleum station next door. Wherever she saw signs of progress in this American town, they came in the form of brash advertisements. Where marketing must leave its print, she preferred to see it rendered in art nouveau.

A bill pasted to a nearby streetlamp caught her eye. The notice featured the sun-bleached and rain-stained image of a girl with light braids and a gingham dress. "MISSING: ANGELA HOUSTON," read the title. Below, in smaller print, the bill read, "IF SEEN, CALL SHERIFF'S DEPARTMENT."

The sound of an approaching automobile engine snapped Jenny out of her reverie. A sheriff's car skidded to a halt on the other side of the goat. A uniformed young man popped out. He fumbled with his deputy's cap before tossing it on the front seat. "Lonnie! Are you all right?"

"Of course I am, Gal," she said. "Got your goat."

"He's not my goat." The deputy's sigh suggested he'd heard that joke before. "Second time this week that rascal's escaped Schrader's farm." Gal edged closer, reaching out for the severed tether. Noticing Jenny, his hand went up to doff the cap he was no longer wearing. "Evening, miss. Excuse me while I – oof!"

The goat butted him in the belly. Gal doubled over. He stood, color rising to his cheeks. Jenny noted with relief that the young man appeared unpunctured.

Gal shook a fist at the goat. "Why, you rotten, ornery..." With an abashed glance at Jenny, he left the rest unspoken.

"That's telling him, Gal!" Lonnie threw an arm around the animal's hind legs, holding him from the side to avoid a kick. "Hurry, get his front legs!"

Gal caught the goat's legs and neck, pressing his head against the animal's neck to avoid the horns. Together they heaved the beast off his hooves and shoved him into the back seat of the sheriff's car. Lonnie slammed the door shut. The goat bleated a complaint and stuck its head over the front seat.

"Oh, no, you don't!" Gal dove in to rescue his cap. With a sigh of relief, he turned to the women. "Thanks, Lonnie."

"You know I don't mind looking after you, Gal," she said. "Why, Miss Barnes, would you believe that when we were in grade school–"

"Lonnie, don't."

Lonnie didn't skip a beat. "–Galeas Morgan here was the smallest boy in our class. Sometimes the other boys would catch him after arithmetic–"

"Lonnie," Gal pleaded. His deep voice reminded Jenny of a baritone she'd met at the Teatro alla Scala. He stood an inch taller than Lonnie, and he was so lean Jenny guessed he skipped meals.

Jenny thought she might need a friendly sheriff's deputy in her search for Izzie. It would be best if she got off on the right foot with this one. "Whatever size he was as a boy," said Jenny, "I think we can all agree he's grown admirably. Thank you for your help, Deputy Morgan."

Gal's eyes radiated gratitude.

Lonnie shrugged, threw a leg over the motorcycle, and kicked it back to life. "Better get moving."

Gal put on his cap and touched the brim. "Enjoy the Harvest Festival, Miss–?"

"Barnes."

"Say, Miss Barnes, you haven't happened to have seen a black or green truck tonight, have you?"

"I've come straight from the train station," she said. She considered mentioning the strange figure on the platform. She decided it would be better not to appear to be a nervous Nellie. Still, curiosity got the better of her. "Why do you ask?"

Gal began to reply, but a tearing sound from the sheriff's car drew his attention. The goat had its teeth in the upholstery.

"Hey, knock it off, you devil!" Gal rushed back to the car.

"Come on, Miss Barnes," said Lonnie. "Papa worries if I'm out too late."

Stifling her laughter at Gal's ridiculous struggle against the goat she now thought of as "Devil", Jenny returned to the sidecar.

"Good luck, Gal!" Lonnie cried as they zoomed away.

Jenny shouted over the motor's roar, "Why did he ask about a truck?"

Lonnie's grin faded. "Somebody saw one near the last disappearance. Sheriff Engle has everybody on the lookout."

They drove along the waterfront until Lonnie turned the bike toward the heart of the sleepy town. She slowed as they approached a colonial-style house with a wide veranda on the ground floor. Yellow light flickered through a pair of garret windows with arched tops. The half-drawn shade in one lent the edifice a snooty air as it peered down at the circular driveway. A sign in the round garden read "The Continental Hotel."

The doorman narrowed his eyes at the motorcycle as gravel

crunched under the tires. Then he noticed Jenny's pearls and hastened forward.

As she stepped out, Jenny remarked, "I didn't notice a ring on Gal's finger."

"What?"

"I mean, he's an eligible bachelor, isn't he?"

Lonnie's eyebrows formed a comical pair of arches. "You don't mean – I mean, a lady like you wouldn't be interested in a fella like–"

Jenny smiled, pleased that Lonnie rose to the bait. Jenny had a knack for identifying affection disguised as bullying. It had been her own modus operandi as a girl. "It just seems strange," she said, "a good-looking young man like that without a wife or at least a fiancée. Perhaps a sweetheart?"

"Ha!" Lonnie slapped her cap against her thigh. "Gal's been too busy looking after his ma and sisters. Ever since his papa and his older brothers… you know."

"The war," Jenny nodded, regretting the turn the conversation had taken. It had been much worse in Europe, but she knew many in the States who had lost someone in the Great War. She handed Lonnie five dollars. "Thanks for the ride."

Lonnie gawped at the bill. "Miss Barnes, it's too much."

"No more 'Miss Barnes' from you." Jenny tucked the bill into Lonnie's overall pocket. "My friends call me Jenny."

CHAPTER 2

After unpacking and freshening up, Jenny donned a glittering black Chanel evening frock. She inspected herself in the mirror and concluded it was a bit formal. She exchanged it for an acid-green moiré dress by Paquin. It was no more subtle than the Chanel, but it was far more frivolous. She brushed her lashes with mascara and her cheeks with rouge. She finished with lipstick and blew herself a kiss in the mirror.

She exchanged her handbag for a beaded pochette. She pulled the matching gloves up past her elbows. As she transferred the necessities from her handbag, she spied the Green Man medallion lying beside Izzie's letters on the bed.

She picked it up, surprised as always at its weight. The circular disc was a little more than two inches in diameter and about a quarter-inch thick. Verdigris obscured the finer details, but the highest edges gleamed deep bronze.

On one side was the image of a man's face, the willow fronds of his hair and beard lifted as if in a strong wind. His features seemed vaguely Mediterranean. His eyes yearned upward, mouth open as if singing – or screaming.

The green patina covered more of the opposite side. Jenny could make out the pattern of willow fronds around the border. Within the fronds appeared concentric circles or a continuous spiral. Jenny could never decide which. She studied the obscured pattern, trying to discern the minuscule shapes that formed its lines, following them deeper toward the center. She grew dizzy and averted her eyes.

Jenny had found the medallion at an archaeological dig she'd funded near Turin. Poor management and labor relations, exacerbated by political turmoil, resulted in a complete fiasco. At least Jenny had collected a souvenir for her trouble, along with a few anecdotes to thrill her fellow expats in Paris. Besides, she liked the Green Man iconography, one of the few ways in which her tastes intersected with her father's obsession with Arthurian lore. She sent Izzie a copy, along with an account of her disastrous investment.

Jenny began to slip the medallion into her pochette but stopped. The color wasn't a perfect match, but it didn't clash with the Paquin, so she fastened it around her neck. She hid Izzie's letters beneath some clothes in the dresser.

Izzie had mentioned moving out of a boarding house in spring, but not the address. Jenny had only a few names of friends and places. Of those, there was only one she could visit so late in the evening. At least it was one of the more interesting-sounding locations.

Jenny donned her coat and swept out of the room.

In the lobby, Jenny found the concierge standing motionless behind an oak-paneled counter. In his old-fashioned suit and with his wavy white hair parted in the middle, he might have been mistaken for a painting of a Puritan. All he lacked, in Jenny's opinion, was a wide-brimmed hat with a big brass buckle.

"Excuse me," said Jenny. "Could you tell me where to find the Tick-Tock Club?"

The man's head swiveled on a neck barely thicker than a pencil. Jenny imagined frost forming over his eyeballs. "I'm sure I don't know, miss. While you might be used to European customs, Prohibition is still the law of the land in the United States of America."

Obviously, he knew the place she was talking about. In Paris, there was always a way to smooth things over with a supercilious functionary. Jenny lay a gloved hand on the counter, spreading her fingers to reveal the color of money beneath them.

The frost expanded across the concierge's face.

Jenny decided to try her luck with a taxi driver, if she could find one. As she passed the young doorman, he whispered, "You'll find the Tick-Tock two blocks that way, miss, around the corner from the watchmaker and down the stairs."

"Naturally." Jenny slipped him the bill she'd offered the concierge. "Is there a password?"

"I'm told it's always midnight at the Tick-Tock." Before Jenny could ask him to explain, he added, "You'll need an escort, miss. Unaccompanied women are not admitted."

"Oh, I'm never unaccompanied, not even when I'm completely alone." Jenny walked off, leaving the doorman to puzzle over her meaning as she puzzled over his. She enjoyed trading in enigma. It was a fair substitute for flirting when no suitable partner was readily available.

Half a block from the hotel, Jenny felt glad she'd brought her coat. She could feel the damp from the river a few blocks away. Only one car drove past during her walk, reminding her just how quiet the rest of the town seemed. In Paris, even in the dead of night, one could always hear distant music, laughter, or the sounds of lovemaking.

As she rounded the corner from the watch shop, Jenny found three taxicabs lined up at the curb, the drivers standing together and smoking. They started at the sound of her footsteps. A cigarette fell from one cabbie's lips.

"So, this is where you've been hiding," Jenny said.

Before anyone could offer her a ride, Jenny turned to descend the nearby stairs. She glanced back when she heard the cabbie grumbling. He fetched his discarded butt and put it back to his lips.

"Serves you right," muttered Jenny, annoyed to find them here when she'd wanted a taxi at the train station. On the other hand, her journey with Lonnie had been much more exhilarating.

A talented artist had painted a jaunty clock on the door. Its oval face and curved arms suggested the swift passing of time.

"Must be fun in there." Jenny heard faint music from somewhere inside. When she opened the door, the sound grew louder. Before her lay a hallway with three doors marked as service entrances; signs indicated the watch shop, a florist, and a cobbler.

A grandfather clock stood at the far end. Jenny approached the clock. She noted the hands showed the time as 8:22, which she guessed was about right.

"It's always midnight at the Tick-Tock." Jenny smiled at the clue. Standing on tiptoe, she opened the glass front and advanced the minute hand, carrying the hour along until both pointed at the twelve. Rather than a succession of chimes, she heard a metallic *click*. As the hands rewound themselves to the correct time, the clock swung outward.

Beyond lay an antechamber draped in burgundy velvet. A burly man stood up from a stool, a folded newspaper in one hand, the stub of a pencil in the other. He frowned to see she was alone.

"No unaccompanied dames," he said, sounding exactly as Jenny had always imagined one of Al Capone's Chicago gangsters might. "Scram, Sheba."

"But my escort is right here." Jenny produced a ten-dollar bill from her pochette. "Allow me to introduce Mr Jackson."

The big man glowered. For a second Jenny imagined he might throw her over his shoulder and deposit her on the sidewalk. How the cabbies would howl!

Instead, the bouncer snatched the bill and jerked a thumb over his shoulder. "G'wan in."

Jenny glanced at his newspaper as she walked past. "Cur."

"What's that?" he growled.

She looked back over her shoulder. "Fourteen down. Three letters for 'mongrel.'"

The bouncer peered at the crossword. "Oh, yeah." He rubbed out "dog" and scribbled in the correct answer.

Jenny stepped into a smoky room. Clock faces adorned every foot of wall space, each in a different style. Some had hands like a churchyard fence, others cartoon arms with big white gloves for hands. The hours appeared as Roman or Arabic numerals, pairs of dice, or numbers drawn by one of Mucha's countless imitators. Every clock indicated a different time.

Every face tells a different lie.

Jenny winced at the tacky floor and wrinkled her nose at the smell of cheap tobacco, but her ears perked up at the music. The writhing clarinet melody was enough to forgive the speakeasy's other deficiencies.

An oak bar stretched across the right wall, its stools vacant. Half-empty glasses filled fifteen or so little tables curling around a small dance floor, where the customers wiggled with more enthusiasm than grace. Jenny recognized a little Charleston, a little Turkey Trot, and a lot of groping.

Past the dancers, Jenny spied the six-piece jazz band on a tiny wedge of a stage. The pianist appeared to be their leader, but the clarinetist was standing for his solo. His houndstooth suit was tight in the shoulders and loose everywhere else. He closed his eyes as his dark brown fingers danced along the keys.

Jenny waved off the girl at the coat check and turned back to enjoy the music until the solo ended. Before the dancers could fill the seats, she claimed an empty bar stool. She pretended not to notice the curious stares she drew as the only single woman in the place. She slid a dollar bill across the bar. Like a ghost in the mirror, the bartender materialized.

"What's your pleasure, miss?" He spoke with a warm Irish lilt.

"What sort of cognac do you have?"

"Bourbon, rye, rum, and gin." His tone cooled.

Jenny realized her mistake. Prohibition aside, Arkham was a far cry from Paris or even Boston. Besides, she ought to acknowledge her return to the United States with a distinctly American drink. "I don't suppose you can build a perfect Manhattan."

"Rye or bourbon?"

"Bourbon, if you please."

The band struck up another song as the bartender created her drink. Jenny was heartened to see him produce French vermouth and Angostura bitters from beneath the bar. He shook the cocktail and strained it into a martini glass. She didn't complain when he garnished it with a candied cherry instead of a lemon twist.

The bartender watched as she took a sip. The drink was a trifle sweeter than she was used to, but she liked it. She raised her glass in salute, and he nodded. It wasn't much of a relationship, but she hoped it would support a few questions.

"I don't look familiar to you, do I?" she asked.

He lifted an eyebrow.

She removed her hat. "Imagine my hair is lighter and curled. Also, I'm two years younger."

He squinted, a puzzled frown on his lips.

"And my name is Isabelle." No one but Jenny called her sister Izzie. Isabelle preferred her given name, while Jenny couldn't stand hers.

The barman's frown became an *O* of comprehension. "Your sister, is it?"

"Isabelle Barnes. She mentioned this place in her letters. Have you seen her lately?"

Rather than answer, he glanced at a plain round clock above the entrance, which Jenny guessed was the one that indicated the actual time: 8:43. Right in the middle of the band's song, he reached up to ring a brass bell in a distinctive three-two-three pattern. "Last call!"

A wave of men crashed against the bar as the ladies queued up at the entrance to the powder room. Jenny shot the bartender an inquiring look, but he was busy pouring drinks and settling tabs.

"I guess I should have warmed him up better," Jenny grumbled.

"You can warm me up, doll."

Jenny turned to see a man standing too close. He was only a little taller standing than she was sitting on the stool. He was clean-shaven with sharp features that might have been passably handsome except for the sneer of his thin lips. He was the only man in the place wearing his hat, a felt fedora that matched his blue suit and tie. Tufts of red hair stuck out on either side.

"Sure," said Jenny. "Got a match?"

He reached into a pocket before getting the joke. "Cute," he said. "And inquisitive, I'm guessing." Jenny noticed the lump of a pistol under each of his arms. He and the barkeep exchanged nods.

Jenny realized the bartender must have summoned this charming character to check her out. He was much too small for a bouncer, so she guessed he was the owner – or an "associate", as the newspapers called rum runners. If she were to learn any information at the Tick-Tock, unfortunately, it appeared she would have to get it from this man. She tried a new tack.

"I'm Jenny Barnes." She offered her hand.

The man's hands were small, even for a short fellow. They glistened, too. Jenny was glad she'd worn her gloves. "Dainty Donohue," he said. His green eyes fixed on hers, daring her to laugh at the nickname. With a big friend at her side, she might have cut him down shorter still, but she hadn't come to the Tick-Tock to trade barbs with this leprechaun.

"Mr Donohue, I was just asking your bartender whether he knows my sister, Isabelle."

"Isabelle?" Donohue shrugged, but he flinched at her name.

Jenny offered up the only other relevant clue from Izzie's letters. "She might have been here with someone named Auggie."

"So, your sister is that dip's girl?" Donohue took a seat.

"She was with a drunkard?" said Jenny.

"Naw, not a dipsomaniac," said Donohue. He reached for her clutch as if to slip his fingers inside. "He takes a dip," he said. "Like so."

Jenny moved the handbag out of his reach. "Izzie wouldn't date a common pickpocket."

Even as she said the words, she knew she was wrong. Izzie had no discrimination when it came to men. She'd never had.

"If it's any consolation, he wasn't all that common. He was a real swell, well heeled. I figure he dipped for thrills," said Donohue. "Had a knack, too. He fleeced the flock for weeks before we caught wise."

"What did you do with him?" Jenny flinched as a woman brushed past, giggling at something her date had said. "What happened to Izzie?"

"Don't get sore." Dainty patted her shoulder. Jenny shuddered at his moist touch. "We shook out his pockets and gave him the bounce. Nobody touched his squeeze. Ain't her fault she's dizzy for a bad egg."

Jenny breathed a sigh of relief. "Where can I find this Auggie now?"

Rather than answer, Donohue accepted the cash box from the bartender and began counting. "Give us a couple of those special cocktails, Pat. Then you can call it a night."

"You got it, Dainty." The bartender began mixing a couple of drinks beneath the counter.

Donohue turned back to Jenny. "Say, I like that accent of yours. Where's it from?"

"Charm school." While she tended to adopt the local dialect in other languages, her mid-Atlantic diction returned whenever she spoke English. In any event, she refused to be distracted. "Mr Donohue, I need to find my sister. At least tell me this Auggie's last name."

Donohue paused in his count. "Never knew it. Sixty, seventy…

Besides, he's blown. I'm bored with him. I wanna know more about you."

"If you don't mind, Mr Donohue–"

"Ninety-five, one hundred… Call me Dainty. All the gals do."

"Listen, Dainty, I haven't seen my sister in years. Now she's in trouble, and I've come back from Paris to help in any way–"

As the last patrons pushed through the exit, the band concluded its set with an embarrassing squeal from the clarinet.

"Wrap it up, you clowns," yelled Dainty. "And don't come back until Reggie remembers how to play that licorice stick."

The musicians chuckled in the self-deprecating manner of employees used to mistreatment – all except the clarinetist. He stared at Jenny, his expression grim.

Pat set a couple of drinks on the bar, one beside Dainty, the other next to Jenny. They were some sort of whiskey cocktail with beads of citrus oil on the surface. Jenny glanced at Reggie, the clarinet player. His gaze flicked down at her drink. Almost imperceptibly, he shook his head.

Donohue finished counting. He compared his tally against the slips of paper in the till and nodded. "G'night, Pat. Lock up on your way out."

Jenny didn't like the sound of that. Whatever Donohue had planned, she didn't expect it included answering her questions about Izzie.

"'Night, boss." Pat slunk away, avoiding Jenny's glare.

Donohue smiled, revealing a plentitude of teeth. He reached for Jenny's knee. "Now we can get to know each other."

Suppressing the impulse to slap his hand, Jenny looked toward the bandstand. Pat and Reggie exited through a servants' door. "Where are they going?"

As Donohue turned to look, Jenny switched their drinks. She sloshed a little of the cocktail on the bar. Donohue turned back before she could wipe it away.

"Don't worry about them. This place is full of nooks and crannies," said Donohue. "You could get lost back there. It's a real maze."

"You've never been to the Khan el-Khalili, have you?" Jenny had a feeling this man didn't even own a passport.

After a blank look, Donohue said, "Sure I have. All the time."

Donohue picked up the drink beside Jenny. Afraid he'd caught wise to her trick, she began formulating a plan involving knocking over the bar stools and making a run for the door. Rather than drink, however, Donohue handed the cocktail to Jenny. He raised his own glass in a toast. "To the Connell Collie."

"The Connell Collie!" Jenny agreed, choking back a laugh at Donohue's ignorance. He was all bluff, and that knowledge gave Jenny courage. She clinked her glass to his. Donohue watched as she tossed back her drink.

"Wow! My kind of dame!" He drained his glass.

Jenny fanned her face with a hand. "That giggle water comes on pretty strong."

Donohue blinked. Jenny imagined the manager of a speakeasy could hold his liquor, so whatever Pat dosed it with must have been strong.

"Too bad you sent Pat away," said Jenny. "I could use another."

"Yeah? Me, too," said Donohue. He hopped off the barstool, wobbled, and steadied himself. "Or maybe a glass of water."

"Water?" Jenny struck a tone of disbelief. "What kind of a man drinks water while he's making a gal a drink?"

As he rounded the bar, Donohue whirled, thrusting up a finger like a professor making a point. "Right you are." He slipped and grasped the bar's edge for support.

"Steady on, Dainty."

He struck the bar gate several times before realizing he had to pull it open. "Say, Pat must have mixed up…" He fixed Jenny with a look of comprehension. "Wait a min–"

He slumped behind the bar.

Jenny boosted herself onto the bar surface, spun around on her bottom, and hopped down beside Donohue. He babbled a few more syllables into a bubble of saliva that disappeared with a sad little pop.

"That's easy for you to say." Jenny went through his pockets for the keys. She raised them in triumph. "Aha!"

A muffled bang came from behind the servants' entrance. Jenny feared Pat had returned.

Donohue stirred. Jenny saw he was reaching under his jacket.

"Oh, no, you don't." She rolled him over and slipped a gleaming .45 automatic from its holster.

Donohue got a hand around her wrist, squeezing with surprising strength. She brought the pistol's butt down on his chin.

"Pat!" he shouted. He reached into the other side of his jacket.

"While I hate to pick on somebody smaller than me," said Jenny, "in your case I'll make an exception."

She cracked him on the forehead, but he kept struggling. It took her two more tries to still him. She held a finger under his nose. When she felt his breath, she heaved a sigh of relief.

She took his second pistol, twin to the first. The engraved nickel plating was beautiful, but Jenny liked the tapered grip even more. She'd fired big pistols before, but she'd found the grips too big for her hands. These fit perfectly.

Another sound from the back startled her. Jenny juggled the pistols, her clutch, and the keys. As she tried to hang onto just the pistols, she dropped everything on the floor. She winced at the clatter, but at least the guns didn't go off. She picked one up and braced it against the bar as the bandstand door began to open.

CHAPTER 3

As a man stepped out onto the stage, Jenny remembered to thumb off the safety. He saw her and raised his hands above the tailored shoulders of his houndstooth jacket.

"Don't shoot!" Despite his alarm, Reggie had the presence of mind to call out in a stage whisper.

Jenny lowered the pistol. "I thought you were Pat. Your name's Reggie, isn't it?"

Reggie nodded. "Pat locked up and went home."

"How did you get back in?"

"Bathroom window," he said. "I reckoned maybe I could distract Mr Donohue before... Well, I figured you'd want to get out of here."

Jenny gathered up her clutch, the keys, and the second pistol. "You came to my rescue."

"It looks like you rescued yourself," he said. "That's good, because I don't know if I could have stood up to Mr Donohue."

"Well, you're a hero in my book."

"We'd better get out of here. Say, are those Mr Donohue's guns?"

Jenny held a pistol over her shoulder and struck a pose. "I think they suit me better than him. Don't you agree?"

"You didn't…" Reggie peered uneasily at the bar.

"No, although he deserved it, the rat."

Reggie sighed in relief. "That would have been more trouble than I could have run from."

"You and me both," said Jenny. "Let's go."

Reggie started leading her back to the bathroom. She showed him the keys, and he took her to the back door instead. She locked up as Reggie collected his clarinet case. Together, they hastened down the street behind the speakeasy.

"A woman oughtn't to go into a place like that alone," said Reggie.

"I wasn't alone," said Jenny. "You were there, too."

"That's not what I meant, miss."

The manic humor that buoyed Jenny in moments of terror began to fade. "I have to find my sister. She mentioned the Tick-Tock Club. Dainty said she'd been there with somebody called Auggie."

Reggie nodded.

"You know him?"

"Not exactly."

"Do you know where he lives?"

"One night, he and his gal got into a big car. He might have told the driver to take them back to French Hill."

"What's that?"

He pointed eastward. "Across town. It's where the rich folk live."

"What else do you remember? An address? Did you see the woman with him? Did she look a bit like me?"

He rubbed the back of his neck. "Maybe a little. I can't remember."

"Think harder," said Jenny. "If it was Izzie – Isabelle Barnes – she's in trouble. Was she wearing a medallion like this one?"

Reggie peeked at the medallion, but only for an instant before looking away. "I'm sorry, miss. Mr Donohue's always warning us not to stare at the women in the club."

Her anger turned to embarrassment as Jenny realized Reggie's situation. He'd taken a risk by warning her about the Mickey Finn. She couldn't help thinking that Reggie would have a better time in Paris, where appreciation for talented musicians outweighed racial bigotry.

Sometimes, anyway.

They walked two empty blocks, the shuttered windows and shadowed doors punctuated by a yellow streetlamp at each corner.

They turned onto the street that led back to the hotel, and Reggie stopped. From across the street, the Continental's doorman stared at them.

"I'd better let you go here, miss."

"Jenny," she said. "Jenny Barnes."

Reggie's brow furrowed.

"What is it?"

"The Barn," he said. "I'd almost forgot about it."

Hope snagged Jenny's heart. "What do you mean?"

"Mr Donohue said Auggie mentioned some place called the Barn. Mr Donohue figured it was another speakeasy, but he'd never heard of it. He wanted to know where it was."

"Did he find it?"

He shook his head. "I don't know, Miss Barnes."

"Thank you, Reggie." She offered to shake his hand, but he recoiled when he saw the money in her palm.

"I didn't do nothing but show up after you'd taken care of yourself."

"You risked your neck to help me, and now it's cost you a job."

He considered the bills in her hand, tempted but proud. "It's too much."

"Share it with the band. They'll need a new job without you to carry them at the Tick-Tock."

"Well, that's true." Reggie indulged himself in a small, proud smile at the compliment. He accepted the money and slipped it into his pocket. "Thank you, Miss Barnes."

"Jenny!" she insisted.

He waited until she'd crossed the street before heading back the way they'd come.

By the time Jenny entered the lobby, the concierge had joined the doorman. He held a stack of folded flyers advertising the Harvest Festival. Unlike the one Jenny had seen at the train station, these featured the image of a young girl sitting in a pile of hay.

While the doorman had the decency to look ashamed for spying on her, the concierge stared at Jenny as though expecting an explanation. Before he could speak, she fired the first volley.

"Burn any good witches lately?"

The concierge choked. The doorman shoved a knuckle against his lips to keep from tittering.

The concierge responded in clipped syllables. "While I have little doubt the staff in French hotels turn a blind eye to such inappropriate fraternization, madam, the reputation of the Continen–"

"Miss," said Jenny.

"Pardon me?"

"I'm not a madam," said Jenny. "Not in any sense of the term."

The doorman retreated, trying to stuff the escaping giggles back into his mouth.

The concierge sniffed at his underling before fixing his eye on Jenny. "In that case, miss, your behavior is all the more scandalous." Jenny became acutely aware of the pistol handles protruding from the clutch.

She turned to strike a defiant pose, which concealed the weapons. "No doubt I can count on you to alert whatever passes for a gossip rag in this backward little village." Under different circumstances, she might have regretted the petty retort, but it pleased her to see it stung him. All she wanted was to find Izzie and escape this small-minded town.

Before the concierge could reply, Jenny waved goodbye over her shoulder and ascended the stairs.

The lights nearest her room had gone out, leaving the hallway dim. At the door, she fished for the keys in her overcrowded clutch.

"Should have taken the holsters," she muttered. Upon reflection, she concluded they wouldn't go with any of the clothes she'd brought. An idea brightened her sour mood. "I could have some made!"

She opened the door and tripped the light switch. The room remained dark. She flicked the switch a few more times, but nothing. Jenny became aware of a dull tingling sensation on her breastbone beneath the medallion.

A cool breeze lifted the curtains. Outside, the corner streetlamp gave off a little yellow light. She heard the slow creak of a floorboard as an unseen intruder's weight shifted.

On instinct, Jenny stepped back, poised to run back down the stairs. She would rather lose all her jewelry than fight a burglar cunning enough to disable the lights both inside her room and in the hall. The only thing Jenny couldn't bear to lose was the medallion, since it was the one tangible clue to her sister's presence in Arkham.

But there were also Izzie's letters.

Jenny drew a pistol from her clutch and thumbed off the safety. "Show yourself." Her voice quavered. "In front of the window, if you don't mind. I'd hate to paint the walls red."

Only silence replied to her challenge.

Holding the pistol ready, she tucked the clutch under her arm and reached out for the lamp beside the door. She felt under the lampshade for the bulb and found it loose in its socket. Before she could twist it down, the intruder shoved the door, smashing her against the door jamb. The pistol flew from her hand and clattered somewhere across the room.

Jenny tried to scream, but a man's hand covered her mouth. His fingers were a vise, squeezing her cheeks tight against her teeth. He slammed her head against the wall. She tasted blood. He fumbled at her chest before his rough fingers closed on the medallion.

Jenny grabbed the medallion's chain with both hands. She kicked low. Her foot struck something hard as a wooden beam where his leg should be.

Jenny released the chain and got her hand around the barrel of the second pistol in her clutch. The intruder tore away the medallion and shoved Jenny onto the bed.

She landed on the corner of an open valise. Pain shot through her hip, but she held onto the pistol. She rolled away, tangling herself in the clothing heaped on the mattress. The intruder's weight followed her onto the bed, a hand grasping at her ankle.

She kicked. Her reward was an angry grunt. "*Nervensäge!*" Jenny recognized the German expression for "pain in the neck".

Rolling off the bed, she shook a silk stocking off the pistol and raised the gun. Her sight had begun adjusting to the dark, and now she had the window at her back. Across the bed she saw the outline of a big man in a long coat rising to his feet. She aimed at his head.

"I'll give you a *Nervensäge!*" She fired.

The pistol kicked harder than she'd remembered, but in the flash she saw a head-sized mass fly back to strike the wall. The man's body fell to the floor. For a sickening moment, Jenny regretted her quip about bloodying the walls.

She was surprised to hear him scrambling across the floor, muttering more curses in German. He rose, his figure indistinct in the feeble light from the window. He replaced the hat – a Homburg with a bullet-sized hole in the crown – and turned toward her. The way he tilted his head, she feared he could see her clearly in the dark. The only thing she could see was that he didn't have the medallion.

He seemed to realize the same thing. He crouched, feeling around on the floor.

"Hands up, buddy," said Jenny.

Shouts and running footsteps approached the room. The concierge cried, "What is going on in there?"

"Get in here!" yelled Jenny.

At the same moment, the intruder lunged across the bed. Gripping the pistol in both hands, Jenny fired and then aimed to fire again, but the man had already leaped past her. He flew headfirst through the open window.

Jenny ran to the window. The man had vanished over the

eaves, but she heard him grunt as he hit the ground. His irregular footsteps receded alongside the hotel.

The door flew open. The doorman peered into the dark room, the concierge cringing behind him. A man in pajamas and a nightcap joined them.

"You're a bit late to the party," Jenny said. She felt around in the dark until she found another lamp and screwed the bulb tight. Everybody winced as the sudden illumination blinded them.

As their vision returned, the concierge gasped. "What in heaven's name have you done?"

The room was a shambles. The sofa cushions had been flung into the corners. Jenny's clothes lay across the bed and floor. Dresser drawers were strewn about the room. Jenny searched until she spied the corner of Izzie's favorite stationery peeking out from beneath a satin slip. She tossed aside the clothing and saw the rest of her sister's letters scattered beneath. "Thank goodness!"

"I demand an explanation for this brawl," snapped the concierge. "For this gunplay!"

Behind him, a sleepy-looking man appeared at the doorway. The doorman stepped aside with a curt bow. By that show of deference and the quality of his jacket, Jenny took the newcomer for the manager.

"You demand an explanation?" Jenny snapped back at the concierge. "I want to know how your hotel security allowed a burglar to sneak into my room and threaten my life."

"I will not be addressed that way by a spoiled flapper," spat the concierge. "A sneering, pistol-packing floozy with no respect for–"

The manager cleared his throat. His tousled hair suggested he'd come straight from bed, but his pencil mustache gave him an authoritarian air.

"Don't interrupt me when I'm–" The concierge froze as still as a gargoyle when he turned to see he had rebuked not an underling but his superior. "Mr Gentry. I beg your pardon, sir."

"One might be prudent to speak with greater civility to an armed woman," said Gentry. His mid-Atlantic accent suggested a certain savoir faire, but his voice turned heavy as a vault door. "Especially one who is a guest of the Continental. Don't you agree, Cecil?"

"Yes, Mr Gentry."

"Prepare another room for Miss … ?"

"Barnes," said the concierge. "Miss Guinevere Barnes."

"Call me Guinevere again and I will shoot you."

"Shall I summon the police?" said Mr Gentry. "Or would you perhaps prefer … ?"

Jenny appreciated that he left the decision to her. For all Mr Gentry knew, she'd just had a violent lovers' quarrel. She considered the matter while fetching up Izzie's letters, her clutch, the medallion, and the second pistol. If she could avoid presenting herself as a victim to the police tonight, she could make a stronger case for soliciting their help later.

Also, she wouldn't like to explain where she'd acquired a pair of .45 automatics.

"Perhaps I should sleep on it." She joined him at the door.

Mr Gentry offered her his arm. "Cecil will have the rest of your things delivered to your new accommodations."

"But sir," said Cecil. "The maids have all gone home."

"Then you will attend to it personally. Don't let me catch you lingering over the lady's unmentionables."

"I would never–!"

"Cecil."

"Right away, Mr Gentry."

Jenny squeezed Mr Gentry's arm in appreciation. Tormenting the concierge was much more fun as a team sport.

"If there is anything I can do to make up for Cecil's behavior, Miss Barnes, you have only to let me know."

"There might be something." Jenny held the medallion tight, afraid someone else might snatch it from her. She wished she knew more about it, but the only person she could think to ask was an ocean away. "A man like you must have a friend at the telegraph office. I need to send a message to London at once."

"I'll have Cecil wake the operator."

"So his name is Cecil?" Jenny allowed Mr Gentry to lead her to a new room. "I would have guessed it was Cotton Mather."

Gentry's mustache appeared far more dashing above a smile. "Oh, I doubt Cecil's ever met a real witch. Anyway, he's far too timid to burn one."

CHAPTER 4

The wind tugged at the brim of Jenny's favorite blue hat. She slapped one gloved hand on top of her head and looked up at the "Ritter's Plumbing and Motor Shop" sign.

In her other hand, Jenny held a round hat box by the ribbons, her handbag swinging on her wrist. With only the necessities and Izzie's letters, the handbag was much lighter. She'd discovered that her coat pockets made near-perfect holsters for the weapons. Now that she'd fired in self-defense, she no longer thought of them as Dainty Donohue's pistols. They were hers.

Even under the wool coat, Jenny's Green Man medallion tingled against her skin. She had planned to have the chain repaired as one of the morning's chores, but a replacement chain appeared on her breakfast tray beside the reply to her telegram, along with an apologetic note from the courteous Mr Gentry.

The medallion didn't match her ensemble, but feeling it against her chest provided a constant reminder that it was safe from thieves. Unfortunately, the tingling sensation reminded her of last night's nightmares. In them, she'd run through a bramble forest, taunted at every turn by the faces of screaming goats.

Another autumn gust sent the leaves scratching across the concrete drive leading to a pair of garage doors. "CLOSED" read the sign through the office window.

From behind the building, tinny radio music rose above the wind. Jenny followed the music. As she entered the backyard, she heard grunting and dull impacts.

Between the shop and a row of parked vehicles, two boxers faced off in a makeshift ring on a cinder-block foundation. They wore leather boxing gloves and headgear, but the sound of each blow made Jenny wince. She feared she'd hear the crunch of bones at any second.

The first pugilist was a man of about fifty years. He'd stripped to his undershirt, revealing lean but muscled arms. He stood in the center of the ring and kept his opponent at bay with quick jabs.

The second fighter had a good thirty pounds on the first, and an inch or two of height. Despite these advantages, every punch met an immovable left glove. Every side-step met a precise turn by the defender.

Even from behind, Jenny recognized those brawny shoulders. "Lonnie!"

As the big mechanic turned, her adversary caught her jaw with a punishing hook. Lonnie spun around, blinked, and grinned as she spotted Jenny. "Hi," she muttered through a mouthguard before sinking in a graceful spiral to sit cross-legged on the canvas.

The older boxer shook a glove at Lonnie. "What is it I am always telling you, girl? Never lower your guard."

Lonnie cringed. "I know. I'm sorry."

Jenny dropped her hat box and slipped under the ropes to kneel beside Lonnie. She glared up at her opponent. "Shame on you!" she snapped. "What kind of man fights a woman?"

"It's fine, Jenny." She groaned and clutched her head. "Meet my papa, Lew Ritter."

Jenny gently removed Lonnie's headgear. Curly russet hair spilled out, softening the contours of her shoulders. Jenny saw a world of feminine possibilities for the tomboy, but this hardly seemed the moment to propose them. Instead, she spat, "What kind of a man beats up his own daughter?"

"Every woman should know how to fight." Ritter's German accent sent a chill down Jenny's spine. "Have you come for a lesson, Fräulein Barnes?"

Jenny couldn't tell whether he was mocking her, but she noted his use of her last name when Lonnie had introduced her only by her first. The gleam in his eye might have been fatalistic Teutonic humor. It might have been something worse.

Lonnie unlaced her gloves with her teeth and pulled them off under her arms. "Papa was the boxing champion of Berlin. If not for his, uh, accident, he would have boxed in the Olympic Games."

"There were no German boxers that year, Lonnie," said Ritter. "How many times must I tell you?"

"But you were there." Lonnie stood up. She grinned again. "You wouldn't have met Mama if you hadn't gone to meet the coaches."

"Less talk, *liebchen*. More listen." He moved closer, dragging his left leg. He stuck out his fists.

"Yes, Papa." Lonnie unlaced his gloves and pulled them off.

"I suppose Lonnie told you about our little adventure," said Jenny. She noticed a thick scar on the back of Ritter's hand. As he flexed his fingers, she saw another on his palm.

"A good daughter tells her father everything," said Ritter. "And she remembers to offer coffee when a guest arrives."

"Sorry, Papa!" Lonnie slipped through the ropes and started to run for the shop before skidding to a halt. She mimed holding a teacup with her pinkie finger extended. "Or does *mademoiselle* prefer tea?"

Jenny's laugh died in her throat when she noticed a black truck in the row of vehicles. The letters reading "Ritter's Plumbing and Motor Shop" seemed yellow in the morning light. She wondered whether they might look green at night. "Coffee's fine."

"*Oui oui, mademoiselle!*" Lonnie practically skipped into the building. From the rear, it looked much more like a home than a machine shop.

"It is good of you to visit," Ritter said. When he saw Jenny raise an eyebrow, he added, "Lonnie has few women friends."

"Perhaps if she had fewer black eyes they'd be less afraid to come around."

"You think me brutal," said Ritter. "But Lonnie is a good fighter."

"Having the best right cross won't get her invited to the Harvest Festival ball."

"Maybe not," Ritter nodded, frowning. "But it will get her home safe if she goes with the wrong fellow."

Jenny pictured Dainty Donohue's piscine grin and decided Ritter made a good point.

She retrieved the hat box and brushed off a knot of yellowed grass. Lew Ritter stepped out of the ring. His left foot touched the yard with a metallic *clank*. Jenny noticed the leather strap of a leg brace around his shoe.

"The accident?"

The lines in Ritter's face hardened. "No accident. Even those who learn to fight cannot always win." He gestured to the house and said no more. He held open the door to a rear vestibule and followed Jenny in. He paused to wipe his arms and neck with a towel before donning a shirt from the coat rack.

A Homburg hat hung from the top post. Jenny saw no bullet hole in the crown, nor any evidence of a recent patch. She reminded herself that a man could own more than one hat.

Ritter's eyes narrowed as he noticed her staring. "May I take your coat, Fräulein Barnes?"

Jenny turned to let him take the coat. Her bare arms prickled with gooseflesh in the cool air of the little room. She smoothed her gloved hands over a few wrinkles around the beaded trim of her dress.

"Hm." Ritter noticed the surprising weight as he put her coat on the rack. Jenny realized she had just surrendered her pistols. "Please, come inside."

Two chairs flanked a little table. Ritter fetched a third and held it out for Jenny. The surrounding countertops were all clean and tidy. On the wall beside the ice box hung a calendar, October's picture featuring a young boy carving a jack-o'-lantern. Written in a precise hand on each day's box were names and times, each one through yesterday's struck through with a diagonal black stroke. Beside the iron stove, Lonnie spooned coffee into a tin pot.

Jenny set the box beneath her chair. Ritter squeezed past to open a cupboard from which he removed a paper-wrapped package the size of a brick. Before he closed the door, Jenny glimpsed a few bottles with handwritten labels: schnapps.

He fetched plates from another cupboard and forks from a drawer. As he set the table, his gaze fell on Jenny's medallion. He frowned and turned back to the kitchen drawer, from which he drew out a long knife.

Behind her, Jenny heard the coffee start to percolate. She couldn't look away from the blade's serrated edge.

"Be right back." Lonnie darted out of the kitchen.

"Lonnie!" Ritter shouted.

"I know! No running in the house." Lonnie pelted upstairs, undeterred by the warning.

Ritter smiled for the first time that Jenny had seen. "Don't worry," he said. "We won't wait for her."

Ritter unwrapped a moist brown apple cake. It smelled so fresh, it might have been baked that morning.

"Lonnie's aunt sends one every week," said Ritter. He placed the knife as if to cut a slice, but suddenly his hand swept up.

Before Jenny could dive for the floor, Ritter snapped his fingers. "The Harvest Festival!"

"What?"

"Your necklace." He pointed at the medallion on her chest. "It is on the flyers for the Harvest Festival."

"Yes," said Jenny, trying to maintain her composure. "I was surprised to see it myself when I arrived yesterday."

Ritter made a curt nod to himself, as if to say that was one problem solved. Yet as he cut a slice of cake, the frown returned. "No." He shook his head as he served the first slice to Jenny. "That wasn't it."

"What wasn't it?"

"I saw the flyers, but also I saw this face somewhere else. Not a drawing." He set down the knife and made a clutching gesture. "Something real, not on paper."

"Another medallion?" said Jenny.

"Not a medallion, no."

"My sister has a copy of this one." Jenny held up the medallion to give Ritter a better look. "Do you know Isabelle Barnes?"

Ritter shook his head. "Lonnie said you came to visit your sister. Her name is Isabelle?"

Jenny decided that Ritter was telling the truth, or else he was a better actor than she would have guessed. "She looks a bit like me, only two years younger and with lighter hair."

Ritter shook his head. "Sorry."

A silence fell over them. Just before it could become uncomfortable, Jenny remembered something Ritter had said in the boxing ring. "Why did you say every woman should know how to fight?"

"Do you not agree?"

Jenny certainly did agree, but she already knew her reasons. She wanted to know Ritter's. She simply nodded.

"Someone has been abducting young women, some little more than girls. A man who does such things does not expect a fight. A girl who can bloody his nose might escape such a man." He made a fist.

Jenny detected a note of personal grievance in his voice. "Do you know one of the abducted girls?"

"Everyone knows one of the missing," said Ritter. "Little Angela Houston lived only two blocks from here. Girls have been taken from all over town. From every neighborhood. From every congregation."

"So they have nothing in common except that they are all young women?"

Ritter considered the question. "There is one thing none of them have in common."

"What's that?"

"Wealth. The girls of rich families do not walk out alone. For them, there is always a brother or a suitor. Those who must work or walk home after dark, they are the ones that are taken." He glanced at Jenny's expensive clothes. He looked away, the bitterness plain on his face.

That much Jenny could understand. While she had been born to wealth, she found it easy to befriend people from all walks of life. In Paris she had met a few fellow travelers who resented the disparity in their stations. The artists had more complicated ways of expressing their resentment of class inequality, usually from the comfort of a café where someone else was paying the check. While Jenny had some sympathy for the socialist argument, she doubted its most vocal proponents performed as much labor in a year as the Ritters did in a week.

Besides, Lew Ritter's indignation seemed more personal than that of a barstool philosopher. Jenny asked, "Are you worried about Lonnie?"

"Lonnie can fight." His expression hardened. "But even a good fighter cannot always win."

Lonnie blew back into the kitchen. She'd changed into blue jeans and a clean khaki shirt with the sleeves rolled up tight around her biceps. Except for a few rebel wisps, her hair was stuffed back into the cap she'd worn when Jenny met her at the train station.

Ritter fetched three cups and a sugar bowl while Lonnie brought out a pint of cream from the ice box.

"Your family is not from Arkham?" said Ritter.

"New York."

"Barnes is an English name, *ja?*"

"Father comes from English stock, but he was born in New York. Mother is French."

"Ooh la la!" interjected Lonnie. Ritter shot her a disappointed glance, and even Jenny rolled her eyes at the stale joke. "Sorry. I got to learn some more French words."

"What sort of work does your father do?" said Ritter.

"He is a professor of Arthurian studies." Recalling Cecil's mention of her given name, she bristled. "Takes it all too far, if you ask me."

"You need a ride somewhere, Jenny?" Lonnie could barely contain her eagerness as she asked the question.

"Actually," said Jenny, "I did hope you'd be free today. I could use a native guide I can trust."

"Can I, Papa?" Lonnie leaned over the table, quivering like a puppy.

Ritter gave Jenny a doubtful look. "We must finish replacing the lead pipes at Schrader's farm."

"There's hardly any more to do there, Papa. Besides, Karl always helps. Please, Papa?"

Ritter maintained his skeptical countenance.

"I'll pay for the entire day," said Jenny. "Oh, and I almost forgot." She retrieved the hat box from beneath her chair and presented it to Lonnie.

Lonnie pulled off the ribbon and opened the lid. Inside, she found two leather helmets with goggles. They weren't genuine aviator caps, but Jenny didn't think Lonnie would mind the difference.

"Jenny!" Lonnie tore off her cap and tried to pull on a helmet, but it was far too small.

"Try the other one, Cinderella." Jenny took back the smaller helmet. "This one's for your fairy godmother."

The bigger one fit Lonnie to a T, and Jenny congratulated herself on the guess. Lonnie adjusted the goggles and put them on before turning a pleading smile back to her father. "Please, Papa. Can I go?"

Jenny maintained her best poker face while struggling to reconcile the self-assured young woman she'd met last night with this overgrown child who begged for her father's permission. She wondered whether it was love or fear that inspired such deference.

Ritter scowled at Lonnie until her lip began wavering. Then a smile cracked the corner of his mouth. "Who am I to tell Amelia Earhart she cannot fly?"

Lonnie nearly flipped the table as she lunged over to buss her father on the cheek. She fled outdoors before he could change his mind. "Come on, Jenny."

Jenny rose from the table, smiling but not entirely convinced by Ritter's apparent warmth. She'd known abusive men who donned a loving face for company. For Lonnie's sake, she hoped Ritter wasn't one of them.

He fetched Jenny's coat, hefting it with a quizzical expression. "Where will you take her?"

"First, to the university," said Jenny. "Then French Hill. Then, I don't know. Wherever the trail leads us."

"The trail?"

Jenny took a deep breath. "I'm not exactly visiting my sister," she said. "I'm searching for her."

Ritter's eyes narrowed. "She is in trouble?"

Jenny started to say she didn't know, but she had a feeling Ritter would have seen through the lie. She nodded.

"Then you must bring her home safe."

"*Danke schön*, Herr Ritter."

"And Lonnie, too. I will not ask you to keep her out of trouble. No one can do that. But bring her home safe, too."

"I promise."

Jenny went out to the garage. Lonnie pushed the Big Chief onto the driveway. In the back yard, Ritter carried a toolbox over to the shop truck. Jenny decided she could disregard the coincidence of the Homburg hat, but the leg brace bothered her. What were the chances of encountering two lame Germans in one small town?

Fairly good, she decided.

The Great War had touched people all over the world. Still, the similarities between Lew Ritter and her assailant troubled her. Jenny put her hat into the sidecar and donned her helmet. "Say, Lonnie, what time did you come home last night?"

Lonnie adjusted her chin strap. "Right after I left you at the hotel."

"Was your father waiting up for you?"

"Most nights he goes to bed early, especially when his leg is bothering him." Lonnie kicked the Big Chief to life.

Jenny stepped into the sidecar, weighing Lonnie's word against the evidence. The way Lew Ritter dragged his leg made Jenny doubtful that he could have leaped over the bed and out the window as her assailant had done. "How did he hurt his leg?"

Lonnie glanced back to see her father loading copper pipes into the truck. She drove the motorcycle off the driveway before answering. "Papa doesn't think I know, but Mama told me the story before she died."

Jenny felt a lump in her throat. "I'm sorry, Lonnie. I didn't mean to pry."

"It's all right," said Lonnie. "A lot of folks lost family to the Spanish flu. What can you do about something like that? You just got to keep living." She drove the Big Chief at an uncharacteristically modest speed. They rode along residential streets where children played and packs of little dogs chased each other across neighboring yards.

Jenny's cousin Iris had died in the pandemic, as had several of her friends from school. And Jenny had gone on living.

Less than a year later, Izzie had her troubles. Izzie's incident was a more personal tragedy than war or pandemic, but it was the sort of thing that happened to young women all over the world. For months, Jenny tried to be the good sister, but Izzie's moods turned hot and cold. One day she would beg Jenny to mount an escape. The next she would accuse her of betrayal. She said such hateful things that Jenny could bear no more.

And so Jenny had fled. In Paris she had gone on living, just without her sister.

Still, sometimes Jenny couldn't shake the dreadful feeling that all the everyday catastrophes of the world were intertwined. On those rare occasions on which she failed to find a diversion, Jenny felt as though an enormous hand hovered over the planet, poised to snuff out a life, or a hundred lives, or ten thousand.

After Lonnie turned onto a main thoroughfare, she said, "Papa killed a man in the ring."

"How awful!" Jenny shouted over the noise of a passing roadster and its occupants, seven or eight young men in varsity sweaters. They hollered at Jenny, but she ignored them. Much as she enjoyed cheering college athletes, this was not the moment.

"He didn't mean to kill him, but that didn't matter to the dead man's friends. They were Berlin gangsters. They cornered Papa one night and taught him a lesson."

"At least they didn't kill him," said Jenny. An insect spattered on her goggles. She tried wiping away the remains with a gloved finger, but that only spread the carnage.

"Only because he killed two before the others ran off. The bulls found him crawling home. Mama told me that's the real reason he left Germany."

Jenny understood. "He figured they'd try to finish the job sooner or later."

"I hope they died in the war," said Lonnie. "Papa volunteered to fight, but the American army rejected him on account of his leg. I think Papa was sadder about that than anything else. He wanted to prove he is an American now. I just wish he'd had a chance to fight the men who hurt him."

It seemed unlikely that gangsters would let themselves end up fighting in a war, but Jenny liked the poetic justice of thinking Lew Ritter might avenge himself with a rifle across no man's land. Stranger things had happened, if one believed the stories told by veterans in France and Italy.

Anyway, she couldn't think of any way Lew Ritter's peculiar history could relate to Izzie's disappearance. She had a good feeling about Lonnie, and for now that was enough to relax about her father.

Lonnie slowed the Big Chief as they approached Miskatonic University. The sun had come out from behind the clouds, revealing the campus in its full glory. The buildings were among the most beautiful Jenny had seen since arriving in Arkham. Most were made of stone or brick. As they passed a sports field, Lonnie pointed out the bell tower marking the center of campus.

"Head that way," said Jenny. "We'll consult the natives for directions to the oracle."

Lonnie grinned at her.

Jenny grinned back.

CHAPTER 5

The second group of students they asked for directions pointed them to the Anthropology Department. Lonnie had to hit the gas to escape the first bunch, who were less interested in helping than in chatting up Jenny.

When they arrived, Lonnie parked the Big Chief beside the quad, where half a dozen young men tossed a football.

"Will you be all right waiting for me here?" said Jenny.

"Sure. I'll show these boys how to chuck a pigskin." She cupped a hand to her mouth and yelled, "Gimme the ball, you bunch o' pantywaists!"

When the young men looked her way, Lonnie charged. Jenny saw terror in their faces. She called after Lonnie, "Try not to break any bones!"

Ivy smothered the three-story Social Sciences building, leaving only the crenellated crown exposed. Jenny stepped into the lobby, deflected an offer to carry her books by pointing out that she hadn't any, and located the faculty directory. She found the abbreviations she sought: Dr T Félix, Assoc Prof Anth Rm 308.

On her way up the stairs, Jenny passed another woman, the first she'd noticed on campus. Before the war, she would have found herself even more alone in a sea of men, so that was some progress. Still, she wished she could see a few more skirts among the trousers, if only to provide cover. Of course, if Professor Félix turned out to be anything like most academics she'd met, he'd be as distracted as the students.

Colorful flyers advertising university events papered the door to room 308. Frosted glass walls to either side of the door revealed hulking silhouettes, suggesting a storage area rather than an office. Through the open transom came smells of incense and tobacco, and a mélange of other scents Jenny associated with bazaars, like Cairo's labyrinthine Khan el-Khalili.

As she raised her hand to knock, Jenny noticed another missing persons bill, this one including photos of two girls and a drawing of a third. Jenny imagined the family was too poor to have hired a photographer. She recognized one of the names: Angela Houston.

Partially obscured by the missing girls notice, Jenny saw her Green Man staring back at her from another Harvest Festival advertisement. This one listed more campus activities whose dates had just passed, including lectures on colonial American history, Celtic fertility cults, and Sumerian harvest worship. Seeing the Green Man gave her a queasy intuition of danger but also some hope that she was on the right track.

She rapped on the door.

"Enter," called a woman's voice.

It was difficult to tell from a single word, but Jenny detected a European accent. She went inside.

Despite the hints she'd seen through the glass, Jenny was

unprepared for the full extent of the clutter. Tall shelves lined the walls and formed two partitions that created three cramped spaces out of the larger room.

Books and papers filled the lowest shelves. The rest supported a dizzying array of artifacts: statuettes, coins on velvet plaques, fetishes of bone and feathers, painted baskets, pottery shards, urns, carved coffers, ceremonial masks, and fragments of ancient garb. There were all manner of other specimens one usually expected to find under glass in a museum: an Australian didgeridoo, Chinese porcelain masks, Egyptian statuary, and a carved wooden disc Jenny guessed came from some pre-Columbian culture.

The far-left corner enjoyed an unobstructed window. Beneath it stood a mahogany desk. A full set of Frazer's *The Golden Bough* stood on one side of the blotter. Stacks of manuscripts lay on the other, with a teak cigarette box in the front.

A woman rose from behind the desk. She wore a charcoal jacket and knee-length skirt, neither of which obscured her gamine charms. A monocle dangled from a black lapel ribbon. Her short black hair swept back from her face to show off exquisite cheekbones. The afternoon light made her hazel eyes appear almost golden, a startling brightness against her olive skin.

"Professor Félix?" Jenny had met other female scholars, but never one who would have seemed more at home on a Paris fashion show runway.

"Yes?" Félix walked around to the front of her desk and leaned on its edge.

"My name is Jenny Barnes. A friend suggested you might be able to help me identify an object."

"What friend is this?"

Jenny decided Professor Félix was a fluent francophone but a native Spaniard, perhaps from Andalusia. She produced the morning's telegram and offered it to Félix. "*Un ami d'une amie*, actually. Howard Carter, the Egyptologist."

Professor Félix appeared as aloof as the Sphinx. She opened the cigarette box on her desk, sniffed at what she saw inside, and let the lid drop. "You are not an archaeologist, I think."

"*Pas du tout.*" Jenny offered the professor her own cigarette case. "Yet I have had the privilege of visiting a few notable digs."

Félix studied the cigarette case as if a sticky child had just offered her a captured salamander. "*Et amis d'amis riches, non?*" Her tone sharpened. "Access to such places is a privilege better given to scholars than to wealthy dilettantes."

Jenny took a slow breath. She tried not to be offended by Professor Félix's ungenerous summation of her character. She helped herself to a cigarette and left the case open, holding it casually within Félix's reach. "I happen to agree, but I could hardly refuse Lady Evelyn's invitation to witness the opening of King Tut's tomb."

"Careful, Miss Barnes. If you drop any more names, you shall trip on your way out of my office." Félix's indifference cracked when she glimpsed the contents of the cigarette case. She snatched a cigarette and smelled it. "Gauloises! No one in Arkham sells them."

"Provisions for my sea voyage," said Jenny.

Félix nodded toward a coatrack and fixed her cigarette to a wire finger clip.

Jenny hung up her coat and removed her ivory cigarette holder from her handbag.

Félix admired Jenny's blue dress, her eyes lingering over the shimmering beadwork. "*Très chic.*"

"*Merci beaucoup.*"

The professor lit their cigarettes from a brass lighter stamped with an image of Atalanta shooting the boar. They drew in the tarry smoke, held it awhile, and exhaled in unison toward the open window. All they needed were two glasses of absinthe, thought Jenny, and they might have been lounging in a Montmartre nightclub.

Lonnie's voice rose from the quad. "Go long. Farther! Keep running! Hey, where you going? I've got your ball."

Jenny felt a pang of sympathy for the burly girl. Perhaps part of the reason she trusted Lonnie was that she recognized in her a wounded soul.

"Call me Tilde," said Professor Félix. "I don't recall Howard Carter's mentioning a Jenny Barnes."

"In truth, I barely know the man." It was a relief to have Tilde warm to her after their false start. If they had met in Paris, Jenny was sure they'd have become friends. "After the Valley of Kings, he became fantastically busy. I was there at Evelyn's invitation."

"How do you know Lord Carnarvon's daughter?"

"We became friendly in London, and she knew I'd enjoy the visit to Egypt for the grand reveal of her father's expedition."

"I know the earl only by reputation." Tilde drew another toke from her cigarette. "I met Carter while inspecting digs for the EAS."

Jenny knew only a little about the Egyptian Antiquities Service. She knew Carter had resigned from the organization after siding with Egyptian site guards in a dispute with French tourists. If not for Lord Carnarvon's financial support, Carter would never have allowed Jenny near the tomb. She glanced around Tilde's office, surprised by the paucity of Egyptian artifacts. "You're an Egyptologist?"

"Not specifically, no. I have studied many cultures to develop a curriculum on world anthropology. We focus so often on the specific that we lose track of the universal."

"So you're applying Frazer's approach?" Jenny nodded toward *The Golden Bough.*

"You've read Frazer?" Tilde sounded dubious.

"I once forgot to bring a novel on a long train journey. A professor of comparative religion rescued me with volume ten."

"*Baldur the Beautiful.*" Tilde took a long drag on her cigarette. She reappraised Jenny and blew another plume of smoke out the window. "You begin to make me envy the idle life."

"It only idles if you don't drive it anywhere," said Jenny.

Tilde nodded at her bon mot. "Why did Lady Evelyn send you to me?"

Jenny indicated the medallion on her chest. "This little trinket."

Tilde's eyes widened. "Is that the original?"

Jenny unfastened the chain and offered it to Tilde. "You know it?"

"It's on flyers all over town." Tilde donned a pair of stained white gloves before taking the medallion. "The detail is far better than on the reproduction." She turned it over and peered through her monocle, which Jenny guessed was a magnifying lens. "I can't make out the text."

"I couldn't tell whether it's writing or a decorative pattern."

"It is hard to tell under all this accumulation of verdigris. Where did you acquire it?"

"I once financed an archaeological dig of my own."

Tilde arched an eyebrow.

"I met Professor Lucius Angstrom at a shipboard fete near Palermo. He wanted to investigate a site in the Susa Valley, near Turin, but he needed a backer. The whole endeavor became a fiasco."

"What went wrong?"

"The locals refused to work for us, even to sell to us. We hired men from Turin and carried on despite some rather gruesome vandalism. Soon after we uncovered a barrow mound, the villagers stormed the site. I was lucky to get out alive."

"Where is the Italian equivalent of the EAS when you need it?" said Tilde.

"Probably loitering with Arkham cabbies."

"Pardon?"

"Never mind me. I'm nursing a grudge."

Tilde sighed. "Were you at least able to date the site?"

"Professor Angstrom identified writing carved into the barrow lintel as Lepontic Celtic. That's an early form of–"

"Gaulish." Tilde sounded annoyed to be instructed by an amateur. "Do you have a rubbing of the text?"

"Sadly, no. Angstrom promised to send me a translation, but," Jenny hesitated, "he hasn't."

"What else did you discover before escaping the torches and pitchforks of these angry villagers?"

"Very little," said Jenny, overlooking Tilde's sarcasm. "There was a statue, but the vandals had spoiled it beyond recognition. Angstrom was beside himself. He'd been hoping for some evidence of a fertility cult."

"Hmm." Tilde raised the monocle again, studying the pattern on the back. She shook her head and flipped it back over. "This screaming face bears a resemblance to other images associated with fertility cults, but it doesn't appear Gallic. Perhaps it came to Italy with a proselytizing priest." Tilde flipped the medallion again and traced her finger along the spiral. "This pattern reminds me of an obscure deity I recently researched. Most sources suggest the pattern is a prayer to a goddess, but some refer to the deity by masculine terms – although that might be the result of confusing the deity with its consort, an entity known as Hastur."

"What's this he-or-she deity called?"

"Shub-Niggurath."

Jenny winced at the unpleasant name. It sounded at once familiar and alien. "That's not even Greek to me."

"I have seen it represented as Shupnikkurat or Ishnigarrab in Greek, Egyptian, and Druidic sources. To be honest, most of what I've read is obscure or contradictory, more myth than history." Tilde turned to face Jenny directly. "Would you permit me to clean the medallion? Perhaps then I can make out whether these spirals form words."

"Will it take long?"

"*Pas de tout.*" Tilde led Jenny to a table surrounded by cubbyholes. In a small dish, she mixed a paste of salt, flour, and vinegar.

"And she can cook, boys," said Jenny.

"This is as close as I come to domesticity." Tilde smeared both sides of the medallion with the resulting goop before working it into the crannies with a brush. "Now we wait a little while."

"What else can you tell me about this Shub – this fertility deity."

"A horrid name, is it not?" Tilde leaned against a shelf. The gesture put her head beside a grimacing African mask. "It appears less often in histories than in legends. Modern occultists often refer to it as the Black Goat of the Woods with a Thousand Young."

"That sounds like a phrase I once heard Aleister Crowley use."

Tilde tensed like a cat who'd spied a snake in the garden. "You're one of Crowley's coterie?"

Jenny held up a conciliatory palm. "In Paris, one cannot attend any party without encountering the loathsome as well as the charming. I found him to be a conceited bigot who took advantage of willing fools."

"You may be a spoiled dilettante," Tilde decided, "but at least you are not one of those cretins."

The backhanded compliment made it more difficult for Jenny to ask her next question. The real history of the medallion was less important than what Izzie might have believed about it. "Let's imagine that we aren't two sensible, skeptical, educated women. If we believed in this 'Black Goat,' how would we use this medallion? What's its purpose?"

Tilde took a last drag from her cigarette, detached it from the clip, and stubbed it out in a stone mortar. "It could allow a high priest the ability to invoke the god's favor. To grant its worshipers gifts."

"So the one with the medallion could ask for a rich harvest?"

"In exchange for a sacrifice, yes. It could also grant fertility to livestock and women wishing to conceive. Or so its worshippers believed."

Jenny felt a pang of guilt at sending Izzie the medallion. Izzie had absolutely no difficulty conceiving, and thus her troubles had begun.

"So, they believed in the power of prayer. Let's think bigger." Jenny stubbed out her cigarette. "Let's say there is real magic – that the worshippers believe in it, anyway. What wonders would the ancient Crowleys promise their followers?"

Tilde shrugged. "Perhaps the medallion could summon a divine emissary, one of the Black Goat's Dark Young."

"What are they?"

"Here, I can show you." Tilde fetched some crumpled papers out of the wastebasket beside her desk. She smoothed out a page to reveal a bizarre sketch. "My first crude effort to copy an illustration from a book on ancient cults."

From three cloven hooves rose crooked legs supporting a headless torso. A wide maw opened in a silent roar, while dozens of smaller mouths gaped like pustulant sores all over the body. Thick tendrils wriggled above the inhuman mass like the trunks of drowning elephants.

"This looks like something drawn by a demented child."

"Wild imagination is not a modern development," Tilde smiled. "Although I must admit that such grotesqueries put to shame the chimeras and centaurs of Greek mythology. What is wrong?"

Jenny realized she'd been rubbing her arms, trying to dispel the chill she felt at the sight of the Dark Young. For a moment it had seemed less fanciful and more – she hated even to think it – archaeological. It felt less like a picture of a dragon than one of a dinosaur, some impossible thing that had actually once existed.

"Don't tell me you believe in monsters," said Tilde.

"Of course not." Jenny raised her chin, indignant and ashamed. "Still, there is something rather... well, something rather numinous about the medallion. Since last night, I've felt a strange sensation when wearing it."

Tilde narrowed her eyes as if deciding whether to call for the men with butterfly nets.

"See for yourself. Go feel the medallion. Is your potion done cleaning it?"

"Ideally, we would let the compound work longer, but let us see what it has revealed."

Tilde returned to the worktable and bathed the medallion in a pan of water. She cleaned the grit with a brush, rinsed it, dried the metal, and buffed it with a small cloth. The result was a shining bronze surface. Scant traces of the patina remained in the deepest recesses, and fine details became evident. Tilde scanned the spiral pattern through her magnifying lens and sighed.

"What's wrong?" said Jenny.

"It's definitely not Lugano text," said Tilde. "That is the alphabet used for Lepontic writing."

"You said it might be from an older culture."

"And so it is. This text resembles Linear A."

"I've heard that name somewhere."

"Don't tell me you haven't a close personal friend who is the foremost scholar of prehistoric writing."

"When the opera is out of season, I sometimes stoop to academic lectures."

Tilde's laugh reminded Jenny of the clink of champagne glasses. "Linear A is the earliest form of Mycenaean writing we've discovered."

"And Mycenaean is?"

"Pre-Greek," said Tilde. "More or less."

"Can you read–?"

"No one can. We've been aware of the existence of Linear A for only forty years or so, Linear B half that long. There aren't enough samples of either to create a syllabary."

"All right," said Jenny. "But there's still the tingling sensation. Don't you feel it?"

Tilde removed her gloves and stroked a slender finger across the medallion's face. She shrugged. "Nothing."

"Try touching it with your whole hand," said Jenny.

Tilde did so, holding her palm over the medallion for a few seconds. She shook her head. "Nothing. Perhaps you are letting your imagination run wild."

"That's odd," said Jenny. "I felt it last night and again this morning." She picked up the medallion and held it between her palms. Nothing. She wondered whether it had reacted to the would-be robber. That made no sense, since she'd felt it again today.

While she was visiting the Ritters, she realized.

Jenny remembered another difference. She hadn't felt the strange sensation in her hands. She pressed the medallion against her chest. After a moment, she felt the tingling as she had before. "It's the heart," she said. "I feel it over my heart."

She passed the medallion to Tilde. After holding it to her breast for a second, Tilde gasped and pulled it away.

"You felt it!" said Jenny.

"I felt something."

"There's some sort of power emanating from the medallion, something connected directly to your heart."

"We've already established that you aren't a fool," said Tilde. "Don't start playing one now." She peered at Jenny's skin where the medallion had rested. "I don't see a rash, but it could be a chemical reaction."

"Then how would you feel it through your blouse?"

Tilde bit her lip. "You make a good point. Perhaps those academic lectures were not entirely wasted on you."

Tilde's compliments were becoming less backhanded all the time. The idea of applying a scientific approach to religious practices reminded her of another illogical fact to challenge. "You said you were recently doing research on this cult."

"Yes," said Tilde. "Oh, you think it is a strange coincidence. Not so. The Harvest Festival committee asked about the medallion weeks ago. There was some controversy over its inclusion on their flyers."

"And that is when you first saw this Green Man? On the flyers?"

"On the flyers, yes. But also on the copy of your medallion. Where else would they have gotten the image for their flyers?"

Jenny froze. "Who showed you the copy?"

"A young man by the name of August Olmstead."

"August Olmstead." The name seemed familiar. Jenny remembered why. "Auggie!"

"I take it you know him."

"My sister mentioned an Auggie in her letters. Last night I confirmed she'd been with him at a local speakeasy. I don't suppose you have his address."

Tilde returned to her desk and produced an appointment book from the drawer. "I have it right here."

"Why did he bring you the medallion?"

"He wanted to know more about it," she said. "He wanted a report on all I could find about its historical origins. I found nothing in the general collection. It was only after visiting the restricted collection that I found anything interesting."

"What was that?"

"Two books with rather lurid titles: *Cultes des Goules* and *Unaussprechlichen Kulten*."

"*Ghoul Cults* and *Nameless Cults*? What did you discover?"

"Several fanciful religious ceremonies, mainly, but also some pseudohistory. Very little of academic value."

"Did you make a copy of your report?"

"Of course," said Tilde. "But I left it with Dr Armitage. I had to promise he could read my report in exchange for access to certain restricted volumes."

Jenny began to feel a bit light-headed. "Was there a woman with Auggie? One resembling me?"

"No woman," said Tilde. She wrote down the address and gave it to Jenny. "There was another man, though. A rather sinister-looking fellow with the Heidelberg scar. Several of them, in fact, all on the same cheek."

"He must take offense easily." Jenny's joke did little to calm her nerves, so she tried again. "Or give it often."

Tilde smirked. "You know that's not why they–"

"I know," said Jenny. She knew that certain foolish young men at the University of Heidelberg fenced without masks, pouring wine into the resulting scars as a badge of honor. She preferred the image of prickly Germans slapping each other's faces with white gloves. "Did you catch his name?"

"He never said a word, and Mr Olmstead never spoke to him. I had the impression he was some sort of servant." Tilde's expression turned reflective. "Or perhaps a bodyguard. Now that I think of it, Olmstead seemed frightened of him."

Jenny considered that information along with what she'd heard of Auggie's being thrown out of the Tick-Tock Club. She hoped there was no criminal element to Izzie's disappearance.

"I need to talk to this Auggie," said Jenny. "I need to find Izzie."

"Your sister?"

"The picture on the flyers and Auggie's name were my only

clues." She held up the address. "Now you've given me a better one. Thank you."

"You're welcome," said Tilde. "But I want more than thanks."

"Oh?" Jenny began to reach for her handbag.

"*Sacré bleu*! I am not asking you for money."

"Of course not." Inside the handbag, Jenny shifted her grasp from money clip to cigarette case. She withdrew it with practiced nonchalance, as if all she'd wanted was another gasper.

"I want your permission to take a rubbing of the medallion. Now that more detail has become apparent, I'd like to compare the text with that found in Armitage's rare books."

"Please do."

Tilde produced a stick of charcoal and paper. She made a quick rubbing of each side before returning the medallion.

"When you come back," said Tilde, "I'll share my findings."

"When I come back," said Jenny, "I'll introduce you to my sister."

CHAPTER 6

Jenny found Lonnie leaning against the Big Chief. Despite the increasing warmth, she wore her helmet with the goggles in place while smoking a cigar.

"That's one way to keep the smoke out of your eyes."

"Yeah."

Jenny might have chalked up Lonnie's thick voice to the cigar, but she suspected the boys' running off had hurt her feelings. That wasn't a problem Jenny had ever faced. She found herself without any advice to offer. Where wisdom fails, she knew, wit must suffice. Unfortunately, she felt less witty than anxious to act on her new information. "I know where Auggie lives."

"Auggie?"

Despite her doubts about Lew Ritter, Jenny felt she could trust Lonnie. She summarized her reason for visiting Arkham, including the gist of what she'd learned at the Tick-Tock Club and from Professor Tilde Félix.

"I realize you didn't agree to more than driving me around town." Jenny handed her the address. "But I hope you'll still–"

"Your sister's in trouble?" Lonnie straddled the Big Chief. "That's all you had to say, Jenny. Let's move!"

They sped east toward a prominent rise surmounted by a church spire. Brick row houses stretched across the western slope of French Hill. They passed a cemetery where a Catholic priest led a funeral procession to an open grave. As the Big Chief ascended, more of the houses seemed to perch rather than rest on the slope, their gambrel roofs hunched like gargoyles' shoulders as they peered at the declining sun. The narrow lanes between houses twisted and rose, with crooked stairs ending at shadowed doorways.

As they crested the summit, Jenny saw that eastern French Hill boasted far grander homes. A few decrepit Georgian manors gave the neighborhood a respectable air, but many of the residences were new wood-frame houses on brick foundations. Driveways, garages, and generous yards gave the homes a little elbow room.

The wind subsided, and the afternoon sun overcame the autumn chill. If the trend continued, Jenny imagined they could expect a balmy evening. She would give half the world to spend it with Izzie, catching up on all the things that had happened while they lived so far apart. The other half of the world she'd save so they could explore it together, as they should have done from the start.

As Lonnie drove the Big Chief downhill, the sidecar shuddered. Jenny gripped the sides.

"What was that?" she yelped louder than she'd intended.

"Probably just a loose bolt," said Lonnie. She slowed the bike as they approached their destination.

The address Tilde had given Jenny led to a narrow brick house. Lonnie pulled into the driveway and parked behind a yellow roadster that seemed designed to keep the driver and passenger as close together as possible. Jenny stepped out of the sidecar before it could collapse.

Lonnie hopped off the bike. The whole rig rose as she took her toolbox out of the sidecar. She wheeled the Big Chief to the grass and turned it on its side to see beneath the sidecar.

"How does it look?" Jenny asked. She exchanged her leather helmet for her broad-brimmed hat.

"Nothing's broke," said Lonnie. She opened the toolbox and hefted the enormous wrench Jenny had seen her use at the train station. "Don't worry, I'll have everything right and tight in a jiffy."

Jenny left Lonnie to the task.

A middle-aged housemaid answered her knock at the door. "How may I help you, miss?" She spoke with a light Irish accent. Agitated voices echoing down the front hall suggested a reason for her wrung-out appearance.

Jenny paused long enough to overhear snatches of a conversation from somewhere off the main hall: "…hardly a serious factor…" "…postpone the exclusive party…" "…finish up at the barn…"

Jenny noticed the maid noticing her eavesdropping, so she said, "Miss Barnes to see Mr Olmstead."

"Barnes, is it?" The maid studied Jenny for a moment and nodded as if recognizing her. "Please come in, Miss Barnes."

The maid offered to take her coat. Remembering the weight of her pistols, Jenny hung it on a peg herself. She followed the woman down the hall. As they approached the open door to a parlor, Jenny heard a woman saying, "…no choice but to dispatch Geiszler again."

"Do you think it wise, my dear?" replied a man. "I mean, if you aren't certain–"

The maid announced, "Miss Barnes to see Master Olmstead."

Three people sat within the parlor. A fire crackled in the hearth. Opposite, light filtered in through gauzy curtains. From the walls hung art prints featuring pastoral landscapes or fantasies of nymphs and satyrs, all related more by subject matter rather than by style. The same appeared true of the mismatched furnishings, which Jenny guessed someone had acquired piecemeal at estate sales. She needed no further evidence to conclude the house was home to a bachelor.

Two men rose at her arrival. The woman remained seated.

The younger man eased into a practiced slouch to cover his momentary surprise. His squinting smile emphasized a pointed chin and crooked teeth. Jenny guessed he was about twenty-five, a bit old for the juvenile haircut that left his blond locks flopping over his brow. He extended a hand. "Why, if it isn't the celebrated Guinevere Barnes."

"Auggie, I presume." Jenny shook his hand. "And I much prefer that you call me Jenny."

"Of course. Isabelle mentioned that. I should have remember-ed," said Auggie. "Jenny it is. Allow me to introduce my father, Winthrop Olmstead."

Jenny was sure she knew that name, but she couldn't remember why.

The elder Olmstead's muttonchop whiskers and stout torso gave him a solid presence. "Miss Barnes." He nodded at Jenny before speaking past her to the maid. "Bring us some refreshments, Nesbitt."

The maid departed. Auggie indicated the seated woman. "My mother, Abigail Olmstead."

It was from his mother that Auggie had inherited the tapered chin and pale blue eyes. Mrs Olmstead wore her fading golden hair in a conservative coif that matched the braid work on her gray woolen dress. Jenny wondered whether the hairdresser or the dressmaker had been instructed to mimic the other.

Mrs Olmstead stared at Auggie until he offered her his hand. She took it and rose from her chair, regal as a queen. She didn't appear to need assistance so much as to insist on receiving the courtesy. "How lovely to meet you, my dear. We've heard such tales of your European adventures."

"I may have exaggerated to entertain Izzie," said Jenny. In fact, the opposite was true, but she sensed the elder Olmsteads would disapprove of the truth.

"Izzie?" Mrs Olmstead turned her head in a quizzical manner. "Ah, your pet name for Isabelle. And you prefer 'Jenny', do you? What a shame. Guinevere is such a lovely name."

"One day I might like to kiss an Arthur," said Jenny, "and I wouldn't want to scare him off."

"I imagine you've kissed more Lancelots." Auggie shot her a lascivious wink.

"August!" grumbled Mr Olmstead. "Decorum."

"More toads, actually," said Jenny, looking Auggie up and down. "I've yet to uncover a prince."

Auggie grinned, missing the point entirely.

"After her time in Paris, I doubt Miss Barnes is sensitive to the coarse insinuations popular among today's youth." Mrs Olmstead fixed a disapproving eye on her son. Auggie shrank under her inspection.

"Jenny or Guinevere, I would have recognized a Barnes sister anywhere," said Mr Olmstead. "Your family resemblance is striking. You even dress alike, right down to the ornaments. Didn't Isabelle wear a medallion like that one?"

Mrs Olmstead leaned forward, squinting at Jenny's medallion. "I've left my spectacles at home. May I see it?"

Jenny unfastened the chain and passed the medallion over.

Mrs Olmstead held the medallion close to her eyes. "It looks exactly the same as the one Isabelle persuaded me to use on those awful flyers."

"What was awful about them?" said Jenny. Now she remembered where she'd seen the name Winthrop Olmstead before. "Oh, you're chairwoman of the Harvest Festival."

"That is correct, Miss Barnes. And it was this medallion that made the flyers so awful. Father Iwanicki informs me that this image depicts a pagan deity," said Mrs Olmstead. "Were you aware of the trinket's origins?"

"Until today, I'd assumed it was an early type of Green Man." Mrs Olmstead's accusatory tone put Jenny on the defensive. She felt the urge to explain and recalled something Tilde had just reminded her of. "You know, like those found in so many English churches."

"Is that so?" Mrs Olmstead re-evaluated Jenny. "A Green Man."

"Izzie may have mentioned our father is an Arthurian scholar," said Jenny. "We grew up steeped in tales of the Knights of the Round Table and all the rest. Naturally, I was surprised to learn this isn't a Green Man at all." Jenny turned to Auggie. "I'm told you inquired about the history of the medallion."

"What? Me?" Auggie cringed like a boy caught with his hand in the cookie jar. "I mean, yes, I did borrow Isabelle's medallion once Mother expressed a concern. I showed it to a woman professor at Miskatonic. She turned up some ancient mumbo jumbo."

"But why did you take it?" said Jenny. "I gave it to Izzie."

"I asked August to inquire," said Mrs Olmstead. "Discreetly. Father Iwanicki is too used to having his way in matters beyond his purview, so I doubted his claims. Unfortunately, I'm afraid that what August learned validated his concerns. The image is completely inappropriate for a family-oriented festival."

Mrs Olmstead was a woman accustomed to wielding matriarchal authority, Jenny thought, and not just over her son.

The maid returned with a tray of cakes and a pitcher of hot cider.

"Ah, here we are." Mr Olmstead poured. He offered the first to Jenny and the next to Mrs Olmstead, who handed the medallion to Auggie. As Mr Olmstead poured another, he sloshed the hot cider over his wrist.

"Damnation!" he hissed.

"Winthrop, please," said Mrs Olmstead. "Must you be so coarse in front of our guest?"

"Sorry."

"Here." Auggie held up Jenny's medallion, offering to place it around her neck. Jenny let him do so.

Mr Olmstead gave Auggie a cup and poured one for himself. "To our unexpected – but most welcome – visitor."

The expression on Mrs Olmstead's face belied her husband's sentiment. Everyone sat. Jenny nibbled and sipped enough for courtesy before pressing her inquiry.

"I came to Arkham looking for Izzie – Isabelle. Can you tell me where she's staying?"

The Olmsteads exchanged furtive glances.

"Where is she?" demanded Jenny. "Where is my sister?"

"We haven't seen her for weeks." Mrs Olmstead glanced at Auggie, who stared sheepishly at his feet. "Isabelle and Auggie had a falling out."

What did you do? Jenny wanted to say. She caught herself and said, "What happened between you?"

"She'd been acting queer lately," said Auggie. "Starting at shadows, complaining of headaches and bad dreams."

"Too much nightlife. That's what it is," said Mr Olmstead. "If only Isabelle had remained involved with the Harvest Festival. The event offers so many wholesome alternatives to gin and jazz and heaven-knows-what-else at seedy talk-easies."

"Speakeasies," said Auggie.

Mrs Olmstead silenced her son with an imperious look. "It pains me that you even know that vulgar term, August."

Jenny wanted to change the subject before the conversation sank under domestic quicksand. "What did Izzie have to do with the Harvest Festival?"

"I had hoped Isabelle would help me organize this year's event," said Mrs Olmstead. "She was bubbling with enthusiasm at the start. She designed the original flyers, the ones that troubled Father Iwanicki. Unfortunately, she soon lost interest."

That sounded like Izzie. When they were girls, Izzie was always the first to grow bored with their latest hobby when the flush of excitement gave way to the realization that there was boring work ahead. She always left Jenny to see things through to the end.

"To be fair," said Auggie, "no one's as invested in the Harvest Festival as you are, Mother."

"That's neither here nor there," said Mrs Olmstead. "Isabelle was committed to the event at the start. It was only later that her behavior became erratic." She turned to Jenny. "Does Isabelle have a history of... well, of fragility?"

Mr Olmstead reached over to pat his wife's hand. "Let's not be indelicate, my dear."

Abigail turned her gaze on him. He withdrew his hand as if from an arching cobra.

"No, it's all right," said Jenny. She reminded herself that once – when it had mattered the most to Izzie – she had been the one to give up. That had been the last time they'd seen each other. "It's all right. It's why I've come to Arkham. It's true. Some years ago, Isabelle suffered... a misfortune."

"I knew it." Mrs Olmstead cast a gaze of triumphant disapproval at her son. "When I caught her weeping at every little mishap, I recommended her to my physician. The very suggestion only exacerbated her distress."

"I told you she doesn't like doctors," said Auggie. He turned to Jenny. "She's been to doctors before, hasn't she?"

Jenny nodded, mute in her guilt. What Izzie had needed wasn't a doctor's care but a sister's support.

"If only you'd come sooner," said Mrs Olmstead. "You might have persuaded Isabelle to seek the help she needed."

The admonition took Jenny's breath away. "I didn't realize how troubled she was until her latest letter. I..."

Jenny had no excuse. She'd had her chance to make amends many times over. After her release, Izzie often hinted that she'd love to join Jenny in Europe. They both knew Izzie couldn't do it alone. Their parents kept her on a modest allowance, thinking it would keep her out of trouble. Izzie considered that a punishment, since Jenny continued to receive generous stipends from her trust fund. With a simple wire transfer, Jenny could have put them both on equal footing.

And yet she hadn't. She didn't want to put herself in her parents' position of looking after Izzie. Jenny loved breaking rules, not enforcing them. She refused to be her sister's keeper.

Jenny felt the Olmsteads staring at her. So seldom at a loss for words, she could only plead, "Don't you have any idea where she might have gone?"

"The landlady at her boarding house said she'd moved without leaving a forwarding address," said Auggie. "I assumed she'd gone home to your parents."

"No," said Jenny. She'd sent her parents a telegram from Paris. Her father replied that he'd had no word from Izzie.

"Perhaps Isabelle has gone to visit another friend." Mrs Olmstead turned to Auggie. "One who hasn't yet spent all his money on nightclubs and the latest French fashion."

"Mother!" Auggie's flicker of defiance wilted beneath her disapproving gaze.

"All I am saying is that she was happiest when you were spending money on her," said Mrs Olmstead. "Her difficulties only arose when your pockets were empty."

"Abigail," pleaded Mr Olmstead.

Jenny wanted to defend Izzie, but she couldn't help thinking there was some truth to Mrs Olmstead's insinuation. Even before the incident, Izzie had always depended on others. At first she relied on her parents and Jenny, later on feckless boyfriends.

As easy as it was to imagine that Auggie had abandoned Izzie for another woman, Jenny knew it was also possible Izzie had tired of him – or of his domineering mother. Perhaps Izzie had begun seeing someone else who had triggered those dire letters.

Whatever the truth, Jenny could no longer bear these strangers who'd seen Izzie at her worst. There was only one more thing they could offer her. "May I have the address of Izzie's boarding house?"

"I already talked to her," said Auggie.

"But perhaps she'll be more forthcoming with me," said Jenny. "After all, I am Izzie's sister."

Auggie glanced at his mother, who nodded. Auggie jotted down the address on his calling card and handed it over.

Mrs Olmstead said, "If you will wait for him to return from washing the car, our man Geiszler will drive you back to the Continental."

Jenny hadn't mentioned she was staying at the Continental. Someone who knew that could also have sent someone to burgle her room, and Geiszler was a German name. All at once, she was certain that the Olmsteads had been deceiving her. She felt a powerful instinct to get away before this Geiszler returned.

"Thank you." Jenny maintained a neutral expression. "I have a driver waiting for me."

Auggie parted the curtains. "And so you do. Golly! Is that a woman with that motorcycle?" he laughed. "She looks strong as a bear! Somebody call the circus!"

Jenny bristled. In other circumstances, she might have cut Auggie off at the knees for mocking Lonnie, but now was not the moment. She had to get away.

"Isabelle always said her sister was the epitome of the modern woman," said Mr Olmstead. "I am only surprised Miss Barnes didn't arrive by airplane."

"Give Lonnie a little time," said Jenny, deciding there was time for a retort. "She'll catch up to Earhart before you know it."

"Earhart?" said Mr Olmstead.

"Oh, you know," said Jenny. "The famous aviatrix."

The Olmstead men appeared perplexed, but Mrs Olmstead frowned. Jenny waved goodbye, regretting none of the cheek that accompanied her returning courage. It took all of her will not to break into a run as she retrieved her coat and felt the reassuring weight of the guns in her pockets.

She stepped outside to see the Big Chief and sidecar standing upright. Lonnie bounced in the sidecar, the big wrench in one hand.

"Good as new," declared Lonnie. "Suspension feels better, too."

"Let's get out of here." Jenny swapped the hat for her helmet.

Lonnie jumped out of the sidecar and dropped the wrench back into her toolbox. "Where to, boss?"

Before Jenny could decide the answer, the sound of a big car approached. A black Packard with burgundy panels coasted into the driveway, blocking the way out. Glare from the descending sun hid the driver from view until he opened the door and stepped out.

He was tall and lean with a face marked with scars, predominantly on his left cheek. He kept his colorless hair combed straight back. Jenny could see that what appeared to be an unfashionable part was actually a scalp wound, still glistening fresh.

The man saw her and grinned, revealing teeth like a row of tombstones. The humorless gesture made a death's head of his face.

"We need to go now," said Jenny.

Lonnie straddled the Big Chief and kicked the starter pedal. The engine cleared its throat but refused to turn over.

Jenny turned around to see the driver limping toward them. His gait wasn't impaired. It was inhuman. On his left foot he wore a leather sheath. Jenny had seen a similar appliance on a club-footed organ grinder in Florence.

"Now, Lonnie!"

"I'm trying!" The starter again failed to live up to its name.

Jenny reached into a pocket and fumbled for a grip on a pistol.

The man – Geiszler, Jenny assumed – halted his advance. He raised his empty hand to form a pistol of his own. The two-fingered barrel pointed straight at Jenny's head.

"*Peng!*" he mouthed.

The Big Chief roared to life. Lonnie drove across the neighbor's lawn and into the street while Jenny hung onto the sidecar with one hand and gripped a .45 with the other.

CHAPTER 7

They sped through the streets of French Hill, turning down side-streets at every chance to shake off pursuit. Jenny kept looking back to see whether Geiszler followed. A few times she spied a car just as they turned, but she couldn't tell whether it was the one she feared.

"Where we headed?" Lonnie shouted over the din of the engine.

Jenny didn't want to return to the Continental, now that she knew the Olmsteads had sent Geiszler there. They might also look for her at Izzie's boarding house, so she didn't want to go there, either.

She recalled something else the Olmsteads had told her about when they'd last seen Izzie. Jenny wondered whether some truth had slipped out along with the lies.

"Back to the university," she yelled. "And don't spare the horses!"

"What horses?" Through her goggles, Lonnie's eyes were a cartoon of perplexity.

"Hit the gas!"

"Why didn't you just say so?" She twisted the accelerator. The front wheel came up off the pavement. Both women whooped until it came back down. Lonnie leaned her shoulders over the handlebars to keep the bike down. Jenny hunched forward in the sidecar to add a few more pounds to the equation.

They startled a pair of horses drawing a delivery wagon.

"These horses?" yelled Lonnie.

Under different circumstances Jenny would have laughed. Her fear of Geiszler and her new belief that the Olmsteads knew exactly where Izzie had gone had her teetering between rage and terror.

The wagon driver yelled and shook his fist. Lonnie twisted the accelerator. The Big Chief left him choking on dust.

Lonnie brought them back to campus in half the time it had taken them to reach French Hill. As she drove onto the walk beside the Social Sciences building, a shrill whistle sounded behind them. Jenny looked back to see a deputy pursuing them on a motorcycle huffing out black exhaust.

"Oh, no!" bellowed Lonnie. "Papa will knock me on my ass if I get cited."

As the motorcycle drew nearer, Jenny saw the driver spit out his whistle. It fell to his chest, hanging from a chain. Despite smudged goggles and puffy red cheeks, Jenny recognized the young man.

"It's all right, Lonnie. It's Deputy Morgan." Jenny nudged her with an elbow. "I think he might let you off with a warning."

"Oh, no, he won't," she said. "I picked on him too much. Jenny, he's going to put me in jail!"

"You're being ridiculous."

Jenny waved as Gal parked his smoking hulk. It appeared to have been cobbled together from several different motorbikes, some car parts, and possibly a bicycle or two. The engine rattled and twitched before subsiding with a hiss. Gal balanced the bike on its kickstand before carefully backing away. Before he got out of range, the tailpipe belched out one last noxious cloud.

"You're going to have to bail me out, Jenny," Lonnie babbled. "Papa won't do it. He'll say I deserve to be taught a lesson."

"Show a little backbone, Lonnie," Jenny whispered. A simple traffic stop was a trifling matter after their flight from French Hill. She turned her brightest smile on Gal. "Good afternoon, Deputy Morgan."

"Miss Barnes." He tipped his hat.

"I didn't mean to scare those horses!" Lonnie blurted out.

"That's not why I'm–" Gal coughed into his sleeve. By the sound of it, Jenny figured he'd be lucky not to contract black lung.

Jenny offered him a handkerchief. "Why on earth are you riding that death trap?"

"Sheriff Engle wasn't too happy when he saw the strips Devil tore out of the department car." Gal declined the handkerchief.

Jenny returned it to her bag. "Devil is the right name for that voracious beast."

"Yes, miss. Now, as to the reason I pulled you over–"

Jenny put a hand on his arm. "Take it easy on her, will you, Gal? Lonnie's already terrified. I'm sure she's learned her lesson."

"I didn't hit nobody!" cried Lonnie. "There's no posted speed limit! Anyway, I can't see through these goggles!"

Jenny leaned over and whispered, "Don't overdo it."

"Ladies," said Gal. "I didn't pull you over for speeding."

"No?" said Jenny.

"Although I should warn you to keep motor vehicles off the campus walkways."

"That sounds entirely reasonable," said Jenny. "You will stick to the streets from now on, won't you, Lonnie?"

Lonnie pushed up her goggles. "I sure will. Promise!"

"See, Gal? You've reinforced public order. Wasn't that easy?"

"I'm not here for Lonnie, Miss Barnes." Gal removed a notebook from his shirt pocket. "I'm here for you."

"For me? Whatever for?"

Gal flipped open the notebook. "We have a complaint from one Wylie Donohue that a woman identified as Jenny Barnes assaulted and robbed him at his place of work."

Jenny laughed. "You can't be serious."

"He says you stole a valuable pair of custom firearms."

Jenny arched an eyebrow, hoping to conceal her surprise while blunting Gal's confidence. She stood, leaving her coat on the seat of the sidecar and raising her arms, knowing full well how the gesture showed off her bare shoulders and the snug fit of her dress. "Does this ensemble look like it would be complemented by a pair of holsters?"

Gal focused on the notebook but couldn't conceal his blush. "The report doesn't mention anything about holsters, Miss Barnes."

It took little effort to exaggerate her indignation. "Even so, Dainty Donohue claims I assaulted him?"

"So you do know the gentleman?"

"See how clever he is, Jenny?" said Lonnie. "I've always said, 'That Galeas Morgan will make a fine detective one day.'"

"Stay out of this, Lonnie." Jenny and Gal did double takes after hearing themselves speak in unison.

"I was just paying the guy a compliment," grumbled Lonnie.

"I met a man called Dainty Donohue," Jenny admitted. Silently, she berated herself for overplaying her bluff. "I assure you, however, he was no gentleman."

"Be that as it may, Miss Barnes, he's a resident of Arkham and a business owner. It's my duty to investigate his complaint."

"Are you kidding me, Gal?" Lonnie dismounted from the bike. "Dainty Donohue is a crook and a rum runner. Sheriff Engle knows that as well as anybody. So do you!"

"That doesn't matter, Lonnie. If he files a complaint, I've got to investigate. So you admit you were at Mr Donohue's place of work last night?"

"You mean the Tick-Tock Club?" said Jenny.

"I have it listed here as O'Malley's Watch Shop."

Jenny held up a testifying hand. "I can honestly say I wasn't in a watch shop last night."

The front door of the Social Sciences building banged open. A flood of students poured out, the deluge splitting into smaller streams headed in different directions. A few of the young men slowed to admire Jenny's legs. One whistled. Jenny wrinkled her nose at him, but she had to admit he had an admirable whistle.

Gal pointed at the whistler. "Mind your manners!"

The student jeered. Lonnie raised a fist and took a menacing step forward. He ran for his life.

Gal looked poised to admonish Lonnie for interfering. Instead, he turned his attention back to Jenny. "But you were with Mr Donohue last night. Isn't that so, Miss Barnes?"

The young deputy was as smart and tough-nosed as he was good-looking. If he were on the take from Donohue and his gang, Jenny's goose was as good as cooked. But if he turned out to be an honest police deputy just trying to do his duty, as she tended to believe, she would need to do more than bat her eyes at him to extricate herself from his interrogation.

"I had a brief encounter with Mr Donohue. I asked after my sister. He responded by adulterating my drink."

"Adul – he did what?" Gal's eyebrows leaped in surprise, an expression soon replaced by a look of grim disapproval.

"Don't be thick, Gal," said Lonnie. "She's saying he slipped her a Mickey."

Jenny suppressed the urge to compliment Lonnie's vocabulary. One moment she misunderstood a perfectly ordinary expression, but the next she grasped an uncommon word. Jenny wondered whether Lonnie played dumb to appeal to men, but if that were the case, she'd expect Lonnie to dress in a more feminine manner. In some ways, Lonnie was a more enigmatic woman than anyone Jenny had met in Paris.

"Miss Barnes," said Gal, "if Donohue tried to drug you, why didn't you file a police complaint?"

"You should have let me come with you last night," Lonnie said. "I'd have given the lout a good crack across the kisser."

"Stay out of this, Lonnie," said Gal. "Well, Miss Barnes?"

Jenny had many good answers to Gal's question, but she knew perfectly well how men in authority responded to such complaints from women. The first thing they asked was why the woman went alone to a place like the Tick-Tock Club. Next, they'd accuse her of asking for trouble. Jenny decided to offer Gal another part of the truth, "Deputy Morgan, I came to Arkham to find my sister. I have reason to believe she's in danger."

"So, did you assault Mr Donohue because you believed he drugged your drink or because he wouldn't tell you where to find your sister?"

"I simply switched our drinks," said Jenny. "If anything, Mr Donohue assaulted himself."

Gal mulled over that point. His expression wavered between acceptance and skepticism. "Maybe you ought to start at the beginning, Miss Barnes."

Jenny saw no other way out of it than to let Gal in on what she'd already told Lonnie, omitting Reggie's role, her theft of Dainty's pistols, and the bruises she'd doubtless left on the gangster's face. The university bell tower chimed three o'clock as she finished her tale.

Gal closed his notebook. "That's quite a story, Miss Barnes." There was sympathy in his voice but also a dutiful tone. "Maybe it'd be best if you came down to the station to make a statement."

"Haven't you heard a word she's said?" Lonnie poked Gal in the chest. "Her sister's in trouble. There's creepy stuff going on. You should be helping her, not bothering with some ginned-up complaint from a lousy crook."

Gal swatted her finger away. "Keep your mitts off me, Lonnie. You need to respect the uniform, even if I'm the one in it."

Lonnie winced. "But I do respect–"

"Save it, Miss Ritter," said Gal. "You're lucky I don't charge you with assaulting an officer of the law. Now step back and let me do my job."

Lonnie cringed at "Miss Ritter." Her shoulders slumped.

A rapid patter of high-heeled shoes approached. "Just what job is that, deputy? Harassing my colleague on the sacred grounds of the academy?"

Professor Félix hurried out of the Social Sciences building, a storm rising in her eyes. With a ball-shaped clutch swinging from one hand and a folder under the other, she looked as fierce as an Amazon wielding flail and shield.

"Tilde!" said Jenny.

Tilde didn't spare her a glance. She focused on Gal, who responded with an expression of confused awe. "Well, Deputy– what is your name?"

Gal tipped his cap while trying but failing not to stare at Tilde. Jenny felt a brief pang of envy at her effect on the deputy. "Galeas Morgan, Miss... uh..."

"Professor Félix."

Gal took half a step back. "Professor."

"Miss Barnes," said Tilde. "I've found the material you requested. I'm afraid it can't wait for this functionary to cite you for whatever misdemeanor he means to conjure from his little notebook."

"Now listen just a minute–" Gal began.

"Honestly, Deputy Morgan," said Jenny. "Do I look capable of overpowering a grown man to you?"

"Well, I wouldn't think so, Miss Barnes."

"And you've known Lonnie all your life, haven't you?"

"Well, sure." He rubbed his chest where she'd poked him. Jenny imagined he already had a fingertip-sized bruise.

"Then if Lonnie vouches for me..."

"Sure, I vouch for you, Jenny. I vouch for her, Gal."

"In that case, Deputy Morgan, don't you agree that your questions can wait until after we've found my sister and ensured her safety?"

Gal removed his hat and scratched his head. "Well, when you put it like that, Miss Barnes, I suppose my duty to ensure public safety includes helping to find your sister."

"That's the Gal Morgan I know!" said Lonnie. She slugged him in the arm before she realized it. She winced. "Sorry."

"Darn it, Lonnie!" Gal rubbed his arm.

Tilde shook her head in annoyed disbelief.

"It's all right, Tilde." Jenny moved close enough to whisper to the professor. "I trust both of them. They can hear whatever you have to tell me."

"That's all very good." Tilde held up the folder. "But you may not trust me after you see what I've discovered."

"We'll try our best," said Jenny. "But tell me something: when did Auggie Olmstead first show you the medallion?"

"What medallion?" The proximity of Gal's voice surprised them. For a flatfoot, he had an awfully light step.

Jenny unclasped the medallion and showed it to him. Gal examined the face, but Tilde flipped it over to show him the back. As their fingers touched, Gal blushed. Tilde seemed not to notice, but Lonnie crossed her arms and scowled at the professor.

"The markings on the back do resemble early Mycenaean script," said Tilde. "But I think it may be even older."

"So there's no way to translate it?" said Jenny.

"Not directly." A sly smile crept across Tilde's lips. "However, I've discovered similar script – including translations of some phrases – beneath a drawing in *Cultes des Goules*."

"Huh?" said Lonnie and Gal.

"*Ghoul Cults*," Jenny translated in unison.

"Ghouls?" Gal frowned. "You mean grave robbers?"

"Worse," said Tilde. "*Cultes des Goules* is a record of bestial cult practices throughout history. This medallion was used in a ritual of blood sacrifices. Fortunately, the translated text is not in some indecipherable language. It is in–"

"French!" Jenny guessed. "Modern French?"

Tilde nodded. "Modern enough for a spoiled American dilettante to read."

"What does this have to do with Miss Barnes' missing sister?" Gal sounded exasperated. "You can't expect me to believe–"

"What has become of the missing girls the Miskatonic County Police Department has failed to locate?" said Tilde. "Perhaps your Sheriff Engle supposes their disappearances are the work of a lone degenerate. But what if a group is behind these crimes?"

Gal swallowed his protestations.

Tilde removed a few pages from her folder. She beckoned to Lonnie. "Here, give me your back."

Lonnie balked. Jenny nodded at her, and she turned around.

"Lower!" Tilde spread a drawing across Lonnie's broad shoulders. In the sketch, tendrils rose above an altar on which a number of sheep had been butchered. "The cultists worship this monstrous god called Shub-Niggurath. They believe animal sacrifices forge a path to the deity, but only human blood can open the way, allowing the Dark Young of Shub-Niggurath to accept their sacrifice."

"A worshipper," Gal frowned. "Of a god."

"I do not suggest these are historical facts," said Tilde. "They are but extracts of a belief system that some modern cultists have apparently adopted. Look here." She produced another drawing, this one a refinement of the hasty sketch she'd shown Jenny earlier. In it, the heavy tendrils of one of the Dark Young of Shub-Niggurath tore apart a sacrificial victim. Dismembered limbs fell into numerous maws gaping from the thing's headless torso.

"That's–" Gal stammered. "That's not even an animal."

Jenny feared these outré details could shatter Gal's tenuous acceptance of cult involvement. "We're not saying this is real, Deputy Morgan. Gal, I think people who believe in these things have got my sister. They've certainly kidnapped the local girls."

Gal's mouth worked for a moment before he closed it. He gestured for Jenny to continue.

"Here's the urgent question, Tilde: when did Auggie show you the medallion?"

Tilde's brows converged as she thought. "He first visited on the seventeenth. Nine days ago."

"That's barely over a week," said Jenny. "Yet he said he hasn't seen Izzie for several weeks."

"You think Auggie did something to your sister?" said Lonnie. She slapped a hand over her mouth. "I mean, you think he's got her stashed somewhere?"

"I don't know," said Jenny. "What I do know is that Auggie Olmstead is lying to me, and so are his parents."

"The Olmsteads?" said Gal. "You mean Winthrop and Abigail Olmstead?"

"Yes," said Jenny. "I just came from visiting them at Auggie's house. They must have sicced their chauffeur on me. I'm sure he's the one who broke into my hotel room last night."

"Jeez, Jenny," said Lonnie. "First the speakeasy, then a burglar? You had one busy night."

Gal tore off his hat and slapped it against his thigh. "That tears it! The Olmsteads are the most upstanding citizens in Arkham. There's no way they'd have anything to do with ghouls or cults or... or monsters. Monsters, for Pete's sake!"

"You're just saying that because they always support the police department's fundraisers," said Lonnie. Gal shot her an angry look. She jutted her chin, refusing to take it back.

"A moment ago, you were ready to arrest me on the word of a known criminal," said Jenny. "Now you're telling me the Olmsteads can't be guilty of a crime because they're rich?"

"I–" Gal swallowed whatever it was he was going to say. "When you put it that way, I guess… But why would they kidnap your sister? The Olmsteads don't need money."

"They aren't looking for ransom," said Tilde. "They are looking for sacrifices."

"I still don't buy–"

"You don't have to believe it all. You only have to believe that the Olmsteads could be lying about knowing what has become of Miss Barnes' sister."

Jenny wanted to hug her. Jenny had seen a few things in Europe and Africa that opened her mind to unorthodox beliefs. She knew it was hard for Gal to accept it, but she'd thought it would be even harder for an academic to credit such ideas. All she knew for certain was that Izzie was mixed up in something, and the Olmsteads were at the bottom of it.

"Perhaps Izzie saw something they didn't want known." Jenny turned to Gal. "It doesn't matter what else they're trying to hide. They're definitely hiding whatever happened to my sister."

"August Olmstead asked me to research this medallion for a reason," said Tilde. She handed Jenny her notes. Even a glance at the dense writing and odd symbols was overwhelming. There was too much information and too little time. Jenny needed it all simplified. She had no time to read. She needed to do something. She needed action.

"If your notes tell them what they need for this ritual, why did they need my medallion?"

"The cultists believe it has magical power." For a moment, Tilde's confident expression cracked. "After the tingling I felt when I put it on this afternoon, I'm not entirely sure they're wrong."

"What tingling?" Gal wrinkled his nose as if he'd caught a whiff of something rotten. "First it was monsters. Now you're talking about magic?"

"Here," said Tilde. She unbuttoned Gal's shirt. He sputtered and made a feeble effort to brush away her hands. Lonnie bristled. Jenny put a hand on her arm, impressed by Lonnie's hard muscles.

Once she had exposed the bare skin above Gal's undershirt, Tilde plucked the medallion from his hand and pressed it against his chest. "There. Feel that?"

Blushing so deep that Jenny worried he might faint, Gal shook his head. "I don't feel anything."

"Sure you don't." Lonnie glowered at Tilde. "Get your mitts off, lady. Don't you know you're assaulting an officer of the law?"

Tilde let go of Gal and handed Lonnie the medallion. "Try it for yourself. Press it over your heart, and tell me you don't feel it, too."

With a dubious frown, Lonnie slipped the medallion beneath her shirt and pressed it to her breastbone. She held it there for a few seconds before saying, "Nothing. This is nothing but a bunch of hooey. Sorry, Jenny. But it is."

"I don't understand." Jenny took the medallion and pressed it to her chest. She felt nothing but the bronze, slightly warmed from contact with Gal's and Lonnie's skin.

"Let me see," said Tilde. She tried it herself before peering closely at the medallion. "This isn't the one you showed me earlier, Jenny. The detail isn't nearly as fine. This is the copy!"

Jenny snapped as she put two and two together. "That little weasel! They threw Auggie out of the Tick-Tock for picking pockets. He must have palmed my medallion at his house. He replaced it with Izzie's copy. He must know where she is!"

"All right, ladies," said Gal. "I can't say I believe this stuff about cults and ghouls and magic. But this medallion is evidence that your sister's been kidnapped. We'd better all go to the sheriff's office and take your–"

"The Barn!" Jenny blurted out. "A musician at the Tick-Tock said Auggie mentioned some place called 'the Barn.' Dainty assumed it was the name of a rival speakeasy, but what if he was talking about an actual barn? The Olmsteads were talking about a barn when I arrived. Do they own a farm?"

Tilde and Lonnie shrugged.

"Do they, Gal?"

"They have a farmhouse out on Harrow Road."

"Is there a barn?"

"Well, I guess there is. But you can't just go running over–"

"There's no time to lose." Jenny stepped into the sidecar.

"Where to, boss?" Lonnie jumped onto the Big Chief.

Jenny realized she had no idea. "Gal, we'll need you to lead us to that barn."

Gal winced. "I can't just–"

"Izzie's life is in danger! Besides, it'll be dark before long."

"It will be darker than you think, *cherie*. Tonight is the new moon – a propitious time for blood ritual." Tilde looked embarrassed to hear the words coming out of her own mouth. "If you believe in such superstitious nonsense, that is."

"Knock it off with the ritual talk!" said Gal.

"They're going to hurt those girls if we don't get there soon," said Jenny.

Gal turned from Jenny to Lonnie to Tilde before accepting that he was outnumbered. "All right. I'll take you there, but I'll talk to the Olmsteads myself. Understand?"

Jenny nodded. "Thank you."

"I don't like the looks of that contraption." Tilde eyed the ugly police motorcycle. "But I suppose I must ride with Deputy Morgan."

"What?" said Gal. "You can't ride with me. Certainly not dressed like – with those very nice–"

"That's right," Lonnie cut him off. "Safety hazard."

"Well, I am not staying behind." Tilde thrust her fists against her hips. "I did all the research!"

"It'll be a tight fit." Jenny squeezed over. "But best you join me."

CHAPTER 8

The paved streets of Arkham gave way to gravel just beyond town limits. Lonnie held back on the gas to keep the Big Chief out of the police bike's oily exhaust. It was no mean feat since – even with two in the sidecar – the newer motorcycle could easily overtake Gal's.

About two miles later, Gal turned onto a dirt road. A column of dust rose in his wake. Lonnie stopped the Big Chief and tied a handkerchief around her face. She looked like a bandit preparing to rob a stagecoach. Jenny and Tilde followed her example. When they were ready, Lonnie twisted the accelerator. The Big Chief leaped back into the chase.

Jenny and Tilde lowered their heads against the dust. With Lonnie's big toolbox on the floor, Jenny felt as if they were crammed into a dumbwaiter.

"Oh no!" Lonnie yelled over the sound of the engine. She pointed to the side of the road. "Devil's on the loose."

On a low hill perched a farmhouse feathered with peeling paint. On one side of the house, a hard-faced woman took in the wash from a clothesline. On the other, a stocky youth carried an armload of firewood. At the sound of motorcycle engines, both paused to stare at the chase. Just as Jenny was about to ask Lonnie what she was talking about, she noticed an iron post in the yard. Hanging limp from the pole was a gnawed rope.

"The same goat?" Jenny shouted over the din.

"We'd better warn Gal!" Lonnie laughed. "If that goat eats his motorcycle, the sheriff will have his hide."

Tilde covered her eyes as the dust lashed their faces. "*Merde!*"

Noticing the professor's distress, Lonnie opened the throttle. Tilde bent over to shield her face beneath the lip of the sidecar.

A little over a mile later, they found Gal by the side of the road. He'd dismounted off the bike and craned his neck to peer around a tree. Lonnie pulled up beside him.

"What is it, Gal?"

He beckoned her over. Jenny joined them. Tilde followed, rubbing grit out of her eyes and muttering French profanities.

"Isn't that your father's?" He pointed to a black truck partly obscured by a stand of sugar maples.

"Looks like it," said Lonnie. "He must've finished at Schrader's."

"What's he doing near the Olmsteads'? He didn't even park in the driveway."

"I dunno." Lonnie pulled her goggles down beneath her chin, leaving a clean mask over her dusty face. "He installed some gas light fixtures a while back. Maybe they had problems."

"It's a weird coincidence." Gal glanced at Jenny. "You're sure the man who broke into your room was the Olmstead chauffeur?"

"He spoke German," said Jenny. "And he had a limp."

Gal looked thoughtful but said nothing.

"Stop right there, Gal." Lonnie sounded more pleading than

angry. "You know Papa better than that. Just because he's got a bum leg and an accent don't mean nothing."

"This is getting more peculiar by the minute. We should have gone to the station." Gal fiddled with the whistle hanging from his neck. "This is no use out here."

"The sun's getting low," said Jenny. "We need to see what's going on over there, and it's better if they don't hear us coming."

Gal reluctantly agreed to leave the bikes behind. Jenny fetched her coat. Even if she hadn't wanted her pistols, the afternoon's warmth was fading fast.

Lonnie ran back to the Big Chief. She caught up with them as they reached her father's truck. She had her big wrench in hand. "In case something needs fixing."

They peered into Ritter's truck and saw no one inside. They crept along the stand of maples until they came to a driveway. About sixty yards away stood a two-story Georgian, grand enough for a family like the Olmsteads, Jenny thought. Parked between the main house and a servants' house was the black-and-burgundy Packard. The driveway curved around to the back.

"Geiszler's here," Jenny whispered. "Probably the whole Olmstead clan, too."

"Look there." Tilde pointed to the opposite side of the house. Jenny glimpsed a tall, limping figure disappearing around the corner.

"Did you see who it was?" said Gal.

Tilde shook her head. "He was carrying something. A stick. Maybe a shotgun."

"That's suspicious." Jenny suppressed the impulse to take charge. Having a deputy at her side could be a great advantage, but only if he felt as if he were making the decisions. "Don't you think so, Gal?"

Gal's hand rested on his revolver. "Stay here. I'll have a look."

"If we stay here, you won't be nearby if he finds us." She held up her empty hands, hoping he didn't notice the sagging weight of the .45s in her pockets.

Gal chewed it over. "All right, but keep behind me. And stay close."

Jenny followed. Tilde kept a hand on Jenny's shoulder, while Lonnie brought up the rear, clutching her wrench.

They hurried across the driveway, conscious of every gravel-crunching footstep. Lonnie ran over to touch the hood of the Packard and loudly whispered, "Still warm."

From somewhere behind the house, the scrape of a garage door being opened or closed startled them. Lonnie ran back to the group. Gal drew his revolver.

They hurried along the side of the house where they'd spotted the limping man, crouching to keep their heads below the windows. Revolver held shoulder-high, Gal peered around the corner.

"Nobody." He led the others behind the house.

The backyard resembled an English garden. Its centerpiece was a concrete birdbath flanked by wrought-iron benches. A green toolshed nearly disappeared into the surrounding foliage. A footpath wound through an ivy-covered arbor and into the woods.

Gal kept near the house, glancing at the woods after every second or third step. Their footsteps were almost silent on the grass, but Jenny couldn't help imagining each soft step was as loud as a falling branch. She pictured Geiszler's nasty grin and the way he pointed his fingers like a gun. "*Peng!*"

The breeze returned. At every *shush* of leaves, Jenny looked around to see whether the Olmsteads' man had found them.

On the far side of the garden stood a brick garage with its door open. Inside they could see a small tractor parked beside a large vacant space. Two pairs of tire tracks led away from the empty spots.

"Room for a car and a truck," said Jenny. "What do you think, Deputy Morgan?"

Gal offered a grim nod.

The sound of a door closing came from around the corner of the house. Jenny slipped a hand into her coat pocket to feel the pistol grip. Gal moved around the corner. She caught up to him at a side door. He touched the doorknob and peered inside the window. He paused to nod at Jenny. He opened the door and stepped inside.

Through a pair of archways on the right was an empty kitchen, its counters clean and tidy. Across the hall, closed doors suggested a pantry and closet. Gal touched Jenny's elbow and nodded at the hallway floor. A faint trail of dusty footprints led to a stairway.

They followed the prints upstairs. They emerged onto a hall lined with burnished gas lamps that illuminated landscape paintings. The trail led to an open door. Slanting light pooled on the hallway floor.

Gal whispered, "If that was the chauffeur, then we've just unlawfully entered."

"Would a chauffeur skulk around his employer's house?" said Jenny.

"We don't know what he was doing." Gal holstered his pistol. "He might have been checking for intruders. Legally, we ought to go back and ring the bell."

"Giving him time to conceal evidence?" said Jenny.

"It was a mistake to come in like this," said Gal. "I'm going to ride back to – hey!"

Jenny rushed past him and through the open door of a library.

Cherrywood shelves lined the walls. Beside the door stood a fireplace. A ring of chairs surrounded a round carpet and coffee table on which sat three enormous books. To one side, a globe of the world rested in a brass cradle. Tiffany-style chandeliers caught the western light and threw motes of red, yellow, and violet across the room.

Jenny's arrival startled a man standing near the fireplace. He turned, a length of copper pipe half-raised. Jenny began to pull the pistol from her pocket as Lonnie cried out, "Papa?!"

Ritter's face reddened. "What are you doing here, *liebchen*?"

"No, Mr Ritter," said Jenny. She left the pistol in her pocket but kept her hand on the grip. "You tell us first."

"I came because of you." He pointed at the medallion around her neck – Izzie's medallion, the copy. "I remembered where I had seen that face before." He indicated the fireplace mantel.

Images of satyrs and nymphs cavorting among trees adorned the molding. They formed a procession rising from the base of one side up to the top, across, and down again. The figures leaped and danced, their mouths open in joyous song.

At each corner of the mantel was a large round junction with the image from Jenny's medallion. It wasn't exactly the same, but the artist clearly intended the same subject. The willow fronds forming the man's hair and beard extended beyond the frames and wove into the forest background. There they entwined the wrists and ankles of unlucky celebrants, dragging them into the darkness between the trees. The expressions on the captured were anything but joyous.

"Is anyone home?" Tilde's voice quavered. Her clutch and folder no longer looked much like an Amazon's armaments.

"I don't think so," said Ritter.

"Stay here," said Gal. "I'll take a look."

Jenny didn't like his leaving, but she was sure she could handle Lew Ritter if he turned out to be lying. On the other hand, she wouldn't like to shoot Lonnie's father. She felt safer with an officer of the law present.

As Gal withdrew, Ritter said, "I know I shouldn't have come inside, but there was no answer to the bell. The door was unlocked."

"It's all right, Mr Ritter." It wasn't all right, of course. Despite her brief encounter with Geiszler, Jenny still wasn't comfortable around Lew Ritter. "I'm told there's a barn on the property. Do you know where it is?"

Ritter pointed northwest. "That way, about half a mile through the woods."

"Why so far away?"

"The Olmsteads own several adjacent properties. I don't think they work much of the farms. They enjoy their privacy."

Especially if they perform cult ceremonies on their property, thought Jenny. She and Tilde exchanged a knowing glance, but neither gave voice to the notion.

A voice came from somewhere on the house's ground floor. Lonnie started to say something, but Jenny shushed her. She strained her hearing to make out who was speaking. She stepped into the hallway.

Near the top of the stairs, Jenny could hear the voice better. It was definitely a man, but before she could make out what he was saying, a shrill cry came from the woods. It reminded Jenny of the goat's scream that welcomed her to Arkham, but the tenor was different.

"Was that a child?" said Ritter.

"An animal, I think," Tilde said hopefully.

Gal charged up the steps. "Did you hear that?"

"We all did. Was there someone downstairs with you?"

"No." Gal's gaze shifted away from Jenny. She knew he was lying.

"Let's check behind the house," said Jenny. They hurried back the way they'd come.

As they crossed the garden, Jenny caught a whiff of the Miskatonic. Its scent had a different character here than in Arkham. There was no bitter tang of coal, no taint of asphalt and engine exhaust. Tree bark and decaying leaves sweetened the air flowing off the river.

Gal led them along the footpath winding away from the house. The farther they walked, the denser the woods became. Through the darkening boughs, scarlet ridges of clouds grew brighter against the deep blue sky. Jenny began to fear they would become lost. Just before the point of despair, they emerged into a twilit clearing.

At their feet sprawled a harvested pumpkin patch, severed vines browning among the furrows like eels asphyxiating after a tidal retreat. To one side lay several more fields, all fallow.

"Look." Gal pointed out a pair of tire tracks running across the fields to a barn. Affixed to its walls were circular plaques painted with strange images.

"Those do not look like hex signs," Tilde said.

As a girl, Jenny had seen hex signs on a tour of Pennsylvania Dutch farm country. Unlike the usual geometric designs, these images were asymmetric sigils and androgynous green faces, hair and beards floating as though submerged in a river current.

The barn doors stood open. The sweet odor of hay mingled with the stink of animal dung. Inside, a row of empty stalls ran along one wall. Along the opposite side squatted three iron cages. Tools hung on the sun-faded walls, along with the silhouettes of missing farm implements: hooks and sickles and knives. Ladders rose to a high loft filled with bales of hay. Loose straw covered the floor, crushed where regular passage had worn a path down the center.

The Ritters stood at the barn door while Gal examined the stalls. Jenny and Tilde checked the cages. The straw in each of them had been pressed down as though by long occupancy. Inside each lay a filthy bucket and a clay jug.

"These were made for dogs," said Tilde.

"But they held something else." Jenny stooped to pluck a scrap of gingham from where it had caught in the wire body of the cage. Before she stood up, she noticed letters scratched in the barn wall: "A. H. was here."

"What do the initials 'A. H.' mean to you, Gal?"

Gal puzzled over the question, but Lew Ritter blurted out, "Angela Houston! One of the missing girls."

Jenny looked for more writing but found none. One of the jugs had been tipped over. "The straw here is still wet," she said. "Someone left this cage recently."

"They went into the truck," said Gal. "But if we follow those tracks across open fields, we'll be seen."

"Come on, Gal," said Lonnie. "You were a Boy Scout. Find us a shortcut."

"A scout, not a bloodhound." Despite his complaint, Gal went outside and peered at the surrounding foliage. He sniffed the air. "Do you smell that?"

"Maybe you're a bloodhound after all!" Lonnie looked to Gal for approval of her joke, but Jenny knew it was not the moment. Lonnie's smile dwindled as she came to the same realization.

"It's coming from the river," said Gal. He pointed out a path

Jenny never would have spied on her own. "Let's try this game trail."

Gal and Jenny led the way. He holstered his pistol, but Jenny noticed his hand never strayed far from the grip. Hers remained inside her pocket, ready to draw the .45 if necessary. Lonnie had her wrench and Lew his length of pipe. Tilde walked in the middle, arms wrapped around her research notes.

The elms and poplars gave way to willows. The undergrowth grew thicker. Roots and vines caught at their toes. The birdsong Jenny had barely noticed earlier became conspicuous by its absence.

A shriek froze them in place.

"That was Devil," said Gal. "I've heard enough of his bleating to know that sound anywhere."

"He was gone when we passed the Schrader place," said Lonnie. "Was he there when you worked on the pipes, Papa?"

Lew Ritter shook his head. "He was always so much trouble, I assumed Mrs Schrader finally roasted him."

"Shush, everybody," said Tilde. She moved forward and beckoned the others to join her. "Listen."

At first Jenny heard nothing, but then the sound of pipes rose above the susurrus of leaves. The melody swirled back on itself. It sounded the way a spiral looked, Jenny thought: simple yet hypnotic.

They moved toward where they'd heard Devil's scream, pausing now and then to listen for the pipes. Soon they heard the rhythmic rise and fall of human voices. Jenny couldn't understand the words. She looked at Tilde, who shook her head at the unspoken question.

They pushed on, crouching at a gesture from Gal. The bleating of goats and a girl's muffled whimpering joined the weird music.

They crept forward, trying to remain behind cover. At last, they looked north onto a meadow separated from the river by a line of weeping willows.

Huge bonfires formed a five-point border around a circle of robed men and women. Sickles and curved knives hung from belts of woven roots and vines. Cowls obscured their faces. They swayed in time with the breeze, not their song, as if they'd surrendered their bodies to nature. The asynchronous motion made Jenny dizzy.

Three pairs of cultists held grass ropes looped about the wrists of girls in homespun gowns. They were all younger than Izzie, with garlands of flowers on their heads. The girls shared a look of gauntness and drowsy bliss.

In the assembly's center stood a platform of fresh pine. Low rails ran along the sides, and thick beams held it a good eight feet above the ground. On the far side nearest the river, a ramp curved up from the ground to the platform.

To the west of the scaffold stood a black delivery truck. Someone had tried to obliterate whatever text or image the truck had once advertised, but the scratched remains looked green in the firelight.

On the east side, a pair of cultists stood well away from a lone goat tethered to a post. Jenny recognized Devil from the red stain around one eye and horn. Several loose tethers hung from the post, suggesting the goat had recently had companions.

The two cultists moved in to catch Devil's leash. The goat hopped back and sprang, knocking one of them to the ground. When the second reached for the goat, Devil shot both rear hooves into his belly. The man fell to the ground and rolled away in a frantic escape.

"Leave the beast, you fool!" a woman from atop the scaffold

yelled down at the would-be goatherds. Jenny recognized her voice.

Abigail Olmstead stood before a gory altar of carved wood. Around her neck hung Jenny's stolen medallion. In the fire-lit glow, her face appeared as red as the blood glistening on the altar. To either side of her stood two cowled figures, a woman and a tall man. Jenny strained to see the shadowed face beneath the second woman's cowl.

"Izzie?" She whispered her sister's name, afraid of attracting attention. Whoever she was, the woman beside Abigail Olmstead did not appear constrained, like the drugged maidens.

Before the altar, two more men heaved a goat carcass off the platform. Their cowls fell back as they moved, revealing the faces of Winthrop and August Olmstead.

The animal's body fell on a heap of goat remains. A cultist awaiting the fresh corpse thrust his fists into its slit belly, rummaged around, and drew out his glistening hands. Crossing the circle, he knelt before one of the dazed girls. He pressed bloody handprints onto her belly. He sketched bloody sigils onto her palms and brow.

At the sight of the blood, the cultist beside Abigail Olmstead let out a little shriek.

Abigail slapped the woman. Her cowl fell back, revealing Izzie's face. Despite the blow, her eyes were locked on the sight of the bloody handprints on the captive girl.

"Izzie!" Jenny choked.

"*Gott im Himmel!*" hissed Lew Ritter. He hefted his pipe and took one shuffling step forward.

"No, Papa!" Lonnie put her hand on his shoulder. "There are too many."

Tilde muttered in French while shuffling through her notes. Gal was also talking to himself, counting the number of cultists. Unless he had a lot of extra bullets in his pockets, Jenny knew he wouldn't like the sum.

Jenny revealed her pistols. "Add another fourteen shots."

Gal looked at her with an almost childish expression of outrage at a lie revealed.

"Strike that." Jenny subtracted the two shots she'd fired at the Continental. "Twelve left."

Gal's goofy reaction transformed into a look of grim determination. He nodded.

Two cultists were leading the anointed girl to the scaffold. As they passed Devil, the goat hopped back, lowered his head, and lunged. The men shied away, and the tether spared them a butting, but the force of Devil's attack loosened the post.

"*Iä! Shub-Niggurath!*" cried the cultists. They raised their arms toward those atop the platform.

Abigail Olmstead thrust her fingers through her perfect coif, freeing her hair. The strands lifted about her head in a wild halo. Light flickered across the medallion, dancing across the bronze like St. Elmo's fire. Together, the Olmsteads responded: "*Iä! Shub-Niggurath!*"

Beside Abigail, Geiszler drew back his cowl. His gaunt face stared out like a skull from a catacomb niche. Together, he and Abigail cried out words in an unknown language. The cultists joined in. At the firelight's utmost edge, willow fronds rose up as though the world had turned upside down. The river howled.

"Stop them!" cried Jenny.

Gal fired a shot into the air. "Police!" he yelled. "Everyone, stop what you're doing! You'll be surr–"

The earth shuddered. Gal fell forward. Jenny tumbled into

Tilde, and they went down together. Lonnie and her father clung to each other to stay on their feet.

The cultists and their captives screamed. All eyes turned toward the source of the rumbling.

The heap of slaughtered goats shifted. For a mad second, it appeared as if they were scrambling back to their feet. Instead, they sank into the earth, consumed by their own ravenous graves. The churning earth formed a circle at the foot of the platform.

The soil flinched, contracted, and flinched again. With each convulsion, the ground shook. Jenny and Tilde stood, crouching to keep from being thrown down again. Gal leaped up, hollering to no avail. The grinding earth and the chanting cultists drowned out his words.

The spasms continued, each time widening a pit that revealed glistening red walls beneath the soil.

A dark mass pushed forth from the earth's womb. Thick limbs like wet branches yearned skyward, high above the platform. They swayed, whether in agony or exaltation Jenny could not tell. Legs like tree trunks slipped out to stand on cloven hooves. Suppurating mouths opened in a thousand dissonant squeals.

Behind the altar, Izzie's scream cut through the din. Cultists and captives screamed with her, all except Abigail Olmstead and her henchman. The high priestess leered in triumph, while the skull-faced Geiszler gazed impassively at the monster.

CHAPTER 9

The Dark Young loomed twice as tall as a man. Its elephantine tendrils reached even higher to writhe above the altar. Cultists fell to their knees, arms raised in supplication.

Lonnie and her father retreated from the creature to stand with Jenny. Beside her, Tilde studied one of her pages and muttered something that sounded like Greek.

"That's your sister up there?" said Lonnie.

"She's not with them," said Jenny. Even as she made the claim, she wondered whether it was true. Izzie had always been biddable, even before her hospitalization.

"We must take the girls away from them," said Lew Ritter. He held the copper pipe as if it were a rifle.

At the sound of another gunshot, Lonnie cried, "Oh, hell. There goes Gal!"

The deputy ran toward the nearest captive. He shot one of her guards, a skinny man with an eye patch. As the first guard fell, the other raised a threshing flail. His eyes widened as Gal charged toward him. Before the cultist could strike, Gal flattened his nose with a haymaker and finished him off with the butt of his pistol.

Lew Ritter ran to the girl, who swayed, mouth gaping. Three cultists ran toward him. Lew threw his copper pipe, striking one, causing the others to shy away. Lew gathered the girl into his arms and ran toward Jenny.

"I'm going to go out on a limb and say Gal and Lew are on our side." Jenny's voice cracked. She had to joke or lose her mind. Izzie couldn't be with the cultists. Jenny couldn't believe it, no more than she could believe that monsters like the Dark Young existed. But there it stood, colossal and impossible. Jenny couldn't stand the look of the creature. Its existence was proof that she didn't know a thing about what was real. She didn't know a thing about her own sister.

Jenny couldn't accept that. She raised her pistols and fired.

The recoil was, again, stronger than she'd remembered. She almost struck herself in the face with one of them. She was lucky she hadn't broken a wrist. She decided she'd be better off firing one shot at a time.

The monster didn't seem to notice her attack. Either she'd missed or else the Dark Young's thick hide was impervious to bullets. Its massive tendrils swept down, rooting through the churned earth as easily as an oar might dip into the water. One emerged with a goat carcass. Three more appendages converged on the body, tearing it apart. It dropped the dismembered pieces into its biggest mouth. The round orifice contracted like a sphincter, each spasm revealing and concealing rings of triangular teeth.

Jenny closed her eyes, but she couldn't block the disgusting sounds of tearing flesh and crunching bone.

Devil's bleating joined the clamor. At the rear of the area, the goat menaced the cultists attempting to drag a girl onto the platform. The robed figures edged carefully onto the ramp, their backs against the pilings.

"Stop them!" thundered an unnatural voice. It came from Abigail Olmstead atop the platform. Abigail's eyes glowed with the same eldritch light emanating from the medallion on her chest. She pointed toward Gal and Lew. "Don't let them interrupt the binding!"

Near the bloodied edge of the platform, Auggie and Winthrop Olmstead cringed beneath the Dark Young.

"Back on your feet," bellowed Abigail. "Prepare to offer the anointed sacrifice."

"There!" Geiszler pointed toward Jenny, Tilde, and Lonnie. "Take them."

Izzie's stunned gaze turned in the direction Geiszler indicated. "Jenny!" Her voice was hoarse, as if she'd been screaming all her life. "Jenny, you have to get away!"

"Izzie! I've come for you!"

"Oh boy," said Lonnie. She hefted her big wrench. "Get ready, here they come."

As her minions charged, Abigail Olmstead resumed her imprecations to the Dark Young. The monster thrashed, one of its tendrils sweeping away a leg of the scaffold.

"Do you understand what she's saying?" Jenny asked Tilde.

"A little," said the professor. "It's a spell from *Cultes des Goules*. She is trying to command the Dark Young, but it has not received its promised sacrifice."

"It just ate those goats!"

"They weren't the anointed sacrifice." Tilde pulled her notes from the folder. "The high priestess cannot control the Dark Young until it receives one of those chosen girls."

"Can you stop her?"

Tilde's face was an etching of despair. "Maybe."

"Try!" Jenny fired a shot past Tilde, wounding a sickle-wielding cultist. The woman raised the weapon to strike Tilde. Jenny put a second bullet through her mouth.

Tilde flipped through her notes, dropping pages in her panic. "I'm trying!" Jenny helped recover the fallen pages. Tilde snatched one from her hands. "Here, this might close the path. Listen, and try to repeat after me. It isn't long." She began intoning strange syllables. Jenny recognized only the repeated "Shub-Niggurath."

"Jenny, look out!" cried Lonnie.

A pair of cultists charged, sickles raised.

Jenny fired again, first with one pistol, then with the other. She missed her attackers, but a cultist guarding another of the captives clutched his thigh. Jenny lowered the guns, realizing how close she'd come to hitting the wrong person.

The first cultist was a husky youth, his beard little more than down on his cheeks. Jenny aimed for his chest and fired while backing away. Her heel caught on a root, and she fell painfully on an elbow. She pushed herself up and saw that the man she'd shot lay still.

The second cultist threw herself at Jenny. Mid-flight, her head jerked to the side as Lonnie brained her with the wrench. Lonnie stood there panting, shocked at what she'd done, eyes scanning the meadow for the next foe. Against the bonfires, she looked like a Valkyrie on the battlefield.

Jenny heard more gunshots near the platform. Gal and Lew advanced shoulder to shoulder like soldiers. Those cultists who made it past Gal's bullets fell to Lew's quick punches. By the time they made it to the ramp, Gal had holstered his empty pistol and begun fighting with his fists.

As he knocked down a cultist twice his size, Devil caught sight or scent of Gal. The goat stood up on two legs, staring straight at Gal. Bleating in panic, Devil pulled away from his tether. The goat ran this way and that, turning at every scream from the Dark Young of Shub-Niggurath.

Before Lew and Gal could ascend the ramp, another group of cultists swarmed them. Gal went down under the weight of three attackers.

"Gal!" said Lonnie. "We need to help them, Jenny. They can't keep–" She paused to kick the legs out from under a young woman in cult robes. She knelt down to give the woman a crack across the jaw, knocking her unconscious. "There's too many of these jerks."

"Stay with Tilde," said Jenny. "Don't let anybody stop her from casting her spell. It's the only way to get rid of that thing!"

"What is she, a witch?" Lonnie shook her head, but a sound from the platform drew her attention.

The monster stamped in impatience. Its tendrils thrashed in all directions, probing for sustenance. They found a bloody-faced cultist staggering away from Lew Ritter. A ropy appendage closed around the man's waist, lifting him off the ground. More writhing limbs encircled the man at wrists, ankles, and neck.

The Dark Young held the man over the center of its alien body. At the juncture of its tripartite torso, hundreds of slimy maws opened like the beaks of hungry chicks. With a violent tug, the monster tore away the man's limbs. A shower of blood preceded the dead carcass into the hungry mouths. Upon hearing the sound that followed, Jenny shuddered.

"Don't let them stop the spell," panted Lonnie. "Got it."

Jenny took shot at cultists reckless enough to approach them. Those she merely wounded faced Lonnie, but only for an instant before Lonnie clobbered them with her wrench or a right cross.

Tilde tugged on Jenny's elbow. Still chanting, she gestured for Jenny to join her. The phrases Tilde uttered were short enough that Jenny soon added her voice to the professor's.

As they completed a full recitation and began another, Jenny felt an invisible connection forming between her and Tilde and the ceremony before the platform. The back of her neck prickled with gooseflesh, and she felt her hair rise. Glancing at Tilde, she saw the professor's eyes widen as she experienced the same sensation. Her black hair rose as if she'd leaned back into the bath.

Back at the ramp, Lew turned his back to his opponents and attacked Gal's foes. He knocked one down and stunned another with a volley of jabs. As the cultists gave way, Lew reached down and pulled the deputy back to his feet.

"Kill 'em, Papa! Get 'em, Gal!" shouted Lonnie. She raised her wrench to strike another cultist. After one look at the unconscious bodies piled at Lonnie's feet, he fled.

Jenny felt the bond connecting her and Tilde to the monster slacken. She looked at Abigail. The high priestess had turned away from the altar. The medallion still blazed upon her chest, but now she raised a long-nailed finger toward Lew Ritter. The words she uttered were different from those with which she had summoned the Dark Young.

"Nyaaaah!" screamed Lew. His right arm rose to point back at Abigail Olmstead, fingers unclenching. His halting movement resembled that of a marionette forced to turn by the motion of its master's strings.

"Papa!" cried Lonnie.

Lew's arm twitched and twisted, his sleeve sagging as the flesh beneath withered. His fingers darkened as they shrank, until at last his arm dropped useless at his side.

"Stop it!" Izzie cried. She raised a fist and struck Abigail on the shoulder. "Stop!" Her voice rang out stronger, braver.

Geiszler struck Izzie with the back of his hand. She fell behind the altar. Geiszler raised his misshapen foot to stomp on her, but Abigail stopped him with a touch on his arm.

"Bring me the anointed girl!" she cried.

Geiszler looked at the cultists holding the captive. He dragged her by the arm and shoved her toward Auggie and Winthrop.

So close to the Dark Young, the girl snapped out of her daze. Her eyes and mouth widened in horror as the Olmstead men took her by the arms and pulled her across the altar.

Jenny felt a wave of hunger surge through her. A glance at Tilde showed she'd had the same sensation. With each repetition of the arcane phrases, Jenny felt a stronger connection to the Dark Young. Rather than simply receive its signals, she tried imposing her own on the beast. She willed herself to be still.

The Dark Young's tendrils slowed. Its thrashing calmed.

Beside her, Tilde nodded.

"We need to help Papa!" yelled Lonnie. Her body tensed as she fought the urge to abandon Jenny and Tilde.

Still chanting, Jenny motioned toward the platform with a tilt of her head. The professor nodded agreement, and together the three women moved. Tilde and Jenny maintained their spell while Lonnie cleared a path with wide sweeps of her wrench.

Gal tried to put himself between Lew and their attackers, but the older man pushed him aside. He pointed with his good left arm toward a lone cultist dragging the third captive girl toward the altar. They exchanged a nod. Gal ran toward the girl. Lew ascended the ramp.

Two cultists blocked his path. He dodged their blows with economical shifts of his body. He jabbed the first in the face. As the man turned away, Lew pushed him off the platform. The cultist landed with a sickening crunch of a broken neck. The second fared no better. Lew caught a wild uppercut with his withered arm, wincing at the pain. He head-butted the cultist, smashing his nose. A quick succession of jabs finished him. Lew stepped over the unconscious man.

Geiszler stepped into his path.

The two Germans sized each other up. Both were lame, lean, and of a similar height. Maimed by Abigail Olmstead's dark magic, Lew Ritter stood with his back straight and his one good fist raised to fight. Geiszler sneered, his shoulders hunched as he reached into the sleeve of his robe.

Lew struck first, turning Geiszler's head with a powerful hook. Geiszler stepped back, raising one hand to block the next blow while withdrawing a blade from his sleeve.

"Papa, look out!"

Geiszler grabbed Lew's wrist, pushing it away as he stabbed him in the belly. He struck again and again, each blow leaving another dark stain on Lew's work shirt.

Wailing, Lonnie ran toward the platform.

Jenny wanted to call out after her, but she could sense the spell's effect growing stronger. She could almost feel invisible iron chains hanging from her heart to Tilde's and together across the meadow to the Dark Young.

From atop the platform, Abigail Olmstead glared at her. Her lips moved in unison with Jenny's. With each syllable, Jenny felt the tug of war between them with the Dark Young at its center. She knew Abigail was stronger, even with Tilde and Jenny working together. Somehow the medallion lent her even more strength.

Abigail dipped for a moment, drawn down by some unseen force. She pulled herself upright, still chanting. At the moment she faltered, Jenny felt the weight of their struggle shift.

A hand reached up to clutch at Abigail's robe. Another appeared, pulling her down. She struggled against it, but the hands continued to rise. Izzie clawed her way up Abigail's robe, shaking the older woman.

"Geiszler!" screeched Abigail. "Get her off me!"

As Abigail abandoned the chant, Jenny felt the struggle shift in her favor. The Dark Young tottered, its massive hooves less threatening than uncertain. The ground beneath them softened.

Izzie clawed her way to a standing position, hands tearing at Abigail's robe and at the medallion.

"No, you little idiot!" cried the high priestess.

Abigail and Izzie fought for the medallion. For an instant, Jenny thought Izzie might tear it out of Abigail's grasp. Then, Geiszler punched Izzie in the back of the head. She fell, limp and dazed. Jenny immediately fired a shot, hoping to blast a hole in Geiszler's face. She missed.

Geiszler caught Izzie by the hair and held her up as a shield.

Jenny faltered in her chant. She almost cried out Izzie's name, but Tilde grabbed her arm and squeezed assurance. They were so close to victory – Jenny could feel it, even though she couldn't understand the unseen mechanisms of the ritual.

Across the altar from Abigail, Geiszler, and Izzie, the Olmstead men struggled with their captive. The horror of seeing the Dark Young dashed the girl out of her confusion. She screamed and thrashed, but the men kept hold of her arms. They dragged her closer and closer to the monster. Auggie's foot slipped as they came close to the bloody edge of the platform.

"Finish the sacrifice, you fools!" Abigail cried. "Geiszler, get me out of here. Bring Isabelle!"

Jenny broke into a run, barely remembering to continue the chant as she headed toward the ramp.

She passed Lonnie, who bashed a cultist with her wrench as another clung uselessly to her other arm. Gal ran up from the other side, a girl in his arms. He kicked the cultist clinging to Lonnie, who stomped the man again as he hit the ground.

"Get the girl out of here!" shouted Jenny. With Abigail's retreat, she hoped Tilde's chant would be enough to send the Dark Young away. She was done fighting otherworldly creatures. She was ready to face the human monsters. She ran up the ramp, pistols raised.

When she saw what awaited her on the platform, Jenny feared she was too late. At her feet lay Lew Ritter, motionless in a pool of his own blood. Beyond the altar, Auggie held the captive girl by the ankles as Winthrop struggled to lift her shoulders. Abigail Olmstead had already slipped down from the platform to the hood of the waiting truck. Geiszler passed the half-conscious Izzie down to her.

Jenny aimed just beneath the bright scar on his bare head, ready to finish the job she'd botched at the Continental.

The sacrificial maiden screamed. Jenny whipped her head around to see what was behind her. The Dark Young's tendrils reached toward the girl.

Jenny aimed at Winthrop Olmstead. The girl thrashed in his arms, spoiling her shot.

"Jenny!" cried Izzie. She stood unsteadily beside Abigail Olmstead.

"I don't want to go!" the maiden cried from before the altar. "Don't let it take me!"

In the girl's pleas, Jenny heard an echo of Izzie's sanitarium screams. She never should have abandoned her sister to an uncertain fate. But if she didn't act now, the harvest maiden's fate was certain.

Jenny fired. Winthrop clutched his arm. The girl fell to the platform, clutching at the narrow spaces between the boards to keep Auggie from pulling her away.

Beneath Jenny, the truck doors slammed shut and the engine roared to life. Behind her, the dreadful sound of Lonnie's anguish rose louder and more painful than any utterance of the monster.

The harvest maiden struggled in Auggie's grip. "Please, let go!"

Jenny shot Auggie. The bullet caught him high in the chest, spinning him close to the platform's edge. His feet slipped on the bloody boards. All at once, the Dark Young's tendrils converged around him. He vanished in the monstrous tangle. As the tendrils spread again, he reappeared, held by wrists and ankles.

"August, my boy!" Winthrop reached toward his son. The harvest maiden slipped in the blood but scrambled across the boards to Jenny's feet.

Jenny turned her pistols toward the truck. She fired, and a shot cracked the driver-side window. She squeezed again, and the hammer struck an empty chamber. *Clack!*

Jenny aimed with the other pistol. *Clack!*

The truck pulled away. Jenny yearned for some sight of Izzie, perhaps her face through the window, but the angle of the retreating truck denied her even that much.

"Izzie!"

A hand fell on her shoulder. Jenny nearly struck back, but it was Tilde, still chanting. Exhaustion etched on her face, Tilde gestured for Jenny to join in. Behind her, Lonnie rose from her father's body. Gal ran up behind her, the girls he'd carried away nowhere to be seen. Together, they joined Jenny.

From hundreds of mouths, the Dark Young howled as it shook Auggie Olmstead above its alien mouths.

"Take my hand, son!" Winthrop stumbled as the abomination smashed away another corner of the scaffold.

Jenny held on to Tilde as the platform slid. Lonnie held on to her and Gal to Lonnie. Following Tilde's lead, they joined in her chant until all sang as one. For a hallucinatory moment, Jenny felt as if they were becoming a single being with many mouths and arms.

A deep vibration rose from the earth, surrounding the platform, the monster, and all the dead or dying cultists in the meadow. The tone settled in Jenny's teeth, spreading out through her bones and veins. Some ancient instinct told Jenny that the sound was a voice from beyond the world – an answer to the words she and her friends chanted.

Behind them, a clatter of hooves ran across the scaffold. Jenny and her friends leaped out of the way as a black blur shot down the platform and smashed into Winthrop Olmstead. Still reaching for his son, the man flew off the platform and into the Dark Young's rending tendrils. The Olmsteads screamed together as the child of Shub-Niggurath tore their bodies to pieces and devoured them both.

In turn, the earth began to devour the Dark Young. The red walls that had earlier disgorged the beast opened to swallow it again. Support beams splintered; fallen cultists slid down into the expanding pit.

Devil hopped and twisted around, hooves scrabbling on wood before he gained traction and ran back toward Jenny's group. Taking their cue from the goat, they fled the collapsing end of the scaffold. Splinters exploded all around them as the platform tilted toward the pit.

Strong arms wrapped around Jenny and carried her off the platform. She fell for a brief eternity, barely feeling the impact as she hit the ground. Lonnie scooped her up, threw her over a shoulder, and ran from the abyss and onto flat ground. She didn't stop there, but kept running until Jenny cried out, "Wait!"

Lonnie set her down. Gal caught up with them, Tilde in his arms. They fell together and rolled away, panting and weeping.

Back at the ritual site, the ground swirled like a maelstrom, grass forming ridges like wave crests, fragments of timber bobbing like flotsam before sinking into the depths. The swirling slowly ground to a halt, leaving only wreckage and a few bodies on the surface.

As the chaos subsided, the three harvest maidens came out of hiding. One went directly to Gal and took his hand. The others huddled close without touching.

Jenny dropped her pistols and sat beside her fellow survivors. One by one they lay back, exhausted in body and spirit. They listened to the Miskatonic River's flow while staring up through the veil of clouds at the indifferent stars. Just as Jenny began to catch her breath, the harsh beams of car headlights raked across the devastated meadow.

Jenny tensed, fearing cult reinforcements. She reached for her guns, even though she knew they were empty. Only then did the whirling police siren begin to sound.

"I called the sheriff from the Olmstead house," Gal explained.

"Why didn't you say so?"

"At the time, I wasn't sure who he'd arrest," said Gal.

"Well," said Jenny, looking around at the churned earth, "we're all that's left."

CHAPTER 10

"Just let us know if there is anything we can do," said Mrs Houston. "Anything at all."

Beside her, Angela Houston held her father's hand. From what Jenny had heard, the girl had spoken little since the night in the woods. She avoided eye contact with almost everyone else, but during the burial she'd looked at Jenny and mouthed, "Thank you."

"Thanks, Mrs Houston," said Lonnie. She looked like an entirely different person in the black dress Jenny had persuaded her to accept. While suitable for mourning, it would also serve her well should she ever attend a formal dinner. It was Jenny's first victory in the battle for Lonnie's wardrobe. "You and everybody have sent so much food, I won't need to cook until Christmas."

As Lonnie received more sympathies, Jenny withdrew and stood beside Galeas Morgan. His dress blues transformed him from merely handsome to downright dashing, but the weary lines around his eyes blunted the effect. He appeared to have aged five years in that one awful night. "Any more word from Sheriff Engle?"

"Barring further evidence, he's set aside the complaint from

Mr Donohue." It was Gal's turn to raise a skeptical eyebrow. With some practice, he'd make that a formidable interrogation weapon.

"Thanks, by the way, for barring that further evidence," said Jenny. "I meant, any word about Abigail Olmstead?"

"There's a hold on the Olmstead bank accounts," said Gal. "Unless Mrs Olmstead had plenty of cash on hand, she won't get far. All her known family are Massachusetts residents."

"So she has people who can hide her."

"Maybe," said Gal. "But I bet most wouldn't if they knew the things she'd done. We found more strange things in the basement of the farmhouse." He shuddered at the memory of whatever he'd seen there.

"What about Izzie?"

"The state police recovered the truck near Ipswich. They're on the lookout for Mrs Olmstead and Geiszler – and your sister, of course. The local sheriff has combed the town, but there's no sign of them. Sheriff Engle thinks they stole another vehicle, but we're still waiting for the owner to report it. Any word from your parents?"

Jenny shook her head. "They still haven't heard from Izzie. I didn't have the heart to tell them what had happened in a telegram. I want to find her myself and bring her home."

"So you're staying in Arkham?"

"For now," said Jenny. "Until I find some clue as to where they've taken Izzie."

"You still think she's a prisoner? The sheriff isn't so sure. He thinks Isabelle sent you those letters to lure you to Arkham with the original medallion."

"You told him about the medallion?"

"Well, yes."

"And about the ritual we used to send the monster back to wherever it came from?"

"I may have left out that part."

Jenny thought that wise. "Maybe Izzie's letters were meant to make me bring the medallion to Arkham. That would explain why Geiszler was watching for me at the train station."

"And you still don't think your sister was a part of this cult?"

"Maybe at first," Jenny said. "But if so, it was because Abigail Olmstead manipulated her."

"And she got the idea after seeing Isabelle's medallion," said Gal.

Jenny felt a cold weight in her heart. "They needed the original for the ritual, but they wouldn't have known about it if I hadn't made a copy for Izzie. This whole thing is my fault."

"That's not what I meant, Jenny."

"I know." She gave him a sad smile. "And thanks."

"For what?"

"For not calling me Miss Barnes."

The last of the mourners finished offering their condolences. The others had already begun leaving the cemetery, raising their umbrellas against the increasing drizzle. A pair of gravediggers stood a respectful distance away, averting their eyes whenever someone looked at them lest they seem impatient.

Father Iwanicki reminded Lonnie that she would always find friends at the church. Then he, too, departed.

Lonnie nodded toward the gravediggers. "We ought to let those boys do their job." She'd already slipped a bottle of schnapps and four of Lew's favorite cigars into the coffin. She took his boxing gloves from a paper bag. She kissed one and then the other before putting them back in and rolling the bag closed. "Goodbye, Papa." She dropped the bag into the grave and turned to walk away.

Dressed in his formal blues, Gal offered Lonnie his arm. She socked him in the shoulder, a little lighter, Jenny noticed, than she'd hit him before. "I can walk on my own, can't I?"

"Of course," said Gal. "I was just–"

"He was just reminding you," Tilde interrupted, "that you don't have to walk alone."

Lonnie started to say something, but instead she turned away. Jenny slipped a hand into her bag to fetch a handkerchief. Before she could offer it, Lonnie's big arm shot up and pointed across the cemetery. "What's that devil doing over there?"

On the crest of a hill less than thirty yards away, the black goat with one red eye and horn munched on a bouquet. Jenny knew the grave site. It marked the uncelebrated burial of a dead cultist.

"I caught him again the other day," said Gal. "Schrader said he didn't want him back. I suppose he's earned his freedom."

"Another deputy will have to catch him next time," said Tilde. She cast a mischievous glance at Jenny before stepping close to Gal and taking his arm.

At the sound of the deputy's gulp, Lonnie whipped her head around. "Knock it off, Frenchie. I'm the one in mourning." She grabbed Gal's other arm and pulled him away with such violence that Tilde released her hold.

Lonnie paused for Gal to open an umbrella before letting him escort her back to the car. Behind their backs, Jenny and Tilde exchanged a conspiratorial wink.

"I'm not sure Deputy Morgan feels the same way about Lonnie as she feels about him," said Tilde.

"I'm not sure he has any say in the matter," said Jenny.

She almost regretted buying the Big Chief, which Lonnie had delivered to the customer who'd ordered it. Jenny offered the man a handsome profit above his cost, and he'd put up no struggle. She was biding her time until a happier occasion on which to present it to Lonnie.

There was a chance the bike would only fortify Lonnie's tomboy nature, but Jenny would continue to advocate the advantages of feminine attire. She might even introduce Lonnie to perfume in a week or so. After all, there was time. Jenny was determined to remain in Arkham as long as it took to discover where the cult survivors had absconded with Izzie.

Tilde opened an umbrella and offered her crooked arm to Jenny, who took it.

"What did Professor Armitage have to say?" said Jenny. "That is, assuming you told him everything."

"At first I gave him an abridged summary," said Tilde. "His response was encouraging. So many in our field take skepticism to its illogical extreme. Armitage seems to have read more broadly on occult subjects than anyone else I have met at Miskatonic. In the end, I told him everything."

"Everything?"

"Well, almost everything," said Tilde. "Sometimes when I wake in the morning, I cannot be sure that it wasn't a dream."

Jenny had slept little since the ritual. "A nightmare."

"Mm," agreed Tilde. "Anyway, I wonder sometimes how much of it was true. Perhaps there were hallucinogens in those bonfires. We all breathed that smoke."

"No," said Jenny. "We all saw the same things. I saw my sister."

Tilde stroked Jenny's arm. "*Oui oui,* and so you did. And believe me, Jenny, you shall find her again, alive and well, and you shall have such a happy reunion."

"Now that's what I call a dream," said Jenny. "But remember,

Abigail Olmstead has the medallion. She's more dangerous than she ever was before I brought it to Arkham."

"That is hardly your fault, *ma chère*."

"Perhaps not," said Jenny. "But it is my responsibility. So is Izzie, although I never accepted that until it was too late."

"Your sister's keeper, are you?"

"Yes. And my friend's keeper, too. I would never have gotten so close to recovering Izzie if it weren't for your help."

"Well, I am only too happy to assist another woman of the world," said Tilde. "Especially one who shares her Gauloises."

Jenny smiled her appreciation. "You weren't alone in helping me. Without Lonnie, Gal, and Lew, I don't know that we would have escaped with our lives. There were others, too. I may not come from Arkham, but this town helped me find Izzie. Maybe it's time I returned the favor."

"You already helped rescue those girls," said Tilde. "What do you call that?"

Jenny looked toward the car, where Lonnie was refusing Gal's offer of a hand while she took a seat. When she pushed past him to enter via the driver's side, Jenny laughed. Lonnie heard her and waved her over. Gal did the same as he hastened to offer Lonnie a hand into the driver's seat.

"What do I call that?" said Jenny. "I call it a good start."

ACKNOWLEDGMENTS

For feedback on an early draft, thanks to Elaine Cunningham, Rachelle Foss, Barb Galler-Smith, Howard Andrew Jones, Jen Laface, Nicole Luiken, Jennifer Kennedy, Liane Merciel, and Greg McKitrick. For consultations on German, thanks to Harald Gehlen. For the invitation to Arkham and directions around town, thanks to Katrina Ostrander.

THE DIRGE
OF REASON

Graeme Davis

*To Jamie Davis, my love, my friend,
and my partner in crime.*

CHAPTER 1

Arkham's dark and pillared police station loomed over the city with what seemed like a disdainful frown. The desk sergeant looked up at Agent Roland Banks with much the same expression when the agent presented his credentials.

"Bureau of Investigation, huh?" He cast a jaundiced eye over Roland's badge. "Well, la-di-da."

"I'm looking for–" Roland glanced down at his notebook, "– Sheriff Engle of the Miskatonic County Sheriff's Office."

The old bull's expression turned half a shade more sour. "I bet you are. That society dame send you?"

"The Bureau sent me."

"Well, hurrah for J. Edgar Hoover. Down the hall, turn left."

Following the sergeant's directions, Roland passed through a glass door with the name of the sheriff's office on the outside in gold letters, and found himself in a narrow lobby with a door on either side and a small desk at which a middle-aged woman sat reading a dime novel. He stood and waited while she finished her paragraph, turned down the corner of her page, and closed the book before looking up at him.

"Can I help you?" Her tone suggested that she would prefer not to.

Roland presented his badge again and was about to ask for Sheriff Engle when the door on the left opened and a head stuck itself out.

"That's all right, Myrna," the man said. "This will be the federal agent we're expecting." He turned to Roland. "Am I right?"

"Agent Roland Banks, Bureau of Investigation."

"Pleased to meet you, Agent Banks. Come on in." Sheriff Engle retreated back through the door, beckoning Roland to follow him.

The office was almost as small as the lobby. Sheriff Engle waved Roland to a chair and edged to his own seat around a desk the size of a matchbox. The desk and the windowsill were piled with papers, and the sheriff hunted through them as he spoke.

"So, what did they tell you in Boston?"

"Not much," said Roland. "Just to come here and talk to you. Something about a house that was destroyed. They weren't big on details." His stop in Boston had been brief. After a day on the train from Virginia, he had been rushed off to Arkham before his half-finished coffee had stopped steaming. The questions he tried to ask had brought the kind of silence that filled an Irish pub right after someone ordered a black and tan.

"Well, welcome to Arkham." There was just a trace of irony in Sheriff Engle's voice. "We've been expecting you."

"You have? I wasn't even expecting me before yesterday."

The sheriff chuckled. "Oh, it was inevitable," he said. "I take it you never met Mrs van Dreesen?"

Roland shook his head. "Never had the pleasure."

Roland did not need to meet Mrs van Dreesen. A Photostat copy of her letter to the Bureau higher-up sat in his valise along with a few other papers they had given him in Boston. From the letter's familiar tone, it was clear that Mrs van Dreesen was a friend of the higher-up's wife, and it did not take a Fed to know that the higher-up would know no peace, either social or domestic, until the matter was resolved to Mrs van Dreesen's complete satisfaction. She even wrote in a Knickerbocker drawl.

"She thought we local bumpkins were in over our heads," the sheriff went on, "and she let us know it loudly and repeatedly. I was half-expecting J. Edgar Hoover in person."

"No," said Roland, "just me."

"I've got everything here," said Sheriff Engle, tapping a fat stack of paper into shape. "Our report on the scene, copies of correspondence between Mrs van Dreesen and her insurance company, and the cable from New York telling us to expect an agent."

Roland took the proffered stack and glanced at the telegram on the top. It bore the same name as the memo in his valise: the name that had made him look twice. He started to turn over the papers as they talked. "I'll be sure to look all of this over," he said. "In the meantime, can you give me the headlines?"

The sheriff leaned back in his chair and counted off points on his fingers. "Pine Beach," he said. "A posh lake house outside of town on Chaumadgee Lake, owned by Mrs Edgar van Dreesen – first name Edith – of Manhattan, New York. About sunset on the fifteenth, it was destroyed. The ground shook as far as here in town, and the noise was heard over two miles away. Thirty-eight people died."

"Thirty-eight? Was it a house party?"

"No – an orchestra."

"A what?"

"It's all in the notes," Sheriff Engle said. "Mrs van Dreesen was a patron, and she lent the house to the orchestra for rehearsals. They were due to open in Boston this week."

"But the house blew up first."

"That's right."

"So Mrs van Dreesen lost more than just a house. She lost an orchestra, too."

"Right again."

"I'm not a society type, but I imagine that would be embarrassing."

"No doubt."

"So it was an explosion?"

"Most likely. But here's the kicker: we can't figure out how it blew up. The gas lines don't run that far into the country, and the house wasn't fitted for propane. It did have a boiler for hot water, but that was wood-fired, and I doubt that even the *Mauretania* has a boiler big enough to blow up with that much force. I was starting to look at the orchestra when my office got orders to do nothing further until you arrived. My guess is, there are things about the orchestra she didn't want coming out. They were a pretty rowdy crew."

"Rowdy? What kind of orchestra was it? Jazz?"

The sheriff looked surprised at the question. "Not jazz," he said. "The papers call them *avant-garde*, whatever that means. What are you thinking?"

"If no one else was there, that makes them suspects as well as victims," said Roland. "*Avant-garde*, you said – so they were artsy types?" Roland waited for Sheriff Engle to nod. "Did they cause any trouble in town?"

"Not in town so much, but they weren't popular with their neighbors. One time they found a dead raccoon and stole someone's motorboat to give it a Viking funeral."

"So they were probably not too concerned about Prohibition?"

"We did have to lock a couple of them up for public drunkenness, but I never did find out where they were getting their booze from." Sheriff Engle's answer was just a little too quick for Roland's liking. "How does that fit with the house blowing up?"

"Could they have been running a still in the house? I've seen a still explosion take down a good-sized cabin."

"You wouldn't ask that if you knew the house. I doubt the DuPont chemical company has a still big enough to do that kind of damage. The place was more like a mansion than a cabin."

"What does that leave? Dynamite? Bootleggers, maybe?"

Sheriff Engle ran a hand over his mustache. "I couldn't say. We've never had anything like that out here before. I guess that's one reason Mrs van Dreesen wanted the Bureau involved. She didn't seem to have much faith in us locals."

"I'm sorry to hear that," Roland said, "although you seem to be taking it well."

The sheriff raised an eyebrow. "I am?"

"Better than any local officer I've ever met before, in fact. Most people in your position don't like getting the high hat from some society type and having to hand over a case to the Feds. How come you're so calm about it?"

Sheriff Engle gave a quick bark of laughter. "I would not presume to comment on my betters," he said. "Mrs van Dreesen felt that the case was beyond the expertise of the local authorities, and I was forced to agree."

Roland hunted through the stack for a letter he had glimpsed and held it up to the sheriff.

"Because of this?" The typed sheet had the letterhead of the

New Netherland Insurance Company, and the letter began, "We regret to inform you…"

"That's right. I wasn't able to assign a definite cause, so the insurance company ruled it an act of God and refused to pay out. That led, from what I heard, to a spirited discussion by telephone, which led in turn–"

"Let me guess," said Roland. "It led to me."

Sheriff Engle replied with an apologetic shrug. "The next day, I got a call from the Bureau telling me to stop everything and wait for you to get here."

Roland heaved a weary sigh. "Of course you did," he said. "And if Mrs van Dreesen doesn't like the report I turn in…"

The sheriff nodded in mock sadness. "That's about the size of it."

"No wonder you've been such a model of cooperation," Roland said. "You couldn't wait to offload this case onto some other poor sap, could you?" Sheriff Engle made no reply. "Is that why you were so quick to reach no conclusion?"

The sheriff leaned back and ran a hand through his hair. "Look, Agent Banks," he said, "I've got nothing against you. I know there's a long and noble tradition of federal agencies swooping in and stealing cases from us honest, hard-working, local bulls, and sure, maybe some might think it's cute to hand a poisoned chalice off to the G-men, but I'm not one of them."

"How do I know that?"

"You don't know it, and that's why I'm telling you. Now, Arkham may look like a sleepy little place, but it has its share of troubles – more than its share sometimes. If I can clear a case by myself, I do it. Why? Because I don't need federal agents coming in and stirring up more trouble than they solve because they don't know anything about this city and its people. That's what you'll do, Agent Banks, whether you intend to or not. And if you think–"

"If I stir up trouble, sheriff, it will be because there's trouble to stir up. The reason you locals don't like G-men is because G-men don't turn a blind eye to handshake deals or special arrangements."

"Sell it someplace else, agent. You know, and I know, you're only here at all because of Mrs van Dreesen's connections, so don't play the altar boy about influence and arrangements."

A long silence simmered as the two men glared at each other across the tiny desk. Finally, Roland spread his hands in surrender.

"All right," he said. "So we both know how the world works. And you're right – I don't know you. You don't know me, either, but the sooner I clear up this case, the sooner I can be gone – and believe me, I want that just as much as you do. No offense intended. I'm sure Arkham's a fine city."

"None taken," said Sheriff Engle with a slightly lopsided grin, "and for what it's worth, I wouldn't wish Mrs van Dreesen on anyone – not even a Fed. If you have more luck figuring this out than I did, I'll be very happy about it. So, what do you say?" He stood and held out his hand. After a moment, Roland shook it.

"I'm sorry." He sat back down. "It's been a long couple of days getting here. I may have brought some old frustrations with me."

"Two days?" The sheriff looked surprised. "I was told to expect someone from Boston."

Roland let out a short, bitter laugh. "Oh, I was in Boston – for about fifteen minutes. They couldn't wait to get rid of me. I got the impression Arkham was catching, somehow."

"It does have a certain reputation," Sheriff Engle admitted. "The whole valley does, going back to the witch times. Somehow, we can't seem to shake it off. So where did they send you from?"

"Virginia," Roland replied.

"Let me guess: you were chasing bootleggers all over Hillbilly Holler, and you ran smack into one of those handshake deals you were talking about. So Mrs van Dreesen is your punishment?"

Roland gave a weary nod. Everyone knew that the BOI had spent the last couple of years in near-constant territorial skirmishes with almost every other federal agency. Director Hoover made no secret of the fact that he wanted to bury the memories of corruption and botched investigations like the Teapot Dome scandal. Since Hoover trusted only himself and the agents under his direct command, conflict with other agencies was inevitable. In Jubal County, the other agency was the Bureau of Internal Revenue's Prohibition Unit. The two government agencies hated each other worse than the bootleggers did.

Roland had never been good at politics. He had never wanted to be. Hoover's anti-corruption stance was what had attracted him to the BOI in the first place: putting bad guys away rather than wasting energy plotting against people who were supposed to be on his own side. Some of the other agents laughed behind his back – called him naïve, a Boy Scout. But no one could get anything on him if there was nothing to get, and that was the only way to avoid being dragged into the mire.

His Boy Scout policy had hit the rocks in a cat's cradle that went by the name of Jubal County. Everyone there was a cousin or an in-law to everyone else, and no one liked outsiders. At some point, someone in one of the federal agencies had made a deal with someone in Jubal County, and the Boy Scout had blundered in and ruined something for someone. Nothing had been said, of course – these things were never openly acknowledged – but suddenly the Boston Field Office needed Agent Roland Banks and no one else would do.

Roland opened his mouth, then closed it, and finally sighed. "I shouldn't discuss Bureau cases with anyone outside the Bureau."

"You didn't. All I heard was you had a long journey."

Roland started to reply, but his stomach interrupted with a sound that bounced off the windows and made the sheriff's eyes widen.

"Don't tell me you haven't eaten yet?"

Roland shook his head. "I came here straight from the station. Professional courtesy: always announce yourself to local law enforcement right away."

The sheriff seemed amused. "I guess you are a by-the-book kind of fellow, aren't you? Well, no wonder you were a little bad tempered. Did you see Velma's on your way here?"

Roland nodded. "I could hardly miss it."

"That sign does catch the eye, doesn't it? It was the first neon in Arkham, believe it or not. Caused quite a fuss when Velma first put it up. Anyhow, why don't you come back in an hour or so, and you can tell me how you want to proceed? I can take you to the site–" he cast a glance out the window, "–and we might have a couple of hours of usable daylight left. Or you could get yourself situated, go through the files, and we could start out fresh in the morning. Just let me know."

Roland nodded his thanks and rose to leave.

"Don't miss the cherry pie," Sheriff Engle said in parting. "You've never had anything like it!"

CHAPTER 2

Roland shouldered through the door of the diner. His stomach gave a skip of joy as the comforting fug of coffee and grill-grease hit his nostrils.

Sheriff Engle clearly had not lied about the food. Roland counted two cops at the counter, two more at a table, and two ministers at another table. Dozens of diners in dozens of towns had taught Roland that uniforms and dog collars were two sure signs of good eating.

The cops at the counter gave him a slow once-over as he entered. They had pegged him for a G-man and they wanted him to know it. Roland returned a brief nod of professional courtesy and scanned the room for an empty table.

"Sit anywhere, hon! I'll be right with you!" A cheery woman with "Velma" stitched on her chest in red script smiled at him from behind the counter. By the time Roland reached the table he had picked, she was already pouring coffee. Roland waved the menu away and ordered steak, hash browns, and three eggs over easy. Then he took a long pull at his coffee and felt its warmth slide all the way down.

The cops at the nearby table gave him a cold stare of their own, like street-corner toughs glaring across an invisible line into rival turf. Roland shot them a beaming grin that stuck one toe over the line into sarcasm, and they turned away sulkily, just like countless other local cops had done before them in countless other towns.

Roland reached in his valise for the newspaper he had bought at the station and opened it on the table in front of him, eating one-handed as he read. The *Arkham Advertiser* was as parochial as its name suggested, but it was local news that Roland was after. The police files stayed out of sight, away from prying eyes. He wrote down the address of the paper's office: reporters were often better friends to federal agents than local law enforcement, especially if they thought a G-man could help take their local story national.

The front page was dominated by follow-up stories about Pine Beach: "Orchestra's Remains Shipped Home," ran the main headline. The newspaper named the thirty-eight casualties as members of the New England Virtuosi, plus a composer named Oliver Haldane.

An unnamed "New York correspondent" described the music world's shock at Haldane's sudden death and reprised several breathless rumors about composer and orchestra, full of bedroom antics, low company ranging from bootleggers to Surrealists to suspected Communists, and every other imaginable form of bad behavior. Mostly, the stories were about how well-connected the paper's correspondent was in New York's arts world, although there was a brief mention of "Arkham's own jazz joint, the Nightingale Club, in Uptown." Roland made a note of the name.

A piece on an inside page wondered whether the van Dreesens would rebuild and whether the summer's trade would be affected by the city's sudden notoriety. Although Arkham clearly was not as dependent on "summer people" as the Hamptons or Cape Cod, it seemed that they did bring welcome cash to the area.

The coverage was exactly what might be expected from a local rag. Roland noted down the names of the editor and a couple of reporters.

"You from out of town, hon?" It sounded like a question, but it was really a test. No stranger could pass unnoticed in a joint like this.

Roland lifted his freshly filled coffee cup, nodding his thanks to the waitress for the refill and for the heaping plate of food she had brought. "That's right," he said.

"A terrible thing, that fire." She heaved a brief, conventional sigh of sympathy, and when Roland did not correct her on the cause of the destruction, she went on with her probing. "So, are you press, insurance, or law?"

"Are those the only choices?"

Velma acknowledged his parry with a raised eyebrow and a low chuckle.

"They have been for the last week, I can tell you that," she said with a conspiratorial smile. "Besides, you don't have the look of an encyclopedia salesman." She glanced down at his valise. "Nor the case, either."

"Good eye. Are you sure you're not a detective yourself?"

Her smile broadened as Roland turned back to his food. Velma already knew he was a G-man – the cops' reactions would have told her even if the cops themselves had not – and from now on it would be a game to see how much she could get out of him. Gossip was currency in a place like this, and fresh gossip brought more customers than fresh coffee.

When Velma came by to take his empty plate and fill his coffee cup for a third time, Roland ordered the cherry pie. "The sheriff said I shouldn't miss it," he said. Velma beamed, and not just at the compliment.

"You're a lawman. I knew it!" she said.

"You knew it before I sat down. Any of the people from the house ever eat here?"

"Those musicians?" She made a face. "I threw a couple of them out when they first got here."

"They made trouble?"

"Not trouble, exactly – just annoyance. They were as drunk as a pair of skunks and wanting all kinds of things that aren't on the menu. Told them I'm not running a fraternity house and they should beat it and not come back. Never saw any of them again."

"What about the owners?"

"Mrs van High-and-Mighty?" Velma snorted. "Imagine her here! For one thing I'm all out of lace tablecloths, and she'd never get the grease smell out of her ermine. She brought her own cook from New York when she came up here, that's what I heard. The summer people don't mix here, not like on the coast. Oh, the paper would mention some grand party or other – debutante balls and whatnot – but we never saw hide nor hair of them in town. Just their people, buying supplies and such."

Velma waited a couple of seconds with an expectant smile on her face, but when Roland offered nothing in return for her insights she turned away to another table. "You be sure and come back, now."

Roland finished his pie and coffee, and left a generous tip. He had got more out of Velma than he had expected to, although none of it was much help. Still, coffee and a hot meal had him feeling almost human again.

Roland returned to the police station and left a message for Sheriff Engle to meet him the following morning for a visit to Pine Beach. He was still bone-tired, and the site that had confounded the Miskatonic County Sheriff's Office would require all his faculties. Meanwhile, he had the stack of documents from the sheriff, plus whatever he could get from the newspaper office. Like a Boy Scout, he believed in being prepared.

With a full stomach and no need to rush, Roland took in more of the city as he headed for the newspaper office. The little square looked somehow different in the afternoon light. Roland noticed a dark, rough-looking stone at one side and a masonry arch marking the western entrance. A handful of locals lolled on benches or strolled across the square on various errands: it was a scene typical of countless small towns, but for some reason Roland felt uneasy.

Perhaps it was the grim, high-walled building that loomed behind the square. It had been unseen behind Roland as he had walked to the police station, but from this direction, it crouched over the city center like a great, gray beast, hunched and threatening. With its brick walls and its many roofs and chimneys, it might have been a cursed mansion from the mind of Edgar Allan Poe or someone similar.

From across the street, Roland read the sign "Arkham Sanatorium" over a sharp-looking wrought-iron fence. He had been to a few asylums in his time – bathtub gin rotted the brain as well as the gut – but he had never seen one so close to the center of a city, not outside of a Lon Chaney movie, at least. Together with the crooked roofs and shadowed alleys, it was easy to see how Arkham had acquired the sinister reputation of which Sheriff Engle had spoken.

After a quick stop at the newspaper office, Roland found a hotel downtown. The Excelsior looked as though it belonged in a larger city and had somehow wandered into Arkham by accident.

The glass panes in the hotel's double doors were etched with its name in an ornate script from the previous century. The lace curtains framing the windows might have been white once, but were now a color that a kindly disposed decorator might describe as ivory. The worn-looking, scarlet and gold carpet was covered by a broad runner of plain red that stretched between the doors and a front desk of wood and polished brass. It was not the Waldorf Astoria, but it would be tolerably clean, if not especially comfortable, and it would be within Roland's Bureau-mandated budget. He had stayed in far worse places.

The bell on the front desk summoned a tall, cadaverous-looking man whose remaining hair fell lank over one side of his head. Dressed in a frock coat and a Celluloid collar, he seemed like a relic from another age, although he complemented the genteel shabbiness of his hotel perfectly. He looked at Roland's badge with no change of expression and pulled a brown paper package from under the desk without comment.

The manager gave Roland a room on the second floor. Seeing no pen on the desk, Roland unscrewed the cap on his Sheaffer and opened the register. A familiar name made him pause and look more closely. Oliver Haldane had registered at the hotel, four months earlier. He spun the book around to face the manager.

"What can you tell me about this guest?" he asked. The manager's face went blank so fast that Roland could almost hear the sound of a door slamming.

"I'm sorry, sir." The voice was respectfully soft, but unyielding. "The hotel's policy does not permit–"

"This man is dead," Roland snapped, "and so are thirty-seven other people. A house was destroyed. I am a federal agent looking into those deaths. Would you like to reconsider the hotel's policy?"

The manager recoiled a hair, but his expression did not change.

"If you wish, I can refer you to the owners' attorneys," he said, "although I doubt anyone here will know anything of use to you. The staff of this hotel are under strict instructions to respect our guests' privacy."

It was clear from the manager's tone that nothing short of a federal warrant would budge him an inch further. Roland took his room key and went upstairs before he said anything he might regret. He was not the kind of agent who went around bullying civilians.

Roland spent the rest of the day going through Sheriff Engle's police file and the stack of notes, photographs, and back issues from the newspaper office. Along with the police report came several photographs, and Roland scoured them with a pocket lens until his eyes felt like sandpaper, but they told him next to nothing. The house had been big, which was hardly surprising, and had been built of timber on a stone foundation. A few older pictures showed it intact: three stories, the lower two enclosed by a broad, double-decked veranda-*cum*-balcony, with dormer windows in the roof and massive stone chimneys poking up like the stumps of primordial trees. A manicured lawn ran down to the beach that gave the house its name, with an Italian-looking fountain of pale stone adding an awkwardly formal touch to the New England woodsiness of the scene.

One photo, dated 1905, was captioned "Worthington-Mullen Wedding, Worthington House, Pine Beach, Arkham, Mass." Roland made a note to find out who the Worthingtons were, when the house was built, and when the van Dreesens bought it.

Perhaps he might find a hint of some inherent instability in the construction or the underlying ground, which had caught up with the house and its occupants that night.

The recent photographs showed rubble and matchwood, and here and there a barely recognizable piece of a human body. It looked more like the result of an artillery bombardment than an accidental explosion. Roland laid the photographs of the intact house on the floor and tried to orient the scenes of destruction around them. He had half of the house to work with, as well as the fountain, which had been reduced to a stump. An ambiguous shadow extended behind it. The lawns were all but lost beneath a layer of debris that extended halfway to the lake.

The back numbers he had picked up at the newspaper office revealed even less. The same photographs were reproduced in grainy dots and credited to "E. Talbot." Roland flipped one of the prints over and found the same name rubber-stamped on the back in smudged blue ink, along with an address in New York. Another summer person – one unlikely to have stayed around after an experience like that. He wrote the address in his notebook.

There were a few stories about the orchestra, starting with a piece from several weeks ago, announcing that they would be coming to Pine Beach. As their patron, Mrs van Dreesen received a respectful number of column inches, and Arkham congratulated itself on being ideally remote and peaceful, yet well-appointed, to attract a renowned orchestra wishing to rehearse an important new piece ahead of a New York premiere. Initially glowing with anticipation, the reports changed after the musicians arrived in Arkham. Now and again, as the sheriff had said, their drunken escapades had led to a night in the cells, but there was no mention of lawsuits or trials. The invisible hand of Mrs van Dreesen at work, most likely: the rich, and the friends of the rich, could get away with a great deal.

Darkness fell, and Roland ordered food from the kitchen. He went over everything again, chewing on a paper-thin piece of cold roast beef between two dry, curled-up slices of bread. After another couple of hours, he opened a window and stuck his head out to get some air, focusing on a distant spire to give his eyes a break. Arkham was layer upon layer of shadows, one behind the other, like the set of a movie he had seen a few years ago, about a sleepwalker in a German town made up of crazy, jagged angles.

Moments later, or possibly minutes, he jerked awake just in time to stop himself from toppling out of the window. He was close to sleepwalking. He put the papers away and went to bed, very little the wiser.

CHAPTER 3

"Sleep well?"

Roland replied to the sheriff's cheery greeting with a noncommittal grunt. He had been with the Bureau so long that he could probably sleep on a bed of nails if he had to, but sleep had done nothing to relieve his frustration. Much of it, he admitted to himself, had little or nothing to do with Arkham or this case – he was just getting started, after all – and a lot more to do with Jubal County and his burning sense of the injustice he had suffered there. He climbed into the sheriff's car, hoping that a visit to the site would give him something to go on – or just something to occupy his mind.

Sheriff Engle drove out of town on the Gloucester Road. Dense woods blocked out the view on either side, just as they had on the train. Once again, Roland felt as though they were trying to close in on him.

"Did you get anything from the files?" Sheriff Engle asked.

"Just a headache," Roland replied. Sheriff Engle nodded sympathetically and kept driving.

"Explosion, cause unknown," Roland quoted. "Did you really expect anyone to be pleased with a conclusion like that?"

"No, I didn't," said the sheriff. "But it was either say that or make something up – something I'd then have to defend in front of Mrs van Dreesen, her insurance company, and probably a judge. I mean, thirty-eight deaths, New York society types – that's not the kind of thing that's going to go smoothly."

"Ain't that the truth?" said Roland. "And you figured that whatever you said, Mrs van Dreesen would kick against it, so why say anything at all?"

Sheriff Engle's nod was a little less sheepish than Roland was expecting. "I barely got the chance to say anything at all. Her lawyers all but ran our people off the scene, so we – what was it they said, now? – so we 'wouldn't compromise any further investigations by more qualified personnel.' That would be you, I guess."

"Lucky me."

They turned left onto a winding dirt road that climbed gently past a couple of small farms before plunging again into the woods. Every few hundred yards, a driveway led off to the right, marked by a stone pillar carved with a name. They passed by Lakeview, Trout Bank, and Sempel's Landing.

"All right," Roland said at last, "let me see if I've got this straight. The house looks like a howitzer shell hit it. You don't know why, and Mrs van Dreesen didn't encourage you to look very hard, so you didn't. There's no gas that anyone knows of, and the hot water boiler was far too small to blow up with that much force. So, unless the house was bombed by a Zeppelin you haven't told me about, there's just one thing left: bootleggers."

"It's possible, I guess." The sheriff volunteered nothing further.

"All right," said Roland, "you're going to make me work for it, so

I'll ask: do you have any bootlegger trouble in Arkham?"

"Did you ever hear of a mug named Johnny V?"

"I've been down south for a while, remember? Who is this Johnny V? Is he local talent?"

"Boston. Real bad news, from what they say."

"And what brought him to little old Arkham? I'm guessing he's not a music lover?"

"Word is, he's been expanding up the coast over the last few months, but there's a local guy who's been holding out."

"Go on."

"Now, this orchestra wasn't exactly the Metropolitan Opera."

"I got that impression. So their quest for booze put them in between these two bootleggers, and someone was a sore loser?"

"It crossed my mind." Sheriff Engle frogged his mouth. "But I can't prove it."

"Did you even try?" Roland asked. "Or are you in with one of these bootleggers? The local boy, at a guess."

The sheriff let out a snort of laughter. "Sure. That's why I'm telling a G-man about him."

"You left out his name."

"Leo De Luca. Happy?"

"So, how come he's still walking around?"

Sheriff Engle spread his hands. "No evidence, no witnesses. There's never been much booze in Arkham, outside of the college. New England Congregationalists, you see."

"I get the picture," Roland said wearily. People almost never gave up their local bootleggers: out of loyalty, out of fear, or from simple distrust of the Feds, they kept silent. "So did this local boy De Luca blow up the orchestra, or did the Boston outfit do it?"

Sheriff Engle grimaced briefly. "You're the expert," he said.

"I just lock up drunks and chase burglars. Anyway, this is it."

The entrance to Pine Beach was marked by two rustic-looking stone pillars, joined by a wrought-iron arch with the name in old-fashioned scrollwork. They bumped down the rutted driveway for another quarter of a mile before the sheriff brought the car to a halt. Roland sat for a moment, taking in the scene.

The trees bowed away from the house, as though some giant had pushed them askew. At the center of the clearing, nothing stood higher than a couple of feet. A crumbling chimney loomed over a jumble of wood and rubble.

"Keep going," the sheriff said with a dark laugh. Roland walked up the path, past what remained of the walls, and took a deep breath.

On the far side of the house, almost nothing remained but hints of the stone foundations. A halo of rubble ringed the scene: shattered timbers and fragments of masonry radiated out from the ruins like the rays on a child's drawing of the sun.

In 1918, Roland had marched through Château-Thierry with Pershing, during the Second Battle of the Marne. The little village had been blown apart by German and Allied artillery in the war's last gasp, but Pine Beach was in even worse shape. The far side of the house looked shorn off rather than blown up: it was reduced to a couple of courses of stone, surrounded by a wide ring of debris.

Boot prints and tire tracks on the muddy ground reminded him that the scene was far from pristine. He turned to Sheriff Engle. "Where were the bodies?"

The sheriff stretched out his arms in an all-encompassing gesture. "All over," he said. "A few were whole, some were in pieces, some were…"

"Some were what?"

"Hard to describe. Crushed, I guess. Like a bug when you step on it and drag your shoe."

"Where were they taken?"

"The morgue at St. Mary's Hospital, first. The last one went back to his family two days ago."

"Autopsies?"

"No. Cause of death was pretty clear."

Roland looked around him and was forced to concede that this was true. "Any identification problems?"

The sheriff shrugged. "You'd have to ask the coroner. All I know is, the numbers tallied. Thirty-eight in the orchestra, including the composer. Thirty-eight in the rubble."

Roland wrote this down. They skirted the foundation in silence. Roland paused to examine a fallen roof beam. Once a pine trunk as thick as a beer barrel, it was shredded like a chewed toothpick. He turned and followed the line of the fallen timber back to the house.

"Looking for something?" asked Sheriff Engle.

"Everything on this side is pointing out from the site of the explosion," said Roland. "Find the middle and we find the origin."

Roland stepped into the foundation and stopped dead. In contrast to the outside of the house, the wreckage within the building's original footprint was a chaotic jumble, without pattern or order. He walked around for a while, trying to make sense of it, but it seemed increasingly that there was no sense to be made.

"Scratch that plan," he said at last. "I never saw dynamite do that before. How about you?"

The sheriff shrugged. "I've never seen dynamite do anything before."

"The joys of a quiet life," Roland said sourly.

Roland walked around the perimeter of the foundation. The

house had been a big one, all right. He had seen smaller castles. Roland widened his path, spiraling outward in the hope of finding something – anything – that might tell him more.

The fountain he had seen in the old photograph was shorn off at the same level as the foundation: ankle height on one of the nymphs. The rest of the marble was nowhere to be seen. Something about the stone caught Roland's eye.

"Sheriff Engle!" The sheriff came trotting over. "Take a look at this." Roland indicated the stump of the fountain.

"You found something?" The sheriff looked where Roland was pointing. "Huh." Sheriff Engle straightened up and pushed his hat back a little.

Despite the evident violence of the explosion, the stone was not shattered. Instead, the top of the stump was smooth, like freshly cut cheese.

"Looks like someone sawed it off," Sheriff Engle said at last.

"That's a good way to put it," said Roland. "Could our merry pranksters have done that, do you think?"

"If they had a quarry saw, maybe," said Sheriff Engle. "My pa worked with granite over in Quincy," he explained in response to Roland's questioning look. "They had one – water powered. It was big, however, and very slow, and it was set up for vertical cuts. Something like this, now… it would take some doing."

Roland straightened up and strode back to the remains of the house. By the time the sheriff caught up with him, he had cleared an area about three feet square. The stone here was darker, a local granite rather than imported marble, but the signs were the same. The top of each stone looked as though it had been sliced off with a hot knife. Roland raised an eyebrow at Sheriff Engle, who shook his head slowly.

"I never saw the like," he said. "And this was done right here, not at any quarry. See how level it is from one stone to the next? No one can lay a foundation that regular."

"Something else is off, too," Roland said. "Have you seen any sign of burning anywhere?"

"Burning?"

"Yes. An explosion's nothing more than a very fast, very intense fire. There should be some charring, especially around the heart of the explosion."

"Huh." The sheriff looked mystified. "That makes sense, now you come to mention it. I didn't see a trace of a fire anywhere. Does that rule out dynamite?"

"I don't know. Between that and the stone, though, it bothers me. Did you say Arkham's a college town?"

"Miskatonic," said the sheriff. "Almost as old as Harvard and Yale." A hint of local pride crept into his voice.

"Good," said Roland. "Maybe a geologist or a chemist can make sense of this. It's got to add up somehow. You said the noise was heard a long way off?"

Sheriff Engle nodded. "Heard – and felt, too. A picture fell off the wall in my office."

"Like an earthquake?"

"Hard to say. I never felt an earthquake before."

"All right. What about the sound? Did it sound like an explosion?"

"Just a rumble by the time it reached town. Something like thunder, maybe. One of the witnesses said it sounded like a locomotive crash – but she was close enough to hear the debris falling."

Roland turned on Sheriff Engle. "What witness?" he almost

yelled. "When were you planning to tell me there was a witness?"

"Not an eyewitness," the sheriff rebutted, "just someone who heard the noise. Name's Talbot, Miss Talbot. She was here with the orchestra – took the photos in the file."

"I remember. From New York? There was an address on the back of the photographs."

"Right. She went back soon after."

"I'll need to talk to her."

Leaving the sheriff still examining the edge of the foundation, Roland returned to his spiral path. Beyond the fountain the lawn narrowed slightly, leaving an avenue of trees framing the way to the lake. Their trunks were bizarrely studded with debris, reminding Roland of photographs he had seen of tornado damage in Kansas. A piece of metal silverware jutted from one tree, pushed in hilt-deep as if the tree were a baked potato. Lower down, something that might have been a table leg jutted out to one side.

Roland turned to look out across the lake. A single cabin was visible on the opposite shore, crowded by trees and much less grand than the Worthington House had been. If Roland ignored the devastation behind him, the place was peaceful and idyllic. A gentle breeze stirred the trees and carried the sound of lapping water to his ears. The only other sound was the crunch of Sheriff Engle's boots as he approached.

"Seen enough?" he asked.

Roland held up a hand for silence. "Do you hear that?" he said. Sheriff Engle stood and listened.

The sound was far off, almost too soft to hear.

"What is that?" Roland asked. "A bird?"

The sheriff listened for a moment longer. "Not any bird I know," he said at last. "Mostly you'll hear loons and woodpeckers around here, maybe a hawk once in a while, some smaller birds."

"I haven't heard a thing since we got here," said Roland.

"Me neither," said Sheriff Engle. "Not even a squirrel."

The wind shifted and the sound became clearer. Thin and monotonous, there was nothing musical about it. The image of a suspended bamboo pipe sprang into Roland's mind, with a ceaseless prairie wind blowing across one end. It was the sound a movie-house musician might conjure up to accompany a blurred and silent newsreel image from out West, of rolling tumbleweeds and abandoned shacks half-buried by drifting sand. For no reason he could fathom, Roland suddenly felt bitterly cold and desperately lonely.

The wind shifted again, tearing the monotonous piping into shreds and breaking the spell that had kept the two men rooted to the spot in silence. They looked at each other briefly, each moved by a sudden need to know that the sound had affected the other in the same way, but broke eye contact immediately. By an unspoken mutual agreement, they turned and walked back toward the house.

It was a few minutes before Roland felt able to speak. At last, he set his shoulders, swept the scene with an overly deliberate gaze, and said, "I got what I need for now. Let's head back." Sheriff Engle nodded silently and they walked back toward the car.

The sound remained in Roland's head, even though he knew his ears could no longer hear it. He looked back at the ruins and shivered: it was as though he saw them – truly saw them – for the first time. The devastation of Château-Thierry suddenly seemed like a ridiculous comparison, its destruction by heavy artillery altogether too benign an analogy. Dynamite was far kinder, somehow, than whatever had happened here.

Roland's mind kept turning unbidden to fragments of the Bible: Sodom and Gomorrah, the Book of Revelation, and pillars of fire from the heavens. He fought a rising sense of panic, and he had to check his pace to keep from running. He forced himself into a heavy marching pace, taking comfort in the automatic, unthinking motion and holding tight to his memories of the Marne like a child clutches a teddy bear in the dark.

Minutes or hours later, the two men reached the sheriff's car and climbed in without a word. The inexplicable fear lifted as they drove back to the road, but neither man spoke until they were back in Arkham. They parted with few words, Roland agreeing to keep Sheriff Engle informed of his progress.

CHAPTER 4

"Welcome back, hon! We missed you at breakfast!"

Roland was relying on the banal cheer of the diner to clear the last of the strange mood that had overtaken him by the lake. Two different cops sat at the counter, giving him the same look their brothers in blue had the previous day. Roland ignored them and chose a table at the back.

Velma's smile faltered just a hair as she took his order – only a trained observer would have noticed, but Roland could tell she had seen something in his face. What had happened out there? How could a half-heard sound shake a grown man so badly? Roland had faced German machine guns and bootleggers' Thompsons, but the only feeling that came close to his experience at Pine Beach was the sudden clutch of panic that had followed the alarm of a mustard-gas attack. He needed to think of something else.

Roland gulped his coffee and pulled out his notebook. An explosion remained the most likely explanation, despite the lack of burning and the strange appearance of the shorn-off stones. He would go to the local college and look for a geologist who could explain it. He also needed to look into Sheriff Engle's bootleg war:

he cursed himself briefly for forgetting to ask the sheriff where the local boy – he flipped to the right page – Leo De Luca could be found. He would also see if the Bureau had anything on De Luca, or on Johnny V, the pride of Boston.

"What's the word?" The waitress arrived with Roland's food and began eyeing his notebook. He flipped the book closed.

"Right now," he said, with his most charming smile, "the word is lunch." He began to eat, ignoring the fact that she stood there just a second too long. He had nothing to tell, not even if it were Hoover himself who was asking.

Roland felt a little calmer by the time he left the diner. He had one line of inquiry to pursue, and that was enough for now. He looked into the police station, but was told that Sheriff Engle had been called to the countryside and no one knew when he might be back. Roland suspected that the sheriff might be taking a little fishing trip about now; Roland himself was certainly looking forward to putting more distance between himself and Pine Beach just as soon as he could.

It came as no surprise that no one in the station would admit that they had ever heard of Leo De Luca. Judging by the strawberry noses on a couple of the older bulls, Roland was probably asking some of the bootlegger's regular customers. Johnny V's name was a little more familiar, or so it seemed. His surname was Valone, Roland learned, and yes, he was from Boston or thereabouts, according to a couple of officers, who had heard it from a distant cousin or passing acquaintance in the city. As for Arkham, Roland was told quite firmly that Arkham did not have a bootlegging problem; Sheriff Engle's comment about New England Congregationalists was repeated almost word for word.

Roland would have to find some other way to track down these two entrepreneurs. Perhaps the Boston Field Office had files on Johnny Valone and Leo De Luca. It was worth a cable to find out.

On his way to the telegraph office, Roland noticed the jazz club again. It was just as obvious as it had been the day before: the very first place anyone would think to look if they wanted illicit booze or the people who moved it, and therefore the very last place that was likely to have any connection with bootlegging. On the other hand, he might have overestimated the worthy constables of Arkham. It could be that they were dumb enough, or confident enough, to let the place move hooch under their noses. It would not be the first time he had seen one place allowed to remain open so that the cops had somewhere to make a show if they needed to – or somewhere to drink if they wanted to.

This early in the day, of course, the place was closed up tight. Roland resolved to come back in the evening and see what he could find out. For now, he would send his cable, go back to the hotel to clean up, and then see if he could scare up a geologist at this famous college. His stomach knotted at the thought of going back to Pine Beach, but next time he would have a scientist with him, to give him a safe and boring explanation for everything that was so strange and disturbing about the scene.

It was just after two when he returned to the hotel. He was three paces across the lobby when a woman's voice stopped him.

"Are you the federal man here about Pine Beach?"

Roland's heart stopped as dead as the rest of him. The last thing he needed was Mrs van Dreesen dropping by to check on his progress. When he turned around, though, the woman who had just risen from one of the threadbare armchairs was anything but a toffee-nosed Knickerbocker. A Louise Brooks bob framed a pair of smoky eyes that held Roland's gaze with disarming frankness and obvious intelligence – and something else that Roland could not quite identify, hidden down deep. She wore country tweeds rather than flapper beads, but she was the type who would look good in silk or sackcloth. Roland cleared his throat.

"Who's asking?"

The young woman pulled a business card out of a jacket pocket.

"Edie Talbot. I photographed the scene. Also–" she hesitated for a fraction of a second, "–I knew Oliver Haldane. I was here to write a profile and report on the new piece for *The Music Trades*."

"The what?"

"*The Music Trades*. It's a magazine from New York."

Roland nodded, remembering the New York address from the back of the photographs.

"Thank you for finding me, Miss Talbot. Or is it … ?"

"It's Miss." Her tone was professional rather than flirtatious, but not unfriendly.

"Agent Roland Banks, Bureau of Investigation." Roland flashed his badge. "Have you been in Arkham since it happened?"

"No. I- I went back to New York right afterward. Somehow, I just couldn't stay on there. I came back when I heard you were in town."

"I'm glad you did, Miss Talbot," said Roland, "and I certainly want to hear what you have to say, but it happens that right now I have to go. Where can I reach you, say, tomorrow morning?"

She looked disappointed, but not offended. "Here. I can…"

"Wait a minute." The first of Edie's photographs had shown no one else on the scene, and she had just implied that she was either staying at Pine Beach or somewhere very close by. Sheriff Engle had said she was a witness, after all. The college could wait: those stones would not be going anywhere. He motioned Edie back to her chair and seated himself across from her.

"I'm sorry, Miss Talbot," he said, "I was a little slow on the draw there. Am I right in thinking you were near the house when it happened?"

"About a quarter mile away. My editor knows someone who knows the Sempels."

"Sempel's Landing? I passed by it this morning."

"That's right. When it happened, I ran out to try and help, but there was so clearly nothing to be done. I telephoned the police, photographed everything I could, met with them when they arrived, and then left to develop the film. It was little enough, but it was all I could think of to do."

"It was plenty, Miss Talbot, and good thinking. Most people would have lost their heads in those circumstances."

"I would have lost mine, I think, if I hadn't had the photography to occupy it." There was the faintest tremble in her voice. "I've never seen anything like it." Roland could think of no answer.

"I haven't explored Arkham yet," he said at last, "so I'm unsure where would be a good place for us to talk in private. Do you have any suggestions?"

"Not the police station?" Edie sounded surprised, but Roland shook his head.

"I'd prefer not," he said. "It might surprise you, but the local law doesn't always welcome us federal types with open arms. The only other places I know are the diner–"

"Privacy isn't exactly Velma's long suit," Edie put in, with a mischievous smile.

"I'd noticed. We could stay here, I suppose, but ..." He tilted his head subtly toward the front desk and the open door behind it.

"I understand," she said. "How about the tearoom at the station? Plenty of noise and bustle there."

Fifteen minutes later, they were seated at a lace-covered table sharing coffee and cake at the train station. After bringing their order, the waitress ignored them as thoroughly as the handful of fellow patrons did. Roland brought out his notebook and uncapped his pen, writing Edie's name at the top of a fresh page.

"All right, Miss Talbot," he said, "in your own words, tell me everything you saw and heard." Edie's face fell a little, but she steeled herself and started talking.

"It was around dusk," she began. "I was inside writing up my notes from the day's rehearsals. I could just hear the music coming across from Pine Beach. It was a hot day, and they would often work with the windows open." She waited for Roland to stop writing, and continued at his nod.

"It was a section I hadn't heard before – the choral passage from the inscription."

"Inscription?"

"Something Oliver had found in a museum. I've got the particulars in my notes if it's important."

"Probably not. Then what happened?"

"Everything shook – just how I imagine an earthquake would be. The sound was…" she struggled, clearly searching for the right words, and then shook her head in frustration. "I think it went dark, just for a second. Then it was still again, with just the sound of falling debris. I ran across as fast as I could, but it was all over. I'm sure the other witness could tell you more."

Roland's head snapped up. "The other witness?"

"Yes – surely you know about him already?"

"I wish I did. Who is he?"

"A strange little local man. I think he has a shack in the woods somewhere. At any rate, the boys would buy moonshine from him and make fun behind his back. He's odd, as I said: the drink's gotten to him, I think. What is his name?" Her brow wrinkled in thought. "Ellis, Elmer, Elwood – El-something, at any rate."

"You saw him there after the… explosion?"

"He was kneeling at the edge of the woods. He looked up at me and just started screaming." She closed her eyes briefly. "A horrible sound it was, truly horrible. When the police came, he grabbed one of them by the jacket and started babbling nonsense at him, something about the sky cracking open and the world ending." She sighed. "Poor man. The shock was too much for him. It nearly was for me, too."

Roland wrote furiously. This Ellis, or whatever his name was, sounded like the first viable suspect Roland had come across. He had known backwoods moonshiners to be vicious and resourceful, if a little reckless and apt to lose control of their chemistry. A scenario sprang into his mind, fully formed: an overheard slight, attempted arson, something going wrong, shock and remorse tipping an already rocky mind over the edge – it made an appealing amount of sense. But what could have gone so catastrophically wrong as to level half of the house to its foundation? Whatever had happened, the moonshiner was Roland's best – and possibly only – chance to find out. "Do you know what happened to him?"

"They took him away," Edie said. "The police did. He was ranting and raving, trying to get someone to listen to him. They wanted us both out of the way so they could examine the- the damage. I went to develop my photographs, but he refused to leave. It took three of them to wrestle him to the ground. They threw him in the back of a car and drove him away."

Roland finished writing and looked up. Edie's face was pale, her eyes large. It had cost her something to remember it.

"I'll be sure to ask the sheriff's office about that," Roland said, slashing a savage underline into his notebook. "Now, you say you were working on an article about this new musical work?"

"Yes – *Rites of Apsu*."

"That's a strange name."

"It's Mesopotamian. Or Babylonian, or something. I don't know the difference, to be honest."

"From the museum piece you mentioned?"

"That's right. It was on display at the Met when Oliver saw it."

"And you came to Arkham at the same time as the orchestra?"

"The same day, at any rate."

"And you've been with them every day?"

"Most of the time, I'd say, but not all. Are you going to ask me if they had any enemies?"

Roland looked up and saw a gleam of amusement in her smoky eyes. "That was going to be one of my questions, although accident hasn't been ruled out yet. But let's start with enemies. I've heard they didn't exactly make themselves popular with the neighbors."

"The business with the motorboat?"

"Among other things. And not just here. I read that Oliver Haldane was a controversial type."

"He liked to play the *enfant terrible*. A lot of artists do."

"Can you elaborate?"

"Well, his *Missa Negra* was condemned from the pulpit because Oliver used a choral section based on a witch's spell book from Salem. He liked the Mesopotamian carving because it came from a cursed city. He always said that it was the responsibility of the true artist to challenge mediocrity by breaking down the conventions of society to free the human spirit from the shackles of civilization. People have called him a Communist, an anarchist, a Satanist – he loves notoriety." She took a brief, shaky pause. "Loved, I mean."

"I see," said Roland. Spiritualism had flourished like a weed after the destruction of the Great War, and the fashionable wasters of the art world saw black magic as a way to seem dangerous and interesting.

"Was there anyone, or any group, in particular who was so outraged that they could have tried to kill him, or his orchestra?"

"No one in particular, no."

"I've heard that bootleggers are active in the area," said Roland. "Based on what I've heard about the orchestra, it seems possible that they somehow found themselves caught between two rival gangs. You already told me that they did business with someone named Ellis, or Elmer, or Elwood, or something similar. Do you know of any other criminal contacts?"

Edie was silent for a moment. Roland waited.

"I don't know of anyone else in these parts," she said at last.

"Does the name Leo De Luca mean anything to you? Or Johnny Valone, also known as Johnny V?" She shook her head.

"Miss Talbot," he said, "thank you for your help. If there's anything else you remember – anything at all..."

"I'll leave you a message at the hotel," she promised.

CHAPTER 5

"The sheriff's still out of town." The desk sergeant did not even bother to look up at Roland this time.

"I'm not looking for the sheriff," Roland said. Sheriff Engle had neglected to mention the old moonshiner earlier; there was no telling what else he might have held back – what else the other cops might let slip if Roland pushed them.

"I need to talk to every one of your people who went out to Pine Beach that day," he said. "Everyone who saw or spoke to the witness – the one that the sheriff forgot to tell me about." He slapped his growing stack of files down on the counter and lowered his voice to a growl. "Right now."

That made the sergeant look up. The two men locked stares for a long moment, but Roland was used to these territorial battles with local law enforcement. The sergeant broke off first.

"You'll need to ask the captain," he said, clearly trying to sound more confident than he felt. "But he's–" Roland was already striding through the wicket to the bullpen.

"Thanks," he said over his shoulder as he headed for a door with "Captain" in gold letters on its frosted-glass window. Two minutes later he was back on the street, having learned that the old moonshiner's name was Elmer White and that he had been taken to the Arkham Sanatorium.

Storming the local police station like an enemy trench was far from standard procedure. Roland was supposed to show up, flash his badge, and invoke the might of the Bureau of Investigation, whereupon the locals were supposed to tug their forelocks and give him whatever he asked for. Standard procedure had clearly been designed by someone who had never left headquarters, but Roland had always gone by the book despite the book's obvious problems. He told himself he was planting the Bureau's flag on the moral high ground, but in hindsight, perhaps he had just been covering his rear, toeing the line so no black mark could ever sully his file. A lot of good that had done him in Jubal County, and he would be damned if he'd let another bunch of local hicks make a fool of him.

The momentum of his anger and frustration carried Roland into the asylum like an express train. With the prospect of an eyewitness hanging before him like a vision of the Holy Grail, the qualms Roland had felt at the sight of the place the previous day evaporated. Roland had become an irresistible force, and heaven help anyone who tried to play the immovable object.

"Bureau of Investigation." He shoved his badge in the face of a startled receptionist. "Agent Roland Banks. I need to see one of your patients: the name is White comma Elmer. Right now."

"Visiting hours are…" The receptionist was made of sterner stuff than the police captain. Perhaps working around asylum inmates gave a person confidence. But Roland was not about to be stalled.

"Never mind visiting hours," he snapped. "This is federal business. Elmer White – where is he?"

"I'm sorry, but…"

"Don't be sorry, be cooperative. Five minutes from now, either I'll be looking at Elmer White or I'll be hauling you off in cuffs for obstructing a federal investigation. The choice is yours." He made a show of looking at his watch as the receptionist reached for her phone. Throwing his weight around was more of a thrill than he expected, and he could see how some agents got to liking it a little too much. *Watch yourself,* he thought. *You're a lawman, not a bully.* But he could not deny that it felt good.

A nurse marched up to the desk, wearing a crisply starched uniform and an even starchier expression. She opened her mouth to speak, but Roland struck first.

"Thank you for your cooperation." His badge was already in his hand. "Agent Roland Banks, Bureau of Investigation, to see your patient Elmer White without delay. Federal business." He pushed past her and set off down the corridor.

"What's the room number?" he shot over one shoulder as the nurse trailed in his wake. He kept talking, giving her no opportunity to protest. "I'll have some questions for you, too. You'd better bring his patient file." He turned a corner to find a heavy door blocked by two burly orderlies in hospital whites. They stood with folded arms like a pair of granite statues, and they looked about as easy to move. Roland was forced to stop walking.

"If I call your superiors," the nurse's voice was cold, "will I hear the same story you just told poor Miss Millicent? Stand aside or face arrest for obstruction?" Roland bit back an ungentlemanly response.

"Nurse…" he began, turning to face her.

"Heather."

"Nurse Heather," he said, trying not to lose his momentum,

"what you will hear is that a house was destroyed, thirty-eight lives lost, and that Elmer White is definitely a witness and quite possibly a suspect. You will also hear that Elmer White is suspected of multiple violations of the Volstead Act and that these violations will be reported to the Bureau of Internal Revenue's Prohibition Unit, which will probably begin its own proceedings against Mr White. I am a federal agent engaged in a federal investigation, and any lack of cooperation on your part will be reported and may result in criminal proceedings for obstruction. Do I make myself clear?"

To Roland's annoyance, Nurse Heather did not look at all intimidated. On the contrary, she looked a little amused.

"Abundantly clear, Agent Banks," she said. "And now, let me make myself abundantly clear in my turn."

Roland raised an eyebrow to let her know she had his attention. He wished those two toughs were not right behind him, and he knew Nurse Heather could see him wishing it.

"In the first place," she said, with a hint of a malicious smile, "anyone who comes in here ranting and bullying and claiming to be above the rules is exhibiting the classic symptoms of paranoid schizophrenia with delusions of grandeur. It is my duty to have any such person restrained until a formal diagnosis can be obtained. In plain English, if you come in here acting crazy, I can lock you up until Dr Mintz has time to examine you. And," her mouth twitched up at one corner, "I'm the one who decides what 'acting crazy' looks like. So, unless you'd like to spend tonight in a padded room and most of tomorrow trying to prove you're sane, why don't you ease up on the gas? OK?"

She was a smug one, all right, and Roland had no doubt she could make good on her threat. Heck, she could probably shoot him full of something and actually make him crazy, and then he would be here for good. Given how things had gone in Virginia, the Bureau might not even try to get him back. Roland found his jaw was clenched too tight for talking, so he answered her with a shrug and a spread of the hands.

"All right, then," she said, turning on her heel. "For one thing, you're heading the wrong way. Follow me." Roland knew that he must have felt more foolish at some point in his life, but right at that moment he could not call the occasion to mind.

Nurse Heather kept talking as they walked, probably to keep the upper hand as Roland had tried to do earlier. The two orderlies followed, just a little too close so that he felt on edge. No doubt that was on purpose as well.

"Did you ever hear the saying, 'a lunatic has the strength of ten'?" she asked, clearly not expecting an answer. "Well, I can tell you it's true. That's why we like to keep our patients nice and calm, and that means that we don't like raised voices or other displays of aggression. It stirs them up, and before you know it, you can have a riot on your hands. And in a place like this, it's nothing like a standard prison riot. It's more like a painting by Hieronymus Bosch. Ever seen his work? Never mind. The point is, don't go bulling around, because it gets the patients excited and that makes problems for everyone. I'd tell J. Edgar Hoover or President Coolidge the same thing, and I'd lock them up just as fast if they didn't listen." She turned her head to look Roland in the eye. "Don't test me on that.

"So – Elmer White," she continued without skipping a beat. "Brought in by the Arkham police on the day the house was destroyed. They said they found him there in a highly agitated state. He wouldn't or couldn't answer their questions, wasn't making sense, and became aggressive. They brought him here in handcuffs, upset and incoherent. He seemed to think the world was ending, or had ended when the house was destroyed. Dr Mintz diagnosed paranoid schizophrenia – remember I mentioned that? – complicated by brain and liver damage from a lifetime of alcohol addiction. He prescribed morphine to keep the patient docile pending a decision on long-term treatment. There's no next of kin that anyone knows of, so the decision will rest with the county."

"How docile?" Roland asked. If Elmer was drugged up to the eyebrows, he would not be much use as a witness, and who knew how long it might take to bring him back.

"See for yourself," said Nurse Heather, unlocking a door to the right and motioning Roland inside.

The first thing that struck Roland was the smell. A nauseating mixture of organic waste, decay, and suppuration assaulted his nostrils, overlaid but not overshadowed by bleach and sharper chemical smells. Surely it could not all be coming from one person. At least none of the stains on the mattress and sheet looked very fresh.

A small, scabby man was strapped to the bed. Roland put his age at about seventy. His slack face was turned to the wall, but it was clear that his eyes saw nothing. Apart from the bed and its occupant, the room was completely empty. There was not even a chair to sit in.

At a gesture from Nurse Heather, one of the massive orderlies muscled in behind Roland. "Cole will stay with you," she said, "for your own safety." Roland looked down at the shrunken, wizened figure strapped to the mattress.

"My safety?" Roland said. "From him?"

"You'd be surprised," said the nurse. "Schizophrenics are like nitroglycerin: one little nudge and they blow up. I saw a patient smaller than this one break out of restraints in less than ten seconds. The bed frame was bent like a banana. And you're here to ask about the house, which can't fail to get him agitated." She flashed Roland a bitter smile and left.

Roland leaned over the bed as Cole settled his impassive bulk across the doorway.

"Best not to get too close." The orderly's voice was surprisingly soft. "They can move fast when they turn: grab your tie or rip your ear off before you know it." Despite himself, Roland glanced down at the thick leather straps that held the patient's wrists to the bed frame. They looked reassuringly sturdy.

"Elmer White?" he asked, as gently as he could manage. The old man gave no acknowledgment.

"Elmer?" Roland repeated. "Can you hear me?" Still nothing. He might as well be talking to a sack of potatoes.

"Mr White." He let an official edge into his voice. "My name is Agent Roland Banks, and I'm with the Bureau of Investigation." An eyelid flickered. Roland decided to treat it as a good sign. He would start with some innocuous questions and see how things went.

"Have you ever done business with Leo De Luca?" Elmer's eyes slid away from the nothing they had been looking at and fastened onto the blank wall. His stillness changed almost imperceptibly, becoming a little more deliberate.

"How about Johnny Valone? Have you ever heard that name before?" White said nothing.

This tack was getting him nowhere. Roland tried a lighter tone. "Tell me, Elmer," he said, "how do you like it here? Cole here, he seems like a real swell guy. I bet you two talk and laugh all the time. That Nurse Heather, too – boy, what a peach! Does she tuck you in just right, make sure those straps are good and snug?" Roland sensed, rather than saw, that his words were getting through the blanket of morphine that enveloped the old moonshiner. Although Elmer had not moved perceptibly, the rising tension in him was palpable.

"And how's Dr Mintz?" Roland asked. "I haven't met him yet, but he sounds like a real smart man. How's he treating you? Do you lie on a couch and talk about your mother? Take cold, refreshing baths? Or is he one of those modern types, with big electrical machines to fix you up?" One of Elmer's hands twitched in its leather restraint: that last question had struck a nerve.

"Yes, I bet he is, Elmer," Roland went on, maintaining his conversational tone. "I bet you're having a whale of a time and getting the most modern treatments. Why, I bet you're having just as much fun as a Vanderbilt princess taking the rest cure in Switzerland. Well, I have good news for you, Elmer. All you have to do is keep stonewalling me and you get to stay here forever. You and Dr Mintz can whoop it up from dawn to dusk, and no one will try to stop either of you. Not unless one of your relatives steps in and stops the party. Do you have a big family, Elmer? Anyone likely to come and get you?"

Elmer's eyes were moving now, sliding foggily from side to side like those of a hunted animal. Roland pressed his advantage.

"That's what I figured, Elmer. Nurse Heather tells me no one's been asking about you – no family, no friends, no one at all. Leo De Luca hasn't come to call. I don't see any flowers with love from Johnny Valone. Not even a bunch of grapes. Well, I guess they don't want to disturb you when you're having such a good time with your new pal, Dr Mintz." Another twitch. Roland had no idea what Mintz had been doing to the old rummy, but he was willing to bet it was more than just the morphine sedation Nurse Heather had mentioned.

"Leo…" The voice was paper-thin, but it was there.

"He's not coming, Elmer. I'm your only way out of here. I know it, and you know it, too. So, what do you say? Just a few little questions?"

"Leo…" It took some effort, but Elmer fixed Roland with one rheumy eye. "Leo 'n' me… got… business."

Roland smiled, deliberately showing his teeth. "There – that wasn't so hard, Elmer, was it now? And you know what? I'm a good scout, so I'm not even going to ask you what kind of business. No sir, I'll just mind my own beeswax on that score. But the thing is, Elmer, I'd really like to talk to your buddy Leo. I hear Johnny V's giving him some trouble, and I want to help Leo out." The bleary eye did not move.

"I get it, Elmer," Roland went on. "You don't trust me because I'm a G-man. But here's the straight dope: I'm not here for you, and I'm not here for Leo. You two can peddle your giggle water all over Arkham and across three counties for all I care. No sir, it's Johnny V I'm after. He's the big fish that's going to get me a promotion and a fat pay raise. And after I fix Johnny's wagon, I'll be far, far away in Washington, smoking cigars with J. Edgar Hoover and telling him how we can pinch a certain Mr Capone. Little old Arkham won't ever cross my mind again. So, you see, we all come up aces – you, me, and Leo."

Roland gave this a moment to sink in. The morphine was not making Elmer's mind any faster, he knew, but he hoped his breezy tone would smooth out any bumps. Elmer's other eye finally caught up with the first one, looking right at him.

"But there's just one little problem, Elmer," he said. "You can see what it is, can't you? I have to talk to Leo so I can clue him in on the plan. Otherwise, it's all for nothing. So be a pal, Elmer, and tell me where I can find him."

After all that talking, it was a kind of agony for Roland to wait for Elmer's answer. The old rummy was trying, he could tell, fighting through the haze of morphine, but it held him almost as securely as the leather straps.

"Leo…"

"Yes?"

"Th… th'Night'ngale." Elmer's voice was getting stronger, although it was still no more than a whisper.

"Well, all right, Elmer," Roland said. "You've done your part and I'll do mine. I'll talk to Leo and get everything set up. Then we'll bust you out of here and we'll all three go fix Johnny V together." He gave the old man a comforting pat on the shoulder. "In fact, I'm going to take care of the paperwork right now."

Roland rose as if to leave, taking a step toward the door before he asked his real question.

"Say, Elmer," he said, "just to double check – it was Johnny V who blew up that big house by the lake, wasn't it? Must've taken a mess of dynamite."

Elmer was very still for a moment, and Roland started to worry that he had lost him to the morphine again. Then the old man's mouth opened wider than the gates of hell and a sound came out like a thousand cats being neutered with dull knives. The bed rocked as Elmer thrashed against his restraints.

"The sky!" Elmer's voice was suddenly as clear as a Baptist preacher's. "It tore through! Licked it up! Licked it all up!" Roland felt himself picked up like a Kewpie doll. Before he could react, he was outside the room and Cole was locking the door. Elmer's voice was muffled, but Roland could pick out a word here and there: "eyes," "tongue," "teeth," "sky," "flute," "balloon," and others, apparently at random.

"Shouldn't have gotten him excited," the big man said in his oddly gentle voice. "Got to get the doctor now. You got to leave." Roland thought for a moment that Cole expected him to comply without argument, but then he realized that it made no difference to the orderly whether he resisted or not. He decided to go quietly.

"Was that how he was when he came in?" he asked.

Cole nodded gravely.

Neither one spoke the rest of the way outside, and Roland felt a little relieved that he did not encounter Nurse Heather as he left.

CHAPTER 6

Outside the asylum, the air felt cooler. Roland took a few deep breaths and reviewed his options. It had been a Bearcat of a day, and he was not proud of some of the things he had done, but he had a few pieces of information to show for it. He had crossed some lines, but he felt far less guilty than he would have expected. He strolled across to the square, collecting his thoughts as he went.

Whatever had wiped out that mansion, it had been big. Dynamite was the most likely explanation, even though the scene did not look quite right. It certainly made more sense than a tongue full of teeth reaching down from a hole in the sky.

The bootlegger war felt like a pretty solid angle, although Roland was not sure yet how it all fit together. It seemed most likely that somebody had blown up somebody else's customers. This Leo De Luca could probably clear up the details.

Roland would need some kind of leverage, of course. The threat of a raid, or the promise of protection from Johnny V or from the Prohibition Unit, would only work if Leo was gullible enough to trust the word of a G-man, and Leo was probably not that naïve. It had only worked on Elmer because the old coot was so befuddled by the doctor's morphine and his own coffin varnish.

Roland needed to know more about both Leo De Luca and Johnny V. It seemed like days, rather than hours, since he had cabled Boston for their Bureau files, but it would be tomorrow at the earliest before he heard anything back. Right now, he could pass either one of them in the street and not know it.

As tired as Roland felt, he was not ready to call it a day and go back to the hotel. He would only end up beating his head against those files again, and there was nothing more to be gained there. He had not yet burned off all the frustration and anger that had propelled him into the asylum like a wrecking ball. He needed to unwind somehow.

That was when he decided to visit the Nightingale Club. The sun had set while Roland was in the asylum, and the place was probably open for business. Maybe he would go inside and see if Leo De Luca was in there, as Elmer had told him he would be. Maybe he would have a drink to settle his mind down. It was the sixth year of Prohibition and his fourth as a federal agent, but despite this – or perhaps because of it – the thought of whiskey gave him the same illicit thrill as his first schoolyard glimpse of a French postcard.

There was always the risk that Roland might run into one of the Arkham cops or some other bigwig in the gin mill. It was not unknown for federal agents to arrest a local police chief or even a mayor in a speakeasy, and Roland had been the kind of agent who relished these collars in particular. If the Bureau were to hear of any transgression on his part, far too many people would be far too happy to have something on the Boy Scout.

On the other hand, Elmer had directed him to the jazz club,

and the bootlegger angle had to be investigated. Rules or no rules, Roland was certain to be pegged as a G-man if he went into a speakeasy and asked for lemonade. He could call it undercover work, and it would be within a stone's throw of the truth. "Close enough for government work," the saying went.

By the time all these thoughts had run through his mind, Roland had crossed the river, the docks, and the university campus. Uptown was newer, cleaner, and better lit than most of Arkham, and the club was bright and bustling. Roland loosened his tie, tilted his hat, and turned up his coat collar, and when he was sure he looked respectably disreputable, he approached the door. A large gentleman in a tuxedo looked him up and down, and waved him inside.

This early in the evening the place was not packed, but there was enough of a crowd for Roland to avoid standing out. He checked his hat and coat at the door and took the measure of the place. The club was decorated according to someone's idea of a Hollywood party, with a healthy dose of luxury liner thrown in. The walls were lined with long curtains of silver tinsel. Needless classical pillars were painted pale gold and rocked a little when the music grew too spirited. Fake palm trees of white ostrich feather erupted from tables painted white and silver. At one end of the room, half a dozen musicians played Dixieland.

To the side of the stage, another large gentleman in a tuxedo stood beside a door marked "Dressing Room." A few minutes' observation told Roland that the password to the speakeasy was green and folded. Arkham was a good deal less sophisticated than New York or Chicago, it seemed. A few minutes after that, Roland was comfortably ensconced in a quiet corner with a glass of whiskey in front of him and a clear view across the smaller room.

The first sip felt so good going down that for the second time in under an hour, Roland almost forgot to feel guilty. He savored the slow warmth, held his glass up to the light, and admired the rich, amber color. This was the good stuff, all right. Leo De Luca must have connections up the coast to Canada. Roland looked around for any sign of Elmer's moonshine – "white lightning", they had called it in Jubal County – but the clientele here looked well-heeled: social drinkers rather than hardened rummies. The rotgut must move in another direction.

Another sip, and Roland felt his shoulders start to relax. He beckoned to a cigarette girl and paid over the odds for a pack of Chesterfields, scanning the crowd with a narrowed eye as he lit one.

Most of them were just here for a good time. In accordance with speakeasy etiquette, they stuck to their own groups, laughing and drinking together but making sure not to notice anyone else. The only ones who looked up were those who were here to work.

Aside from the bartender, the cigarette girl, and a couple of strategically placed bouncers, Roland noticed three other people looking around. A greasy-looking cove in dove-gray pinstripes sat at the bar, talking to an older gent. Something changed hands – all Roland saw was a glimpse of brown paper – and the fellow pocketed a thin wad of bills as his customer drank up and left. Roland dropped his eyes to his drink as Pinstripes cast a look around.

The other two were a team. They sat together as though they were on a date, but all their attention was directed outward rather than toward each other. They reminded Roland of a picture from *National Geographic* magazine: two cheetahs on an African anthill, watching for slow-looking antelopes.

The woman was in her mid-twenties, with dark, natural curls forced into a Marcel Wave and pale, natural curves forced into a tasseled red dress. Her shoes looked sharp, but Roland noticed they were low in the heel: she could move fast if she needed to. He glanced at her beaded handbag, trying to estimate whether it was big enough to hold a gun. A .22, he decided, or a .32 snub in a pinch.

Her companion wore a dark suit, a thick coat of Brilliantine, and a patient expression. They were clearly waiting for someone, and that someone was not expected at any particular time. Roland wondered whether the someone was expecting them. He thought not.

Roland finished his whiskey and ordered another. It was a fine line: drink too fast and he would be slowed down, perhaps fatally, when the time came to act; drink too slowly and the staff would get suspicious, which was never a good thing in a place like this. Just as his drink arrived, the door opened and a young flapper came in. She was solo, which was not typical of her ilk, and her face looked strangely familiar. It took Roland a minute or so to recognize Edie Talbot, the tweedy magazine writer he had spoken with earlier in the day. He started to blame the whiskey for dulling his wits, but on second thought he doubted her own mother would recognize her in that getup.

She looked as though she were stepping into the Cotton Club rather than a small-town speakeasy. A turquoise plume danced above a silk helmet of the same color, perfectly matching a knee-skimming, beaded dress set off with a double rope of beads. A few heads turned, but she ignored them and scanned the room coolly. Not finding whomever she was looking for, she drifted over to the bar and settled herself on a stool. A tall, heavily iced measure of gin appeared at her elbow as she fitted a cigarette into a holder that was only a little shorter than her arm.

Pinstripes materialized at her side with a gold-plated lighter and a smile like Rudolph Valentino swallowed an accordion. She favored him with a chilly smile, but he was clearly used to rejection and settled in to wear her down.

Roland sipped at his whiskey to cover a smile. He was tempted to intervene, but she knew he was a Fed and in this company that could be bad for his health as well as his investigation. Miss Talbot was used to New York, so she could probably handle a small-town masher like this guy. He thought of the earnest, tweedy woman from the hotel lobby with amusement. She was clearly a woman of many parts, and he should not let himself forget that if their paths crossed again.

To Roland's surprise, Pinstripes seemed to be getting somewhere. Now and again, Miss Talbot would grant him a word or a nod in response to something he said. She was not exactly leading him on, but she was not giving him the brush-off either, and he was clearly prepared for a long siege. After a few minutes she turned a little toward him; a minute later she favored him with a raised eyebrow. She asked a question, and he grinned even wider and thumbed his own chest. Whatever she was looking for, Pinstripes was her man.

Pinstripes signaled the barkeep for another round of drinks, and when they came back, he talked in the man's ear. The barkeep looked surprised, and then Pinstripes talked some more and got a reluctant nod in return. A few greenbacks changed hands and the barkeep went out back, returning a moment later with a nod for his benefactor.

Just as Roland was wondering what seedy delight Pinstripes was in the process of organizing, another man came out of the back. Roland's first thought was that this fellow could almost make it in moving pictures: he was tall and well built, with chestnut-brown hair swept back from a strong face. He was in shirtsleeves, dressed for work rather than for going out, and he made quite a contrast with the lounge lizard who had summoned him.

Miss Talbot clearly thought so, too. Roland could not see her face as she turned to the new arrival, but he felt a momentary pang of jealousy at the way her back straightened when she saw him. Then a few things happened at once.

The handsome fellow's smile slid from his face as he looked beyond Miss Talbot to Marcel Wave and her broad-shouldered friend. He nudged the bartender, who reached beneath the bar and came up with a sawed-off shotgun. Taking his cue, the tuxedoed gorillas at the door started toward the unwelcome pair.

The two interlopers looked around them like cornered animals. Pinstripes had just figured out that something bad was about to happen and was edging out of the line of fire as fast as he could shuffle, leaving Miss Talbot alone at the bar. So much for chivalry. Roland instinctively reached for the .38 revolver under his jacket, but kept it out of sight. There was no sense in making a tense situation worse.

Marcel Wave dipped her hand in her handbag and came out with a nickel-plated .32 just in time for one of the bouncers to grab her wrist and point it at the ceiling. The palooka's other arm wrapped around her waist and lifted her off her feet. Her knight in worsted armor looked at the shotgun in front of him and the second bouncer approaching from the side, and he weighed his chances for a long second. In that second, Roland made his move.

Two loping strides took him to the bar. He half-tackled the writer and his momentum carried them both out of the line of fire. His movement, and Miss Talbot's shriek of surprise, broke the tableau: there was a scuffle and a curse, the smack of knuckles on flesh, and a clatter of footsteps toward the door. When Roland looked up, the unwelcome pair was gone and the two doormen were heading after them, one with a pronounced limp. The barkeep's eyes were on Roland, but his hands were uncertain of where to point his shotgun; Handsome was nowhere to be seen; and Pinstripes was cowering in a corner. Roland lifted Edie to her feet.

"Are you hurt?" He tried to ignore the way her perfume filled his head.

"I'll live, but I'm not so sure about my stockings."

Roland turned to Pinstripes.

"Put her in a cab for the Excelsior Hotel – and don't go with her." Pinstripes managed to look scared, disappointed, and offended all at once, but nodded. Roland turned to the bartender.

"Neutral party," he said, looking the man square in the eyes, "just looking out for the lady. Got a message for Leo from his buddy Elmer."

The barkeep's eyes twitched involuntarily toward the back door, confirming Roland's suspicion: Handsome was Leo De Luca, the local hero, which meant that the unwelcome pair must be scouts for Johnny V. Roland made a big show of holstering his .38, and the barrels of the shotgun lowered slowly.

"I'm going to leave now," he said, locking eyes with the man. "If you want to shoot me in the back, I can't stop you." He turned and walked out the door slowly and calmly, despite every nerve in his body screaming at him to run.

As soon as the door swung to behind him, Roland circled around the building at a sprint. Leo had a lead on him, and so did

Johnny V's people. Nerves were taut, trigger fingers were twitchy, and the darkened streets were a far better place for a kill than a crowded speakeasy.

Reaching the back door, Roland stopped to listen. The night was quiet, almost unnaturally so: Arkham was one of those old, old towns where the darkness seemed to absorb sound as well as light. Roland hesitated, unsure of which way to go.

The crack of a gunshot made the decision for him. He pulled his .38 and followed the sound, hoping he would get there before the party was over. A couple of blocks later he heard another shot, closer this time. He skidded around a corner and ran slap into a standoff.

Marcel Wave and her friend had Leo backed up against a stack of crates in an alley. His shotgun was sawed off shorter than the bartender's, giving it a lot of scatter. The out-of-towners tried to spread out, but in that tight space a two-barrel blast had an excellent chance of hitting them both. The dame had her .32 and her friend was hefting a big, black Colt .45.

Roland fired before anyone could react, getting rid of the big Colt and sending its owner skedaddling down the alley clutching his wrist. Roland pointed his gun at the moll with the .32.

"Drop it," he said. She considered the matter for a little longer than he liked, but eventually let the pistol fall. Roland looked over at Leo, but left his gun pointed at the woman.

"I saw your pal Elmer this afternoon," he said. "He gave me a message for you. If you blow a big hole in me, you'll never get it." Leo searched Roland's eyes, and then gave a tight nod. Clearly, he had no idea that Elmer was no longer capable of giving anyone a coherent message.

"All right, then," Roland said. "Let's keep this short. You–" he nodded at the woman "–are pals with Johnny V down in Boston, and Leo here doesn't want to roll over and play nice. That about the size of it?"

"Take a hike, flatfoot! Yeah, that's right; I got you pegged, and I ain't sayin' nothin'!" Her eyes would have thrown fire at him if they could.

"Suit yourself." Roland gave her a shrug. "I'm not from the Prohibition Unit anyhow. I'm just trying to figure out why Johnny would blow up a whole orchestra from New York. I heard they were the types to make great customers."

"What orchestra?" she spat back. "You're all wet!" As soon as the words were out, her eyes went down, and her mouth went tight. She had spoken despite herself, and that convinced Roland that she was telling the truth. He bent an eye over to Leo, who looked equally confused.

Roland pretended to consider her words while he decided how to end this standoff. The Boy Scout clamored to run them both in, but he was alone and Leo was still armed. For all he knew, the wounded gunman had gone for help and more of Johnny V's troops would arrive any minute. The book was no help to him here; he would have to choose the least of all evils.

"Get out of here," he said to the moll. "Go find your friend and go back to Boston. Tell Johnny the Bureau of Investigation's in Arkham because some rich lady's mansion went boom, and they'll be around for a while. He'd be well advised to let things cool off a little. Now scram, before I change my mind."

The woman gave Roland a look like a fisherman who had just had a thirty-pound trout jump up and kiss him. She took one hesitant step, glanced back, and then was out of the alley faster than a bullet in the back. Roland turned to Leo.

"I'd prefer not to be here if she comes back with reinforcements.

Where can we talk in private?" Leo said nothing. The barrels of his shotgun came up a hair.

"Now, now," said Roland, raising his .38 squarely into the bootlegger's face. "That hurts my feelings. Didn't I just run off the opposition for you?" The shotgun stopped moving, but Leo's face did not soften.

"Just so you know," said Leo, "I flatter myself that I had things under a pretty good measure of control back there at the club. Those two were no more trouble than a fly on a cow's rump, until you decided to play Douglas Fairbanks. And there's also your federal affiliation to consider, which isn't meant to be comforting to the likes of me, now, is it? Not to mention–"

"–not to mention that you don't know what I might have done to poor, addled old Elmer," Roland finished the sentence for him. "I get it. But right now, the question is, do you want to be here if she comes back mob-handed?"

"A change of scene sounds like a fine suggestion to me," Leo conceded, "although I'm not overkeen on continuing our chat in a police station, if that's your thinking. And I'll keep ahold of my shotgun, if it's all the same to you. Or even if it's not."

"Fair enough," said Roland. "We're just two new acquaintances, taking the night air and talking as we wander. Pick up the .45, too, if you like. I'll take the .32. No sudden moves, that's all." Keeping an eye and a gun on each other, they picked up the goods as slowly as two circling tomcats. Leo nodded down the alley, and they moved cautiously forward.

"I know nothing about that mansion," Leo volunteered. "Let's make that plain from the start."

"I figured as much," Roland said. "Where were you when it went up?"

"Reading the Bible to my ailing grandma. She's taken awful bad with the damp at this time of year, and the sound of scripture brings her comfort."

"Serves me right for asking," Roland admitted. "Seems Elmer was at the mansion, though, and he saw everything. It shook him up real bad."

"And how bad would that be?" Leo's tone darkened. "If you've done anything…"

"Not me," said Roland. "The sheriff swept him up and he's in the asylum right now."

"The asylum? Lord save us." There was shock in Leo's voice, and a touch of fear, too.

"Yeah. Just staring at the wall till I mentioned you. He seems to like you."

Leo sighed softly. "He was a good man once, although not the master distiller he thought himself. It was his own hooch made him soft in the head, but he was never certifiable."

"Must have been some shock, then," said Roland. "Did you see the mansion lately?" Leo shook his head.

"A casualty of your little bootleg war, I figured," Roland continued. "It would take a truckload of dynamite to do that much damage. Anyone else around here in the import-export business and able to lay their hands on that much explosive?"

"And what possible reason would I have for giving you everything on the local trade, chapter and verse, for the asking?" Leo shot back. A sneer twisted the side of his mouth. "It's certainly not the pleasure of your company or the charm of your conversation. No, let me see if I can guess." He held up a hand and counted on his fingers. "In the first place, you saved me from those two and I now owe you my life: a weak argument, since you did nothing of the kind. Of course, you want me to understand that Johnny V's the big prize, and I'm just a charming local rogue who's doing no harm to anyone. Indeed, we're getting acquainted, and you've decided to like me and turn a blind eye to my business so long as I repay you with sweet words and useful intelligence: an offer I wouldn't trust if it came on oath from the Holy Father himself. And then, there's the prompting of your tender heart, which urges you to spring Elmer from the madhouse, just so long as I give you a measure of cooperation in proportion to your trouble." He turned back to Roland with a grin. "Was there anything I missed, or is that the sum of your argument?"

Roland considered for a moment. "Just one more thing," he said. "Assuming we don't kill each other before this conversation is over, which I would rather avoid, I can place one long-distance phone call and have a few dozen Prohibition agents tearing the city apart by lunchtime tomorrow. Starting with your speakeasy back there."

Leo thought this over for a moment and then sighed.

"And you'd threaten such a thing after drinking my whiskey," he said. "It's true that you government men have no souls. Ask your questions, then, though you'd best hope, as I do, that I don't live to regret my choice." The shotgun vanished beneath the bootlegger's coat, but he kept the .45 in his hand.

As they walked, Roland learned a thing or two and came to suspect a couple more. The first was that Leo had grit. Despite the fact that he was gun to gun with a federal agent, he kept a cool head and gave almost nothing away regarding his own operation. He said he did not have dynamite on hand, but admitted that he had been thinking of investing in a few sticks in case things turned heated with Johnny V's people. He also said he had heard Johnny blew up a couple of places in Boston while he was eliminating the competition there. He neither admitted nor denied supplying the orchestra with enough booze to float a battleship, and he absolutely refused to be drawn out on the reasons why the local police took no interest in the Nightingale Club, or in any other business dealings Leo might have in and around Arkham.

They were approaching the river docks when Leo stopped and turned to face Roland.

"This is where we part ways," he said firmly. The .45 made an ominous bulge in his coat pocket, pointing right at the G-man's stomach. Roland gave a grunt of amusement.

"What, you don't want me to walk you to your door?"

"You know better than that. Johnny or no, we both know which side you're on. I'm in a generous mood, though, so here's how it's going to be: I'll watch while you walk away, and you have my word that I won't shoot you in the back unless you do something I don't like the look of. That's a better deal than you'd get from most in my profession, and you'd be well advised to take it." Roland mentally filed away the fact that Leo likely had a place somewhere by the docks, turned around, and started walking.

CHAPTER 7

The walk back to the hotel reminded Roland just how tired he was. It had been a long, long day. The stairs to his room felt like Mount Everest. Closing the door behind him, he eased off his shoes, threw his jacket over the back of a chair, cursed when he remembered his coat and hat were still checked at the club, and fell face down on his lumpy bed.

It was still dark when his eyes opened. The music had woken him – or was it the dream? Or was the music a part of the dream, or the dream a part of the music? He shook his head to disperse the cold, damp slab of dread that was lodged between his ears, and he fumbled for the light.

Fragments of the dream still clung to him. It had been cold, colder than he ever thought possible. There was no ground beneath his feet, just the night sky all around with stars in unfamiliar patterns. The music had drawn him, pulled him to that place – that no-place – as though it were a physical force. A formless and monotonous piping enveloped everything, its random notes somehow familiar. In the dream Roland had looked around for the source of the noise and had glimpsed the strange, unnatural pipers gyrating slowly in a blasphemy of dance – and he had seen the vast and formless monstrosity around which they circled.

Roland rose from the bed and looked around the room, desperate to fix on anything real and solid in this world that would take his thoughts away from the memories of the nightmare. His jacket and shoes were still where he had dropped them; his valise stood at attention beside the small and slightly battered table with its paunchy lamp of dull brass. He strode over, turned the desk lamp on, and then went to the switch by the door. The extra light was comforting, but the haze from the nightmare still lingered in his mind.

He hesitated a moment at the window. The air outside would be cool and bracing, he knew, but the thought of sticking his head outside into the darkness roused an inexplicable dread. Shaking his head and cursing himself for a fool, Roland wrenched the sash up and thrust head and shoulders out into the night air.

A few deep breaths cooled his imagination down. Roland listened intently, giving his mind something else to focus on: he could hear the rustle of the wind through unseen trees, the distant yowl of an alley cat – and beyond it, something that undid all the good work of burning lights and fresh air.

It was that music again. Although it was very distant and only audible in brief snatches, Roland knew it immediately. The same music that had haunted his dream – and the same music, he now realized, that he had heard drifting across the lake the previous morning. Roland tried to tell himself that he was imagining things, that the formless piping was nothing more than random shreds of sound that his mind was putting together under the influence of the dream, that no sound could possibly travel from the lake all the way to the heart of Arkham; his mind knew that this must be the case, but his ears, and some deeper part of him, clung to the irrational belief that the half-heard piper from the lake was still playing – had never stopped playing, perhaps.

With no clear idea of what he was going to do, Roland pulled on his shoes and jacket and crept from the hotel. All was dark and quiet downstairs; the clock above the reception desk read a little after two. Half-dreaming still, he followed the snatches of weird piping through the dark and shadowed streets.

He paused at the city limits, listening for a hint of the mindless music to direct him further. It was with a paradoxical mix of dread and relief that he heard it again. It was coming from the direction of the distant lake.

The journey to Pine Beach had taken a few minutes by car. On foot, Roland slogged along semiconscious, much as he had slogged through the mud of the Marne, seeing nothing and thinking of nothing beyond taking one step and then another. He stumbled along the road almost blindly, barely noticing the dark trees that crowded the roadside and hung over him like the vault of some ancient cathedral, reducing the sky to mere shards of lesser darkness. All his attention was focused on the sound: he heard it more frequently now, and more clearly too, and it drew him with a strange, almost hypnotic power.

A pair of tall shadows loomed out of the darkness, strange and misshapen. As Roland's stiff legs brought him closer, he recognized the freestone pillars flanking a dirt drive. His groping hands found a carved plaque and traced out a name: Lakeview. Dimly remembering his journey in daylight, he turned away and kept walking. Hours seemed to pass; the bizarre piping continued, neither closer nor farther away. He passed by another pair of pillars, and another, until he saw "Pine Beach" written in iron scrollwork against a sky of hematite. Without pausing, he turned and walked along the rutted track.

The ruins were faintly silvered in the starlight, all their colors flattened down to shades of gray. The debris that surrounded them bobbed and jutted strangely in the gloom, and more than once Roland fancied that he saw a skeletal arm or leg reaching up to drag itself free of the chaos. The remains of the fountain gleamed obscenely white, like a broken tooth. He found himself standing by the same tree he had noticed earlier, looking at the metal fork that sprouted from its trunk.

The piping drifted across the lake in ripples, seeming nearer and then farther, then nearer again. Roland found himself on a wooden jetty without knowing quite how he had gotten there. He had been so deep in the thrall of the repulsive music that it seemed only by chance that he had not walked right off the end and into the lake. Stopping himself, he turned this way and that, trying to locate the source of the piping, but without success. It seemed to be all around, somehow coming from every direction yet also out of reach.

Retracing his steps to dry ground, Roland started walking along the shoreline. The surface of the lake almost amplified the sound, but he still had no sense of being any closer to its source. He walked like a man in a dream; a dim and distant part of his mind wondered whether he was still asleep in the hotel. Perhaps he had merely progressed to a different level of dreaming. Certainly, the blend of inexplicable horror and powerless fascination that the hideous music inspired in him smacked more of nightmare than reality. And yet, another part of him recognized that if he did not track this unnatural sound to its source, he would surely lose his mind. Without some form of resolution it would haunt him for the rest of his life, and he would never sleep peacefully again.

So he followed the sound, stumbling through the gloom like a drunkard. He did not know how long he walked, but slowly the hideous whine of the pipes became louder. He stumbled upon a trail of sorts; bushes and undergrowth were flattened as if something large and heavy had rolled over them. Some instinct told him to follow the trail, even as a deeper part of his mind screamed at him to turn his back on it and run.

The trail twisted and turned, seemingly at random. With every step he took, though, Roland felt a growing certainty that he was closing with the source of the noise. He followed the trail around a clump of trees and up a low ridge. As he stood at the top, he saw the piper at last.

What the creature was, Roland could not say. It bulked oddly in the dim light, and he felt strangely grateful that the scene was not better lit. If he had seen the thing clearly, he might have lost his mind entirely.

Before he knew it, his gun was in his hand and he was firing as fast as he could. He emptied the magazine and pulled the trigger three more times before he realized that he had no more bullets. Then he turned and ran.

The creature ignored him completely. He saw his bullets strike its gelatinous flesh, but it kept rolling on its way and it piped its unspeakable tune without missing a note. The muzzle flash burned hideous images of the creature into Roland's mind, like the flickers from a hellish movie: the toadlike bulk; the rippling, blubbery skin; the inexplicable appendages that rolled it along; and the long, flaring pipes that might even have been part of the creature's anatomy. As he fled through the woods, those nightmare visions kept on flashing before his eyes, goading him faster and faster until there was nothing left of him but the need to run and run and never stop.

Branches lashed at Roland's face as he ran, and brush snatched at his legs. He ran on, willing himself into wilder and faster motion, hoping that his sleeping body, safe back in the hotel room, would begin to thrash sympathetically and force him to wake up.

Eventually Roland found himself at the lakeshore. He saw a boathouse in the distance. Some tiny remaining grain of reason associated this with human habitation, and human habitation with a measure of safety. Behind the boathouse stood a house, and behind that, a driveway, which led to a road. The road led him back to Arkham.

The old town's shadows seemed no less sinister, yet Roland found their human architecture comforting after the stark unreason he had seen in the woods. Somehow, he was walking rather than running; his returning sanity told him that he must have stopped running some time ago, that the human body could not sustain such exertion for long, but he could not remember slackening his pace. Finding his gun dangling useless from one hand, he holstered it and staggered back to the hotel. He needed to get back to his bed, he told himself, because that was where his sleeping body was. He must get back there so he could wake up, so he could find his way back to the real world of science and reason, the world where everything made sense and horrors did not pipe in the woods.

CHAPTER 8

The soft tap at the door made Roland twitch a little but did not properly wake him. It was the young woman's gasp that brought him to full consciousness.

"I'm so sorry," she stammered. "I thought…" Roland blinked twice and she came into focus: mousy looking, about nineteen, and wearing a maid's uniform. A couple of brush handles sprouted from the metal bucket in her hand.

"What time is it?" The maid stopped backing out of the room, but her eyes did not get any less wide. Roland realized with relief that he was fully dressed. He must have just fallen right over when he got back from the speakeasy.

The chambermaid's brow wrinkled in thought. "It was ten when I started," she said. "I never start before, in case folk sleep late. But I…" Roland's involuntary curse sent her scuttling from the room.

He hauled himself all the way upright, wincing. Everything ached. His head felt like Jack Dempsey was inside trying to get out.

He grabbed his wash kit and lurched along the passage to the bathroom. The mirror told him he looked as bad as he felt, and he couldn't escape the feeling that it enjoyed doing so. He had broken a few rules last night and a couple of laws into the bargain; maybe this pain was the price he had to pay. It took forever to wash and shave.

Back in his room, Roland took rueful stock of his clothes. He remembered a fight – and even some shooting – but it must have been worse than he thought. His shoes were scuffed and muddy; his pants were muddy, too, and torn in a couple of places. He got rid of the mud as best he could and fixed the worst of the tears with the small sewing kit he always carried. The result would not pass close inspection, but it would have to do for now. Then he dragged his aching bones and roiling stomach to the diner for a late – very late – breakfast.

The waitress was as inquisitive as ever, but Roland could not have given her anything if he had wanted to. If the truth were known, he could barely form a complete sentence. He could only trust that ham, eggs, and coffee would get his mind working again.

Back in his room, he picked up his valise and prepared to keep beating his head against the case file. If he knocked hard enough, perhaps something would shake loose and make sense of the few things he had learned since his last attempt. The feeling that he was waiting for something nagged him until he remembered that he had requested Boston's files on the two bootleggers.

He shuffled the papers he was holding, intending to put them back down and go to see whether the files were waiting for him downstairs, but then something stopped him: a faint trace of perfume, slightly familiar. He lifted the papers to his face and sniffed. It was faint, but it was definitely there. Then he sat bolt upright and cursed. It was the same perfume he had smelled on Edie Talbot when he tried to get her out of the fracas at the speakeasy. He stuck his face into his valise and sniffed again. The perfume was there, too, beneath the smell of leather.

Roland flung the door open like a gunport and headed for the stairs. That sanctimonious old relic of a manager was going to get a piece of his mind. Roland would jam the hotel's policy as far down that chicken neck as it would go. Then perhaps he would ask if those reports had arrived.

He was partway to the stairs when the little chambermaid emerged from a room. She gave him a frightened look, and suddenly she became very interested in her bucket and brushes. That was unwise because it made Roland shoot an involuntary glance in the same direction and notice the bottle neck poking out from behind a feather duster.

All the anger and frustration of the past couple of days came welling up again at the sight of a more or less legitimate target. A part of Roland knew he would hate himself later, but for the moment that part was in the minority. He grabbed the bucket, ignoring the maid's squeak of fear.

"What's this?" he demanded. The maid backed against the wall as he thrust the bottle in her white face.

"I... I..." She struggled for words, but they had gotten clean away and left her high and dry.

"Do you make a habit of filching from the hotel's guests?" he demanded. "Or are you delivering rather than picking up?" The maid looked desperately at the ground, silently pleading with it to open up beneath her feet.

Roland let the silence stretch on. He knew it would eventually become unbearable and she would have to say something. But she just kept looking at the floor. A few seconds more and her shoulders started to shake. If she started crying, she would become useless.

"All right," he said, in a softer voice. "I can see you're not Al Capone. Heck, you're not even Leo De Luca." She looked up in surprise, clearly not expecting him to know about the local bootlegger. He handed the bucket back but kept hold of the bottle, waving it back and forth to punctuate his words. She could not tear her huge, scared eyes away from it.

"I tell you what," he continued, "I'll give you back your grandma's rheumatic medicine, and we can say no more about it. Provided–"

The maid's gasp cut him off. "Never!" Her back straightened and she fixed him with what she clearly hoped was a defiant, outraged glare. "I'm not that sort–"

"–and I'm not that sort of guest," Roland interrupted. "I just want to know one thing – no, two things. If I like what you tell me, I never saw this bottle. And you," he added, "never saw the state I was in this morning. Is it a deal?"

The maid's eyes were almost back to their usual size, but her face was still pale. She nodded silently, and the bottle found its way back into her bucket.

"First question," Roland said. "When did you let the lady from New York poke around my room?" He waved away her protest. "I know she was there. You don't use her brand of scent."

"Yesterday," the maid said sullenly. "I was cleaning in there and she gave me three dollars." Her eyes widened with a sudden thought. "Say, she didn't steal nothin', did she? She only wanted to look around, she said. I ain't no thief! Honest I ain't!"

Roland knew he had better ask his second question before the maid's composure abandoned her entirely.

"No, she didn't steal anything. Now – what's your name?"

"Hannah," the maid said miserably, "Hannah Stowe. Officer." Her eyes had fallen to the carpet again.

"Now, Hannah," Roland said, "I want you to think back four months or so." Hannah looked puzzled, but nodded. "Do you remember that composer fellow who stayed here then? What can you tell me about him? Where did he go, who did he see, and who came to see him?"

"I only saw him here," she said. "I don't know where people go."

"All right," Roland persisted, "but you cleaned his room, didn't you? Maybe you saw something and you don't know it."

"Oh, I saw plenty," Hannah said. Roland guessed from her tone that Haldane had given Arkham's gossipmongers plenty to chew on. He nodded, but she didn't need much encouragement.

"In the first place, he didn't even want his room cleaned," Hannah continued. "He had papers everywhere, and he didn't want them disturbed. Mr Pendergast insisted, though, because he could have set the room on fire and there were the other guests to think of. But Mr Haldane, he gave me a few bucks to leave the papers alone. I just made the bed, emptied the ashtrays, and took out the empty bottles."

"What kind of papers?"

"A lot of music paper, I guess. That was most of it. There was a big drawing he fixed to the wall with thumbtacks. It was kind of creepy, like something from a museum."

Roland remembered that Edie Talbot had said something about an inscription that had inspired the work Haldane was rehearsing. He would have to ask her when he confronted her about her snooping.

"Did it have writing on it? Hieroglyphs, anything like that?"

Hannah thought for a moment. "Maybe," she said. "But it wasn't like any writing I ever saw. Little triangles all over, like birds had walked on it." That meant nothing to Roland, but he filed it away for future attention.

"That's all you remember?" Hannah nodded once, and then her eyes widened a little.

"No!" she gasped. "There was a letter – right next to the drawing – from the university!" She beamed at him, temporarily forgetting how much trouble she thought she was in.

"The one here in town?"

Hannah nodded happily. "Miskatonic University," she said, as proudly as any alumna. "Why, I'll bet he was talking to someone there about that creepy old drawing! Those professors are awful clever with rare old languages, you know!" Roland gave her a smile in return.

"Thank you, Hannah," he said. "You've been a great help. I'll keep my word about that bottle–"

Her triumphant smile slipped a little at the reminder.

"But if Miss Talbot asks you for a peek at my room again, you tell her to come and ask me. What did she give you, three dollars?" Hannah nodded.

"All right, then. I'll see her three, and raise three." The little chambermaid looked at the six dollars like they were the treasure of the pharaohs. Actually, they represented a healthy chunk of Roland's expenses for the whole trip. "And not a word to Mr Pendergast from either of us. Agreed?"

"Yes, sir!" she said. "I mean, officer, detective, sir!"

"Agent," he corrected her. "Roland Banks, Bureau of Investigation." She looked at him for a moment like he was one of King Arthur's knights, and then she scurried off to the next room on her rounds.

The conversation had put Roland in a much better mood. Part of it, he admitted to himself, was because the chambermaid had been so much easier to impress than the bootleggers, the asylum staff, or anyone else he had met since coming to Arkham. He was actually civil to Mr Pendergast when he asked whether a package had arrived from Boston, and he walked away without a peep when the old buzzard told him it had not.

Miss Edie Talbot was due for a reckoning, but that would have to wait. He sat on the bed and ran his fingers through his hair. If Haldane and his friends had not been killed by the warring bootleggers – and it seemed increasingly likely that they had not – then the university was his only lead. At the very least, he needed to find a geologist to tell him what had happened to the house's foundation and the base of the fountain. If it was not dynamite that tore the house apart – and again, the lack of burning made dynamite look unlikely – then he needed to know what did.

The drawing – inscription, whatever it was – might amount to something, or it might not. The earlier work with the Salem witch stuff had raised a stink against Haldane, Edie had said, so it was just possible that someone wanted to stop this new work from ever being heard. It was thin, desperate stuff, but since he would be at the university anyway, it could not hurt to see if he could track down whichever egghead Haldane had consulted and find out what was so special about this carving. At worst, he would be able to rule it out – and who knew, he might find himself with some new suspects.

He inspected the repairs he had made to his clothes again and decided they would pass muster. He wished he had his hat and coat, but they were still at the speakeasy and it would likely be dark before he had a chance of getting them back. He grabbed his valise just in case Edie outbid him and got Hannah to let her into his room again, and set out for the university.

CHAPTER 9

The campus lay across the river, in the older part of Arkham. After Roland crossed the bridge, the buildings got smaller, and darker, and closer together. Some of the streets even had cobblestones.

He passed an ancient burying ground, where worn headstones leaned at crazy angles. A huge, old willow tree crouched in the middle, looking like it might stand up and trample the surrounding cottages if it took a mind to. Roland half-expected a headless horseman to ride out from behind it.

At last, Roland emerged from the dark tangle of streets and alleys and onto the broad and well-kept grounds of Miskatonic University. The university had clearly been around for a considerable time. Its buildings were a mixture of old and new, with colonial brick and timber staring across broad and leafy walks at modern stone and concrete.

Roland found a building with "Administration" over the door. The inside smelled of beeswax, floor polish, and time. A young woman sat behind a tall counter of dark wood like the judge at a witch trial, absorbed in an ancient book that was almost as big as she was. She did not notice him until he cleared his throat.

"I'm sorry," she said. "Can I help you?"

"I hope so," he said, showing her his badge. "Have you worked here long?"

"All this year," she said. "What's this about?" Roland opened his valise and fished a picture of Haldane out of the police file.

"Have you seen this man before?" he asked. "I believe he might have come to the university about four months ago, possibly making inquiries about an ancient inscription."

She studied the picture briefly.

"Oh, yes," she said. "Lord Byron."

"Pardon me?"

"Sorry – that's just something I do." She smiled. "He reminded me of Byron, the poet. Mad, bad, and dangerous to know."

"That sounds about right."

"He was killed at Pine Beach, wasn't he? With all those other musicians? Is that what you're investigating?"

"That's right. Why did he come here, four months ago?"

"He had a picture of the Tell La'anat inscription," she said. "He wanted help with the cuneiform." She smiled at Roland's blank look. "It's a writing system from ancient Mesopotamia," she explained.

"Like bird's feet?" Roland asked, remembering the chambermaid's words. She suppressed a chuckle.

"You could say that," she said. "Anyway, I sent him to Professor Rice. Left at the top of the stairs, and all the way to the end. You'll see his name on the door."

"Thanks," Roland said. "Do you have any idea why he came to Arkham for this? He lived in New York, and, well, no offense, but..."

"Oh, that's easy. The Tell La'anat expedition was one of ours. Professor Rice was actually on the excavation team."

"But the inscription's in New York?"

"It was. The Metropolitan Museum was one of the sponsors, so they got to display the finds before anyone else."

"You seem to know a lot about it. Are you a student here?"

"Graduate student." She nodded down at the massive book. "And I'm making some extra money filling in until they find a replacement. Everyone knows about the expedition, though: it was a real feather in the Classics Department's cap. I hear Geology is planning to go to Antarctica, just to get even."

"That reminds me," said Roland, "I'll need a geologist as well." He ignored her questioning look; clearly this conversation was more interesting than the huge and moldy book, but he was not here to socialize.

"Geology's in the Science building," she said, indicating a vague direction out of the door. "You can't miss it. It's…"

"A big building with 'Science' written on it?" said Roland. "I saw it on the way in. Thanks!"

Roland decided to see Professor Rice first. A broad staircase led up to a narrow landing with dark corridors leading off to left and right. The last door on the left had a handwritten card reading "Dr W Rice, Languages" stuck into a brass holder. Roland knocked and walked in.

The paneled office was a good size, but the clutter made it seem a good deal smaller. It looked something like a library might look, if a giant hand had picked it up and shaken it like a snow globe. A bearded, bespectacled man in his late forties looked up with a surprised expression.

"Professor Rice?" Roland said.

"I am," said the man, a little peevishly, "and who are you?"

"Agent Roland Banks, Bureau of Investigation." Roland showed his badge. "I'm investigating the incident at Pine Beach, and I…"

"You found out that fatuous composer was interested in the Tell La'anat inscription," Professor Rice interrupted. "Don't tell me the Bureau of Investigation believes these ridiculous stories?"

"What stories?"

The professor snorted. "The curse that destroyed the city somehow transferred itself to the orchestra, striking them down like the Curse of the Pharaohs. Utter nonsense."

Roland rubbed his jaw. "I heard the story of the curse appealed to the composer," he said, "maybe even inspired the music he was working on, but I'm not planning to arrest any ancient ghosts. Can you confirm that Oliver Haldane came to consult you about a carving from the site?"

"I can."

"And when did he do that?"

The professor made an impatient gesture. "I have no idea. Weeks ago. I'm rather busy preparing the excavation report for printing."

"But you did speak with him?"

"Why is this important?"

"It might not be, professor," Roland admitted, "but I need to account for all his movements in Arkham, both then and more recently. It's looking like the explosion was no accident, so I need to find out whether he made any enemies locally."

Professor Rice let out a short, bitter bark of laughter.

"Professor?"

"He was the sort of man who makes enemies wherever he goes, in my opinion," he said. "One of those irritating pseudo-Romantics who poses as… as…"

"As Lord Byron?" Roland remembered what the graduate student at the reception desk had said.

"Yes!" The professor seemed pleased with the comparison. "Exactly so. You met him?"

"No," Roland said, "but I've been hearing a lot about him."

"He was certainly irritating – and persistent. In the end I transliterated the inscription just to make him go away. But murdered, along with so many other people? I can't imagine."

"He wanted you to translate the inscription for him?"

"Transliterate," the professor corrected him. "Cuneiform is an alphabet, of sorts, used by several ancient languages. I simply rewrote the inscription in our own Roman alphabet. Translation is proving more difficult – it seems to be in an unknown language. Luckily, all he wanted to know was how the text sounded."

"So he could set it to music?"

"That is what I gathered. He also wanted to know more about the alleged curse on the city."

"I don't want to take up any more of your time than I have to," said Roland, "but in case there is some link to the excavation, would you tell me what you told him?"

Professor Rice ferreted through a stack of paper and brought out a photograph.

"Here is the inscription," he said. "The original is currently on display at the Metropolitan Museum of Art." The picture showed a large slab of dark stone, carved and polished in low relief. Panels of strange characters covered the slab, engraved right over the figures beneath.

The figures themselves stood in stiff poses with their arms raised, looking across the panel to something beyond the broken edge. One held a drum, and two or three others held strange-looking rattles. At the top of the panel, near the break, something that might have been a flute jutted into the picture; only a few fragmentary lines indicated the thing that played it, but Roland found the partial image horribly suggestive.

"Why was he so interested in this particular inscription?"

"You didn't see the exhibition?" The professor seemed genuinely surprised.

Roland shook his head. "I've been – away from civilization for a while," he said.

"Tell La'anat is a remarkable site. It would not be going too far to call it unique." The irritated tone had left his voice, replaced by the erudite drone of a college lecturer. Clearly, he had delivered this talk before.

"Even its name is unusual," the professor went on. "A tell, of course, is an artificial mound created by centuries of continuous occupation, with each successive rebuilding taking place on top of the ruined foundations of its predecessor, and so adding to the tell's height. *La anat* is a modern Persian word that translates as 'cursed' or 'forbidden.' The site is called Tell La'anat today, but its actual name was lost thousands of years ago. 'Tell La'anat' is purely a description: 'the forbidden city' is as good a translation as any. Similar terms appear in various languages, in documents from the Ottoman Empire, the Crusades, the Roman Empire, the travels of Herodotus – all appearing to refer to the same city, but with no name beyond 'the forbidden city' or 'the cursed city'. The locals tell all kinds of ghost stories about the place; in fact, it was very hard to find laborers for the excavation. We had to bring them in from some distance away, and even then, they ran off constantly."

"And Haldane was inspired by the idea of a cursed, forbidden city," Roland offered. "But why did he pick this inscription, in particular?" He tried not to glance down at the part of the photograph where vague lines suggested something unholy.

"There were no other panels of any size that survived the city's destruction," Professor Rice answered. "It came from a large structure that we interpreted as a temple. In fact, it was the centerpiece of the eastern wall. Where the other stones were shattered, this one was apparently knocked flat when the wall fell, and that is what saved it."

"That's all?" Roland asked. "Just because it was the only thing left from a cursed city? What if the inscription turned out to be a no-spitting sign or something?"

The blunt analogy made the professor smile briefly. "I put that to him, more or less," he said. "I thought at first that it might be some law code, based on its length: most cuneiform public inscriptions are either law codes or accounts of battles. But Mr Haldane was quite certain that the presence of musicians meant it was a song of some kind, most likely a hymn to some ancient god."

"That sounds like him," Roland said. "He already set a witch's spell book to music, so I suppose he couldn't resist a hymn from a forbidden city."

"If it was a hymn," Professor Rice put in dryly, "and not, as you say, a law against spitting."

"What made you think the building was a temple?"

The professor smiled a little sheepishly. "To be honest, it was because we could find no other explanation for the size and shape of the structure. It was located more or less in the center of the site, and there were no remains of any trade or craft within its walls." He lowered his voice conspiratorially. "Between us," he said, "archaeologists often use the designation 'ritual' as a synonym for 'we have no idea'. It is one of the secrets of our profession."

Roland could not suppress a smile, and his eyes dropped to the stack of photographs from which Professor Rice had pulled the image of the inscription. He snatched the picture from the top and stared at it closely.

"Don't tell me you have a better idea," said the professor. "A police station, perhaps?" His sardonic expression fell away when Roland met his eyes.

"The stone here," Roland pointed, "how would you describe it?" Professor Rice took the photograph, and one eyebrow twitched up as he looked.

"That was another unusual aspect of this structure," he said. "The city as a whole had been destroyed by burning – well, first it had been burned down, and then the ruins had been demolished in a very deliberate and painstaking fashion. But here, there was no sign of burning. No ash or charcoal among the rubble, no calcination of the stone – just a strangely smooth finish on the floor of the temple."

"What caused it?" As far as Roland could tell from the photograph, the foundation of the ancient temple looked very like the shorn-off stone of the ruined mansion.

"Several theories are being pursued," he said. "Perhaps some kind of vitrification from extreme heat…"

"You said there was no ash or charcoal."

"True, and that is a problem, but the Geology Department still thinks it the most likely theory. They say no human force could have produced this effect."

"Are they right?"

"The Archaeology Department favors the theory that the wall was cut or polished using some unknown technique…"

"Like a modern quarry saw?" The professor looked surprised.

"Yes, perhaps – although this was an early Bronze Age site with little metal of any kind, let alone the kind of high-grade steel required to make a quarry saw. Why is this so important to you?"

"The foundation of the house at Pine Beach looks a lot like this."

Professor Rice made a small, choking sound. Roland looked up to see that all the color had drained from his face.

"How was the city destroyed, and when?" Roland could not keep the urgency out of his voice. "I need to know everything you can tell me."

"It was destroyed..." he began, "well – no one knows exactly when. The cuneiform is of an early pattern, at least as old as the oldest Sumerian cuneiform from Ur. The earliest Akkadian and Elamite sources speak of the accursed city as a ruin haunted by evil spirits. The stories all say that the people of the city were wicked, and that a god stretched forth his hand and destroyed them. The city was burned by its neighbors afterward, to cleanse it of its taint."

"Which god?"

"The later sources name whichever deity the neighbors themselves happened to follow: Ashur, Ishtar, Marduk, Allah. But the earliest sources say the people of the city were destroyed by their own god, who was evil and delighted in suffering."

"And what was the name of that evil god?"

"They don't give a name. Some sources imply that the name itself is too dangerous to speak or write."

"You said the Geology Department was studying the effect on the stones?"

"I'll take you." The professor rose from his desk with the movements of a man twice his age. The two did not speak further as they crossed the campus; Roland did not hear the running footsteps behind him until a hand clapped down on his shoulder.

CHAPTER 10

Roland turned and found himself looking at Leo De Luca. The bootlegger seemed worried.

"I need your help, Mr G-man," he said. "Our mutual friend Miss Talbot's run into a spot of trouble."

Professor Rice looked uncertainly from one to the other. Roland quickly shook his hand.

"Thanks for your help, professor," he said, "but this sounds urgent. I guess I'll have to talk to your geologists another day." He trotted after Leo, who was already three paces away.

"What happened?" Roland asked. "And how do you know Miss Talbot anyway?"

"A shared interest in contemporary music," said Leo, "and in other things that lift the spirits."

"And in spirits themselves," said Roland. "What happened?"

"That hellcat from the speakeasy happened," he said, "along with her tame gorilla. They must have seen her talking with me and reasoned that she could be used to exert pressure on behalf of their boss, Johnny V."

"Talking? When?"

"Around the orchestra, sometimes. She was covering them for a fancy New York magazine, as you probably know, and I've always had a soft spot for a pretty face and a lively wit. This morning, though, she came to me with questions about the house, and the progress of your investigation, and who knows what besides, and before I could turn her away those two jumped up like the devil from a tinker's hearth and the big fellow stuck a shotgun in my face as the hellcat wrestled her away. She said they'd be in touch and not to come after them."

"So, naturally, you thought of me – we're such close friends."

"You looked out for the lady last night, and you showed you can shoot straight. Was I wrong?"

"No," said Roland, "you weren't wrong. I don't suppose you know where they took her?"

"As it happens, I do have some idea," said Leo. When Roland raised an eyebrow, he continued, "I'm a well-liked fellow, you see, blessed with friends all over town. Usually, they watch out for members of your own profession, but they will also notice a car that has a lady beating on the windows. If I were a betting man – which I am – I'd say they found Elmer's cabin, back there in the woods."

"Any of those friends of yours willing to come with us?"

"They'd be of little use," Leo answered. "They've keen eyes, but soft fists. Which left me no choice but to find you. This is me." He indicated a Model T stakebed parked at the edge of the campus, and they jog-trotted toward it. "I put a couple of shotguns under the canvas. You still have the guns from last night?"

It took Roland a moment to remember the nickel-plated .32 he had taken from the moll.

"I have them," he said, "but let's not get trigger-happy. I'd prefer to get Miss Talbot back in one single, unventilated piece."

Leo gunned the engine and peeled away from the curb.

The first part of the drive followed the same route Roland and Sheriff Engle had taken to Pine Beach the day before. Mostly to distract himself, he pulled out his .38 and checked the chambers. All six were empty.

His oath brought a sharp look from Leo, but the bootlegger kept driving. Roland had fired one shot the previous night, wounding the big gunman who followed Leo along with the tough-talking moll. That should have left him with five bullets. He had not fired a shot after leaving Leo the night before – except in his nightmare, where he had emptied his gun into the horrific piping creature. But surely, that had only been a dream: creatures like that could not exist in real life.

If Roland's gun was empty, he must have really fired on the weird piper. The thing was real – as real as the mud on his shoes and the tears in his clothes. Something unspeakable roamed the woods above Pine Beach, something that mocked reason by existing when it should not.

The truck jerked to a halt, breaking Roland's reverie. The road had come to a dead end by the edge of the lake. The ruins of Pine Beach stood a few hundred yards behind them, and a steep ridge rose up from the end of the track.

"Come on," said Leo, jumping down from the cab. "The rest of the way's on foot." He threw back the tarpaulin that covered the truck bed and picked up a shotgun, jamming a box of shells into his pocket. Then he pulled the gunman's .45 from his other pocket, checked the magazine, and tucked it into his belt.

"So close to all these houses, and no one knew the cabin was there?" Roland asked. Leo shot him a pitying look.

"And just as I was starting to have hopes of you," he said. "Are you sure you're a G-man at all?" Roland grimaced. Of course everyone who lived around the lake knew the cabin was there. It might even have been built specifically to service them. That would certainly explain why old Elmer had been on the scene so soon – had even witnessed the destruction, and lost what was left of his mind.

Leo fished a metal toolbox from the back of the truck. He opened it and pushed it toward Roland. "Help yourself to shells," he said. "There's a box of .38 Special in there too, if you're out." Nodding his thanks, Roland reloaded his .38, scooped a handful of shells into his jacket pocket, then picked up the second shotgun and followed Leo up the hill.

When they reached the top of the ridge, Leo stopped walking and checked his weapons for a second time.

"No talking from now on," he said in a low voice, "and walk quietly. We don't want them to hear us coming." He straightened up and looked around with a perplexed expression. "It's odd, this," he said. "I never heard the woods this quiet before."

It had been just as quiet the previous morning. The silence felt almost solid. No wind was blowing; no squirrels rustled in the leaves or shook the branches with their jumping; no birds sang in the trees; and no waterfowl honked, quacked, or wailed across the lake. It was as though nature had fled – or was holding its breath and praying not to be discovered.

Even though he had not consciously realized it the previous day, Roland knew now that this unnatural silence was part of the reason he had felt so uneasy – even before he had heard that piping. Treading as lightly as he could, he followed Leo along the ridge.

Elmer White's cabin was a one-room shack that leaned like a fairground funhouse. It looked as though it had been built by a gang of enterprising kids in a comic strip. Its windows were boarded up, and although the door hung crookedly in its off-kilter frame, it was too dark to see inside. Leo raised a hand and crouched behind a tree to watch the place. Roland crouched beside him.

The silence pressed in on Roland as they watched the shack. At the edge of his hearing, far in the distance, Roland fancied he could hear the weird piping again. It came and went maddeningly, as if toying with him. When he listened for it all he heard was silence, but when he focused his attention elsewhere the monotonous squeal stole in at the furthest limits of his hearing.

The footfall, when it came, sounded like a rifle shot against the enveloping silence. Leo pointed: a burly figure was approaching the shack from the opposite direction, carrying a bundle of deadfall. Roland recognized the goon from the alley even before he saw the crusted brown bandage around his gun hand. He carried the wood inside, letting the door creak shut behind him.

Roland raised an eyebrow at Leo, and the bootlegger nodded. Hefting their shotguns, they moved toward the shack as quietly as they could, trusting that those inside would be too busy making a fire to hear them coming.

Leo was first through the door. There was a gasp, a curse, and a scuffle before Roland could see what was going on. He stepped out from behind the bootlegger to see the big guy with his hands in the air and the moll crouched at bay by the stone chimney, wearing an expression that would not look out of place on a wolverine. The only thing that looked more dangerous was the wooden crate by the door. It had been built to hold a dozen bottles of beer, but two dozen sticks of dynamite, lashed together in pairs, stuck out instead of bottle necks.

Edie Talbot was tied to a chair in one corner of the shack, with a rag gag in her mouth and a fresh cut across one cheek. Apart from her and the dynamite, everything looked as though Elmer had just stepped out: the rickety, unmade bed, a warped and graying table littered with an assortment of empty bottles, and a dingy overcoat hanging from a ten-point rack of antlers on the wall. A curled and spotted calendar hung beside the coat, showing the month of September, 1912, beneath the faded image of a bare-shouldered Gibson Girl and the legend "Pacific Brewing and Malting Company, Tacoma, Washington, USA".

Roland motioned with his shotgun, and the moll stood up, going to stand by her large friend.

"Guns," said Roland, "nice and easy." The moll showed her empty hands and nodded toward a leather handbag beside the hearth. The big guy opened the left side of his jacket to reveal another big .45 in a shoulder holster. At a nod from Roland, he took it out with thumb and forefinger, put it on the ground, and slid it across with his foot. Roland did not bend to pick it up, but kept both eyes and both barrels on the pair as Leo flipped a clasp knife open and bent down to cut Edie free.

Edie stood up, ripping the gag from her mouth. One quick step took her to the stone hearth, where she pulled a pistol from the handbag. It was not as big as the nickel-plated model from last night, nor as good looking, but it seemed convincing enough in the writer's hands. Roland was just wondering what sort of company she kept back in New York when she took two more quick steps and dropped the moll to the floor with a blow to the temple.

"She had that coming," Edie explained, using the gun barrel to indicate the cut on her own cheek. She hoisted the handbag and turned a hundred-watt smile on her rescuers.

"Shall we go?" she said, just as though she were talking about a picnic in Central Park.

"Not so fast," said Roland. "You'll find a pair of handcuffs under my jacket, on the left side. Why don't you put 'em on your new friend here? Unless you'd prefer to keep on pistol-whipping her, of course."

"I only owed her the one," Edie replied. "More wouldn't be ladylike." With quick, sure hands she found Roland's handcuffs, wrenched the groaning moll's hands away from her bleeding head, and pinioned her arms behind her back. Leo had already trussed up the gunman with some spare rope.

With both prisoners secure, Roland stooped to pick up the discarded .45 and then pulled the dynamite box closer.

"Did you have any more of this stuff?" he asked.

"Jeez, mister, you have trouble with your hearin' or somethin'?" A trickle of blood ran down her cheek from the goose egg above the moll's eye, but she did not seem to care. "I told ya already – it wasn't us that blew the nice lady's mansion all to bits!" Roland fixed her with a skeptical look, and she subsided a little.

"That was for this dope," she muttered, jerking her chin toward Leo, "only we never found out where he keeps his stock."

"And you never will," Leo chuckled. The moll stuck out her tongue at him, a curiously childlike gesture.

"You two are adorable," said Roland. "I guess you realize you're under arrest? I'll start with kidnapping, but I'll be happy to throw in suspected ties to organized crime, bootlegging, and waving guns around. We'll figure it all out when we get back to Arkham. Your names will do for now."

The moll opened her mouth to speak, but Edie forestalled her.

"Miss Vicky Serra," she said, "of North Boston." She held up a piece of paper she had just fished out of the handbag.

"Pleased to meet you, Miss Serra," said Roland. "Now, who's–"

This time, they all heard the strange piping.

It drifted through the woods, as formless and monotonous as before but closer and clearer than Roland had ever heard it. He felt suddenly dizzy, as though he might fall over, and he could not stop himself from dropping the shotgun and clapping his hands over his ears.

Leo kept his hold on his own shotgun, but dropped into a crouch in the doorway and scanned the woods with desperate intensity. Roland could tell from his face that all Leo wanted in the world was to find the source of the infernal noise and keep shooting until it fell silent.

Vicky Serra spat curses at the unseen piper, fighting with all her strength to tear free of the handcuffs. Roland looked at her unnamed companion, just in time to see him break free.

The big man's face was a mask of horror. His eyes bulged out and his mouth opened wider than Roland would have thought possible. His screams were almost as awful as old Elmer's as he pulled and pulled with his massive arms until the ropes tore. Then he ran out of the shack, right over the crouching figure of Leo.

"Maury!" Roland learned the big gunman's name at last. Vicky Serra shouldered him aside, vaulted over Leo, and set off in pursuit of her cohort. Her arms were still pinioned behind her, giving her an awkward gait, but she was quickly lost to view among the trees. Leo sent a shot after her, but it had no apparent effect. The bootlegger reloaded, almost without looking. His skin was so pale, and his jaw clamped so tightly shut, that he might have been carved from ivory.

Roland looked at Edie. Her fashionable pallor had turned faintly gray. The fine thread of blood stood out shockingly scarlet against her cheek. "What…?" Her voice was barely a whisper, but her eyes were clear. She seemed to be in control of herself.

"Take this," he said, pulling the .32 from his pocket. "Can you handle two guns at once?"

Edie shook her head briefly, as if to clear it, and took the nickel-plated gun. "I'm willing to try," she said.

"Get as far away from that sound as you can," Roland said. "Go back to the hotel, and if I'm not back by morning…"

"Not a chance," she said firmly. "This has something to do with the house, doesn't it? With Oliver?"

"I think so," Roland replied. "Just don't ask me what."

"Then I'm going to find out," Edie said. "It's my job."

"I can't let you do that," said Roland. "If I'm right about the sound – I just can't."

"Forget it, Sir Galahad," Edie shook off his restraining hand. "If you're so determined to keep me safe, come with me." She tried to twist by, but Leo was blocking her way. Roland took hold of her arm.

"All right," he said, "but we're going to be smart about this." He hoisted the box of dynamite onto his shoulder.

CHAPTER 11

Leo fired another shot from the doorway. Roland placed a hand on his shoulder and he jumped like a startled animal. His eyes showed no sign of recognition.

"Come on," Roland yelled, his voice unnecessarily loud. "Keep us covered!" The bootlegger's eyes flicked to the dynamite and back to Roland. He nodded tautly and the three left the shack together.

Roland turned his head this way and that, but the piping seemed to come from everywhere and nowhere. It filled the woods as water envelops a drowning man, existing as much in the minds of the three listeners as it did in the world outside. Direction and distance were somehow meaningless next to the cosmic cold and loneliness woven through the terrible dirge.

It was impossible to say how long they stood transfixed by the formless music. At last, Roland set off down the slope, his two companions trailing behind him.

They might have been walking toward the music or away from it. For hours, or minutes, they wandered at random, pushing through the weird cacophony with their shoulders set as though against a high wind. Now and again, they looked up, but mostly they kept their eyes on their feet. The twigs and dry leaves underfoot were natural and banal, reassuring signs of normalcy compared to what they might see if they looked up. Even so, the rustle and crunch of their progress syncopated disturbingly with the formless piping.

After a few minutes, Roland paused and looked back. Edie's face was still gray apart from the trickle of blood on her cheek and the startling white of the tooth that bit down on her lower lip. Her arms hung limp at her sides, as if the two pistols weighed a hundred pounds each. Her arms barely moved as she walked. Leo De Luca scanned the woods like a hungry animal, his head and his shotgun's barrels always moving. There was something in his eyes that could break either way, into headlong flight or berserk violence.

Beyond his companions, Roland saw the ruins of the house. Pine Beach should have been screened in by lush trees, but those closer to the ruins had been reduced to bare sticks. The lake lay like a sheet of tarnished silver, and an occasional chimney or roofline could be seen through the trees on the far shore. There was no wind: the trees were as still as a photograph in the motionless air. Against that overall stillness, the fleeting glimpse of motion was like a lighthouse beam.

Roland set off at a run. Whether his companions followed, he neither knew nor cared; in truth, he was only half-aware of his own motion. Like that of a child confronting a schoolyard bully, his fear had turned to rage and his rage to something like courage. Without consciously deciding to, he sang and shouted so he would not have to think about the creature from his dream, the creature he was about to confront again. Blistering invective, snatches of opera, vaudeville, bawdy barrack-room fare from his army days – anything to compete with the maddening piping.

They came upon the creature in a small hollow. Leo's face contorted into a terrible mask and he began firing and reloading, firing and reloading, over and over with an unstoppable, mechanical intensity. Edie gave vent to a banshee wail and raised both her guns, firing with eyes closed rather than look at the abomination. Roland dropped the dynamite and reached for his .38, but something stopped him from drawing and firing.

The formless, toadlike, tentacled abomination seemed unaffected by the hail of fire. Here and there its warty, gelatinous hide ripped with the impact of a shot, but just as it had done the previous night, the horror took no more notice of the gunfire than it would of a gentle rain.

Roland forced his eyes up the gully, trying to fix the creature's position without looking directly at its impossible form. Cursing like a drill sergeant, he pulled out a double stick of dynamite and lit the fuse. His throw was good; the stick fell directly beside its target. Roland hit the dirt and waited for the explosion, vaguely aware in the intervening seconds of the steady boom from Leo's shotgun and the clicks from Edie's emptied pistols.

The explosion echoed off the sides of the dell, kicking up a brief shower of dirt and debris. Roland looked up, shaking his head to clear the ringing in his ears. Leo was climbing to his feet; Edie was on the ground in a fetal position, with her arms wrapped around her head. Her stockings were shredded and thick ribbons of blood trickled down her muddy legs from countless small scratches. One of her shoes was missing, and Vicky's handbag lay where the journalist had dropped it at her first sight of the creature.

Leo laid a heavy hand on Roland's shoulder and stared

desperately into his eyes. Leo's mouth moved, but Roland could hear nothing. He shook his head and pointed to his ears.

"Is it dead?" The bootlegger's voice seemed very far away, but it was clear he was yelling. He had both hands on Roland's shoulders now, and he punctuated each word with a shake.

There was a small crater where the dynamite had landed. The creature was nowhere to be seen. Roland scrambled down into the hollow, searching for any sign that they had killed or even wounded the thing. He found nothing.

Turning to look up at Leo, he saw Edie standing beside the bootlegger, staring down at him. Her hands hung limp by her sides, the empty guns forgotten in her hands. Her eyes were wide and did not quite seem to focus on him. Roland climbed back up to join them.

"It's gone," he said. It was all he could say. "It's just gone."

"But is it … ?" Leo sounded desperate. He needed to be sure the thing was dead, that it would not be coming back, that he would never have to see or hear it again. He needed proof.

Roland could do nothing but shrug. If this was victory, it was hollow without the body of their foe. The woods looked normal, as though nothing unnatural had taken place, but all three of them knew those woods might never be the same again – could never be the same, until the monster had been found and its taint cleansed with fire. The oldest of rituals: burning evil to destroy it completely. Nothing less would serve to exorcise what they had witnessed.

"No!" Edie gasped and dropped to her knees, her face a mask of horror. Roland and Leo looked down at her, confused for a moment, until they heard it, too. The obscene piping was fainter, distorted perhaps by the shape of the dell, but it was unmistakable.

For a long moment the three looked at each other. The same

questions filled all three minds, and they searched each other's faces for the answers.

Unlike the piping, the screams had a direction. The first was a man's scream, and it was followed by a woman's. Leo snatched his shotgun off the ground and set off at a dead run; Roland hoisted the box of dynamite onto his shoulder and followed.

"Get out of here!" he yelled over his shoulder at Edie. "Find a road, get back to Arkham!" She shook her head defiantly and matched his pace despite her missing shoe, the empty guns still in her pumping fists.

They found Vicky Serra in a glade near the lakeshore, screaming curses that would make a sailor blush. She had somehow managed to step through Roland's handcuffs so her hands were no longer behind her back, and she was throwing rocks two-handed as quickly as she could pick them up. Her target, a few yards away, appeared not to feel the rocks any more than it had felt their bullets and buckshot earlier.

The creature had seemed smaller when they looked down upon it in the dell. Now that they were on the same level, Roland could see that its body – if the shifting, greenish-purple mass could be said to be a body – was a little larger than a car, and its lashing tentacles made it seem larger still. Everything else about the creature was changing constantly: its shape, its color, the texture of its skin, all seemed to shift and bubble, as though they were looking at a movie frame that had come too close to the projector bulb and was endlessly repeating the last, boiling second of its existence.

What did not change, though, was Maury. The big man was caught in the creature's tentacles, struggling with all his might and screaming like a steer that had just smelled the slaughterhouse. His massive arms ripped one tentacle away just in time for another to wrap itself around his waist, arm, or leg, the process repeating endlessly like an obscene dance to the sound of the monstrous piping. His clothes were in shreds from the struggle, and sucker marks the size of dollar pancakes adorned his arms and torso.

Leo had skidded to a halt and was looking at the unspeakable tableau slack-jawed. His shotgun hung at his side, all but forgotten. Edie stopped beside him, similarly mesmerized.

Roland, slowed down by the box of dynamite he still carried, was the last to arrive. Dropping the box, he drew his gun and took careful aim. Perhaps there was a trick to hurting this thing: a soft spot, or at least a spot that was vulnerable at some point in the creature's shifting and roiling. If not, he would save his last bullet for Maury. He sighted along the barrel, looking for details that might betray a weakness. It was good to narrow his focus, rather than looking at the whole of the monster's impossible shape.

Seeing something that looked like an eye, Roland fired. The slug struck the creature's skin and vanished with the slightest of ripples. His second shot hit the base of a tentacle, with the same lack of effect.

A boom made Roland turn his head. Leo was reloading his shotgun. Either he had had the same idea as Roland, or he could not bear to stand by and would rather do something useless than do nothing at all. Roland was about to resume his own desperate strategy when a piercing whistle split the air.

Limping on one heel and one bare foot, Edie advanced on the creature, whistling with two fingers in her mouth like a bedraggled, jazz version of Huck Finn. She shot Roland a warning look when he reached out an arm to stop her and kept walking, slowly and steadily. Her whistle slid up and down the scale in a jarring succession of flats and minors. Now and again, she was able to replicate one of the creature's formless phrases more or less perfectly. Ignoring the steady boom of Leo's shotgun, Roland lowered his own weapon and watched.

Edie's whistling was a human sound, and she could not match the foul piping precisely. Occasionally the creature's piping and Edie's whistling collided in a scraping harmonic that made Roland wince: it was these notes, rather than the matched phrases, that seemed to have an effect on the beast. The first time, it stopped as if in thought, its only movement coming from Maury's struggles against its grip. The second time, its piping changed key subtly. The third time, it lashed out with a tentacle, farther than it should have been able to reach. Edie was thrown back like a rag doll, hitting a tree twenty feet away with sickening force. Rage made Roland fire three more shots, even though a part of him knew they were useless.

Maury's struggles were growing weaker. He was fighting for breath, his face darkening as a tentacle crushed his chest. One of his huge arms strained against the grip of a smaller appendage, and his legs kicked in the air as the creature lifted him off his feet. At a place which might have been the top, front, or side of the formless beast, a nauseating, rippling movement created something that looked like a mouth. More tentacles wrapped around the fading gunman, guiding him inexorably toward the yawning maw.

Something like an electric charge shot through Roland. Before his conscious mind truly knew what he was doing, he had dropped his gun and picked up the crate of dynamite, lighting the fuses of the two sticks nearest the center. Apparently of their own volition, his feet took two steps forward and his arms swung up, lobbing the fizzing crate in an arc that led exactly where the unfortunate Maury was headed.

"Get down!" Roland heard himself yell. He caromed into Leo, bringing him down in a clumsy tackle. Vicky, he saw, stood open-mouthed for a second, watching the dynamite sail through the air before throwing herself down with a despairing wail. There was a sound like the end of the world, and everything went black.

Unconsciousness beckoned with velvet fingers, but Roland forced his eyes open. He felt blood trickle down from one ear. Everything ached as he hauled himself to his feet and looked around.

Vicky was still on the ground, writhing in apparent agony. Her eyes and mouth were both wide, and somewhere far, far behind the cacophony of tiny silver bells that filled his head, Roland could hear her keening wail. Maury was nowhere to be seen. Leo, on hands and knees, was retching and coughing helplessly; Edie was still as death against the base of the tree where the horror had thrown her. It was only then that Roland thought of the monster.

Hanging in the air above the glade was a mist, of a color that was either something more than a color or something less. There was no word for it in the language of any artist who had ever lived; it was utterly repellent, yet Roland could not take his eyes off it. The mist hung in the still air, fading slowly like the light from a guttering candle. Eventually it was gone.

Beneath the place where the mist had been, the ground was flat. Twenty-two sticks of dynamite should have produced a sizable crater – should, perhaps, have killed them all, as close to the explosion as they had been. Whatever property of the horror's body that made it impervious to bullets from the outside must also have trapped the explosion inside.

Walking like a man in a dream, Roland went to the tree where Edie lay. He found a pulse; her breathing was shallow but regular.

He soaked his handkerchief in the lake's cold water and blotted her forehead and neck until she stirred. There was a large knot on the back of her head, but miraculously her skull did not appear to be broken. He lifted her in his arms and directed Leo toward Vicky Serra with a jab of his chin. The tough moll seemed completely undone – whether from the sight of the monster or the loss of her cohort, Roland could not tell. She gulped and sobbed hoarsely in Leo's arms as they made their way back to the bootlegger's truck.

CHAPTER 12

"So, what are you going to say?"

Roland looked up from his notes to see Edie Talbot in the doorway of the borrowed office, with a notebook in one hand and a pen in the other. Apart from the healing cut on her cheek, there was no sign that anything out of the ordinary had happened to her – or at least, not until he looked at her eyes. Somehow her bright, businesslike smile did not quite reach them.

Roland gathered up his papers and covered them with a file jacket before beckoning her inside. She closed the door and sat down.

"Are you here to snoop on my investigation again?" he asked. "I should have run you in for breaking into my hotel room."

Edie held up her hands and rolled her eyes.

"Shoot me instead," she said. "Have you seen what they make you wear in a women's prison? Is that why you borrowed Sheriff Engle's office – to thwart my journalistic skills? Say, can I quote you on that?" She gazed a little over his head and waved her pen like a conductor's baton. "'G-Man Goes Gruffly to Ground, Cuts Cute Correspondent Cold.' What do you think?"

"I think I'd get posted to Alaska if I put that much alliteration in my report," he said.

Edie laughed. "Well, my readership is more sophisticated than yours. So come on, agent, how about a quote for the masses?"

Roland leaned back in his chair and ran his fingers through his hair. "How about I crib from you this time? What are you going to say killed the New England Virtuosi? I heard all the music papers are clamoring for your story."

"Not just the music papers," she corrected him. "I've got *Time* and *Life* magazines in a bidding war by cable." She sighed, a little wistfully. "Oliver's getting more press now than ever. If only he knew."

"I'm sure he'd be proud," said Roland, "and from what I've heard of him, he'd be even prouder of going out the way he did. It was his music, wasn't it? Something he took from that inscription brought that thing here?"

Edie's smile faded and she suppressed a shudder. "I don't know what else to think," she admitted, "although did it do that to the house, all by itself?"

"Elmer said there was something bigger," Roland said, "something that just reached through from – from wherever it was. Professor Rice reckons it might have been the evil god of the cursed city. His guess is the thing we saw fell through by accident."

It was a moment before either of them could speak again.

"Too bad I didn't have my camera," Edie said at last. "Without proof, no one's ever going to believe us. Especially with Elmer and – what was the big lug's name?"

"Maury," Roland hunted through his notebook, "Maurizio Trappeto. Johnny V imported him from the old country four years ago."

"Luckily, though," Edie said, "there is still the charming Miss Serra. Or did she chew her way through the bars and bust out?"

Roland smiled despite himself. "No," he said, "some guys from the Boston Field Office picked her up before Johnny's fancy lawyers could get here. They were on the next train back, and I wish Miss Serra and my Boston colleagues great joy of each other."

"So at least you got a bootlegging collar while you were here," Edie said. "That's got to help you."

"Maybe a little, although it hasn't impressed Mrs van Dreesen."

Edie made a sympathetic face. "Yikes," she said, "I'd almost forgotten about her. What did you tell her?"

"She'll have to read the report like everyone else," said Roland. "If I ever figure out what to write in it."

"I don't suppose you can tell the truth." Edie was suddenly serious. Roland shook his head.

"If you'd asked me that question a week ago..."

"I know," she said. "They'd lock you up, and me along with you if I told the same story. I doubt Mrs van Dreesen's insurance company would be swayed by a story of an evil god." Roland gave vent to a brief snort of laughter. "What?" she asked.

"You know," he said, "their first report said it was an act of God. That's why they didn't pay out, and why I was sent here in the first place."

"Not quite the god they had in mind," she said, "although I doubt even Mrs van Dreesen's policy covers her against ancient curses. The heck with it – I may just head to the Nightingale Club and get bent. Maybe the spirits will move me and I'll dream up the perfect story. Care to escort a lady?"

"I'm still a federal agent, you know."

"And you were a federal agent when you dragged me out of

there the other night, as I recall. Was that whiskey I smelled on your breath, or your own special hair lotion?"

"I was casing the joint incognito. I had to have a couple of drinks, to avoid suspicion."

"Any sacrifice in the line of duty. They should give you a medal."

"Are you here to give me a hard time, or do you want to help?"

"Help? Are you putting me on the case, agent?"

"You came here to find out what's going to be in my report, didn't you?"

"Except you have even less than I do."

"So help me write it."

"You couldn't afford my word rate."

"Consider it a trade for not running you in."

"Why, Agent Banks! Are you soliciting a bribe in kind?" Edie's eyes widened in mock offense.

"Enough," said Roland. "We have to figure something out. Have you heard from Leo? What's he saying?"

Edie shook her head. "He's taking a trip, is what I heard. He took off as soon as we got back, without a word to anyone. The boys at the Nightingale think he's in Canada buying stock. Or maybe the Bahamas."

"I can't say I blame him. A bracing sea voyage does sound good right now."

"I'll meet you on the lido deck," she said. "So, assuming we don't mention – you know – then what kind of story makes sense? Some kind of explosion?"

Roland shook his head. "That was the first thing I thought of, but it won't fly. There was no gas on site, and the boiler was too small to level the entire house. I thought maybe the orchestra could have been running a still of their own–"

"They did like a gargle," she put in.

"–but it would take a commercial-sized still to make a big enough explosion. Besides, none of that can account for the second explosion."

"Second explosion?"

"I think you missed it. It happened right after your argument with that tree."

"Oh, right," said Edie, involuntarily putting a hand to the back of her head. "What about the dynamite? Can you pin it on Johnny V?"

Roland shook his head wearily. "I spent all morning trying to figure out a way to do that," he said, "but it's just not adding up. The dynamite's gone, so I can't produce it in court, and besides, I'd have to put Miss Vicky in the witness box. Who's to say what she might come out with?"

Edie let out a *pfft* of air. "Who cares? She's getting locked up whatever she says, I imagine. In an asylum if she tells the truth – in jail, otherwise. There has to be some room for negotiation there."

"Maybe," said Roland, "but the last time I saw her, she was cursing me out for what happened to Maury. I wouldn't put it past her to try to smear me for not taking Leo in as well as the two of them – making some case that the local boy's paying off the cops and bringing the Prohibition Unit down here poking under every rock."

"Hell hath no fury," Edie quoted, a little out of context. "I guess she really liked the big guy. But–" She turned to Roland with a worried expression. "What's to stop her from doing that anyway?"

Roland shrugged. "I'm guessing she knows better."

"What?"

"Right now, she's only facing charges for kidnapping you to put pressure on Leo. My guess is that Johnny will get her out on bail, and then she'll disappear before her trial. Some nice little island in the Caribbean, maybe, or down to Mexico, or somewhere else out of the way. But it all depends on Vicky getting bail."

"So?"

"So, if she accuses a federal agent of corruption, or looks like she's willing to turn state's evidence against another bootlegger – say, Leo De Luca – then everything changes. She becomes a valuable witness for the government, and instead of bail she gets protective custody. That means that Johnny V and his lawyers can't get within a mile of her, and *that* means that Johnny won't be able to keep from worrying that she might spill the beans on him as well as on your pal Leo. All of which means that Miss Serra's life gets a lot more complicated very fast."

"I hadn't thought of that," Edie admitted. "But do you think she's smart enough to figure all that out for herself?"

"I gave her a few pointers between curses," Roland said. "She had to pause for breath now and again."

"I hope she got the message," Edie looked only half-convinced. "So what's left, an earthquake?"

"I checked with a geologist at the college, and New England isn't exactly earthquake country. The last one was in 1755 – and earthquakes don't usually stop at destroying a single house."

"Sheesh, professor," Edie looked offended. "I only asked."

"Don't blame the messenger. There might be something in the geology angle, though."

"I'm all ears."

"What if there was some kind of underground gas pocket? Suppose it leaked into the house and blew it up?"

"That sounds good!" Edie said. She chewed the end of her

pencil as she thought. "How about this? It must have continued to escape and build up, because when we were chasing those bootleggers a stray spark from a ricochet or something set off the second explosion!" She started writing rapidly. "And that whistling noise–"

"Don't remind me." Roland shuddered at the memory.

"–that was caused by gas escaping through fissures at various points in the woods." A triumphant expression stole across her face. "And since the whistling's stopped, we can be sure there's no more gas escaping. Everyone's safe, and no one has to worry about their own lake houses going boom!"

Roland thought about this for a minute.

"That does cover pretty much everything," he said. "Where do you think that will leave Mrs van Dreesen?"

"Off your back, and onto someone else's," said Edie. "My guess is the insurance company will cite natural causes and keep on refusing to pay, so her lawyers will try to find someone else to blame. Could be a local mine or quarry, if there is one, or even the Worthington estate for selling her a house on top of a gas pocket."

Roland gave a grunt of amusement. "She'll spend more on lawyers than it would cost her to rebuild the house," he said.

"Oh, probably," said Edie, "but the thing you have to understand with her type is, it's never about the money. Worrying about money is vulgar. You keep going until you've won, no matter what it costs."

"I just hope this works," Roland said. Something in his tone made Edie look up.

"Why wouldn't it?" she asked.

"I don't know," he sighed. "Making up stories, lying in an official report – it just doesn't feel right."

"What's the alternative? Tell the truth and get locked up? Even if we had undeniable proof…" She let the sentence trail off.

"I guess you're right," Roland conceded. "But don't we have a duty – shouldn't people know?"

"What good would it do them if they did? Do you feel happier for knowing? I know I don't."

"I know," he said, throwing up his hands. "I know. It's just that – well, my whole career I went by the book, never put a foot wrong. I told myself I was just trying to stay out of trouble, that federal agents had to hold themselves to a higher standard. But ever since I got here…"

"That's Arkham," said Edie.

Roland looked out of the window. "Sheriff Engle said something similar, when I first got here," he said. "There's just something about the place that's off somehow."

"I know I'll be glad to get back to New York," said Edie. "Hell's Kitchen looks positively welcoming after all of this. How about you? What's next for the fearless G-man?"

"It looks like I'll be sticking around," Roland said.

"Sticking around? Does someone really hate you that much?"

"Something's off about this place," he repeated. "Sheriff Engle knows more than he's telling, and so do those eggheads at the university. I get the feeling that what we went through is just a taste of whatever's wrong around here. If I cut and run, then my report is just a lie – nothing more. We can talk about protecting people from a truth the world isn't ready for, but really I'm just ducking out."

"What does the Bureau have to say about that?"

"That's the strange thing," Roland said. "I got a cable from the Boston Field Office saying I'd been seconded to a special agency of some kind. No name or anything – just orders to stay here, keep my eyes open, and wait for further instructions. I get the impression that someone in the federal government has a clue what's going on. Maybe I'll get some answers."

"Or maybe you'll get killed or driven buggy," Edie said. "That would be too sad, because I've kind of gotten to like you." She gave Roland a pretty little pout, and he laughed as he felt his cheeks redden.

"Come on, is anyone really that much of a choirboy?"

"Boy Scout."

"Say what?"

"That's what they used to call me," he said. "The Boy Scout. I used to believe it, too, but now, I don't know what I am. I broke just about every rule in the book on this case."

"It can't have been much of a book, then," Edie said. "Maybe it's time to write your own. If Arkham makes its own rules, you should, too."

IRE OF THE VOID

Richard Lee Byers

Part One

THE BARN

CHAPTER 1

Norman Withers was accustomed to empty seats. He was not a popular instructor, he did not take attendance, and his lectures were redundant with the textbook. Still, today, the classroom was emptier than usual, and for no reason he could think of.

"Mr Davison," he said, addressing a perpetually sweaty, twitchy student who never missed a single one of Norman's classes or, in all likelihood, any other professor's.

Davison gave a start as if he had been caught doing something reprehensible instead of paying scrupulous attention and writing copious notes. "Yes, sir?" he squeaked.

"Where is everyone? Is something else going on today?"

"Well, sir, Claus Schmidt is giving a guest lecture. I think some people went to hear him." The boy cringed as though he feared Norman would be offended and take out the resentment on him.

In truth, even had Norman been so inclined, he was too busy feeling shocked that he'd heard nothing of this to bother with such a vindictive response. Perhaps, as the secretaries were forever scolding him, he should check the cubbyhole that was his faculty mailbox on days other than payday.

"*The* Claus Schmidt?" he asked. "The one who collaborates with Albert Einstein?"

If so, this was the physicist widely acclaimed as Einstein's brilliant young protégé. While still working toward his doctorate, Schmidt had participated in Eddington's expedition that provided observational verification of general relativity, and had since aided Einstein himself in calculating the cosmological constant and establishing relativistic cosmology. It was extraordinary that such a luminary – a European luminary, at that – had suddenly materialized in Arkham, Massachusetts.

"Yes, sir," Davison said.

"Where is he speaking? The big auditorium in the Science building?"

"Yes, sir."

"Class dismissed."

Norman hurried from the classroom ahead of any of his students, rushed past the foundation for the new observatory, and broke into a run at the Miskatonic University quad, breezing by its silver maples and sycamores. Strolling or lounging on benches, young scholars smirked or chuckled as he dashed past.

Their amusement prompted him to duck into one of the Science building's men's rooms and try to make himself presentable. The mirror showed a scarecrow of a man. His scraggly white beard needed trimming, and his hair stuck up every which way. His tie was loose and askew, and his tweed suit had gone weeks without a pressing.

It was too late to remedy all of that, but he would do the best he could. He reached into his pocket, found he had no comb, and smoothed down his hair with his hand. Then he fixed his tie, straightened his lapels, and proceeded to the auditorium. As he reached for the door, laughter pealed on the other side. Apparently, the young physicist seasoned his lectures with humor.

Norman found a seat in the back of the hall. Claus Schmidt was a stout, cheerful-looking young man dressed in what was, for a scientist, a surprisingly stylish Lindbergh jacket. His English was excellent, only lightly accented, and he clearly relished American slang, slipping terms like "razz" and "bushwa" into his discourse.

Taken altogether, the jokes, the slang, and his friendly, animated manner made his subject matter all the more accessible. He was speaking on Theodor Kaluza's attempt to extend general relativity into five dimensions – an abstruse topic to say the least, but he was clearly holding his audience's attention.

The lecturer concluded to enthusiastic applause. A significant portion of the audience rose from their seats and headed for the front of the auditorium to congratulate him. Although he tried not to be *completely* rude about it, Norman elicited glowers and complaints as he squeezed and jostled forward. He did not want the physicist to disappear through one of the side exits before he reached him.

As he neared the podium, the German said, "I didn't come here expecting to lecture. I hope I didn't ball it up."

Professor Grant smiled, his bald crown gleaming, spectacles slipped halfway down a prominent nose. "It was wonderful. Now, can we offer you some lunch? The roast beef in the Faculty Club is excellent."

"*Danke,*" said Schmidt, "thank you, but I really should be about my business. If you found me a car and driver–"

"I'll drive you!" Norman called.

Grant and several other faculty members turned to eye him askance. The bald academic cleared his throat. "That is kind of you,

Professor Norman. But someone has already made arrangements."

Norman turned to the youthful Schmidt in his modish clothes. "I know Arkham. Wherever you're going, I'll get you there and take you in style. I've got a Stutz Bearcat." The sports car was left over from better times when he – and his wife – took pleasure in such extravagances.

Schmidt's blue eyes opened wide. "Is it a breezer?"

"It is indeed."

The physicist turned back to Grant. "Thank you for all you've done. But since Professor… Norman, is it?… is here now, offering, I might as well take him up on it."

Grant grimaced. "Well, should there be a problem… that is to say, should you require another driver for any reason, just let me know."

CHAPTER 2

Norman had not lowered the Bearcat's canvas top in years. But it was a mild, sunny September day, and his companion was excited that the two-seater with its doghouse hood was a convertible, so he fumbled his way through the half-forgotten procedure.

Schmidt stowed a black leather valise in the trunk and then handed Norman a list of addresses. "In any order," he said. "Whatever's convenient."

There was nothing about the list to indicate why the German was interested in these particular locations. Norman supposed Schmidt would enlighten him in due course. "We might as well start in Southside and work our way north," he said.

Once the trip was underway, Schmidt availed himself of the unobstructed view to take in the city's Georgian houses with their dentilwork cornices, side-gabled or gambrel roofs, and double chimneys. "Charming," he said.

"I suppose," Norman said, "at the moment." When he thought of Arkham, he thought of gray skies, gray walls, and decay.

Schmidt chuckled at Norman's dour tone. "So, level with me,

old boy. Why didn't Grant and those others want you to drive me? What's their beef?"

Norman winced. "I am not sure what you mean."

"Tell it to Sweeney! You're on the outs. So am I, back home. That's why I came with you. Well, that and the car. I'll tell you about it, but you go first."

Norman needed to confide in the younger man, or Schmidt could not possibly help him. Even so, he felt reluctant. It was pleasant being in the company of a colleague who did not see him as eccentric, if not unhinged. It would pain him to lose the physicist's good opinion if that was how things worked out.

Peering squarely through the sports car's monocle windshield – so as not to see how Schmidt reacted to his story – he took a long breath and began. "I am an astronomer. Some of my work involves discovering and cataloging new stars. On March 11th, 1916, I found six faint stars in the vicinity of Canis Major. Then they vanished all at once, literally within seconds of one another, and have never reappeared."

"Given interstellar distances," Schmidt said, "I don't know of a phenomenon to account for that."

"Nor do I," Norman said. "Nor did anyone. Without exception, other astronomers deemed it more plausible that I never really observed the stars in the first place. Eyestrain, they said. Smudges. Meteors. But I know what I saw!"

"And you've never been able to let it go," said Schmidt.

"It's that obvious, is it? Yes, I never stopped looking for the answer, and it's blighted my scientific reputation. I don't suppose I'd have retained my position at Miskatonic if not for tenure and the fact that I still put in time doing conventional research and publish the occasional journal article."

He could have added that as he had grown increasingly obsessed with the mystery, it had blighted his marriage as well. Eventually, Bernadine divorced him and moved to Los Angeles to be near their daughter, but why pick at that wound? It would only make him look even more pathetic than he likely appeared already.

"If the vanishing stars are the focus of your work," said Schmidt, "and you were so eager to make contact with me, then you must believe I can help you somehow."

"Yes. You – you, Einstein, your circle – are discovering revolutionary new truths about the workings of the universe. I hoped that if I prevailed on you to consider my findings, you'd have some fresh insight to offer."

"I have to confess, nothing is springing to mind. But you're helping with my research. Afterward, it seems only fair that I take a serious look at yours. Then we'll see if I might actually be able to contribute."

Norman hesitated. "I hope you aren't just humoring me. If you think I'm babbling nonsense, you can say it."

"But I don't think it, or at least I don't *assume* it. Now that I've been told that my own current line of research is a load of horsefeathers, I'm less inclined to dismiss the ideas of others out of hand."

Norman pulled the brake lever at one of Arkham's four electric traffic signals, erected two years previously. "What is that line of research? I have to say, I am puzzled as to what problem of physics is better investigated driving around Miskatonic County than in your laboratory in Berlin."

"How familiar are you with general relativity?"

"Reasonably so. Your discipline is relevant to mine." The traffic signal turned green. Norman waited for a horse-drawn wagon to clear the intersection, then put the Bearcat in gear.

"Then you know the theory connects the curvature of space-time to the density of mass in the vicinity. To gravity."

"Yes. By so doing, it explains the anomalous perihelion advance of Mercury and the deflection of starlight Eddington observed during the solar eclipse of '19."

"Exactly. My own scientific heresy has been to connect the idea that space-time can be curved, twisted, warped not just to what we observe in the sky but also to phenomena here on Earth. People disappear mysteriously. Sometimes they even appear just as strangely, peculiar souls who don't seem to belong in the times or places in which they're discovered. If there are discontinuities – folds or holes – in the structure of reality, people could blunder into them and find themselves transported."

Norman frowned. "Surely these disappearances are either legends or events that, were we privy to all the facts, would prove to have a mundane explanation."

"There are more such incidents than you may suppose, in every land and era, and some have been extensively studied without any convincing explanation emerging."

"Well… fair enough, I suppose. But unless I misunderstand them entirely, Einstein's field equations don't allow for the extreme distortions you're proposing. Not on a body with the mass of the Earth, and not at one point on the surface but not another."

"But what," Schmidt asked, "if general relativity, though predictive at a certain level just as Newton's laws are, is similarly incomplete? What if something other than mass is also capable of bending space-time? I hope to prove it is, and then science can figure out the what and the how."

"And you can prove this by touring Arkham?"

Schmidt smiled. "I hope so, old boy, because of your history. You may not realize it, but since the town was founded, it has had an amazing number of unexplained disappearances. My plan is to collect data in the places where they happened."

Norman mulled that over. "This was your 'scientific heresy.'"

"Einstein is sure it's applesauce. But he can't be right *all* the time, can he?"

Perhaps not, but in this instance the eminent physicist seemed far more likely to be right than his protégé. Norman sighed at the realization that Schmidt could not really help him, after all. Once, conceivably, but not now that he had given himself over to nonsensical pseudoscience. Perhaps it was not too late to make an excuse, foist the German off on the driver Professor Grant had offered, and salvage the rest of the day.

Suddenly, it occurred to Norman that he was dismissing Schmidt exactly as his fellow astronomers dismissed him, and for pursuing a line of investigation arguably no unlikelier than his own.

Damn it, he wasn't going to be like them! Not because he believed Schmidt's notions were correct, but because the young man's attitude was. A scientist shouldn't bow down to an argument from authority, even if the authority was Albert Einstein. He should go where his instincts led him and collect evidence to confirm or deny a hypothesis.

Besides, it was pleasant driving the Bearcat around on a sunny day with the top down. He had forgotten. He was a bit sorry when he and Schmidt arrived at the first spot on their itinerary.

CHAPTER 3

The old house stood with the steeple of South Church peeking over the hipped roof like a priest suspicious that someone was robbing the poor box. Even under a blue sky, the structure's appearance was in accord with Norman's impression of Arkham as a crumbling, decrepit habitation. Sickly yellow paint peeled from the clapboards, and the multi-pane windows were grimy. One was cracked.

As soon as Norman pulled up at the curb, Schmidt jumped out of the Bearcat. "Open the trunk!"

For a moment, a smile tugged at the corners of Norman's mouth. His companion was as impatient as a child at the entrance to a carnival. "I take it you have high hopes for this place."

"In 1774," Schmidt replied, "responding to the Suffolk Resolves, five of Arkham's community leaders entered a room in this house to discuss the organization of a militia and never came out. That's the space we're going to investigate."

Norman was half-embarrassed, half-amused that he did not know what the Suffolk Resolves were when a foreigner did. He picked up the valise, and metal clinked inside it. As he carried it toward the portico, he spotted the sign beside the panel door: *Apartments for Rent.*

"If someone has altered the floor plan–"

"We should still be able to identify the right spot," Schmidt replied. "We just need a little luck." He opened the door, stepped into a foyer, and headed down the hallway that ran past a staircase toward the rear of the building. "I think we want the last door on the right."

A tinny radio was playing "Riverboat Shuffle", as performed by Bix Beiderbecke and the Wolverines, on the other side of the door, which had a brass number five screwed onto it. Schmidt knocked, and after a moment a small woman with a face like a fist and mouse-brown hair in curlers responded.

"Good evening, madam," said Schmidt. "My colleague and I are scientists from the university. We're conducting research that requires us to take some readings in your home. I promise it won't take long, and we'll leave everything as we found it."

The woman scowled. "Mr Page – my husband – says never let anyone in when he's not here." She started to close the door.

Schmidt whisked a folded dollar bill from his pocket. "Naturally, we wouldn't dream of asking without offering to compensate you for your trouble."

Mrs Page hesitated. "I'd have to leave the door open."

"Of course," said Schmidt.

She grabbed the money. The physicist shot Norman a wink as the door swung open.

The cramped apartment seemed an unlikely place for a scientific breakthrough, but Schmidt's enthusiasm remained undiminished. He took the bag from Norman, flipped up the latches, and brought out a thermometer. He then moved about the apartment, repeatedly stopping and recording the temperature in various spots. Mrs Page regarded him with perplexity writ large on her pinched, blotchy face.

Norman knew how she felt. "What does this have to do with space-time?" he asked at length.

Schmidt shrugged. "I had a hunch. Maybe it was wrong, or maybe the differential is so slight the thermometer can't detect it. Either way, what comes next is more important."

He returned to the valise and produced a carpenter's level and squares of cardboard. Inserting the latter under the legs of Mrs Page's dining room table as needed, he rendered it rock-steady despite the uneven flooring beneath.

After that, he brought out a small triple beam balance scale, set it on the table, and put a lead one-gram weight on the platform. Unsurprisingly, it turned out to weigh one gram.

Despite himself, Norman felt his earlier disgruntlement creeping back. He had not known what to expect, but surely a revolutionary discovery in physics required more than pointless fiddling with the most basic of instruments.

Then again, Einstein had supposedly arrived at his extraordinary insights through thought alone. After all, a telescope was simply pieces of glass in a tube, and now that Norman had come this far, what did he have to lose by seeing the venture through? If it all turned out to be "bushwa," he could at least take comfort that, for once, he wasn't the one who looked the fool.

"What did that accomplish?"

"Nothing yet," Schmidt answered, "but now we move the table. We'll have to re-level it with each placement."

"I would assume so." Norman took hold of an end.

They shifted the table about, and for the first half a dozen placements, one gram was one gram. Then, when the platform was partway across the yellowed linoleum floor of the kitchen, the weight registered ever so slightly less. Schmidt crowed and clapped his hands together.

The German seemed so elated that Norman rather hated to dampen his moment of triumph. Still, Occam's razor and simple common sense obliged him to speak. "It's likely," he said, "that we simply didn't get the table leveled properly. Or else the scale slipped out of adjustment."

"Then we'll check both," Schmidt replied, "and weigh again."

They did. The reading was the same as before. The physicist brought out a tape measure and used it to define the scale's position in relation to fixed reference points in the room.

As he held his end of the tape, Norman felt lightheaded. Could the variance possibly be real?

One obvious alternative was that, at some point in his life, Schmidt had acquired the skills of a prestidigitator and was using them to perpetrate a hoax, possibly switching one weight for another. But Norman could not imagine why a scientist with a first-rate reputation and bright future to protect would stoop to such a fraud, nor did the notion jibe with his sense of the young man's character.

No matter how carefully the two scientists leveled the table and checked the scale – and how keenly Norman watched Schmidt, just in case the latter was attempting chicanery, after all – the next several placements yielded similarly anomalous results. Gradually a pattern, a gradient, emerged. Objects became ever so slightly lighter, which meant gravity became marginally weaker, as one approached the icebox in the corner of the kitchen.

As he helped shift the table and held his end of the measuring tape, Norman's initial stupefaction gave way to an excitement akin to Schmidt's. He was no nearer to solving his own scientific puzzle, but he was not quite so fixated on it as to render him indifferent to someone else's amazing discovery, nor was it lost on him that his participation, even in a secondary role, might redeem his colleagues' disdainful opinion of him.

Gradually, though, as he and Schmidt shifted the table progressively closer to the icebox, his emotions altered once again. His interest remained, but a growing uneasiness undercut it. Eventually, like an image coming clear when one focused a telescope, the anxiety resolved itself into the suspicion that he and the German were being observed.

As they were. When he glanced around, Mrs Page was viewing the work with an expression that proclaimed her conviction that her visitors were out of their minds.

Clearly, her scrutiny must be the source of Norman's edginess, but to his annoyance, realizing that did not banish the feeling. His mouth remained dry, and a clumsy tightness persisted in his limbs.

The moment came when the table was flush with the icebox and the final weight recorded. Schmidt reached into the corner.

Norman wanted to shout, *Don't!* But he didn't want to appear ridiculous, so he remained silent.

Schmidt felt around the space where one wall met the other. Unlike the weighing, nothing about the manner in which his fingertips tapped the faded wallpaper was peculiar. Still, Norman's sense of being observed intensified, and although he assured himself it was just some fleeting, meaningless agitation of nerves, he nonetheless felt relieved when Schmidt drew back his hand.

They restored the table to its original position, and Schmidt repacked the valise. Giving Mrs Page a smile, he said, "Thank you for your patience. Should it prove necessary, may we call again?"

She shrugged. "If you keep making it worth my while."

CHAPTER 4

After returning the valise to the Bearcat's trunk, Schmidt clapped Norman on the back. "The first house we checked!" he exclaimed. "The very first!"

"What we found was remarkable," Norman replied. "That is, assuming there isn't another explanation, and the observations can be replicated."

Schmidt waved the comment away. "They will be."

"If so," said Norman, "unexplainable fluctuations in gravity are an extraordinary discovery. But we *didn't* find a discontinuity in space-time."

"True. We're not hitting on all six yet. But what a start!" The physicist extracted a silver case from a pocket of the Lindbergh jacket and offered a celebratory cigarette to Norman. Hoping for some exotic European flavor, the American was a bit disappointed that the tobacco tasted pretty much the same as the Chesterfields that were his accustomed brand.

Exhaling smoke, he said, "Do you have any thoughts as to why no discontinuity was in evidence?"

"At this point," Schmidt replied, "we know so little that any speculation is little more than guesswork. But, that said, what if the discontinuity was unstable? The unfortunate patriots disappeared all the way back in 1774. That gave the breach a century and a half to close. Or shrink to microscopic size."

"Maybe. If the discontinuities come and go, that would explain how people like the Pages can live in the same places where others disappeared and never notice anything odd."

"It also raises the possibility that there may not be any open breaches left in Arkham. But I refuse to be pessimistic after such a promising beginning! I prefer to believe that if we simply work our way down the list, we'll find one. Let's get a wiggle on!"

CHAPTER 5

The scientists' next stop was South Church itself, or rather, the small graveyard adjacent to it. As they began their work, a priest who introduced himself as Father Michael arrived to ask what they were doing but, invoking his status as a professor at Miskatonic, Norman satisfied the man as to their bona fides.

Unfortunately, the outdoor site posed longer-lasting hindrances, such as the lack of Mrs Page's dining room table and the floor on which it sat. Schmidt's valise proved to contain a folding table with stubby telescoping legs that was just big enough to hold the balance scale, but it was less convenient to keep bending over it and more difficult to level it on the ground.

The greatest hindrance, however, was that while the accounts that had drawn Schmidt to this location indicated that three people had vanished – a sexton digging a grave in 1845, a widow come to put roses on her husband's final resting place in 1889, and a pair of truant schoolboys as recently as 1909 – they did not indicate where in the cemetery the disappearances had occurred. Thus, it was necessary to perform exploratory weighing all around the rectangular space within the waist-high fieldstone walls.

As the two men labored among crumbling tombstones and ivy-covered mausoleums, gray clouds smothered the sun, threatened rain, and brought a hint of autumn chill. Still, Schmidt worked on with cheerful enthusiasm. Something, pride perhaps, compelled Norman to try to match the younger man's energy even when his lower back began to ache.

Eventually they made their way to the northeastern quadrant of the graveyard. As he slipped cardboard under a table leg, Norman abruptly felt a renewed suspicion of scrutiny. With it came another pang of trepidation, even though the feeling of being spied upon was plainly more baseless than before. Mrs Page was not here, and Father Michael had gone back inside the church.

Schmidt set the weight on the scale. "Voilà! Only this time, the weight is heavier instead of lighter."

Norman tried to keep any irrational anxiety out of his voice. "What do you make of that?"

"I have no idea, but it's interesting. Now we have to figure out where the trail of anomalies leads from here."

Norman hesitated, then shoved away the pusillanimous urge. He pointed to the spot where the low cemetery wall took a right-angle bend. "We should try that direction first."

Schmidt cocked his head. "Why?"

"In Mrs Page's apartment, the gradient led to a corner."

"It's difficult to imagine that's any more than a coincidence, but I don't have a better suggestion. So why not?"

It soon became apparent that Norman's hunch was correct. Schmidt whooped and gave him another clap on the shoulder.

As before, the gravitational disturbances spread out in a fan shape from a presumed point of origin. Only this time, in place of a steady gradient, the weight was too heavy at one spot, too light at the next, and too heavy again at the third.

His heart thumping, Norman conjectured the difference reflected the fact that the previous discontinuity had opened in 1774 and this one as recently as 1909. Perhaps when they did, they created gravitational chaos, and after they closed, the anomalies settled toward a more orderly resting state.

But that was not how the situation *felt*. Crazy though it was, his imagination suggested that gravity was more disturbed than before because the invisible watcher was staring more intently. Or more *maliciously*. He wondered if he and Schmidt were like prey obliviously approaching a hungry tiger hidden in tall grass.

He reached to pick up the scale and nearly knocked it over. "Are you all right?" asked Schmidt.

Norman swallowed. "Fine."

"Are you sure? Your hands are trembling,"

Norman forced a smile. "I'm not as young as you, but I'm not going to fall over dead, either. Not and miss out on all the excitement."

Had he been candid about it, he would have said he was not going to disgrace himself by succumbing to groundless fear. He did not know what ailed him – maybe he would see his doctor when he had the chance – but he was a scientist, and he was going to behave as such.

They reached the juncture of the two walls. Schmidt waved his hands through the air above. Norman held his breath, and… nothing happened.

Schmidt dropped to one knee and Norman's anxiety ratcheted up another notch. He had to struggle not to wince despite himself as his thoughts returned to the crouching tiger he had imagined previously. No such beast was present – obviously – but if one entertained the fantasy that it was, Schmidt had just put himself eye to eye with it.

The physicist felt around the gray, fitted fieldstone, and the corner proved to be as solid as it looked. No hitherto undetected hole in the substance of things yawned in response to the probing.

Schmidt rose and brushed off his pant leg. "Do you want to try?"

"No!" Norman yelped. He took a breath. "I mean, I don't see a point. You were thorough. I wouldn't do anything you didn't mere moments before."

"Suit yourself. I just don't want to hog the fun." Thunder rumbled, and a first raindrop plopped on Norman's shoulder. "Let's pack up and get some supper. My treat, and I insist on somewhere expensive."

As they walked toward the cemetery gate, Norman's sense of being watched faded, as did the anxiety that accompanied it. He resolved that he would not succumb to such idiocy again. Or permit himself to harbor the suspicion that he and Schmidt had now been lucky twice.

CHAPTER 6

Paneled in dark oak with frosted art nouveau wall fixtures providing soft illumination, Drew's was one of Uptown's better restaurants. Once, Norman had been a regular. After he witnessed the six stars vanishing, though, a visit to any such establishment came to feel like a waste of time better spent in his study. Now, dining on shepherd's pie, he rather felt he had been cheating himself.

The unavailability of wine or beer to accompany one's meal had provoked Schmidt into a humorous lamentation on the puritanical American character and the absurdity of Prohibition, but now that the food had arrived, he did not appear to miss alcohol all that much. He was attacking his broiled Boston scrod with the gusto he brought to everything in life.

Norman sipped his coffee. "It's good, isn't it?"

"It's the elephant's eyebrows," the German replied, "and there's nothing like discovering something to give a scientist an appetite."

Norman grunted. "I suppose."

"What's eating you, partner? Most of the time, you seem as excited as I am, but every once in a while, you turn into a bit of a wurp."

Norman's immediate impulse was to deny it. Then, however, it occurred to him that he could in some measure acknowledge his edginess without mentioning imaginary watchers or admitting to irrational anxiety attacks.

"I just wonder," he said, "if you're being a little reckless."

Schmidt cocked his head. "How so?"

"Your hypothesis is that the discontinuities exist and people occasionally blunder through them never to be seen again, and there you are groping around for them with your bare hands. What if *you* fall in?"

The physicist grinned. "Then I'll have the most glorious adventure any scientist ever had."

"I'm serious."

"So am I. Well, in principle, but in practice, perhaps you raise a valid point. Suppose I do the initial probing with a stick. Will that make you feel better?"

"Yes." A little, anyway.

"Then that's how we'll do it." Schmidt pushed his plate away, dabbed at his lips with his napkin, and set it on the table. "Are you game for one more site before we seek out one of these juice joints I've heard so much about?"

Norman frowned. "It's dark, and it's raining."

"I'm sure we can find flashlights and umbrellas, and we'll choose another indoor location. Come on, what do you say?"

Norman reminded himself that he had resolved to put irrational anxiety behind him. "All right. One more."

CHAPTER 7

The farm – if it still was a working farm – lay beyond the city limits of Arkham, on a narrow unpaved road that twisted west from the Aylesbury Pike. The land near the road was overgrown, and no lights shined in the house in the distance. If not for the flashes of lightning, Norman might have missed seeing the vague black mass of it and the larger shape that was the barn.

A chain hung across the drive with a tin *No Trespassing* sign wired to the middle of it. The wind tugged at their umbrellas as he and Schmidt shined their tungsten-filament flashlights on the sign. The chain was not rusty, and weather had yet to fade or stain the lettering.

That felt incongruous, but Norman supposed it shouldn't, really. Whether or not anyone was farming the land, someone presumably still owned it.

"It's a good thing the equipment weighs no more than it does," said Schmidt. "We can ankle the rest of the way."

Norman frowned. "The sign says–"

"Oh, come on! We're not going to hurt anything. No one will even know we were here." He grinned. "For science!"

Norman returned a grudging smile. "Very well. For science."

He opened the trunk, and Schmidt took out the valise. Norman gave the Bearcat a last look, decided no harm would come to it parked where it was on the side of the lonely road, and followed his companion as the German stepped over the chain and headed up the drive.

The wind gusted, and cold rain slipped beneath his umbrella to spatter him. The brush rustled and swayed as though animals were moving through it, although only blackness showed in the gaps between branches. Norman resisted the urge to play his flashlight beam across the overgrowth just to make sure.

"Do we want the house or the barn?"

"The barn," Schmidt replied. "In 1871, a farmer went in and never came out. In 1910, virtually the same thing happened again, this time to the missing man's eldest son."

Up close, the farmhouse and barn looked as abandoned as before. The barn had big doors on the front where wagons, traction engines, and such had presumably gone in and out. Schmidt ignored the large doors in favor of a smaller entrance around the side. He tried the knob, and the door opened.

The dark space inside still smelled of hay, but it was not open and empty the way Norman expected. As he and Schmidt stepped inside, their flashlights' glow flowed across stacks of wooden crates on pallets. He was still trying to figure out exactly what they had stumbled across when a baritone voice barked, "Don't move!"

Norman turned toward the sound. A square-jawed young man in his shirtsleeves and braces was aiming a pistol at the intruders. Behind him, too far away for Norman to have noticed its light from outside, a hurricane lantern sat on a small table where it illuminated a pack of Lucky Strikes, an overflowing ashtray, and a facedown issue of *Western Stories Weekly*.

"Don't shoot!" Norman exclaimed. It was all he could think of to say.

The gunman peered at them. "You don't look like cops. Or hijackers, neither."

"We're scientists," Norman said, his pulse beating in his neck. "I'm Professor Norman from Miskatonic, and this is Professor Schmidt from the University of Berlin. We came here for purposes of research. We thought the property was abandoned."

"Well, it ain't," the guard replied. "And Old Sadie Sheldon don't like others sniffin' around his properties." According to the *Arkham Advertiser*, Sheldon was a bootlegger, so the crates presumably held Canadian whiskey. "And now that you've seen that, what the hell am I supposed to do with you?"

"Nothing?" Norman ventured.

"Oh, yeah? How does *that* work?"

"Why would we talk to the police?" Norman asked. "We enjoy a drink the same as anybody else, whereas we *don't* care for the prospect of experiencing whatever it is that Mr Sheldon does to informers."

The gangster grunted. "OK, that's smart. Scram. And remember, you told me your names."

Schmidt cleared his throat. "Actually, now that we're here, may we proceed with our investigation? We won't disturb the merchandise or do anything that would draw attention."

The bootlegger frowned. "I don't know much about science, but ain't the whole idea to tell people what you figure out?"

"Yes," Norman said, "but we might not find anything in this particular location. We may just check it and cross it off our list.

If we *do* discover something of interest, we'll still say nothing without Mr Sheldon's approval. You have my word."

The guard stood and pondered while scratching his cheek with the muzzle of his automatic. Finally he said, "Go on, then. But don't take all night, and leave the brown alone. I'll be keeping an eye on you."

"Thank you," Schmidt said, and then, in a softer voice, as he set down the valise, "Nice work double shuffling him, old boy. I didn't know you had it in you."

Norman smiled. "Maybe your bad example is rubbing off on me. I take it we're following the usual procedure?"

"Actually," said Schmidt, "I hope to find a shortcut. The disappearance of Zachariah Mayhew – the son – differed from the others we've investigated in one respect. He left behind a pool of blood on the floor."

The satisfaction Norman had felt at persuading the hoodlum, and at Schmidt's approval, gave way to a fresh pang of trepidation. Annoyed with himself and trying to resist the resurgence of his timidity, he said, "Then we look for a stain. If we find one, that's the right area in which to start recording weights."

"Exactly," Schmidt replied.

Shining his flashlight on the floor, Norman headed down one of the aisles between the stacks of liquor crates. The edginess was trying to worm its way back into his head and he felt an urge to hurry, to be done with this task and away, but he made himself go slowly anyway. With the boxes blocking the yellow glow of the guard's lantern, the barn was even darker than before. The bloodstain, if still present at all, was likely to be faded and difficult to distinguish from the general dust and grime. If he did not proceed carefully, he might very well miss it.

From time to time, a shadow with a single luminous eye appeared at the end of an aisle to make him flinch and squint at the glare. It was the hoodlum, prowling with lantern in hand to make sure the scientists were not opening any of the whiskey crates. The bootlegger did not appear very often, however. Apparently, he had decided his uninvited guests truly were harmless, and he was enjoying the stories in his cowboy pulp.

Somewhat more frequently, a band of rain fell hard enough to rattle on the roof, or the wind gusted hard enough to make the old barn groan and creak. The former sounded like claws tapping. Rats – or something bigger than rats – scuttled nearby but out of sight. The latter made Norman imagine the unknown force of Schmidt's hypothesis pulling apart the juncture of two walls to reveal a gash in the flesh of the world itself.

Idiocy. Norman had to get hold of himself. He halted and took several deep breaths. His heartbeat slowed, and some of the tension shivered out of his limbs. Then someone screamed.

Norman recognized the voice, although the wordless cry of terror was unlike anything he had heard it produce hitherto. "Schmidt?" he called.

"Run!" the physicist wailed. The next instant, he shrieked again.

"What the hell!" the bootlegger shouted. With that, he was presumably up and moving to discover the reason for the disturbance.

Norman yearned to do as Schmidt had bade him and flee, but he couldn't just abandon the German. Resisting the lure of possible escape as if it, too, were some sort of gravitational anomaly, he managed to take a step in a different direction, and then another after that.

Due to the way sound echoed beneath the high roof and

through the aisles of crates, he hadn't been able to tell exactly where Schmidt's cries originated, but he suspected it was somewhere near one of the far corners of the barn. Breathing in short little rasps, he crept toward the closer of the two. The pattering he'd heard before returned and now seemed to move with him, as though the phantom rat pack he'd imagined previously was stalking him.

Amber light pushed at the gloom ahead. The guard stepped into the intersection of Norman's aisle with his automatic leveled and his lantern held high.

Norman drew breath to call out to the other man, but before he could, the guard let out a yelp. His eyes wide, he stretched out his shooting arm and fired three times.

A moment later, he lowered the automatic, and Norman's shoulders slumped in relief. The bootlegger's behavior seemed to indicate the gunfire had killed the source of his cries or had at least alarmed it into retreat.

Then wood crashed, and glass shattered. Startled, Norman peered about in an effort to find the source of the new disturbance. The bootlegger did the same, then hastily backpedaled out of sight. As he disappeared, he raised his pistol and fired upward.

Ahead of Norman and to his right, stacks of crates swayed. Dark shapes leaped to the stacks on the left in what seemed to be a pursuit of the gunman. The forms were sufficiently high above Norman's flashlight beam and departed so quickly that his eyes registered nothing more than a surge of movement. But their mass and the vigor of their springing dislodged the upper boxes, and the crates smashed to the floor.

More shots rang out. Additional crates fell. Silence followed. Norman crept up to the intersection and peered around the corner.

There was nothing to see but a splash of light where the

bootlegger had tried to retreat down a different aisle. The glow wasn't dimming, however, which meant both the lantern, and the man who carried it, had stopped moving. Norman imagined the man lying torn and dead with *something* crouching over him.

Surely poor Schmidt had been the first to die. Norman would be crazy to linger in this place a moment longer. Worried fear would make him clumsy, *noisy,* he gathered himself to sneak toward the exit. Then the physicist resumed his shrieking.

Convinced that whatever had killed the bootlegger would rush to silence Schmidt's cries, and in so doing charge within arm's reach of him, Norman flattened himself against the wall of crates. The cringing, reflexive action produced a thump, and the stack above him began to rock and sway, making his discovery seem all the more likely.

But nothing came. Maybe the *things* were too eager to eat the bootlegger to react to Schmidt's screams or, in this isolated location with rain falling, wind blowing, and thunder booming outside, didn't regard the racket as cause for concern.

Whatever the explanation, Schmidt was still alive, and perhaps Norman could help him to safety without the *things* being any the wiser. At least the ongoing cries now revealed the German's approximate location. It was near one of the corners of the barn, precisely where Norman's colleague had expected to find the source of the anomalies.

With the smells of gun smoke and spilled whiskey now hanging in the air, Norman skulked across the intersection. *Just get there*, he told himself, *just get there. It's only a few more steps.*

That was true, but unfortunately, the walls of crates would make it impossible to catch even a glimpse of what awaited until he was quite close indeed. As he approached the end of an aisle, vapor, invisible except for where it tainted the white beam of the flashlight, swirled through the air. For an instant, he imagined it was smoke, but he didn't know what would have started a fire. The hoodlum and his hurricane lantern were behind him, not ahead.

An instant later, he caught a whiff of the vapor and all but gagged in revulsion. The stench was also suggestive of smoke in that it called to mind the incineration of a rotting corpse. Norman had never smelled such a thing, but had he attempted to imagine it, he might have hit on something foul and acrid like this.

Holding his breath, he peeked around the end of the stacks of crates and spied Schmidt at last.

Or rather, Norman spied most of him.

Still screaming despite growing hoarse and short of breath, Schmidt lay on his belly in the corner with his upper body pointed outward. His hands clutched and scrabbled at the floor. From points midway down the calves, his legs were simply absent, as if sticking out of a hole in the wall of the barn. But there was no such opening, merely denser twists of the malodorous fog.

Schmidt hitched backward, gradually losing the struggle to anchor himself as *something* pulled him into nothingness. Breaking cover, Norman dashed forward to grab his colleague's hand and haul him free.

As though Schmidt's unseen captor had only been toying with him hitherto – or as if it had waited for Norman's arrival to tease and frustrate *him* – the German's body shot backward faster than the older man could close the distance. The corner swallowed Schmidt's torso, head, arms, clawing hands, and then nothing at all remained.

CHAPTER 8

Off balance as he was, Norman couldn't stop in time to avoid banging into the juncture of the two walls. The impact jolted him and bounced him reeling backward, as a collision with solid matter should.

He stepped forward again and, hands shaking, stooped to examine the base of the walls, which was to say, the exact spot through which Schmidt had disappeared. It was as solid as the walls that surrounded it.

An instant later, a sense of malevolent attention pierced him through. As though, having dealt with Schmidt to its satisfaction, the physicist's abductor had swung its head back toward the camouflage behind which it hid like a trapdoor spider. Then it howled.

Partly, the cry hurt Norman's ears as any loud noise would. But there was also a component of it that seemed to rip directly into the mind itself.

Other howls answered. The *things* still in the barn were signaling their readiness to deal with him. He bolted.

After several strides, he realized his flashlight was likely to help his pursuers find him. Fumbling, he clicked it off and could see nothing. He continued in what he thought was the right direction and banged face first into what must be a stack of crates. He gasped, less at the jolt of pain than at the telltale noise.

Blundering onward, he ran the fingertips of one hand over the rough wood of the crates. It helped him avoid another collision but *didn't* avert the moment when a panicky sense of disorientation suddenly overwhelmed him. Exactly where was he in the barn? Was he still moving toward an exit? And where were the creatures? Their howling was hideous, terrifying, but at least it had provided some vague sense of their location. Now he could hear nothing but the clatter of rain on the roof.

His fingers slipped from splintery wood to empty air. He'd reached the end of a wall of crates. He groped forward and pushed against a barrier. Believing it to be a barn wall, he started to turn away, then realized it had given ever so slightly under the pressure of his hands.

He reached lower and found a bar in brackets. He'd blundered his way to the big double doors and, thank the Lord, only this simple mechanism secured them. He was going to get away!

He grabbed hold of the bar, shoved it, and it stuck. Either it, the brackets, or both were warped and swollen.

The creatures howled anew. They had spotted him, and they were coming.

Screaming, he pushed with all his might, and, scraping and squealing, the bar slid sideways. He threw himself at the door on the left, knocked it open, stumbled through, and sprinted toward the road.

Every instant of the way, he expected a *thing* to overtake him and rip him apart, or drag him shrieking through a hole in the world. It was only when he had the Bearcat speeding as fast as the sixteen-valve, four-cylinder engine could manage that he decided that, for whatever reason, the creatures had abandoned the chase. Then tears blurred the darkened road and the lights of Arkham ahead. He pulled over and broke down, sobbing.

CHAPTER 9

Seated across the table from Norman, the pages of the astronomer's typed and signed statement lying between them, Sheriff Engle took another drink of coffee. As Norman had previously discovered, the stuff tasted awful, but with his bloodshot eyes, puffy lids, and unshaven jowls, the lawman looked like he needed it, and that was understandable. Some subordinate had woken him in the middle of the night to report that one of the professors from the university had turned up raving about a vanished German, a harrowing chase, and the Lord only knew what else.

In truth, Norman lived and worked in Arkham and had automatically run to the Arkham Police Department in Easttown. There, however, the man on the night desk, one Officer Galeas, determined the "incident" had occurred beyond the city limits and, radiating a certain mischievous relish, handed him off to the Sheriff's Department, who conveniently shared the same building.

Lanky, with a thatch of straw-colored hair, Deputy Dingby looked as dyspeptic as his superior and with an arguably better reason: the sheriff had tasked him with visiting the barn where

Schmidt had disappeared. As a result, he was now as rain-soaked and disheveled as he was tired.

"Well," the sheriff said, addressing Norman, "you've had some time to think." He didn't add *or sober up*, but Norman suspected the latter possibility was in his thoughts. "Do you want to change your story?"

"No," Norman answered. In retrospect, it should have been obvious that his account was unbelievable. But when a man was abducted before one's eyes, by whatever and to wherever, what was there to do but report it to the authorities?

"You sure?" the sheriff persisted. "Because I can imagine it happening this way. You and this German fella drank some bad coffin varnish and went a little crazy. Started seeing things. He got scared and ran off through the fields. Once he comes to his senses, he'll likely turn up. If not, we can track him down in the daylight."

Norman shook his head. "It all happened just the way I told you."

"With holes in the world."

"Yes."

"And monsters."

"Yes."

"Although you didn't really ever see either of those things."

Norman hesitated. "I saw Professor Schmidt slide through the discontinuity. Apparently a person can't see the breach itself."

"You saw him go through. But when you felt around the spot just a second later, the walls were solid."

"Yes. Still, there has to be some kind of evidence." Norman turned to Deputy Dingby. "You searched. What did you find?"

Sheriff Engle waved a hand in a gesture of acquiescence. "Sure, why not? Run it down for us, deputy."

"Well," the deputy said, "the black case with the scale and such was there. So were umbrellas, flashlights, a lantern, a pulp cowboy magazine, and all that whiskey, some of the crates fallen and broken open." He smiled a crooked smile. "The Prohibition Agents are going to be happy."

The sheriff made a spitting sound. "That's wonderful, deputy. I live to make the prohis happy. But what's important here and now is that we can be fairly sure the two professors really were there like our witness claims. Maybe the bootlegger guard, too. Now let's hear the things you *didn't* find. My guess is that bodies are at the top of the list."

The deputy took a breath. "That's right, sir. There were no bodies."

"There wouldn't have been," Norman said, "if the creatures dragged them back through the breaches."

"Any big pools and splashes of blood," the sheriff asked, "where it looked like somebody got mauled? Like by a bear or a rabid dog or something?"

Deputy Dingby swallowed. "No."

"What about the mysterious holes? Did you tap around in the corners like I told you to?"

"Yes, sir. Everything was solid."

The sheriff looked at Norman and spread his hands palms up. "There you have it."

Norman fixed his gaze on the deputy. "When Sheriff Engle asked about bodies, you hesitated. When he asked about pools of blood, you did it again. I don't accuse you of lying outright, but I believe you held back *something*."

The deputy hesitated once more, obviously torn between the inclination to be honest and the desire to please his boss by helping to speed the importunate crackpot academic on his way.

Sheriff Engle heaved a sigh. "Deputy, if you found *anything* funny, lay it out for us."

"Yes, sir," he replied. He reached into the pocket of his brown uniform trousers, brought out a folded handkerchief, unwrapped the contents, and set the object on the table between the two men. It was a fingernail with a trace of dried blood encrusting the bottom.

"You found it on the floor," Norman said, "in the southwest corner of the barn."

The deputy frowned. "Yeah."

Norman turned back to the sheriff. "This proves what I told you! It's Schmidt's fingernail! It tore loose when he was clutching at the floor and the beast was dragging him backward!"

"Come on, professor. You're supposed to be a scientist. You know damn well it isn't proof of anything."

"It..." Norman faltered. It was maddening that the sheriff still doubted, but he made a valid point. By itself, the fingernail *wasn't* enough to demonstrate the truth of the story. "Look. You know Professor Schmidt was with me in the barn. You know he's gone now. What's *your* explanation?"

"You already heard it."

"He wandered off in an alcohol-induced delirium."

"If you don't like that story, I can think of others."

Norman felt a pang of trepidation. "Meaning what, exactly?"

"If you two just got pie-eyed, that's not so bad. Plenty of people drink, the Volstead Act be damned. But you don't look lathered now, and you're still telling the same story, so maybe that was never really the problem. Maybe you're crackers."

"That's ridiculous."

"Is it? I made a couple calls, woke up a couple people from the university. Apparently, you have a reputation for being strange. Maybe you're strange enough that I should check you into the asylum for observation."

"There are no grounds! You wouldn't dare!"

"I might. I might also *dare* to consider you a suspect if your German friend doesn't turn up. From what I understand, you were pretty damn eager to drive him around. And you were the last person to see him before he disappeared. A young fella already at the top of his profession when you're getting on in years and something of a joke…" Sheriff Engle shrugged. "Who could blame you for being jealous?"

"So I murdered him and then came straight to you with a wild story you were all too likely to disbelieve?"

"If you're insane, maybe you didn't realize just how unbelievable it was. You thought you were giving yourself an alibi."

Norman looked the sheriff in the eye. "Whatever else you believe or don't believe, you don't really think I killed Professor Schmidt or need to be institutionalized. Why are you trying to intimidate me into retracting my story?"

"Maybe I'm trying to protect you from what everyone else is likely to think."

"I'm not asking you to do that."

The sheriff settled back in his chair. "OK, then let me tell you about a sheriff's job. Mostly, it's what you expect. If there's a thief stealing people's chickens, I catch him. If a landlord evicts a tenant who then refuses to leave, I boot him out. Straightforward problems with straightforward answers."

Norman scowled. "How is this relevant?"

"Bear with me. I'm getting there. Once in a while, though, something comes up that's bad or scary and *doesn't* have an easy answer. In those situations, maybe the best a sheriff can do is keep a lid on what's really happening. That way, people don't panic."

"Are you saying you *do* believe me?"

Sheriff Engle shook his head. "Don't flatter yourself. But I know funny things happen once in a while, and I've been doing this job long enough to wonder if they don't happen more often around here than in some other places. Anyway, what it all comes down to is this: my men and I will look for Professor Schmidt the same way we'd look for any missing person, but we're not going to act like men from Mars kidnapped him or whatever it is you think happened. Because even if that were true, what the hell could we do about it?"

Norman's emotions – the urgency, the anger – crumpled into a kind of exhausted resignation. "What exactly do you want me to do?"

"First, forget you ever said this bullshit." The sheriff picked up the pages of the statement and tore them in two. "Then give me something that will enable me to declare Schmidt missing and start a search without making it look like we're both out of our minds. You were helping him do research. You don't know what the point was because he's a physicist and you're an astronomer. He wanted to go to the farm, so you took him. The whiskey was there, but you didn't see a bootlegger or anybody like that. You wandered off from Schmidt to take a look around the barn. When you came back, he was gone. And that's all you know."

"Got it," Norman said.

CHAPTER 10

As soon as he entered the classroom, Norman decided he had made a mistake.

Given his ordeal, and the hours with the Sheriff's Department that followed, lack of sleep alone would have provided him with a more than adequate excuse for taking the day off. But he knew he would not be able to rest, and the presence of others and the resumption of routine seemed as if they might protect him from the shuddering fits that could otherwise afflict him.

The problem, though, was that every seat was filled, with more students standing along the back wall. In many cases, they were young men and women whose faces Norman had never seen before. Plainly, the majority of those present had come to gawk at the Science Department's resident eccentric, now more than ever an object of curiosity by dint of his involvement in a celebrated colleague's disappearance.

Well, damn them all. This was an astronomy class, not a circus sideshow. To spite them, he launched into his discourse on Neptune, and Lowell's unsuccessful search for planets beyond, more forcefully than he had delivered any lecture in years.

Unfortunately, neither his energy nor the intrinsic interest of his subject matter sufficed to divert his audience's curiosity into the appropriate channels. When he turned his back to write on the blackboard, they whispered back and forth. The chatter was too soft for him to make out, but he did catch "nuts," "crazy," "did *something*," and "involved *somehow*."

No doubt it would have been far worse had Sheriff Engle permitted his original statement to stand. As it was, the speculation and suspicion might fade in time. Still, teeth gritted, Norman bore down until the chalk snapped in two.

He stretched out the lecture without acknowledging any of the waving hands that sought to interrupt him. Someone might want to ask a question that actually pertained to astronomy, but he was unwilling to chance it. The instant the bell rang, he slammed the textbook shut, snatched it off the lectern, and rushed for the door.

Sadly, his haste merely served to fling him into the clutches of a smiling, apple-cheeked man in a polka-dot bowtie and homburg. Absurdly, a press pass stuck up from the hatband as though Arkham were a major city like Boston or New York.

"Professor Withers," the journalist said, "a moment of your time?"

"Sorry," Norman said, circling around the man, "I'm in a hurry."

The newspaperman scrambled to catch up and fell into step beside him. "Come on, professor, be a sport. I'm Doyle Jeffries. I edit the Advertiser, and I came down here personally just to hear what you've got to say."

"Nothing. It's all in the information the sheriff already released."

"You sure? It seemed to me there were lots of holes in that story."

"It's everything I know. Please excuse me." Norman quickened his pace, and this time Doyle allowed him to escape.

He stamped onward into the Science Department offices, ignoring the stares and awkward greetings of secretaries and the other faculty. He entered his own cramped little sanctuary, with its overflowing bookshelves, stacks of journals, star charts and examples of astrophotography, and slammed the door. Copious torn-paper bookmarks and Moore Push-Pins indicated the locations of data he had, at one time or another, believed might shed light on the puzzle that had consumed the past decade of his life.

Two new items reposed front and center on his crowded desk. One was a note informing him the dean wanted to see him. Yesterday, Norman, cranky recluse that he knew himself to be, would have responded expeditiously. But currently, it simply was not in him.

The second item was the new issue of *The Astronomical Journal*. He opened it and, as was his habit, set out to read it cover to cover.

He had spent countless hours engaged in such study, yet now, for the first time since adjusting to the finalization of his divorce, he had difficulty concentrating. He perused paragraphs or whole pages only to realize he had retained none of the information. The image of Schmidt wailing, scrabbling in vain for handholds, and vanishing kept appearing before his inner eye.

But that was not the only thing distracting him. The office itself was not alarming, and his instincts did not warn of some invisible predator poised to spring. But the space seemed dusty and dingy. Oppressive to the point of claustrophobia. The odd thought came to him that if he heard of a convict sentenced to years of solitary confinement in a cell like this, he would feel sorry for the man.

Still, it was more tolerable than being stared at. He stayed where he was until he heard the sounds of the rest of the department going home for the day, and for some time thereafter. When his pocket watch informed him night had fallen, he emerged from his hiding place and skulked from the Science building onto the quad. A few people were wandering around in the dark, but no one noticed him as he headed for the Administration building, at the top of which was his telescope.

He entered to find the place empty of administrative staff, custodians, and anyone else for that matter, which was just as well.

Norman threw himself into the process of operating the telescope. Here, behind the lens, was where he truly belonged. This was what his life was all about, not the nightmare Schmidt had led him into. If he immersed himself in it anew, surely he could purge himself of the emotions tearing at his insides.

His preparations complete, he pressed his eye to the eyepiece. The portion of the sky that was his abiding preoccupation appeared, looking as it had always looked through years of repeated viewings. The six vanished stars had not returned. There was nothing to provide a clue as to what had become of them. God had not parted the black, spangled curtain of the firmament to expound on the question.

Norman felt a sudden urge to pound on the telescope with his fists. He did not succumb to it, but he stepped away from the instrument for fear that he would. He was breathing heavily, and his chest and arms felt tight.

Over the years, he had often been keenly aware others viewed him as a laughable or pathetic figure. He had told himself that when he finally made his great discovery, they would amend their opinions. Now it came to him that, doing the same things day and night after day and night, it was all but certain he never would solve the mystery. It also struck him that even if, by some extraordinary stroke of fortune, he did, his life would *still* look pitiful and in large measure misspent. Somehow, that thought was the worst of all.

He assured himself it was merely fear provoking such dismal notions. Once he calmed down, his chosen path would seem as worthwhile as it always had.

But truly, anxiety was not the problem. He was still afraid. For an aging academic who had never before faced any sort of danger, it could scarcely be otherwise. Yet, the occasional stab of dread notwithstanding, now that he had put miles and hours between himself and the barn, he actually felt more safe than not.

No, when he took inventory of his tangled emotions, it came to him that his current wretchedness stemmed less from residual fear than from shame. He felt guilty that he had acquiesced to Sheriff Engle's decision to suppress the truth, and guiltier still about what had happened to Schmidt.

Idiocy! If there was anything he should have learned from the way his life had unfolded, it was the folly of espousing a truth no one would believe. He clearly wasn't to blame for the physicist's fate. He'd *tried* to rescue Schmidt but had simply been no match for the *thing* that took him.

True. But he was not trying anymore, was he?

More idiocy! Schmidt was surely dead.

Well, no, not *surely*. Norman lacked evidence to confirm any such conclusion. He did not know why the German had been taken. If the breaches were a manifestation of twisted space-time, he could not even know how much subjective time had passed for Schmidt since his captor yanked him through. Perhaps it had only been an instant.

Which, although an interesting speculation, shed no light whatsoever on how to go about retrieving him. Norman hauled the long-legged chair out from under the telescope, lit a Chesterfield, and climbed up into the seat to ponder what he knew.

He quickly decided that was almost nothing. Schmidt had come looking for holes in ordinary reality and, tragically, found them. But nothing in the physicist's rudimentary hypothesis explained why the breaches seemed to occur only in the corners of man-made structures, why they opened and closed like doors at the behest of creatures lurking on the other side, or what those entities were. A man would have to understand such things to have *any* hope of rescuing someone who had been taken, and Norman had no idea where to look for the requisite information.

Or did he? He still had the list of locations Schmidt had given him at the start of their time together. The majority remained to be explored, although the prospect of doing so made a chill slide up his spine.

Intuition told him he had somehow escaped the *things*. Was he really contemplating offering them another crack at him? What had befallen Schmidt was horrible, but it was not his responsibility to fix it. He had his own life to think about.

Except that he had already examined that life and found it wanting, certainly when compared to that of a brilliant, exuberant young man with many years of "glorious adventure" still before him. If unclouded by fear or selfishness, any rational mind would put a bitter old failure like Norman at hazard if there was the slightest chance of winning the German back thereby. Indeed, he had a sense that turning away would be tantamount to throwing away the final chance for his own life to mean something.

Dear Lord, he thought, astonished by his own audacity, *I'm going to do it*. He opened his notebook and wrote a note explaining he was taking a leave of absence. For the moment, the dean could be content with that.

Part Two

THE HOUSE OF
POWDER MILL STREET

CHAPTER 11

Somewhat to Norman's dismay, it proved impossible to find a parking spot right in front of the offices of the *Arkham Advertiser*. He had to pull up to the curb outside a gray box of a shoe factory a block away. Norman climbed out of the Bearcat feeling somewhat like a man condemned to run the gantlet.

But to his relief, in contrast to the unwelcome attention he had attracted at the university, no one on the street looked twice at him. With its factories, warehouses, and tenements with clotheslines hanging above the alleys that sliced between them, Northside was too busy with commerce to take note of a stray academic. Even one linked to a mysterious disappearance. Besides, Schmidt likely did not seem like such a celebrity hereabouts as he did to his fellow scholars.

Still, the receptionist at the newspaper recognized Norman, or at least his name, and made haste to summon Doyle Jeffries. Clad in a green eyeshade, vest, and shirtsleeves with garters holding them up, the editor ushered his caller back through a crowded space where machinery rumbled and vibrations shivered through the floor.

"The presses," Doyle said, raising his voice to make certain of being understood. "We print next door."

Norman had noticed the factory building attached to this one. "Is it time for a new edition already?"

"The advertising inserts you print ahead of time." Doyle waved his hand. "Here we are."

The editor's office proved to be a modest space partitioned to afford a measure of status and privacy. As he squeezed around behind the desk, Doyle said, "So, you decided to give me an interview after all?"

"Actually," Norman said, sitting down opposite the journalist, "I came to ask for help."

Doyle raised an eyebrow. "We reported the facts to the best of our ability. The way Sheriff Engle gave them to us, and you supposedly gave them to him. If people think they don't add up, if they're looking at you funny, that's not the paper's fault."

Norman sighed. "I don't want you to run an editorial asserting my innocence or anything like that. This is something else. I need information. Facts about the history of Arkham."

As Doyle started to answer, someone screamed. Norman jerked in his chair and then realized the noise wasn't Schmidt – or any human being at all. It was a train whistle sounding from the station to the south.

There was no chance Doyle had failed to notice his jumpiness, but the newspaperman did not see fit to remark on it. Instead, he said, "Well, in that case, let's make it tit for tat. You give me my interview, and afterward we can rummage through the morgue together."

Norman frowned in momentary perplexity, then realized the morgue in question was the newspaper's archives.

He did not want to be interviewed and repeat the falsehoods he and the sheriff had agreed upon, but he had come to Doyle recognizing that it might be necessary to secure the editor's cooperation. So he repeated the gist of his statement and answered questions as required.

They were shrewd, skeptical questions. Despite Doyle's genial manner, the inquisition made Norman feel as if his story were a balloon and each query a needle likely to pop it. He struggled against the impulse to try to make it more plausible via embellishment and over-explanation. He suspected such tactics might well result in non-sequiturs and inconsistencies.

Finally Doyle gave him a grin. "You hate lying, and you haven't had a lot of practice."

Norman tried to wrap himself in stiff scholarly dignity. "Naturally not."

"Even so, you're pretty good at it."

"I have no idea what you mean."

"Yeah, you do. Do you think you've delivered on your half of the bargain by peddling the same bunkum as before?"

"I think," Norman said, "that if you run an exclusive interview with the only witness to Professor Schmidt's disappearance, it won't matter if there's actually any new information in it. It will sell papers and keep interest in a sensational story alive a little longer."

Doyle laughed. "I'd almost think you'd been in the newspaper game yourself."

"No, but over the years, I've read enough of the popular press to notice how it goes about its business." Norman hesitated. "No offense."

"None taken, professor. You've got us dead to rights. What information do you need?"

Norman removed Schmidt's list from his pocket, unfolded it, and handed it to the editor. "Whatever you can tell me about these places."

He had already decided he would be either revisiting the sites he had already seen, exploring ones he had not, or both. He had no other avenue of investigation. But before he did, he meant to learn everything he could about them. Although it seemed unlikely, there might be something that would shed light on how to reach Schmidt. Or at least, keep himself from suffering a similar fate.

Norman had started with the *Advertiser* on the supposition that a newspaper might record lurid stories or trivial oddities that more staid and scholarly sources would neglect. But if Doyle and his resources failed him, he would move on to the Arkham Historical Society and the stacks of the university's own Orne Library.

Doyle frowned at the paper. "This is Schmidt's list. The places you went together – including the farm – and the ones you hadn't gotten to yet."

Norman saw no hope of persuasively denying it. "He'd want his work to continue."

"This would be the same work you claimed not to understand? I think you're playing detective, professor. Trying to find your friend. Does the sheriff have this list?"

"No." Sheriff Engle had not asked for it, nor had it occurred to Norman, still in shock from his ordeal, to offer the information.

"Great! Then it'll be just you and my photographer poking around like Sherlock Holmes and Dr Watson."

For a moment, Norman felt a surge of excitement. It had never occurred to him that he might find a comrade to accompany him in his endeavors. To shore up his courage and share the danger–

But no. It was impossible. Without experiencing what he had, any such companion would think him demented, and even if it were otherwise, Norman could not ask someone else to face a peril that, for all he knew, was beyond any man's ability to withstand or even comprehend.

"I have to do my searching alone," he said, "but I promise you this. If I find Professor Schmidt, you'll be the first journalist to hear about it."

Doyle snorted. "And while the story you two are telling will probably just be more bunkum, at least it will be the *Advertiser's* exclusive bunkum?"

"Well… yes."

"I guess that will have to do." Doyle stood up. "Old editions are in the cellar, all the way back to when the *Advertiser* was the *Gazette*. Hope you don't mind a little dust."

Norman didn't, particularly, but the darkness and the shelving loaded with boxes reminded him of the dark barn and the stacks of whiskey crates. Dread knifed through him, and he paused on the creaking stairs.

Sensing his hesitation, Doyle glanced over his shoulder. "You all right?"

Norman took a breath. "Fine." He resumed his descent.

Over the years, someone had made an attempt to index the newspapers, but the results were sketchy at best. Still, this meager organization seemed to suffice for Doyle who, displaying an instinct for searching old documents that most academics would envy, unearthed the proper musty, yellowed newspapers with remarkable efficiency.

The accounts of the various locations described the disappearances that had captured Schmidt's interest, but, to Norman's surprise, they outlined other unfortunate occurrences as well. For example, in a house on Pickman Street, a young man and woman had hanged themselves on their wedding night. Off the highway that led to Newburyport, a superstitious mob had dragged a suspected witch from her cottage and kicked the poor old woman to death. A man living on Boundary Street had suffered from a phobia of bats and had gone to extraordinary lengths to trap and kill the animals, until the night a black cloud of them reportedly descended on him and ripped him to pieces. The stories suggested the sites on the list were unlucky, dangerous places, but Norman knew that already.

"Yeah," Doyle said, "I remember–" He sneezed. Apparently floating dust had tickled his nose.

"Remember what?" Norman asked.

"This fella. Jonathon Hobart Stane."

Norman frowned. "I've heard the name…"

"Well, you've lived in Arkham long enough that you would have." Doyle reached for a pocket handkerchief, remembered he was currently in vest and shirtsleeves, and settled for wiping his nose on his cuff. "But probably not for a while."

"Refresh my memory, please."

"A young man – well, young back when the paper was reporting on him and you were hearing about him – from one of those rich old families in French Hill that was hell-bent on giving away his inheritance. If you were collecting for a worthy cause, Stane was the soft touch you called on first."

Norman recalled seeing Stane's name on plaques around the university honoring donors for their contributions. He thought he might even have met Stane back in the days when he and Bernadine sometimes attended the college's social functions. But only a vague impression of a tall, good-looking young man escorting an equally attractive young lady remained.

"What happened in the Stane house?"

"In 1859, twin baby boys vanished from their cribs. The mother eventually threw herself out an upper-story window. In '81, a family member had a breakdown, spent some time locked up in the asylum, and lived out the rest of his days as a hopeless drunk. All in all, over the years, the Stanes picked up a reputation for being peculiar or at least unlucky. Although for a while, it seemed like Jonathon would turn that around. He had everything – money, looks, brains – and he was such a nice young man that nobody begrudged it to him." Doyle sighed. "Well, almost nobody."

"What do you mean?"

"After Congress declared war in '17, Jonathon was one of the first Arkham men to enlist. He and his fiancée were spending a last night together before he was due to report. Someone broke into the house, killed her with a big knife, like a Bowie, and probably left believing he'd killed Jonathon, too. But Jonathon held on until the surgeons at St. Mary's could patch him up. Later, he went to a private hospital in upstate New York for more operations. Obviously, he never made it to Europe."

"Did the police catch the culprit?"

"No," Doyle said. "It was an odd case. No forced entry, nothing stolen, no one with a motive. Just… savagery. The fact that no suspect was ever arrested may have helped to change Jonathon's temperament, not that it necessarily needed help after everything else he'd suffered."

"How did it change?"

"He came home from New York a recluse and something of a miser. So far as I know, he never gave another penny to charity. Not even to St. Mary's, where they saved his life."

"That's sad." Albeit understandable. Norman could imagine himself slipping into a similar misanthropy were he in Jonathon's place. "What finally became of him?"

"As far as I know," Doyle said, "he's still there, shut away in the mansion on Powder Mill Street. Nobody sees him anymore, though. He long ago fired the staff and has his groceries delivered."

"In that case," Norman said, "I know where to go next."

CHAPTER 12

In Arkham, new money lived in Uptown, and a number of wealthy older families had moved there as well. With its imposing Huguenot, Georgian, and Colonial Revival houses, French Hill still proclaimed that in its day, *it* had been the city's fashionable, affluent district. But many buildings were now in disrepair, in some cases manifestly derelict, with roofs half-denuded of shingles and lawns nearly as overgrown as the fields surrounding the barn where Schmidt had disappeared. A fair number of the yards were small enough that the old homes seemed to wall in the narrow, cobbled streets. Or huddle together, as if conspiring.

As he climbed out of the Bearcat under a sky mountainous with thunderheads, Norman saw that the Stane family home, a two-story Georgian Colonial with a roof balustrade and three small gables protruding below, was not one of the dilapidated ones. Hermit or not, the occupant must occasionally have someone cut the grass and possibly even slap on a new coat of paint. But every shutter was closed, which gave the astronomer the feeling that such cosmetic measures amounted to a mask intended to disguise a subtler form of decay.

With a scowl, he pushed trepidation away. He already knew the mansion, like the other sites on Schmidt's list, was unsafe. There was no use fretting over that. What mattered was that an ally might await him inside. He dropped the butt of his Chesterfield, crushed it under his brown Oxford, marched up to the door, and banged the knocker clasped in a brass lion's mouth.

No one answered. Perhaps, given that Jonathon Hobart Stane preferred solitude, Norman should have expected as much. He switched to knocking with his fist, then switched back when his knuckles started feeling tender. A housemaid came out onto the porch of a Victorian house across the street, peered at him, shook her head, and went back inside as though abandoning him to his folly.

"I didn't order anything," came a bass voice on the other side of the door, startling Norman even though it was exactly what he was trying to evoke with his repeated knocking.

"I'm not a delivery man," the scientist replied. "My name is Norman Withers. I'm an astronomy professor at Miskatonic, and I need to talk to you, Mr Stane."

"Find another sucker. I don't give handouts anymore."

"So I've heard. But it's not about that, either. I know about corners and the creatures that come out of them."

Stane hesitated a tick. "I don't know what you're talking about."

"I think you do. I think it was really one of the beasts that attacked you and your fiancée. You just couldn't say so for fear of being thought insane. I believe it because I survived such an encounter, too. Only I never actually saw one of the brutes. If you did, you have information I need."

"I don't care what you need."

"Please. It's urgent. So much so that I'm prepared to stand out here and knock all day if need be."

Stane barked a shrill, truncated little laugh. "You are, are you? Well, why not? The memories fester in a man's mind. It might do me good to lance the boil. Wait here."

Soft footsteps retreated and after a minute or so returned. The door swung open.

Stane was still a tall man, but above the waist, his body crooked to the left, presumably the result of his injuries. He wore slippers, pajamas, a silk dressing gown, and, over his head, a sack-like hood of dark red cloth. A blue eye gleamed behind the single hole on the right.

Norman offered his hand. Stane did not shake it.

"Come in if you're coming."

The interior of the house was every bit as gloomy as the closed shutters might have led one to expect. The air was close and stale, and every surface was dusty. Evidently Stane cared about keeping up appearances outside, but not within.

It was clear what he truly did care about. Strips of molding filled every space where wall met wall, floor, or ceiling, turning what would otherwise have been right angles into curves.

Similarly, every entry had a door, and each of those doors was shut, changing open rectangles into filled space. Stane opened one long enough to show his guest into a parlor sparsely furnished with Art Nouveau pieces made all of curves. The walls here, like those in the foyer, were devoid of picture frames.

"All of it, steps in the right direction," said Stane. Evidently, he had noticed Norman taking in the details. "None of it sufficient. No one can eliminate every right or acute angle in a big old pile like this. Still, if I make it difficult enough for the creatures to find their way through, maybe I delay the inevitable. Sit."

Norman lowered himself onto one of the chairs. Insofar as he had ever thought about furniture at all, he liked the sturdy simple forms of William Morris and the Arts and Crafts Movement, but the somewhat flimsy-looking seat proved comfortable enough.

"It seems you've been rather hard at work trying to avoid another encounter with the beasts. What can you tell me about them?"

"You first," the hooded man replied.

Given that he was the one seeking assistance, Norman supposed that was fair. He told the story of Schmidt's disappearance and of his intent to rescue him.

At the end, Stane laughed. "You can't possibly believe the German's still alive."

"Can you be certain he isn't?"

Stane hesitated. "Well, not *absolutely* certain, I suppose. But the creatures are devils. The enemies of humanity in every sense."

"You say that because you've actually seen one?"

Stane laughed another sharp, short laugh. "Well, I have, and the slightest glimpse would be enough to convince a person of their maleficence, wouldn't it? To say nothing of watching the sweet, wonderful woman you love ripped apart by one of them and then feeling its claws tear into you. But I have more than firsthand experience to draw on. I've made a study of them."

"How?" Norman asked. "They aren't merely a species unknown to science. They normally exist in a place or a condition science can't even observe."

"You only think that because you don't realize the ancients knew truths modern scientists have yet to rediscover. Einstein, and his disciples like your friend Schmidt, are just starting to walk the paths others trod before them." Stane yipped his hyena laugh. "And now you know where those paths lead."

Norman sighed. "It sounds like you're talking about mysticism."

"And you sound like you've just decided I can't possibly have anything worthwhile to tell you. Open your mind, professor. Rutherford proved the things we perceive as solid are mere ghosts, empty space with a haze of tiny particles suspended in the void. Hubble demonstrated the universe is vast beyond comprehension, with the Milky Way only one of countless galaxies. Einstein taught us time and space are one, and malleable to boot. In each case, the ancients – well, a few of the ancients – were there before them. More to the point, they recorded their observations of the particular phenomena that now concern you."

It was the final comment that gave Norman pause. Although he remained skeptical that Stane's "ancients" truly had anything to teach the twentieth century about theoretical physics or astronomy, it was not beyond the realm of possibility that some philosopher had observed something about the creatures or the opening and closing of breaches that might prove of practical use. In any case, if he needed to listen to a load of mumbo jumbo to hear what Stane himself had experienced, so be it.

"Please excuse me," Norman said. "I'm eager to learn whatever you can tell me. If my manner seemed to indicate otherwise, it's because this is all very new and strange."

Stane laughed. "You have no idea how strange. The creatures that took your friend are Hounds of Tindalos."

"Hounds?"

"Sometimes they hunt in packs like hounds. They howl like hounds. But of course they aren't really. We don't have a word for what they are. We probably aren't even capable of seeing them as they truly are. So 'Hounds' is as good a name as any."

"And 'Tindalos'?"

"That might be the name–" Stane turned his head from side to side. He seemed to be listening. Stiff with alarm, Norman did the same but heard nothing.

The hooded man relaxed. "Sorry. I jump at shadows sometimes. As I was saying, Tindalos might be the name of the place they come from. Or the god they serve. Or maybe the place and the god are somehow one and the same."

Norman grunted. "Your ancients don't appear to have been certain of much."

"Naturally not. How easy do you think it was to study something that spends most of its time removed from the world as we experience it and kills whoever's around when it does come through? Still, they discovered a few facts and built some interesting hypotheses around them. They conjectured that the Hounds' home is so far in the past that time itself takes on a different aspect. In our age, it's curved, just as Einstein proclaims. In theirs, it's angular."

Norman frowned. "I'm not sure what that would mean."

"Nor am I. Nor, quite possibly, were they. But let's suppose they were right. Your hero Einstein tells us time and space are ultimately the same thing. Then maybe right and acute angles provide trails and doorways for the Hounds to reach us here in our reality."

Norman mulled that over. "If everything you're suggesting is true, and if Schmidt's ideas are also true, a disproportionate number of those trails lead to Arkham. Do you have any idea why that would be?"

"I can only guess. Perhaps once a Hound opens a 'breach', as you call them, its pack mates can sense the path and the doorway. That makes it somewhat more likely that a second creature will eventually push through somewhere nearby. And if your luck is running bad enough that you get to the point where there's a whole spider web of entry points..." Stane shrugged his crooked shoulders.

Norman realized that, despite himself, he was starting to take these notions seriously. Perhaps, when one encountered a phenomenon utterly beyond the realm of normal human experience, one grasped at any explanation, no matter how dubious the source.

"But why do they come here?" he asked. "Can't they catch prey in their own time?"

"Perhaps not the right sort of prey." Once again, Stane stopped abruptly, then sniffed with sufficient force to indent the fabric of his hood. Norman took a wary sniff of his own without detecting any trace of the putrid vapor from the barn.

"One source claims," Stane continued, "that we humans have something special inside us that the Hounds either hunger for or lust to destroy, and so they kill us to get at it."

"And Schmidt attracted their attention by repeatedly poking around at the discontinuity points."

"Possibly. It seems like it."

Norman pondered his next question. So much remained unknown, so much that he needed to understand, that it was difficult to pursue an organized line of inquiry.

"When the bootlegger fired his pistol," he said, "it seemed to stop the Hound that was stalking him, at least momentarily. I hope that means they can be hurt."

Stane laughed. "I haven't discouraged you yet? Heaven knows, I'm trying. I think they can be *startled*. Disconcerted by fleeting twinges of pain. I doubt they can truly be crippled or killed."

"What's your basis for thinking that?"

"The pistol didn't save the bootlegger, did it? And on the night I was attacked, I'd hauled out my father's old revolver and cavalry saber from his Rough Rider days. I suppose I thought looking at them would put me in a military state of mind for the AEF," Stane laughed.

"When the Hound lunged out of the shadows and pounced on Barbara," the crooked man continued, "I grabbed the sword. By the time I turned back around, the creature was springing at me. It bore me down and savaged me, and I stabbed it as best I could. Eventually it broke off and disappeared."

"Isn't that reason to think you *did* hurt it?"

"I don't think so. It retreated too quickly. Too nimbly. It seems more likely that it had fed well enough to satisfy it and had grown tired of the repeated pinpricks."

"Well, making the creatures slow down and with luck even turn away is better than nothing, I suppose. Now tell me this. How do they open and close the holes, and is there a way for a human being to do the same?"

"They don't need to 'open and close' anything. For them, corners are always passages into our time and place. They simply have to find their way to them."

Norman waited for more. When Stane failed to offer anything further, he said, "You didn't answer the second half of my question."

"You can't *still* be thinking of trying to rescue Professor Schmidt. The man is dead!"

"You conceded we don't know that."

"Even if he were alive, you couldn't do anything for him. You'd only throw away your own life and risk stirring up the Hounds. Imagine the slaughter if they started hunting in Arkham every day instead of once every several years."

That was a ghastly thought, but Norman hoped it was also pure speculation. "The fact that you're working so hard to dissuade me makes me think there must be a way for people to go through."

"Well, there isn't. So go home and forget all this."

"If I can't open a discontinuity myself, the other option is to station myself at a breach point and wait for a Hound to notice me. Perhaps if I'm prepared…" Norman realized Stane was no longer paying attention.

Rather, the hooded man was jumping up from his seat and casting about more wildly than before. "They're here!" he screamed. "They're here!"

Norman looked around just as frantically. He saw, heard, smelled, and felt nothing that would lead him to believe the Hounds were coming.

Taking a ragged breath, his heartbeat slowing, he decided that even if some of Stane's information was accurate, the poor man's ordeal had left him with a nervous disorder from which he had never recovered. Perhaps a well-wisher could calm him down, at least temporarily. He turned to try, then froze when he saw the little revolver in the hooded man's hand. It was pointed at his torso.

Stane must have taken advantage of Norman's distraction to whisk the weapon from the pocket of his dressing gown or from under a cushion. Now he laughed and laughed at what was no doubt the stupefaction on the older man's face.

CHAPTER 13

"There's no reason for this," Norman said, his voice tremulous. "I'm not your enemy."

"Maybe not on purpose," Stane replied, "but it's clear you aren't going to leave this matter alone, and I really don't want a fool stirring things up. Who knows where it would lead?" He shifted the barrel of the revolver to indicate the door that opened on the foyer, then shifted it back. "Out, then right, then down the hall to the left."

As he approached the door, Norman wondered if he could lunge through, slam it behind him, and dash outside the house, all so quickly the hooded man wouldn't be able to shoot him in the back. To say the least, it seemed improbable, and the moment passed without him finding the boldness to make the attempt.

Instead, he said, "People know I'm here. My car is parked right outside."

"That complicates things," Stane replied, "but it's not all that difficult. I can call a man who'll drive your car away, no questions asked. And the police aren't likely to pry into the affairs of a wealthy invalid all that aggressively. Should worst come to worst, I have a firm of excellent attorneys on retainer."

"Look," Norman said, "I see now that I was on the verge of making a terrible mistake. If there's nothing a human being can do against the Hounds, then of course I should leave them alone. Just let me go, and I swear I won't say anything about this…" He groped for an inoffensive word, a word that wouldn't incite a lunatic to instant violence. "Misunderstanding."

Stane laughed. "Nice try, professor. Truly. But I'm afraid there's another side to it, too."

"What other side?"

"I'll tell you once you're through that door straight ahead."

The door in question looked like it belonged in a prison or asylum for the criminally insane, not in a mansion like this. An oversized steel deadbolt latch held it shut, and a round, barred window not much bigger than a fist provided a glimpse of the darkness waiting on the other side.

Norman opened the door. He didn't realize Stane had stepped up close behind him until the hooded man shoved him through. Norman stumbled, nearly fell, and the door slammed behind him. The latch clanged as Stane twisted it down to secure it to the strike plate.

A moment later, the light in the ceiling came on, revealing an unfurnished room with a bricked-up window. Unlike every other portion of the house Norman had seen, this room had right-angle corners unaltered by molding. Painted in dark blue and ocher pigment, geometrical designs adorned the walls with some sort of glyphs written around them.

Norman pivoted back toward the door. Stane was peering through the peephole with his good – or was it his only? – eye. Norman felt a sudden furious and quite uncharacteristic impulse to try to gouge the eye through the bars.

But even in the unlikely event that he could accomplish such a feat, it wouldn't help him. He took a ragged breath and said, "All right. Now tell me."

Stane laughed. "Back in the parlor, I didn't get around to explaining *everything* I've gleaned about the Hounds. It hasn't been easy, but the hints are there in the *Livre d'Eibon*, the *Pnakotic Manuscripts,* and even comparatively modern sources like Prinn and d'Erlette if a person knows how to interpret them. One thing I picked up and rather to my dismay–" The crooked man interrupted himself with another shrill titter of mirth. "On those rare occasions when a man escapes the Hounds, he doesn't always *stay* escaped. Sooner or later, they're apt to come after him."

On another occasion, that revelation would have chilled Norman, but now he had more immediate problems. "Don't you see? That's all the more reason for you to work with me to find ways to thwart them."

"You'd think so, wouldn't you? But I already have a strategy. Appease them. Feed a dog, and it's less likely to take a bite out of you. Or in my case, *another* bite," Stane giggled.

"You're sacrificing people."

"If you care to think of it that way. It's easier than you'd imagine. Some theatrical makeup combined with the bad light outdoors at night and I don't look too horribly ugly. And the people I approach on one pretext or another – hobos, drunks, whores, Ethels – aren't picky. I collect them out of town, and a nip from a drugged flask keeps them docile until I get them home."

"It's monstrous! How can you live with yourself?"

"Ever since that night, I've seen life differently. I *remember* loving Barbara, but I've never cared that the creature tore her apart. Better her than me. I don't care when a Hound kills one of my offerings, either. To tell the truth, I like to watch."

"So you intend to hold me prisoner until a Hound shows up?"

"Ah, that would be grounds for hope, now, wouldn't it? Under normal circumstances, it could be weeks, months, or even years before a Hound manifests in this particular space. Plenty of time for someone to come looking for you. But I'm not leaving the entity's arrival to chance. 'Mysticism' affords me the means of lighting a beacon to draw it here. It's actually rather easy for someone in my psychically aberrant condition."

With that, Stane took a step back from the door and began to recite. The sounds had sufficient differentiation and cadence to suggest actual words and sentences, but they weren't in any language Norman had ever encountered. The shrill, staccato yips and snarls were more reminiscent of a hyena than the madman's laughter.

Lightheaded and short of breath, Norman told himself that, despite all the uncanny events he'd experienced hitherto, arrant witchcraft was a step too far. Clearly, Stane was delusional, and nothing would happen in response to an incantation.

Then a pulse of blue and ocher light illuminated the door and the wall around it. Norman turned. The painted designs and symbols were glowing, brightening and fading in a rhythm like a heartbeat. They looked three-dimensional as well, but inconsistently so. One moment, they stood out from the walls, the next, they seemed farther away, like lamps shining through mist.

Stane brayed laughter at his prisoner's consternation. Norman's light-headedness whirled into outright vertigo, and his stomach churned with nausea.

He scrambled to one of the geometric figures, a tangle of

octagons pierced by isosceles triangles. It flattened back into two dimensions when he came within reach of it, and he clawed it with his fingernails. Chips of paint flaked away from the plaster beneath.

"Good thought!" called Stane. "But you can't possibly do enough damage in the time you have left."

The assurance in the hooded man's voice made Norman believe him. But what else was there to do except attempt to deface the paintings? He cast about for an alternative and found nothing. The cell was empty, the window sealed, the sturdy door secured from the other side–

Or was it? The door hung on three-barrel hinges. When it was closed as it was currently, the screws that held the hinges to the frame and door were inaccessible, but the pivots and cylinders were on his side of the barrier.

He emptied his pockets. They proved to contain his wallet and paper money, his keys, a Mercury dime, two buffalo nickels, a pencil stub, a crumpled pack of Chesterfields, and a matchbook with two matches left. Why wasn't he carrying his Barlow knife?

Too late to worry about it now. He'd have to work with the makeshift tools at his disposal. He scurried to the door and inspected the hinges.

The pivots had screw caps on top to anchor them in the cylinders. Experimenting, he found that the dime just barely fit the notch in the uppermost. He gripped the coin between thumb and forefinger and attempted to twist the cap counterclockwise. It resisted.

As he strained, a familiar sense of malevolent scrutiny stabbed through him, and he gasped. Evidently sensing it, too, Stane giggled.

But the Hound didn't burst from whatever corner it occupied.

Not yet. Perhaps, for all its ferocity, it possessed a measure of caution as well.

"What are you doing?" asked Stane. The small window didn't afford a view of a person at the edge of the door.

Norman didn't answer. He was too busy struggling with the screw. Finally, grudgingly, it yielded a hair, balked once more, and then rotated all the way out.

With it removed, he slid the pin out the bottom of the cylinder. He stuck it in his hip pocket and went to work on the middle one.

Unfortunately, the second cap was screwed down even tighter, and the groove seemed narrower and shallower, or perhaps fear was making Norman's fingers clumsier. In any case, the dime skipped repeatedly out of the notch while the fastener refused to yield.

The sense of being watched intensified. Surely the Hound would soon emerge into the sacrificial chamber.

That meant Norman had no hope of removing all three pivots in time if, in fact, it was possible at all. Terrified, frustrated, he slammed the heel of his hand against the door. With the top pin extracted, it shook a little in its frame.

"What are you doing?" Stane repeated, only now in a different tone. Gloating cruelty had given way to alarm.

Norman realized that while *he* knew he wasn't going to get all three hinges disassembled, his captor didn't. Was it conceivable that he could "double shuffle" Stane into doing something foolish?

Not if he sounded desperate. Swallowing, he resolved to imitate the cool, superior confidence with which Sherlock Holmes, A. J. Raffles, and Boston Blackie spoke to their adversaries. He'd read their exploits in his younger days, before he decided he had no time for such diversions anymore.

"I'm taking down the door," he said. "I'll have it open in a few moments." He gave it another thump.

"That's impossible," Stane replied.

"Did you hang it yourself? I suppose I shouldn't be surprised you did such a flimsy job of it. Rich boys don't have much experience with manual labor, do they?"

"You're wasting your time. The deadbolt will hold up the door."

"All by itself? Don't be ridiculous. And with the way open, I wonder whom the Hound will attack: A stranger? Or the man it mauled years ago and has been sniffing around for ever since? You told me they like to finish what they start." Norman pulled the pivot from his pocket and dropped it to clink on the floor. "That's two pins out."

Metal scraped as the barrel of Stane's revolver slid through the bars at an angle. Norman cringed, but when the gun flashed and banged, the shots missed. The window was too small and the bars too close together for the firearm to swivel far enough to the side to hit a target in his current position.

"Nice try," Norman said, dropping to one knee. Stane couldn't see him, but he might be able to tell from what height his voice was coming. "I'm going after the last pin. Here it comes." He gave the door another thump.

A putrid-smelling gray vapor, so thin it was difficult to see in the inadequate light of the ceiling fixture, washed over him. The Hound was surely coming any second now.

Stane seemingly caught the stench as well, and it spurred him to further action. "Damn you!" he screamed. The deadbolt latch clanked as he disengaged it to enter the cell and eliminate the supposed threat to the integrity of the door.

Norman stood up. When the door swung open, he waited an instant, then shoved it as hard as he could.

The door caught Stane halfway in, halfway out, and slammed him into the frame. Norman pulled the heavy door back and pounded it into the hooded man again. Then, praying he'd stunned his captor, he scrambled around the door. At his back, the Hound howled.

Stane wasn't stunned, at least not sufficiently so to keep him from aiming the revolver at Norman. A shock ran through the floor as the Hound made a first bound forward.

Norman flailed and, more by luck than any pugilistic skill, swatted the firearm out of line. He grabbed hold of Stane's robe and swung him out of the doorway and into the cell.

In the process, he caught a glimpse of a rearing serpentine shape with crocodilian jaws and a long tongue lashing beyond. But Stane's reeling, floundering body partially blocked the view, and for that he was grateful. He suspected that, had he seen it any more clearly, he might have frozen despite the urgency of the moment.

He fled through the space he'd cleared, yanked the door shut behind him, and secured the deadbolt latch. An instant later, an impact jolted the barrier so violently that, even though he'd really only removed one pin, he feared it actually would fall down. Trembling, he backed away.

More thuds followed. So did a snapping sound that was presumably gnashing jaws. So did Stane's screams.

The crooked man's face abruptly appeared behind the window. The hood was gone, revealing a left profile ridged and grooved with scar tissue and an empty eye socket in the midst of the ruined flesh. "Help me!" he wailed.

Despite what he now knew about Stane's murders, despite what the man had tried to do to him personally, at that moment, Norman *wanted* to help. But it was impossible. Even if he could muster the courage to reopen the door, doing so would only be throwing his own life away.

Neither hand nor paw but something in between, smeared with a bluish grease or slime and terminating in a bristling bundle of hooked claws, reached over Stane's head. It snagged the talons under its victim's mouth and pulled upward, tearing his face away and obliterating his remaining eye as it ripped its way along. Then the beast yanked Stane down and out of sight.

The thudding and screaming lasted a few more seconds. Then came a sucking or slurping sound. Then silence, at which point the vile-smelling vapor drifting through the round little window began to dissipate.

Ready to turn tail at the slightest new sound, the merest hint of renewed activity on the other side of the door, Norman crept forward. His judgment told him the danger was probably past. His raw nerves, however, screamed that the Hound was still there, that it was just waiting for him to come closer. Then it would find a way to seize him, the barrier notwithstanding.

He peered through the bars and could see nothing but walls, floor, ceiling, the sealed window, and the designs and sigils. The glow that had shone from the latter had all but faded away.

Unfortunately, Norman could not see the entire cell any more than Stane had been able to. He gave the door a thump from this side thinking that might provoke the Hound into revealing itself if it was still present. There was no reaction.

Probably he should let it go at that, but his very dread impelled him to make absolutely certain the creature had departed. He took a breath, slid back the deadbolt latch, and eased open the door, ready to yank it closed again at any sign of danger.

The Hound was gone. As was Stane, and, as far as Norman could see, every drop of spilled blood. Only the madman's hood remained, the scarlet cloth now smeared with bluish sludge. Two more streaks of the same jelly led to the far-left corner.

CHAPTER 14

Norman prowled through the shadowy, sparsely furnished house with its molding softening every corner and its shutters holding in its secrets. The air was as stale and dusty as before. Now that the Hound had taken its prey and gone, the only sounds were the soft ticking of a clock somewhere and the creak of floorboards under his feet.

He did not *want* to linger here but had resolved to stay in order to search for the documents Stane had mentioned. He had learned a good deal since his arrival – albeit, none of it encouraging – but he still did not know how to reach Tindalos, if that was really the name for the realm of the Hounds. Although the crooked man had claimed otherwise, perhaps his research held the answer.

To Norman's disappointment, the library on the first floor contained only mundane material, volumes by Twain, Melville, Hawthorne, and Scott, business ledgers, and the 1911 edition of the *Encyclopedia Britannica*. But when he explored the upper reaches of the mansion, he found that Stane had transformed one of the three small gabled rooms into a more idiosyncratic place for study.

More painted sigils and hieroglyphs adorned the walls, and grotesque little carvings, one a jade figurine of a seated figure with a betentacled head, reposed on the curved shelving along with an assortment of books. To Norman's surprise, some were the works of men like Plato, Aristotle, Bentham, and Kant along with commentaries hereon. Books on philosophy, with an emphasis on ethics. They pointed to a time when Jonathon Hobart Stane had pondered the question of how to live a moral life, and the depraved murderer he had become had evidently believed the musings of conventional philosophers had at least a little bearing on the esoteric matters that preoccupied him later on.

Norman closed the door. He did not want any open rectangular spaces, either, not in this house. Then, guided by Stane's references to the ancients, he scanned the shelves for especially old-looking books.

There was only one, bound in cracked and crumbling blue leather. Apparently Stane had somehow managed to consult other tomes without acquiring them for his personal collection.

Careful not to damage the book more than time had already, Norman opened it. Faded and difficult to make out against the brittle and blotchy-brown title page, woodblock printing in blue ink proclaimed this was the *Livre d'Eibon*.

Norman started looking through it and discovered a consistent patter of two printed pages followed by two blanks. For all he knew, that had some arcane significance, but he suspected it was an artifact of the archaic production process.

The book also interspersed blocks of text with diagrams and

glyphs like the ones in the cell and on the walls of this room, evidence, if more were needed, that it truly did contain information concerning the Hounds.

Near the end was a different sort of drawing. Dots radiating lines – representing stars, perhaps? – hung in a void, and a clawed, six-fingered hand reached as though to pick them like berries or perhaps simply crush them from existence.

Norman stared at the page in stupefaction. He had determined that, bizarre as it seemed, Stane's ancients truly had comprehended space-time, and the entities that prowled its hidden pathways like game trails in a jungle, in a way modern scientists did not. Was it possible they had also known something about the heavens that shed light on his own astronomical conundrum?

With an effort of will, he forced himself to stop staring. The crude picture could mean anything, and there would be time enough to investigate it further if he survived his present course of action. For now, his priority was using what he had found to go after Schmidt.

Assuming he could. The text appeared to be in French, possibly medieval French. Whatever it was, Norman could not read it.

Perhaps he could prevail on one of his colleagues at Miskatonic – maybe Professor Rice from Classical Languages – to translate. But he would not be able to convince the man that time was of the essence. He would only sound crazy if he tried.

Half a dozen identical, slim, black-bound journals sat on the shelf between the spot the *Livre d'Eibon* had occupied and a soapstone carving of a man in a pharaoh's headdress with an expression of sly mockery on his face. Norman opened the first of the books, beheld the initial words handwritten therein, and exclaimed in satisfaction.

Stane had taken notes as he made his studies – notes in English. Norman flipped through the volumes in turn.

It appeared that, as he had more or less indicated to Norman, the madman had consulted four books of esoteric wisdom: the *Livre d'Eibon*; the *Pnakotic Manuscripts*; *Cultes des Goules* by Francois-Honore Balfour, Comte d'Erlette; and *De Vermiis Mysteriis* by Ludwig Prinn. From each, Stane had gleaned something of the nature of the Hounds of Tindalos. Some of it, he had already relayed to Norman. Other bits were new, including the revelation that the creatures possessed allies: the "Dholes" – whatever they were – and satyrs.

Could the latter possibly be correct? Norman imagined the goat men from classical mythology, as depicted in ancient paintings and sculptures, and decided it was unlikely the Hounds made common cause with anything that close to being human. The term as employed here almost certainly applied to entities more alien and malign.

After a second, he surprised himself by laughing. It may have been an inappropriate response, possibly even a warning sign of an impending breakdown, but he was already in so far over his head that, at this moment, the discovery that he might have to contend with other monsters in addition to the Hounds seemed more comical than alarming.

He continued skimming. In the fifth volume was the incantation for "lighting the beacon" to call the Hounds. And in the sixth, another spell, likewise rendered phonetically, for "splitting the angle" and walking through time in the flesh.

Of course, the spell could be nonsense. Norman's understanding of science insisted it had to be. But after what he had experienced in the cell, he could only believe that somehow, in some fashion, magical conjurations sometimes did what they were alleged to, and in all likelihood, this was one of them.

If so, he supposed he should be glad that, against all odds, he had accomplished a crucial step on the way to his ultimate goal. Yet he felt cold with the knowledge that now it was actually possible to follow through on his resolve.

Part Three

TINDALOS

CHAPTER 15

Norman had never frequented Arkham's speakeasies – or "juice joints", to use Schmidt's parlance – but other faculty and students at Miskatonic had a propensity for doing so. Over time, as if by osmosis, Norman had absorbed a little information about them. Supposedly there were a couple with some pretensions to "class". The Nightingale Club in Uptown was one, and the Tick Tock Club in the Merchant District was another.

Located outside the city limits on the highway to Boston, Hibb's Roadhouse affected no such airs. Sawdust covered the floor, the walls were made of bare planks, and the place shook when a train clattered past on the tracks nearby. The air stank of beer and the sweat of the factory workers and farmers who had crowded in to do their drinking. Some of those regulars eyed Norman curiously as he made his way through the press.

He wondered why, as a phone call to Doyle Jeffries had revealed, Old Sadie Sheldon frequented Hibb's and not some fancier establishment. Maybe the bootlegger was a silent partner in the roadhouse. Or perhaps roosting here was a way of proclaiming that, born and raised on a little farm outside Dunwich, he still retained the common touch.

If it was the latter, Sheldon was only willing to put up with so much to foster that image. Despite the general crush, the bootlegger and five associates had the back of the room to themselves with the adjacent tables vacant. A big man in a sack suit intercepted Norman as he approached.

"You can drink at the bar," the hoodlum said. He waved his hand in that direction.

"Thank you," Norman replied, "but I came to speak with Mr Sheldon."

Eyes narrowing, the big man looked him over a second time. Norman got the distinct impression that people with a scholarly air about them did not seek out Old Sadie Sheldon very often. "And who are you?"

"Norman Withers. The person who told the police about the barn full of whiskey outside of town."

"Damn," the hoodlum said. "Wait here." He went to the table, talked back and forth with his boss for a moment, and then waved Norman forward.

Old Sadie Sheldon was a small man with a high forehead over dark, deep-set eyes in nests of wrinkles. He still projected a gamecock toughness despite his advancing years. He wore his steel-gray thinning hair brushed straight back and slicked down with brilliantine.

Like his subordinate, he took his time looking Norman over. At length he said, "After people interfere in my business, they mostly go out of their way to avoid me."

Norman put his hand on the back of an empty chair. "May I sit?"

Sheldon snorted. "Sure, why not?"

Norman took a seat while Sheldon continued to grin silently.

"Like I was saying, normally, if you'd found the brown and run to the cops, I'd be annoyed. Hell, maybe I am. I haven't decided yet. But I understand there was more to it. You had a friend go missing. One of my boys went missing, too, same place, same night, although from what I understand, you and the German never saw him."

"That's what my statement said," Norman answered, "but it's not true. Professor Schmidt and I did run into him."

The gangsters at the table tensed. "Then tell us what happened to him."

Norman sighed. "You wouldn't believe it so it would only get in our way. Suffice it to say, I regret that your associate is probably dead. *Not* by Professor Schmidt's hand or mine, I assure you. But if he's alive and I can restore him to you, I will."

"What is this shit?" Sheldon snarled. "What are you beating your gums about?"

"I know it's frustrating. This is difficult to discuss, and I'm handling it awkwardly. I apologize."

"To hell with *you apologize!* Do you think that because we're meeting in a public place, you can play games with me? I can come pay you a visit anytime I want!"

Norman waved his hand. "Obviously. But there's no reason it should come to that if we conduct ourselves like reasonable men."

Sheldon glared for another moment, and then his gaze softened. "You're not even a little bit afraid of me, are you?" he asked.

With a twinge of surprise, Norman realized it was so.

He had no illusions that he had transformed into a courageous man. The terror he had felt in the presence of the Hounds and the recurring stabs of dread that afflicted him afterward sufficed to disabuse him of any such notion. Yet his recent experiences had transposed fear up an octave into the register of the otherworldly. Ordinary human beings, even hardened criminals, were no longer striking the proper notes.

"I'm not," he said. "Sorry."

Sheldon laughed. "What *are* you doing here if not to tell me what happened to Frankie – my fella standing guard?"

"I need some things. Perhaps I could buy them myself, but not without people who already have their suspicions about me wondering why. I imagine a man in your position could obtain them discreetly." He extracted a piece of notepaper from his breast pocket and handed it over.

Sheldon's eyes widened as he read the list. "Hell, professor, haven't you heard? The war's over. They signed the Armistice back in '18."

"I still need them. I'll never tell anyone where I got them. And, of course, I expect to pay for them." Norman removed an envelope from his jacket's inner pocket and handed it across the table.

Sheldon rifled through the bills. "Teaching college must pay pretty good."

"After my wife – my ex-wife – remarried, I didn't owe alimony anymore, and I worked such long hours that I didn't have the chance to spend much money. My pay just accumulated in the bank. It's all yours if you help me."

Frowning, his eyes narrowed, Sheldon pondered through three sips of whiskey. Then he said, "I probably shouldn't. But scratch is scratch, and I'm curious to see if you'll show up in the *Advertiser* doing something crazy."

"With luck, the *Advertiser* will never find out about it. I do have one condition before we make a deal."

"Oh, yeah? What's that?"

"Someone will need to show me how to use the items." Norman smiled. "I am just a college teacher, after all."

CHAPTER 16

The Prohibition Agents had smashed all the whiskey crates and the bottles within, filling the old barn with the lingering smell of whiskey. After that, they had had no reason to remain. No one challenged Norman when he entered, set his fused bundle of dynamite in the corner where Schmidt had vanished, and then stood facing the juncture of the two walls with Stane's copied incantation in hand. He assumed that if any pathway would take him to the physicist, it was the one that ran from here.

He felt ridiculous with the M1921 Thompson submachine gun and its ammunition, like a little boy playing soldier. Or an aging pack mule weighted down with too much baggage. Yet in a way, the absurdity was welcome. It provided a distraction from the fear.

He had twice survived the Hounds' attentions by running away. It was surreal that he, a mild-mannered academic his whole life through, now proposed to venture *toward* them. Indeed, to invade their home territory.

Certainly, he had little faith that his new weapon would actually enable him to survive. Stane had said it likely would not. Still, if it could improve his chances even marginally, it was worth having.

Of course, that was assuming the Hounds even got the chance to accost him. For all he knew, he was about to step into a place without oxygen, or where blazing heat or unbearable cold would destroy him in an instant. Stane's notes claimed that the same incantation that opened the way protected a traveler from adverse conditions, but Norman wondered how far he could trust that given that the madman had surely never made the journey himself. Stane had done his homicidal best to stay clear of the Hounds except under the safest conditions he could devise.

All in all, Norman would be taking a colossal risk when it did seem all but certain Schmidt was dead. Yet despite all the factors that might have deterred a wiser man, he realized he was going through with it.

He owed it to Schmidt to attempt a rescue so long as there was even the slimmest hope, and the scientist in him wanted to see what lay beyond the human world, even if that meant plunging into horror. To deny those instincts would diminish him, possibly shrivel him back into something he no longer cared to be.

Or maybe it was simply that decisions and events generated momentum, and now that he had come this far, turning back would be the greatest absurdity of all. Whatever his motives, he supposed he should stop pondering them and get on with the task at hand before his nerve failed him.

Norman started reading from the paper. He had rehearsed by practicing this a sentence at a time, out of sequence, to minimize the chances of botching the recitation or casting the spell prematurely. Stane's notes suggested that could be dangerous, although he was vague about the specific consequences.

The yipping, rasping words strained his throat, but as best he could judge, they came out properly, and as he declaimed the final sentence, the world changed. Although the corner he was facing looked no different, it *felt* not just open but profoundly so. As if a door had swung open on a vast desert or a gulf as deep and broad as the Grand Canyon.

The sensation made the hairs on the back of his neck stand on end, but at least he did not feel the attention of a Hound lurking beyond the threshold. He took a breath, walked gingerly forward, and this time penetrated the point where two walls came together with a light sensation like the strands of a bead curtain brushing over his body.

CHAPTER 17

Beyond the corner, twilight waited. Taking a first look around, Norman found himself on a white path that zigzagged forward over gray emptiness without any form of visible support. The way was ten feet wide and broad enough that someone who kept to the center need not fear falling over the side. Even so, the drop-off into what appeared to be infinite depths made him feel dizzy and sick.

He took a breath and then a small experimental step that felt no different than walking on a sidewalk. Turning, he discovered that he stood on the end of the path and that the very end was shaped like a right-angle notch. He reached beyond it and felt the bead-curtain sensation on his fingers. They disappeared, presumably back into the barn, and reappeared when he retracted his arm.

So, everything was all right so far. Either because somehow there was naturally air here, or through the intercession of the spell he had cast, he could breathe. The temperature was cool but not cold. There was light to see by. Gravity and friction made ambulation possible even though he could discern no planetary body beneath him. The path looked smooth as glass, and the way back to the human world was open.

All in all, conditions were as favorable as he had any right to expect. Still, he needed three more deep steadying breaths before he could impel himself farther down the path.

As he neared the first jag, the vast space around him stirred and seethed. Sure the Hounds or their allies were converging on him, he let out a choked little cry.

But no creatures had noticed the intruder and roused themselves to destroy him. Not yet. Rather, by advancing deeper into the void, Norman had somehow brought his environs into clearer focus. His was only one of countless paths, the others suspended above, below, and to either side of him, receding until they faded into the gloom. Some were angular, and some curved. Here and there, one met another. Where they ran on the same level, they crossed via a simple intersection. Where they existed at differing elevations, ramps slanted and spirals coiled.

Once he recovered from the misapprehension that the Hounds had discovered him, Norman still found the spectacle before him, if not terrifying, at least disconcerting. A moment ago, it had appeared he was on a road that, however dangerous, ran straight to his destination. Now it seemed he needed to pick his way through a labyrinth.

As if in response to his dismay, a hitherto unsuspected faculty, surely another product of Stane's magic, opened inside him. He *felt* he was heading in the right direction. In the same way, perhaps, that a flower sensed the sun. When he thought of the barn, the sensation flipped to point back the way he had come.

The faculty guided him through two choice points. Then, sharpening into something akin to clairvoyance, it began providing glimpses of what lay at the ends of the paths he was passing by.

One led to a darkened dormitory in what might have been a Dickensian workhouse, where gaunt, pale women slept motionless as corpses in their cots. Another to a room with paper walls where an Asian man was cutting open his own abdomen with a short sword. A third, to a sidewalk where a mother and child stared up at some sort of airship about to crash into one of two prodigious towers.

If all was going as intended, Norman's route was taking him from the present into a past remote beyond imagining, but the branching trails led to sites and moments in both the past and future, essentially randomly. The one constant was that the termini were rooms, streets, constructed places, because, far more than nature, they provided the clearly defined angles required for breaches. It was strange to reflect that if humans had never invented their arts and sciences, they would have lived lives that were, to borrow Hobbes's phrase, "nasty, brutish, and short", but they might largely have avoided the predations of the Hounds.

The next side trail zigzagged through emptiness to a room where several brown, beetle-like creatures, each standing on its hind legs and with tools hanging in metal loops riveted to their carapaces, were working to construct or repair some type of machine. As one, they turned in Norman's direction. Their split black eyes stared, and their antennae quivered.

Dear Lord, could they sense him in the same manner he'd sensed the scrutiny of the Hounds? He hurried onward.

No beetle-thing entered the maze to pursue him, but the incident nonetheless served to remind him he was in danger with every step he took. He needed to stop sightseeing down the intersecting paths and stay focused and vigilant.

He adhered to that resolve and several minutes later – if

"minutes" was a word that meant anything here – approached an intersection different than any he had traversed hitherto. Before him, his zigzagging path crossed a curved trail coiling up from below. At the spot where they met, a red circle eclipsed the whiteness of the walkways.

As far as Norman knew, there was no inherent reason why a point where angular and curved time intersected should pose a problem, but on the other hand, any new feature of the maze could prove hazardous. He prowled forward even more warily than before.

Nothing appeared to threaten him. He sighed, slumped, and in that moment of relative relaxation, something gleamed at the periphery of his vision. Reflexively, he turned toward the light.

At the end of the curved trail, a Stutz Bearcat sped down a highway between wooded green hills on a sunlit day. Norman's vantage point put him in the car, perched behind the two seats and affording him a close-up view of himself and Bernadine, both joking and laughing, her hair golden with the dye that covered the gray. He caught a whiff of the orange-blossom smell of the Caron Narcisse Noir perfume that was her favorite scent.

Dear Lord, he missed her! He had forgotten how much until recent events had unearthed buried feelings.

It came to him then that his life need not be the lonely thing it had dwindled into. The remedy was mere paces away. If he entered his own past and contrived to keep his younger self away from a telescope on the night of March 11, 1916, that Norman would never see the six stars vanish, and from that point forward, everything would be different.

Except, not *everything*. In due course, Schmidt would still come to conduct research in Arkham.

Only this time, he would have no companion trying to reach him after a Hound dragged him away.

Besides, much as Norman regretted the disintegration of his marriage, he still could not bear to deny himself the sight of the most extraordinary astronomical phenomenon he had ever witnessed. There were many things he would change if he could, but not that.

With a grunt, he thrust temptation away, and when he did, the sheer statistical improbability of what he had just experienced struck him. If the paths snaked everywhere throughout space-time, what were the odds of stumbling across one that ran to a moment in his own little life?

Steeling himself, he took another look and discovered the scene had changed completely. Now two groups of savages were fighting, or rather, they had been. The ones who resembled the men of Norman's time had gained the upper hand while the short-legged ones with the low, sloping brows were trying to flee. Unfortunately for the Neanderthals, though, victory did not incline the Cro-Magnons to mercy. They chased down their enemies and stabbed them from behind with flint-tipped spears.

Norman suspected that in reality the path had always led to the prehistoric slaughter. Something had tampered with his perception to distract him while it sneaked up on him. With a gasp, he spun around.

The creature stalked on cloven hooves and shaggy legs that bent backward like a goat's hind limbs. From the navel up, it was somewhat less hairy and more manlike, albeit with pointed ears and horns stabbing upward from its brow.

Yet as Norman had feared, it was far different from the satyrs of classical myth. It was nine feet tall, and the non-caprine parts exhibited a burliness more suggestive of an ape than a human being. Scarlet from top to bottom and giving off a butcher-shop stench, it sweat blood, slavered blood, and someone – itself, in some ghastly ritual? – had hammered iron spikes into its eye sockets.

Baring crooked fangs, it roared and lunged.

Norman recoiled, and his foot plunged through empty space. Screaming, arms windmilling, he toppled into the bottomless void.

CHAPTER 18

Norman just had time to wonder if, in a realm that existed outside time as human beings normally experienced it, he might live and fall forever. Then he slammed down on his back.

The impact jolted the wind out of him and made him fear he'd injured himself, but when he tried to roll over, he could. He'd landed on a section of the curving path that twisted underneath the intersection.

The satyr peered down from the crossing above, then turned away and disappeared. No doubt it would reappear momentarily when it started down the curved path in pursuit.

Norman's impulse was to flee in the opposite direction. He turned and found that the path he was on only extended several more feet before ending in a convex curve. On the other side waited a white sand beach with blue waves breaking beyond. The directional instinct magic that the incantation had bestowed was like an insistent tap on the shoulder, warning him that the vista before him lay in the wrong direction.

At the moment, however, it might provide a safe haven. Evidently haunters of the curved portions of the maze in the same way the Hounds roamed the angular pathways, the satyrs might be similarly capable of exiting its confines. But Norman's experiences suggested the creatures of Tindalos never ventured far from the breaches, and it seemed a reasonable hypothesis that the horned men didn't either. If so, a dash down the sunlit strand might take him out of danger. If not, perhaps he could hide in the tropical forest that lay inland.

He poised himself to run and then remembered that Stane's magic enabled a mystic to "split the *angle*." What if he ended up in some island wilderness where no one had ever built anything? A place without corners.

Given time, maybe he could create something suitable, but even if so, who was to say a second spell would enable him to navigate his way back to the barn and Arkham? It might only be capable of leading him back to the place from which he embarked. To put it mildly, he didn't understand the sorcery well enough to know one way or the other.

He needed some other way to stay ahead of the satyr. He stepped to the edge of the trail in hopes of spotting another path within jumping distance, preferably an angular one where his pursuer might be unable to follow, but there was nothing but gray void directly below for as far as the eye could see.

The action, however, made the object slung over his shoulder swing and bump against his body, and it was then he recalled he was armed. It angered him that he hadn't remembered sooner, although really it had only been a matter of seconds since the satyr startled him into blundering off the edge of the crossing overhead.

He fumbled the Thompson submachine gun into his trembling hands. At the same instant, the satyr bounded into view and seemed to recognize the threat of the firearm despite the spikes that had put out its eyes. Spraying a mist of bloody spittle, it roared and ran down the curving path.

Norman recalled all that Old Sadie Sheldon himself had taught him about the "trench broom's" Blish lock, "open-bolt" firing position, and what have you. Still, his hands felt clumsy as he sought to cock and point it, as though in a nightmare where a seemingly simple task proved impossible to complete.

At last he was ready to depress the trigger. The gun roared and rattled and, despite the practice he'd put in, the muzzle climbed higher with each round that blazed out of it until he was all but shooting straight up. Unharmed, the satyr charged closer.

Terror screamed for Norman to lower the gun and keep blasting away. Intellect, however, insisted that a shaky novice shooter like himself was unlikely to hit his attacker until it came closer. He forced himself to release the trigger, take a breath, and aim anew.

He resumed firing when the satyr was twenty feet away. This time he did a better job of keeping the submachine gun pointed, and the creature staggered as the rounds slammed into it.

It staggered but wouldn't go down. It kept springing forward, apish hands outstretched to seize its prey.

Norman recalled the breach waiting at his back. Still, hoping he wouldn't take a step too far, he backpedaled as he fired.

The satyr was within three bounds of him. Then two. The trench broom stopped discharging, the fifty-round drum depleted.

An instant later, the satyr's hand fell on his shoulder. Fortunately, it then slipped off, leaving a gory streak down his jacket as the creature collapsed.

His heart pounding, Norman gasped for breath. It seemed incredible he'd survived and perhaps even more so that he'd accomplished it by shooting a firearm and killing something monstrous. He hadn't been in so much as a barehanded scuffle since childhood.

Arguably, his victory was cause for optimism. He had just demonstrated he could at least fight the Hounds' allies and prevail if it proved necessary.

But he couldn't find it in himself to celebrate, not when the Hounds themselves were essentially impervious to human weapons, and not when he'd expended an entire magazine's worth of ammunition – half his supply – killing a single satyr. It seemed all too likely he'd run out of cartridges before the labyrinth and the place beyond ran out of horrors.

Still, he'd vowed to go forward, and he would. He loaded fresh ammunition in the drum, reminded himself that if he didn't hold the trigger down, the tommy gun would fire in semiautomatic mode, not expend every last round in a matter of seconds, and he climbed back up toward the scarlet circle and the crossing of curved and angular time.

CHAPTER 19

As Norman hiked onward, zigzag trails became more frequent, while the curved ones became less so. At one point, he spied a reptilian form scuttling on a path far to the left and just a hair lower than his own. Although he could now discern that it possessed shorter hind limbs and a dragging tail in addition to the arms he'd observed through the window of Stane's sacrificial chamber, the long neck curling up from the body still made it seem snakelike as much as lizard-like or anthropoid.

The Hound turned, revealing it sensed him as well. He gasped, clutched at the trench sweeper, and had to insist to himself, *Not yet!* The creature was still so distant that he could barely make it out in the ambient gloom.

Perhaps the distance spared him a second skirmish. Maybe the creature mistook him for some ally with the right to travel the maze. Or conceivably, the lack of nearby connecting paths persuaded it to leave his destruction to its fellows. At any rate, after a moment, it continued on its way, and, exhaling, so did he.

Several minutes later, at least according to his faltering sense of the passage of time, he reached a point where angular paths continued to divide and proliferate but none of the curved ones remained for as far as he could see. Instead of merely indicating, his mystical sense of direction now all but tugged him forward like an eager dog on a leash.

Yet other sensations pierced him to offset the feeling of impending arrival. Had he thought about it, he would have said that, except perhaps for interplanetary space, a gulf could scarcely seem more of a void than the emptiness through which he crept. With every step, however, although nothing *looked* different, the feeling of infinite depths intensified. It occurred to him that, whereas before he had been moving through four dimensions, the three conventional ones plus time, now, somehow, he was traversing more than four.

With that realization came a feeling of warning or forbiddance. It seemed a sign he was encroaching on a place that, even more than the labyrinth, was hostile to human existence. Had he been a religious person, he might have taken it for the whisper of a guardian angel imploring him to turn back.

Whatever it was, he declined to heed it, and gradually Tindalos took form in the murk ahead.

CHAPTER 20

The Hounds' native realm wasn't like Earth, with its gates into otherness hidden. When Norman looked back, the void and the jagged path he'd just walked were still there in place of the ground and sky the mind expected. The sight of two different realities jammed against one another was enough to make a sane man flinch.

Norman resolved not to look again until he had to. He stared instead at what lay before him.

It was night here. Perhaps it always was. There were no stars visible, so why should there be a sun? A celestial object like a broken moon infested with phosphorescent fungus cast a sickly green light that gleamed on the pyramids and trapezoidal prisms in the distance.

With Norman's departure from the maze, his unnatural sense of direction had dimmed as though it felt it had done the hard work and he should be able to manage the rest himself. Perhaps that meant Schmidt was somewhere in the cluster of buildings, if that was what they were. Hoping it was so, and that the guiding instinct would wake when he needed it once more, the astronomer skulked forward over cracked, barren soil.

Somewhere off to the right, a Hound howled. Norman froze and clutched the tommy gun for a long moment before deciding the cry had come from far away and, more likely than not, had nothing to do with him. Because, so far as he could tell, the call had elicited no reaction from any creature lurking among the angular shapes ahead.

Norman had now crept close enough to make out doorways and windows, confirmation of his initial impression that the masses were buildings, but as yet, he could see neither lights nor motion within. Nor was there anything to hear but the intermittent whisper of the breeze.

Perhaps, for the moment, every Hound was elsewhere. Conceivably they spent most of their time in the labyrinth searching for prey. Dry-mouthed and heart pounding, he made his final approach as stealthily as he could.

Viewed up close, the buildings appeared to be made of charcoal-colored stone polished to a glassy sheen at the edges. To all appearances, the Hounds had carved each from a single huge rock. It was even possible the entire complex was one colossal stone, the seemingly separate pyramids and trapezoidal prisms aboveground extrusions from an even larger mass buried below.

The entryways lacked doors to seal them. The windows were similarly empty, asymmetrical holes without glass, the ones on the ground floors positioned lower than in a human habitation. Norman couldn't have passed beneath them without crawling on hands and knees, so he settled for striding by quickly.

The fetor of the Hounds wafted from doorways and windows alike, a warning that, even if the complex seemed deserted, the creatures might appear at any moment. Norman swallowed repeatedly and bore the stench as best he could. The half-hysterical thought came to him that if he died here, he didn't want to do it with vomit in his beard.

He peered around another corner. Soft blue light shined through the doorway and windows of a smallish pyramid a few yards ahead.

Perhaps Schmidt was inside. If not, maybe Norman was about to get his first really good look at a Hound, a prospect that inspired curiosity and trepidation in equal measure. He skulked forward and peeked in the entrance.

He hadn't found the physicist. He had discovered a Hound, but despite the light, proximity, and the unobstructed view, he still couldn't make out how such creatures looked when intact because the one before him was deep into the process of vivisecting itself.

It lay on the floor in a pool of dark fluids, its wormlike body split lengthwise with the flaps of flesh folded back. Employing its elongated arms, each possessed of two elbows, and the claws at the end of those limbs, it had mostly emptied itself of the organs within and set them around it, and, showing no sign of weakness due to the self-inflicted damage, was busy tearing out the pulsing, twitching tubes and ovoid masses that remained. Its hind legs and tail thumped the floor as the viscera came free.

A long tongue protruded beyond the jagged fangs. Periodically, it writhed toward one of the detached organs and stabbed its pointed tip into it. The proboscis then swelled rhythmically as the musculature inside it worked and matter flowed down what must be a hollow channel at its core. Meanwhile, the punctured organ deflated like a balloon.

Sickened yet fascinated, Norman wondered if he was watching

a Hound commit suicide. If Stane had been correct about their regenerative capabilities, quite possibly not. Perhaps the thing could put itself back together or grow new organs to replace the discarded ones.

But if that was the case, what was the purpose of the seeming self-destruction? Was the Hound undertaking a natural part of its life cycle analogous to molting? Performing a ritual of atonement? Doing something that gave it pleasure? In all likelihood, Norman would never know.

The only thing that was clear was that here was additional reason to believe earthly weapons were unlikely to do a Hound any lasting harm. Grateful that the one Hound he'd thus far seen in the complex appeared incapable of harming him – at least until it regenerated or reassembled itself – Norman prowled onward and after another turn discovered Schmidt.

The German lay in the middle of an open space suggestive of a plaza or park with half a dozen stone buildings looming around it. Soil covered all of him except the head in a way that reminded Norman of his daughter burying him in sand at the beach. Schmidt wasn't moving, and in the gloom, his would-be rescuer couldn't tell if he was alive or dead.

Norman hurried toward him. "Schmidt!" he called, keeping his voice low.

To his relief, the physicist rolled his head. He seemed dazed, but that was preferable to deceased.

Norman quickened his stride. "It's me," he said. "I'm going to take you home."

Schmidt's eyes focused, and the slackness in his face gave way to alarm. "No!" he croaked. "Get back!"

An instant later, Norman heard a sibilant, susurrate sound rising from the ground. He looked down. Long, humped ridges in the earth were slithering away from Schmidt and toward him.

They appeared to be burrows with some sort of creature inside. But when one flowed over the toe of his right shoe, he discerned there was nothing there but soil given life or at least the semblance thereof by some unimaginable process. Once it had his foot looped, it hardened.

CHAPTER 21

Norman gasped, kicked, and broke the dirt-thing into pieces before it could finish altering its consistency to grip him like concrete. But already, others were trying to coil around his ankles and crawl up his legs. Half-tripping with every step, he made a frantic, floundering retreat while resisting the urge to fire the submachine gun at his attackers. He'd likely riddle his own feet if he tried.

He hoped that if he retreated far enough, the dirt-things would break off the pursuit. But there was no sign of it. With every staggering moment that passed, they seemed ever closer to bringing him down. Then they'd surely immobilize him as they had Schmidt. Or simply crush and smother him to death.

He made for a lightless pyramidal building and lunged through the trapezoidal doorway. He swept the Thompson gun from left to right as he looked for new menaces stirring in the gloom.

Nothing. Panting, he turned around.

For the next few seconds, the dirt-things crawled and coiled beyond the threshold that divided ground from stone floor. Eventually they balked and slithered back in Schmidt's direction.

Norman didn't want to step back out of the pyramid. For all he knew, some of the dirt-things had remained to ambush him. He had no way of telling what might be hiding under the surface. But he couldn't help Schmidt from where he was.

He slowly set one foot on the ground. Nothing struck at it. He kept tiptoeing forward until he was close enough to Schmidt for them to converse in low tones. Fortunately, that appeared to leave him outside the circle in which the dirt-things were lurking.

"I never dreamed it was possible for anyone to find me."

"It took some doing."

"Thank you. But you have to go back if you can. There's nothing you can do for me."

As far as Norman had been able to observe, the dirt-things had no eyes, ears, or noses. It seemed plausible they sensed intruders through vibrations in the ground, and he proposed to give them something to orient on besides his own footfalls. He readied the trench broom and, reminding himself again not to squander ammunition, fired three shots into the earth on the far side of the captive.

A horde of dirt-things writhed away to investigate. Norman ran forward. "Dig your way out!"

He hoped the younger man still had the strength to accomplish something in that regard, but Schmidt merely squirmed to no effect. Norman bent over him to tear at the soil cocoon with his hands.

The dirt bulged into elongated humps, revealing itself to be made of additional creatures. Some crawled over Norman's feet, and many of those he'd diverted with the gunshots were already turning around. He saw no choice but to make a second hasty retreat before he could be snared.

When Norman emerged from the pyramid once more, Schmidt said, "The gun made too much noise! You have to run!"

The sensible part of Norman was in full agreement. As it had before, it assured him he'd already attempted more than any rational person could expect, and no one could blame him if he now gave up.

He pushed that part down and once again did his poor best to imitate Holmes, Raffles, and Boston Blackie. "Don't worry about it," he said. "I have this figured out now." He fired more shots into the ground on the far side of Schmidt. The jolts sent a horde of dirt-things crawling away as they had before.

That still left the ones that had remained with Schmidt, but this time Norman was ready for them. As soon as he reached the German, he fired the submachine gun into the ground, down one side of his body, then the other. Or anyway, he hoped he was missing the physicist's body. It looked like the cocoon pressed Schmidt's arms up against his flanks, but it was impossible to be certain.

The humps of dirt atop and around Schmidt heaved and broke apart. The physicist struggled again to drag himself out of the now-lifeless earth and made a little headway. Norman worked his hands into the soil, managed to grip the younger man under the arms, and pulled until his kicking feet emerged.

Norman glanced around. The rest of the dirt-things had already turned and were crawling back in his and Schmidt's direction.

"Run!" the older man cried. He bolted for the doorway of the stone house that had sheltered him before. Schmidt ran after him.

Norman didn't look around again until he and the German crossed the threshold, and then he saw the ground immediately outside bulging and sliding. By the end of the chase, pursuit had been mere inches behind.

He took a long breath and told himself that it didn't matter by how narrow a margin he and Schmidt had won the race, only that they had. "Are you all right?"

"Thirsty," Schmidt rasped.

In addition to his more destructive military equipment, Norman had brought a canteen. He unscrewed the cap and offered it to the man on the ground. "Go easy at first."

Schmidt took a couple sips, then tilted his head back and drank more deeply.

"The bootlegger from the barn," Norman said. "Do you know what became of him?"

"The things killed him," Schmidt answered, "then threw the body off the white path into the void."

Norman felt a guilty surge of relief that he needn't attempt to rescue the gangster as well. He scrutinized the patch of earth immediately outside the doorway. The swelling and stirring had subsided. "Then let's go."

Schmidt peered. "Are you certain the things are gone?"

"They didn't linger long before. Once they lost the scent, they crawled back to where their masters stationed them. Anyway, you were right. *We* can't linger here, either. We have to get away."

"Very well, then."

Despite the reassurances he'd just given, it took an effort of will for Norman to shift a foot from the safety of the stone floor to the soil beyond. He held his breath until it was clear that nothing was going to grab him.

He and Schmidt turned in the direction of the maze. At a distance, in the darkness, the boundary where one world met another was invisible, but Norman felt a vacancy even more profound than the starless sky behind and above him.

To his relief, he likewise felt his directional instinct bestirring itself now that he was ready to make the return journey and, although Schmidt had started out hobbling, his stride was growing brisker. The possibility of escape was emerging in him despite whatever torments and privations he'd suffered.

That possibility still seemed the slimmest of hopes. But the two scientists made it out of the complex without any new creatures accosting them.

Was there any chance at all that the noise of the gunfire had failed to rouse the Hounds? After all, they weren't human. They might not even be animals in the truest sense of the term. Perhaps their senses and minds worked in such an alien fashion that the commotion failed to register as cause for action.

It was an encouraging notion while it lasted. Then, however, in the low hills off to the right where Norman had heard the sound before, a Hound howled. An instant later, others answered. An intimation of onrushing malice, like a tidal wave hurtling toward shore, proclaimed that the things were coming.

CHAPTER 22

"Run!" Norman cried. He suited his actions to his words only to realize moments later that he was outdistancing his companion. His grit and determination notwithstanding, in the wake of his ordeal, Schmidt couldn't keep up.

At least he was running. Norman slowed down to allow the German to catch up and then took care not to leave him behind once more.

Gradually, the gloom ahead turned from black to gray. Like the edge of a sheer cliff, the division between realities appeared and, looking dainty as white threads in the distance, pathways zigzagged out into the void.

"Over there!" Schmidt gasped.

Norman pivoted. One Hound was out in the lead of the pack that Norman could sense charging in its wake. A murkier shadow amid the gloom, it covered ground in bounds that put the satyr he'd encountered to shame.

The fugitives had scant hope of reaching their entry into the labyrinth before the Hound cut them off. Making a little whimpering sound he was helpless to suppress, Norman readied the submachine gun. *Wait until it gets close,* he reminded himself. *Then fire.*

He delayed as long as terror would allow, then began squeezing the trigger. Was he hitting the Hound as it bounded nearer and nearer? He couldn't tell. He certainly wasn't slowing it down.

Perhaps, Norman thought, the only hope was to switch the tommy gun to automatic fire, conserving ammunition be damned. How else was he to inflict enough damage to have *any* hope of keeping the Hound away? He held the trigger down.

The Hound made another leap. Then another. But at the end of the second, it *didn't* immediately spring again. It hesitated a moment, then whirled and scuttled behind a hump in the ground that provided it with cover.

"You hurt it!" Schmidt cried. "You hurt *der Sohn von einem Weibchen!*"

"I doubt I hurt it badly," Norman replied. "It just doesn't feel like taking all the punishment itself when it can just as easily wait for the rest of the pack to catch up. We have to keep moving!"

They ran on.

CHAPTER 23

Norman and Schmidt reached the start of the white path ahead of their pursuers but with a chorus of howls ululating at their backs. The calls fell silent as the two men scurried out into the hyper-dimensional chasm that sundered Tindalos from the beginning of curved time.

"Did they give up?" Schmidt panted.

"I doubt it," Norman said. "It's just that we've entered a different aspect of space-time. We'll hear them again when they've crossed the threshold, too."

"Of course," the German said. "I should have inferred as much." He smiled a grim little smile. "I'm not at my best."

"That's understandable." Norman took a drink from his canteen and then gave it to Schmidt.

Schmidt drank and returned the bottle. "How much ammunition do you have left?"

"Only a few rounds, I'm sure. Our one chance is to stay ahead of the pack."

They hurried onward as fast as Schmidt's condition would allow. The physicist was plainly doing the best he could but flagging nonetheless. The reserve of energy he'd tapped when Norman freed him was running low.

Norman felt disgusted with his lack of forethought. He had embarked on this enterprise carrying a submachine gun of all things, yet he had neglected something as basic as food. It was a ghastly joke that he and Schmidt might meet their ends for want of an apple or a Hershey bar.

Still, they reached the portion of the labyrinth where the psychic pressure of infinite depths multiplied beyond the limits of perception abated and curving trails began. Then, however, the howling of the pack rang out behind them. Worse, other Hounds answered the baying from reaches of the labyrinth that still lay ahead.

Schmidt's shoulders slumped. "Perhaps, my friend, if you go on without me—"

"Stop it!" Norman snapped. "We're scientists! We can think our way out of this!" He strained to make good on that declaration. "The Hounds that are after us may or may not recognize me, but they surely have a sense of who you are and where they caught you. If we take the same route back to the barn, they're bound to overtake us. If we make a detour, perhaps we'll throw them off the scent."

Schmidt frowned. "Won't we get lost? Even if we don't, if we take an indirect route, won't the creatures cut us off?"

"There's a great deal I haven't had a chance to tell you. At the moment, I have a sort of compass in my head pointing the way home. As for the rest, do we really know how distance, time, and geometry work in this place? Or how the Hounds think?"

The German grunted. "We do not. Lead on, then."

As Norman took a branching path that snaked to the left

and downward, he hoped his homing instinct would prove as accommodating as he'd suggested it would. In truth, he had no way of predicting the capabilities and limitations of the magic, but he'd wanted to sound sure of himself to encourage his companion.

When he and Schmidt descended the "wrong" trail, the directional intuition manifested as the same tap-on-the-shoulder insistence that he reverse course. The sensation remained as the fugitives passed truncated pathways that ran to a stone chamber where men with the heads of snakes huddled over a parchment map, and another to a hilly city on a bay – San Francisco in 1851? – in flames.

Dear Lord, Norman thought, he'd lost his gamble. If he and Schmidt didn't retrace their steps, they'd never find a route back to Arkham; if they did, they were sure to run headlong into the pack. The only viable alternative was to accept exile in a place and era not their own.

He drew breath to confess as much, and then, with a swinging sensation that dizzied him for a moment, the homing instinct realigned itself. However grudgingly, it now pointed forward, not back.

Norman sighed and marched on.

CHAPTER 24

Concerned with shaking the Hounds off the trail, Norman conducted Schmidt through another wrong turn and then another. Each triggered the urging to go back and the attendant anxiety that he'd pushed the magic too hard and broken it, or that he'd blundered down a path from which it would prove impossible to reach the barn. Fortunately, on both occasions, after a minute or so, the compass needle inside his head pivoted in deference to his decisions.

The Hounds bayed from time to time, but as best he could determine there were no longer several howling from the same spot. Apparently, the pack had dispersed to seek the fugitives down various paths. Perhaps that was grounds for hope that his evasive tactic had done some good.

He needed that to be the case, for at the moment, neither Schmidt nor his aging, sedentary rescuer could muster the vigor to press on faster than a quick walk. Norman supposed that meant they could spare the breath to whisper back and forth. At least that way, even if worst came to worst, he and his fellow scientist would perish with their curiosity satisfied.

"Do you know," he asked, "why the creatures took you alive and held you captive in Tindalos?"

"'Tindalos?'"

"The name of their world. Possibly."

"Ah. Well, no, truly, I don't know why they took me prisoner. Except... you realize the brutes are in some measure telepathic?"

Norman thought of how he had sensed Hounds spying from the other sides of corners and the manner in which an element of their howling bypassed the ears to stab straight inside the head with a filthy intimacy. Presumably those phenomena were examples of one mind brushing another. "I suppose so."

"Well, after the one that captured me dragged me home, a dozen of them clustered around me and all dug into my thoughts at once. I don't know what they were looking for, or why. I wasn't able to see into *their* heads. But it wasn't pleasant. I..." Schmidt swallowed. "After I while, I wasn't myself anymore."

"I can imagine," Norman said, although he couldn't, entirely, and for that he was glad.

"After that was over, they left me alone. Buried like a dog buries a bone to dig up and eat later, I imagine." Schmidt laughed in a way that reminded Norman of Stane.

The astronomer gripped the younger man's shoulder. "Hang on. You're away from them now, and we have to be quiet so you can keep away."

Schmidt nodded. "Of course. Forgive me, and tell me how you managed to come for me. The story will keep me from dwelling on things I shouldn't think about."

Perhaps it would even though it, too, centered on the Hounds. Norman related it as he and Schmidt hurried along watching for shapes and movement ahead, behind, and on nearby paths.

Toward the end of his account, the homing instinct became a veritable pull to indicate he was nearing his destination. This time, he followed straight where it led.

The other pathways blurred and faded. After several more steps, only the one he and Schmidt were traversing remained, zigzagging up to a right-angle notch of an endpoint. He sensed the barn beyond.

Something in his manner must have communicated his elation. Schmidt asked, "Is that the way home?"

"Yes!" Norman answered. He hurried forward.

"Wait!" the physicist cried.

For a moment, Norman didn't know why Schmidt was alarmed. Then he felt what the younger man had: the malevolent scrutiny of an entity just out of view.

The Hound didn't remain that way for long. Perhaps it had lurked in hiding until its prey ventured close, but now, sweating bluish slime, eyes like black pearls staring, it sprang out of nothingness onto the trail to block the doorway back to Earth.

CHAPTER 25

Norman opened fire. The Hound snarled as the bullets struck but stalked forward anyway, as though the wounds were as inconsequential as gnat stings. After a few seconds, the tommy gun clacked empty.

Now there was no choice but to flee, or at least he imagined so for an instant. But as he turned, howling sounded at his back. The rest of the pack was closing in fast. If he and Schmidt turned tail, they'd simply run into the creatures.

Norman felt a surge of emotion. For a moment, he mistook it for a recurrence of the terror that had so often afflicted him of late. But it wasn't. Here at the end of his race, with the normal human world just yards away but out of reach nonetheless, fear had given way to anger.

Blast it, it wasn't fair that he'd dared and endured so much only to have it come to nothing! He could die, he surely would die, but he wasn't going to fail. Schmidt had to get away.

"Here's what we're going to do," Norman said. "I'll advance to meet the thing. Provoke it into focusing its attention on me. When it attacks, you dash past it and on through the breach." He just had to hope that, even though he was the one who'd cast the spell of opening, Schmidt would be able to pass through from this side without him.

"No," said Schmidt.

"Don't be quixotic. It's better that one of us lives than neither, and if that's the best we can achieve, logic indicates it should be the young genius with a bright future before him. Now do as I told you."

Norman took a deep breath and walked forward, and, seemingly in no hurry, savoring the moment, the Hound prowled toward him. Its neck curved like a question mark to counterbalance the crocodilian head stretched out far ahead of the rest of its body. Its tongue writhed through its jagged fangs, and its stench suffused the air.

"Well," said Norman, "what are you waiting for?" He raised the Thompson gun to club the creature with the butt end.

Unfortunately, he didn't get the chance. The Hound reared and backhanded him, swinging one forelimb in such a way that the claws didn't pierce or rend him. Everything shattered into confusion, and when he came to his senses, he no longer had hold of the weapon and was lying on his back with the creature crouching over him.

The long tongue writhed at him. The Hound touched the point to Norman's forehead, then poised it before his right eye, then pressed it lightly against his throat, as if playing with its now-helpless prey. Then, seemingly tiring of the game, it plunged the needle-sharp member into its prey's shoulder and began to suck his blood.

The pain was hideous. Norman thrashed and battered futilely with his fists.

Then the Hound's body hitched to the side. Schmidt was pushing on it. He hadn't fled to safety after all, merely waited until the Hound was distracted to launch an attack.

Unfortunately, the effort had accomplished nothing. The creature had only shifted position slightly, and now, slipping its proboscis out of Norman's flesh for the moment, it twisted to bring its jaws to bear.

As it turned, though, Schmidt's hand slid in the Hound's coating of slime, and his finger jabbed into one of its round little eyes. The creature flinched and faltered. Injury and the attendant pain couldn't truly stop it, but they could balk and fluster it for an instant.

"Push it again!" Norman shouted. "Fast!" He scrambled to his knees, planted his hands on the Hound's body, and shoved. With both men pushing, the beast lurched sideways off the edge of the path and toppled into the gulf.

The sudden absence of resistance made Schmidt stagger forward to the brink. As he teetered, Norman threw his arms around the younger man's legs, anchoring him until he regained his balance.

Afterward, Norman peered over the side. He half-expected to see that, as he himself had done when the satyr surprised him into a fall, the Hound had landed on a path just a few yards down and was even now rallying to hunt its prey anew. But there was nothing except gray emptiness directly below for as far as he could see.

CHAPTER 26

"Are you all right?" panted Schmidt.

Norman inspected his shoulder wound. It was deep, but it wasn't spurting. The Hound hadn't punctured an artery. "I'll survive," he said, standing up and applying pressure with his hand. "What about you?"

"I'm all right, too."

"Then let's move." As they hurried up the path, Norman added, "You should have done as I told you."

"Are you truly complaining?"

Norman smiled. "Well, maybe not as such."

With Hounds baying in the maze behind him, the two scientists stepped from the end of the path back into the barn. The whiskey-scented space was dark. Norman had been gone long enough for day to turn to night.

He felt, or imagined he felt, a slight, sourceless trembling that reminded him of being in proximity to Doyle Jeffries's printing presses. It made him hesitate for an instant, and then he decided that in all likelihood he was simply feeling his own shakiness, brought on by fear, exhaustion, and the shock of his injury. In any case, there was no time to stand and puzzle over the source of the sensation.

"Wait just a moment," he said, then stooped, groped, and found the bundle of dynamite. He lit a match and then the fuse which, once it flared to life, provided a bit of illumination. "Blow up the corner and you destroy the doorway. Or at least I hope so."

"Look," said Schmidt. He sounded ill.

Norman turned. The debris on the floor was shivering. After another second, the shaking became forceful enough for scraps of wood and pieces of broken glass to clink together.

"The Dholes," he said, feeling sick himself. He should have remembered the Hounds had one more ally and thus potentially one last trick to play.

Something immense and vermiform, distantly related to the Hounds, perhaps, exploded up from the center of the floor and, coated in sludge, swayed back and forth. All but featureless beneath its mask of muck, its head brushed and bumped the rafters as it seemingly took its bearings.

The creature would orient on one of them in another moment, and it had better be the one who had the desperate idea of how to contend with it. Norman pulled a stick of dynamite from the bundle awaiting the touch of the flame crawling up the fuse. Then, sidestepping along the wall, he shouted, "Look at me!"

The huge head swiveled, tracking him. The mouth opened wide, clearly discernible now despite the gloom and the curtain of slime dripping over it.

Norman took out the fresh matchbook he'd procured for this expedition and struck a match. He started to touch the flame to the dynamite as the Dhole's head hurtled down at him.

He flung himself aside and just avoided the enormous creature's jaws. Unfortunately, the frantic evasion blew out the match.

More quickly than anything so huge should be able to recover, the Dhole reared, oriented on him, and struck at him a second time. Once again, he barely managed to keep the thing from snatching him up in its jaws.

He faked a sidestep left and then dodged right instead. That confused the Dhole long enough for him to strike a match and set the entire matchbook burning. Surely that much fire wouldn't blow out!

The Dhole struck. He lurched out of the way and, teeth clenched against the pain of the flame searing his fingers, touched the burning matchbook to the dynamite's remaining nub of fuse. It caught, and he threw the explosive. The Dhole was huge enough and the barn sufficiently spacious that he hoped to land it where it would hurt the creature but not Schmidt or himself. With luck, its body would actually shield them from the blast.

The enormous head descended at him, and then the stick exploded. The Dhole flew into convulsions that hurled wood and glass through the air and crashed portions of its bulk against the walls.

In this confined space, the gigantic worm was scarcely less dangerous in the throes of agony than when trying to kill. Norman retraced his steps and found Schmidt scurrying along the wall to meet him. They hurried onward together.

A flying piece of crate bashed Norman on the hip. A second later, his peripheral vision revealed something huge hurtling in his direction. He recoiled, jerking Schmidt back with him and, charred and torn by the grenades, the Dhole's tail slammed into the wall and smashed a section outward.

The two scientists ducked through the hole and rushed on to the Bearcat. The roadster was halfway down the drive when the bundle of dynamite exploded and blew out the southwest corner of the barn.

Schmidt's better judgment told him to keep moving, but he found he had to see what would happen next. He pulled the brake lever and twisted around in his seat for a better look.

Quicker than he would have imagined, leaping yellow flame engulfed the barn. Perhaps the spilled liquor provided an accelerant. In any case, nothing enormous and wormlike was crawling out of the conflagration. Still shaky with adrenaline but somewhat reassured nonetheless, he drove on.

"Good," Norman said. "The hard part's done."

Schmidt peered at him. "What's the easy part?"

"Stane believed the sites on your list form a sort of pattern that makes it easy for the Hounds to find their way to Arkham. By that logic, if the pattern ceases to exist, it will spoil their road map. Well, we've already made a start, and thanks to some checking I did at the *Advertiser*, I know three of the other locations are empty houses. I have cans of gasoline in the trunk, and I intend to finish the evening with a little arson."

CHAPTER 27

When Schmidt and Norman entered the Science Department, colleagues clustered around to congratulate the physicist on being found safe and sound – give or take – and the astronomer on discovering him lost and disoriented in a patch of woods west of town.

It seemed to Norman there was something tentative about the felicitations that came his way. Probably people still thought it odd that he had ever lost track of the eminent visitor in the first place, and they might well find the whole fabricated sequence of events – the chance fall, the concussion, wandering off in confusion, and all the rest of it – peculiar.

Surely Doyle Jeffries did. The journalist knew the derelict houses that had burned were locations on the physicist's list. But in lieu of any better explanation, he had printed the two scientists' account as they'd provided it.

Norman found the approbation of his fellow faculty members, uncertain though it might be, pleasant. A part of him would have been happy to linger and savor it, but that bit was no match for the imperative that had driven him for a decade, and when the two of them could manage it politely, he shepherded Schmidt to his office.

Schmidt peered into the corners before entering. His ordeal had left him haggard and jumpy, Norman hoped not permanently so.

He, too, was prone to start at shadows and unexpected noises and bolt awake from nightmares. Yet paradoxically, when residual fear was not nagging, he felt surprisingly well. As though the hellish episode had been good for him.

He removed the books and journals from the extra chair so Schmidt could avail himself of it. Then he set a stack of notes and astronomical photographs in front of him.

"This is everything that might be relevant," Norman said. "The rest–" he waved his hand to indicate the remaining contents of the office, bookmarks, Moore Push-Pins, and all, "–amounts to false leads, all of it."

He all but held his breath as Schmidt went through the material. At length the German looked up and said, "I'm sorry. All you did for me, and in the end, I don't have anything for you."

It was disappointing, but not, Norman realized, as bitter a blow as it might once have seemed. "That's all right. I appreciate you trying."

"So, what becomes of us now, my friend? Are we safe?"

Norman shrugged. "In theory, a Hound could emerge from any corner anywhere and anytime, but under normal conditions, it's not something that happens often. If destroying the pattern threw them off our scent, we should be fine. Of course, you change your odds if you go searching for discontinuities again."

Schmidt shivered. "Not likely. Yet we made incredible discoveries. If they don't amount to an entirely new paradigm, they come close. There must be some safe way to study them." He smiled for an instant. "And to pursue such research without the scientific community deciding the researcher is hopped up."

It was good to hear the physicist slip into American slang. It seemed a promising sign for his eventual recovery. "Good luck with that."

"What about you? Will you keep chasing the mystery of the missing stars?"

"Yes." But he would try to keep obsession from isolating him as it had before. His students and colleagues deserved better of him. He deserved it of himself.

"Do you know how?"

Norman thought of the *Livre d'Eibon* and the six volumes of Stane's notes sitting in his bookcase at home. "I have an idea."

THE DEEP GATE

CHRIS A JACKSON

This story represents two of my greatest loves: the sea, and fantastical stories. For the former, I thank my father, who taught me that you could love something that occasionally tried to kill you, and the latter, my mother, who taught me that books are better than television.

CHAPTER 1
Arkham River Docks

Silas squinted through the rain-slashed pilothouse windows as he maneuvered *Sea Change* gingerly toward the Arkham quay wall. The rain-gorged Miskatonic River ran like a millrace, eddies and whirlpools wrenching the small boat about and making an otherwise simple operation tricky. With one hand on the wheel and the other on the throttle, he gunned the engine against a surge of current and eased closer to the tall pilings.

"Come on, dearie, don't fail me now..."

The slogging run up from Kingsport against the flow had taxed the small boat's engine and her captain's nerves to the limit, but the trial wasn't over yet. He had to get a bow line secured without allowing the current to push the boat downriver. A glance over his shoulder at the looming river barge docked just behind verified his worry. One mistake and the current would drag *Sea Change* right under the barge's sloped bow.

"Come on, Silas, you've done this a hundred times..." *Of course, it'd be easier if I could see a damned thing.* He leaned out the pilothouse door, squinted his one good eye against the rain, and ducked back to adjust his speed and course. Bow into the current, running just hard enough to keep from drifting backward, he steered her closer. Finally, he felt the gentle nudge of the rub rail meeting a piling. He tied off the wheel and stepped out onto the foredeck.

Rain plastered his hair flat and ran in rivulets down his bare chest, but Silas barely noticed. Born and raised on the New England shore, he'd swum in the Atlantic in late fall and early spring as a boy. This September nor'easter was certainly blowing like a banshee, but it wasn't promising snow. Besides, people weren't far off when they said he had enough hair on his chest to make a wool sweater blush in shame. He looped a dock line twice around the piling, secured it to the bow cleat, and stepped back into the pilothouse. Wiping the water from his face, Silas pulled the throttle lever all the way back and jerked the gear shift into neutral. The engine all but sighed in relief as it settled to a slow, soothing idle.

"Good girl." He patted the wheel, stepped aft down into the boat's main cabin, and bent to open a hatch in the deck.

Silas blinked through the wave of heat rising up from the thrumming engine. A veteran of both sail and steam, he considered internal combustion engines to be cantankerous beasts prone to unpredictable failure. He'd come to rely on *Sea Change*'s sturdy Knox Model-G with few reservations, but if an engine died at sea or in the turbulent flow of the Miskatonic, he couldn't simply walk to the nearest service station. Consequently, every mariner worth his salt was also a mechanic.

"Hot as a two-dollar pistol," Silas muttered. He left the hatch open to let it cool off before shutting down, happy with the boat's performance if little else. He hadn't wanted to make the trip up to

Arkham, but the opportunity to get some answers dragged at him like a sea anchor. He'd returned to New England to find someone who could tell him if his recurrent nightmares were some kind of family malady – like dropsy or ulcers often were – but there seemed to be a pall of silence hanging over everyone he talked to. Every cousin or childhood friend he asked told him they didn't know what he was talking about, or warned him not to let on that he was plagued by nightmares lest he risk getting locked up in the loony bin. A few days ago, however, he'd contacted another relative by telephone and had been encouraged.

Maybe this time I'll finally understand…

Silas strode through the small cabin and out to the aft deck, and then finished securing *Sea Change* to the quay. After decades at sea, serving aboard every manner of vessel from coal-fired steamers to Singapore junks, he knew ships like he knew the scars on his hands. In the few months he'd owned *Sea Change*, he'd come to love the little boat. She was sturdy, comfortable enough to live aboard, and equipped to serve his many needs. The familiar tasks of tending her lines and tidying up the deck settled his nerves, but as he turned back to the cabin to shut down the engine, a booming voice from the pier drew his attention from his chores.

"Silas Marsh, you old sea dog, don't you *ever* wear a shirt?"

Shielding his eye from the rain, Silas squinted up at the figure there. Swathed in slicker and sou'wester, the man's face was cast in shadow, but he recognized the voice easily enough. "Why wear somethin' that's just gonna get soaked through anyway?" He smiled up at his cousin, although the expression felt forced. *Too many sleepless nights, and too many nightmares.* "Come aboard, Martin. I've got a pot of java on the stove."

"Best offer I've had all day." Martin stepped down onto the deck with practiced ease. The man had been a stevedore, a deck hand, and a longshoreman all over New England, and had only recently settled down in Arkham. "Wicked nor'easter brewin'."

"They come earlier every year." Silas shook his cousin's hand firmly and waved him into the cabin. "Watch your step. Engine room's open."

Martin and Silas had grown up together in Innsmouth, but that seemed a lifetime ago. Silas left that dismal place for a life at sea when he was but a boy, so Martin undoubtedly knew the oddities of the Marsh family better than he. News of Silas's parents passing two years ago, and now these recurring dreams, had called him inexorably back here. Martin would surely know if Silas's incessant nightmares and the constant yearning he felt to be at sea were some kind of family madness or just guilt for abandoning his parents.

Martin stepped inside, shook out his slicker, and doffed his hat, which he hung on a peg in the wet locker. "Ah, the warm's a welcome, ain't it?"

"If you say so." Silas preferred a cool breeze on the open sea. He waved a hand to the tiny chart table and two bench seats. Atop the adjacent potbelly Franklin stove, a coffee pot secured by fiddles bubbled merrily. "Pour yourself a cup and have a seat while I shut this noisy beast down."

"Thanks!"

Martin pulled two tin cups down from their hooks and filled them while Silas stepped past him, knelt to shut down the engine, and closed the hatch. The rain drumming on the cabin top seemed to amplify in the sudden quiet.

"Can't say I wasn't surprised to get your call, Silas. Haven't seen you since you were barely old enough to shave." Martin raised his cup and sipped. "Heard you finally gave up the high-seas trade and came home."

"I've been living down in Kingsport for about half a year." Silas sat and sipped his coffee, the bitter brew scalding a line down his throat.

"Looks like you gained some tattoos and lost an eye on your adventures."

"Lost the eye to a fellow with broken bottle and a temper in Bangkok, and I don't rightly remember where I got all the tattoos."

Martin laughed and grinned again. "And now you're back and you bought this little tub? With your experience, you could captain one of those big trawlers scooping up haddock off Stellwagen Bank and make a fortune."

"Oh, that's not for me." Silas shook his head with a rueful smile. "I'd rather be my own boss and run my own boat." He patted the cabin side with real affection. "*Sea Change* is a stout little ship. I can hand-line cod and haddock by myself, and run pots year round."

"Lobster?" Martin made a disdainful face. "You'll go broke. Didn't know there were any left."

"A few if you know where to look," Silas shrugged. "I pick up other jobs, too. I've got a diving rig and do some deep-sea salvage work that pays pretty good."

Martin's face blanched. "You mean you go *underwater* in one of them hard-hat contraptions?"

"Sure." Silas grinned at his cousin's reaction. "It's not all that dangerous."

Martin snorted in disgust. "You couldn't pay me enough."

"Well, I may not get rich, but I don't have anyone but myself to answer to."

"And what brings you up to Arkham in this weather? More work?" Martin looked honestly curious.

"Can't go to sea in this blow, so I took a job from Old Man McIntire to haul a load of lobster pots down to Kingsport in the morning." Silas sighed and wiped the water from his brow. He'd come to Arkham to talk to Martin, but couldn't say that was the main reason he'd come. He had to ease into this. Just like bringing his boat into the dock, these waters were turbulent. "Truth be told, Martin, I wanted to talk to you about some things, too. Part of the reason I came back to New England."

"And what reason's that, besides drivin' all the young ladies to distraction by walkin' around shirtless in the middle of a nor'easter?" Martin laughed at first, but he sobered when Silas didn't respond. "What is it, Silas? What's happened?"

"Nothing's really *happened*, but ..." He rubbed his eye and tried to think of how to put it into words. "I went to sea to get away from Innsmouth. You know what the town's like. No place for a kid to grow up. But the sea felt right, too. I always felt better on the ocean, but the last couple of years, I just ..."

"Just what?"

"I can't say exactly, Martin." *Not without sounding completely insane.* "You heard my parents passed away, didn't you?"

"Yes. A shame, too. They weren't that old."

"Thanks." He sipped his coffee and searched for words. As usual, he came up short. "After I got the news, I felt this need to come back."

"Well, that's natural."

"I thought so, too, at first, but ..." He sighed in frustration and blundered on. "Do you ever dream of the sea, Martin?"

"Sometimes." Martin looked perplexed at the sudden change of subject. "Doesn't everyone who's been a sailor?"

"Not like mine." Silas stared down into his coffee. "I have

nightmares, Martin. They were just a few at first, and I thought it was guilt for my parents, but now they come every time I sleep. They're so vivid… I dream of the sea, but not like I did when I was a kid, not with the feeling like I wanted to be a sailor."

"How then?" All humor had fled Martin's voice, and his lips were set in a hard line.

"I dream *under* the sea, and I see faces, bloated faces with bulging eyes. They remind me of people I knew as a boy, half-drowned, but not dead." Silas shivered, but not from the chill gusts blowing through the open door. Pointed teeth grinned, webbed hands reaching for him, glowing eyes in the darkness… He couldn't tell Martin those details, of course. Some things you couldn't say aloud if you wanted to stay out of the madhouse. "I wanted to know whether you ever had dreams like that. Dreams of people you knew turned into… something horrible. Voices calling you to join them. We both know the Marsh family's an odd lot. I need to know if this is some family affliction, if I'm going crazy, or if you've ever had any–"

"No." Martin downed his coffee and stood so abruptly his leg jostled the table. "Nope, I never dreamed any such thing, Silas, and you best forget you ever did, too!"

Martin turned for the door and grabbed his slicker, but Silas clutched his arm before he donned it. "Martin, wait. I just want to ask you–"

"Don't ask me anything, Silas." Martin glared at the hand gripping his arm. "I got no answers for you."

Silas didn't release his grip. "You don't have answers, or you just won't *give* me any?"

"I don't *have* any." Martin jerked away and pulled on his slicker. "You want answers to questions like that, you go talk to the main family in Innsmouth. I made my peace with them years ago. I don't bother them, and they don't bother me."

Martin stomped out the door into the weather.

"Martin, wait!" Silas grit his teeth, then spied his cousin's sou'wester hanging on a peg. He snatched it up and stepped out onto the deck. "Martin, your hat."

Martin was already up on the quay, but stopped and turned back. Silas stepped up onto the boat's gunnel and held up the hat. When Martin reached down to take it, Silas refused to let go.

"Don't just run off, Martin. You're the last person I can talk to."

"No, I'm not." He jerked the sou'wester out of Silas's hand and put it on, his face set in a hard scowl. "You talk to the old family. Get your answers there. But I'll warn you, Silas, you may not like what they have to tell you. You've been gone a long time, and you know how they feel about strangers, even ones who share their name." Martin whirled away and strode off down the quay.

Silas stood in the rain glaring at his cousin's receding back. *Answers… why is it always so hard to just get a simple answer?* His cousin knew something about the nightmares that plagued him, but he wouldn't or *couldn't* speak about it. Why? The main family of Marshes harbored many secrets – everyone from Innsmouth knew that – but were they also hiding some hereditary malady of madness or delusion?

Silas suppressed a shiver of revulsion. He'd visited Innsmouth briefly upon his return from abroad, but the pallid faces and watery eyes of his cousins there gave him chills deeper than any nor'easter that ever blew. He'd left without speaking to anyone, feeling as if he'd rather walk into the sea and never return than face the Marshes of Innsmouth.

Better to untie *Sea Change* and head downriver, sail out to sea and never come back. But that wasn't an option. Only a fool went to sea with a nor'easter brewing, and yet, only at sea did he feel at peace. *No wonder people think I'm strange… a sailor who only ever wants to go back to sea.* He looked up into the weeping sky and knew in his bones the weather wouldn't clear for at least three days. Three days sitting on a dock, listening to the siren call of the sea echoing in his head.

"Nothing to do but keep busy," he grumbled, bending to shift some of the deck gear to make room for Old Man McIntire's lobster pots.

As he bent to that task, however, a piercing whistle and call from up the pier drew his attention. *Did Martin change his mind?* But when he looked up, what he saw stopped him cold. "What in the name of…"

A woman walked down the quay, but a woman unlike the usual sort seen on the waterfront. Ramrod straight, wearing a gray dress buttoned up tightly from throat to waist, but no coat, she walked with quick, stiff steps that reminded him of a partridge. She clutched a black umbrella in one hand to fend off the rain, and, of all things, a thick book in the other. The latter she held close, as if it could shield her from the three men who had stepped off a barge to block her path.

Silas grit his teeth. He couldn't hear what they said to her over the hiss of rain, but he didn't have to. Her eyes darted between them as she stopped short, a look of wide-eyed desperation on her face. He knew where this was going. He'd seen this too much in his travels, women accosted and treated like chattel, and not just abroad. Even after the government gave women full suffrage, some men treated them like they should be subservient. The sight of it happening here prickled his skin like a plague of nettles.

Not on my watch… Silas grabbed a slicker from the pilothouse and pulled it on. Men didn't go shirtless in front of ladies, after all. By the time he'd climbed up to the quay, however, the three men were backing away from the woman. One of them turned with a look of unease on his face. The woman took a step toward them, but he couldn't hear what she said.

"Off with you, ya crazy cow!" the largest of the men bellowed, flicking a meaty hand in a shooing motion, although it was he who was retreating from her.

The woman's eyes followed them beseechingly. "Please, I just…" But the men weren't listening, muttering under their breath as they stepped back aboard their barge.

Not knowing what she'd said to send them packing, but admiring her spunk, Silas took a closer look at her. She was younger than he'd guessed from her conservative clothes and severe hairstyle – maybe late twenties or early thirties. Her plain gray dress, speckled black by the rain, looked like something a spinster of sixty might wear. She was slim, straight-backed, with brown hair pulled into a low bun, a few curls escaping to dangle upon her furrowed brow. The book she clutched to her chest was large, thick, and leather bound. Her eyes flicked around, searching, desperate. Her earlier distress hadn't been about being accosted at all. She was looking for something – or someone – and her gaze alighted on him.

Silas turned away, not wanting to look like another ruffian. But a conservatively dressed woman wandering the wharves alone, out in a storm without a coat, clutching a book was nigh strange. Whether she was desperate or mad as a hatter, Silas had no desire to get involved in someone else's problems. As he started to climb back down to *Sea Change*, however, her voice called him back.

"Sir?" She bustled toward him, her birdlike gait closing the distance with surprising speed. "Please, sir, I need the help of a sailor. Please! The… the end of days is fast approaching, and I don't know where else to find help."

"The *what*?" *Desperate* and *mad, maybe,* he thought, but he couldn't simply ignore her. His own pleas for help had gone unanswered for too long.

"The end of *days*!" She tottered up, stopping barely a step away, her eyes wide and her knuckles white on the book clutched to her breast. Her lower lip trembled, her weak chin quivering. "All the works of man will fall. The stars… the travelers will come… everything… *everyone* will perish. The tome foretells it all! You have to *help* me."

"I…" Silas closed his mouth to keep from saying something offensive. He didn't know if she was truly touched in the head or some kind of religious fanatic, but the book she clutched so fervently wasn't a Bible. The tooled leather looked more like some of the things he'd seen in the Far East than anything from a church, and although the woman dressed primly, she didn't talk like a Bible-thumper. *Not your problem, Silas…* "I really can't help you, miss."

The words sounded gut-wrenchingly familiar. No help… no answers… no one who trusts enough to help.

"*Please*, sir." She tilted her umbrella out of the way as she stepped closer, and the nor'easter filled it like a sail, jerking it out of her grasp and flinging it into the river. She didn't even glance after it, but she clutched his arm. "I know this sounds mad, but I need a sailor, someone who knows how to navigate with the stars, to interpret something from this tome." She sheltered the book with her body even as rain soaked her hair. "Lives… no, the very *world* depends on this. Please!"

"The stars?" Not crazy, maybe, but clearly disturbed, she obviously needed help, and having just been refused by his cousin, her desperation struck Silas like a blow. *If you turn her away, what kind of hypocrite will you be, Silas?* Perhaps if he could just talk her down a little, she would move on to a safer area of Arkham. Ladies like her didn't belong on the docks. "You mean celestial navigation? You need someone to take a fix from some numbers in that book?"

"Yes. Precisely." She withdrew her hand and clutched the book closer in a futile attempt to protect it from the rain. "I'm sorry. My name is Abigail Foreman. I'm a librarian at the university. This tome speaks of the end of mankind, a path between stars opening, horrible things entering our world at a very specific time and place. The place is denoted by celestial data, but the time and numbers keep changing."

"Changing?" Now that *did* sound crazy. Books didn't change. But a closer look at the tome's tooled leather cover confirmed that this was no mariner's log, almanac, or explorer's diary.

"*Please*, Mister…"

"Marsh. Silas Marsh." Her plea finally broke his reticence. Crazy or not, maybe if he spoke to her, offered to help, he could calm her down. "You're getting soaked, Miss Foreman. You best step aboard and have a cup of java to warm you while you tell me what you need."

"Oh, *thank* you, Mister Marsh." She followed him to the edge of the quay, but then peered dubiously down at the deck of the boat. "Are you sure…"

One look at her hard-soled shoes and he knew she'd have a problem stepping onto the gunnel. Doing so without letting go of the book she clutched so dearly would make it perilous. Falling into the raging Miskatonic River would be deadly for someone dressed in heavy skirts.

"Here, miss. I'll help you." Silas stepped down to the pitching gunnel and braced one foot on the quay wall. His stance sure, he held up two hands. "Don't worry."

"Thank you, Mister Marsh." She inched forward and started to step down, both hands still firmly gripping the book.

Her shoe met the rain-slicked cap rail and shot out from under her as if she'd stepped on ice. A clipped cry escaped her lips, but before she fell, Silas's hands closed around her waist, and he lifted her down to the deck as easily as plucking a lobster pot from the sea. She wobbled as *Sea Change* rolled, but he was down and gripping her elbow firmly in a flash.

"Here, miss, just step inside and have a seat." Silas guided her into the cabin and waved her to the bench beside the chart table. He hung up his slicker and grabbed a towel from the wet locker. "Sorry for the rough handling. Let me just get a shirt on." He handed the towel over and hurried forward to get a shirt from the fo'c'sle. The thick flannel felt sticky on his wet skin, but he didn't want to offend the poor woman.

When he reentered the cabin, however, he found her drying off the book with the towel, not, as he'd intended, her dripping face and hair. Perhaps librarians cared more for their books than their own condition. He quickly poured her a cup of coffee and put it down on the table.

"Here you go." He topped up his own cup and sat down across from her. "Now, what's this about that book? You said it changed? How can that be?"

"I don't know *how*, Mister Marsh, but the entry *does* change," Abigail finished dabbing at the rain-specked leather and pressed the towel to her face, then dried her hands meticulously before touching the volume. "This is a book of prophecies written by an excommunicated monk in the sixteenth century. I became interested in this particular prophecy because the date of its occurrence is very near to today's date."

Silas arched an eyebrow. Although the edges of the leather were cracked with age, the book looked remarkably well preserved for being four hundred years old, and he suddenly understood her concern for its condition. The cover was deeply tooled with strange symbols and figures around the foreign title: *Prophesiae Profana.*

"I should never have taken it out of the library, but I needed proof." Abigail sighed and finally noticed the coffee he'd placed before her. She wrapped her hands around the hot metal cup and lifted it to her lips, sipping carefully. "I'm afraid I was rather… distraught when I discovered the date and stellar data had changed. I grabbed the tome and my umbrella and completely forgot to put on a coat." She fumbled a tiny notebook out of a handbag she held clutched beneath the book. "But look here."

Abigail pointed to two rows of numbers beside the names of planets and stars. Silas recognized the names of celestial bodies commonly used for navigation, the angles of their sightings from the horizon, and the exact times of the sightings down to the second.

"I jotted this first note down to convert the dates from Julian to Gregorian."

"From what?" Had she slipped into some foreign language?

"The commonly used calendar changed after the tome was printed, so I had to convert it. Then, I took the stellar data to Professor Withers, the university astronomer. He told me he was too busy to help, that there was some strange phenomenon occurring in the heavens that he had to study. He said I should seek out a sailor who knew celestial navigation." She pointed to the second row of data. "When I returned to the library, the date, time, and stellar data had changed to these. I wrote them down immediately, thinking I must have made a mistake, but then realized I couldn't have. There's only one entry in this entire passage, and I couldn't have gotten the information from nowhere. So, I grabbed the book and came down here to find a sailor who could tell me where on Earth these entries point to." She looked up at him. "Can you do that?"

"Yes, but …" Silas didn't want to tell her that two scratched notes in a notebook weren't proof of anything.

"Just let me show you the prophecy. It's in Latin, but I can translate."

Silas clenched his teeth against a sarcastic retort. How convenient that this book was in a language he couldn't read. She could tell him the book said anything she wanted, and he'd be forced to accept her word. Calling her a liar, however, wouldn't do him any good.

As Abigail gingerly opened the tome, Silas found his eyes drawn to the pages, their hand-written block print framed by artistic illustrations that filled the margins. He'd seen books like this before, old texts crafted by monks in distant monasteries, artfully decorated with depictions of holy scenes or relics. She turned the pages carefully, one at a time.

"Please, look here, Mister Marsh." She opened her notebook and put it down beneath the celestial notations in the book. "This passage explains that a door will open to issue forth the hordes of fiends from another place, a hellish place, and those hordes and the… beings that rule them will destroy the world of man and all our works will fall into ruin."

"I'll have to take your word on that, Miss Foreman." He tried not to sound derisive, but the passage could have been a recipe for goulash for all he could tell.

"And these numbers here are…" She pointed to a row of text, but then gasped, "Oh, dear Lord."

"What?"

"Look." She turned the book so he could see and pointed to the line of stellar names and numerals. Even in Latin, Silas recognized the names of Altair and Jupiter. Then Abigail placed her open notebook flat and pointed. "I recorded that second set just *hours* ago. Now they've changed again. See?"

Silas looked at the notation, then the text, and indeed they were different. The one in the tome itself was only five days hence, but that also didn't prove anything. A simple error or some delusion on Abigail's part could explain the disparity. Books simply didn't change. But as he opened his mouth to reiterate this point, his eye drifted to the illustrations filling the margins of the tome. Cold fingers gripped his heart, twisting his guts into knots. Abigail's voice faded into the roar of rain on the cabin roof as his mind stumbled in disbelief.

Nightmares writhed along the periphery of the pages, twisted limbs, deformed and misshapen faces with bulging eyes and needle teeth like some sort of misbegotten serpents. But it was the faces that most gripped his attention, for Silas had seen them before. He saw them every night when he closed his eyes to sleep.

"Mister Marsh?" Abigail looked at him with concern. "Is there something wrong? You look…"

"Nothing." Silas swallowed half of his cup of coffee, biting back a curse at his burned tongue. He looked away, out the porthole, across the cabin, anywhere as his mind spun. *Impossible. It's a coincidence, some trick or other.* He'd never seen this book before, but images such as these were surely copied from others, and he'd seen a lot of strange inscriptions in the distant ports of Indonesia and the South Pacific. He gulped the rest of his scalding coffee and heaved a sigh to steady his nerves. No, it had to be a coincidence. "Now, about these changes... I don't see how–"

"I assure you, Mister Marsh, I am *not* making this up."

Silas looked at the data again. "When was this book written?"

"1541 AD," Abigail said, her voice trembling. "But this piece of text was transcribed from a scroll much older."

Silas looked at her skeptically. "I don't think they had clocks or sextants so accurate that long ago. As for prophecies about the end of the world, I've heard dozens. Every culture has one."

Her lips thinned into a hard line. "I'm *not* crazy, Mister Marsh."

"I'm not saying you're crazy, Miss Foreman, but think. Books don't just change. There has to be an explanation. Someone must be playing an elaborate trick on you or something."

"How? The tome hasn't left my hands since this afternoon."

"I don't know, but whoever's doing this isn't as smart as they think." He tapped her notes, then pointed to the page. "The calculations for celestial navigation are tricky, and working up fixes from nothing would require real expertise. If these are someone's idea of a sick joke, something just to scare you, working out the fixes should show it."

She looked puzzled. "I don't understand."

"Making up numbers like these will more than likely give nonsense results if I do the calculations." He pointed to the data. "See how each fix uses two celestial bodies?"

"Yes."

"Well, if someone made these up as a trick, chances are that these two fixes won't point to any spot on the globe." That certainly made more sense than some moldy old book accurately foretelling the end of the world down to the second, let alone the text changing as if by magic from one hour to the next. "If they *are* made up, I should be able to tell you so."

"Very well, Mister Marsh." Abigail snatched up her notebook and wrote down the third set of numbers, then ripped out the page and handed it to him. "I'll pay you ten dollars to calculate the locations from these celestial fixes or prove them false."

"What?"

"Prove to me this is a hoax," Abigail rooted through her handbag and came out with a wad of banknotes. She thrust the cash at him. "*Please*, Mister Marsh. I'll sleep better if you do prove this is some sick joke."

"Call me Silas." He pushed the money away and stood, dragging his eyes away from the tome that so accurately depicted his nightmares. "I'll work up the numbers for you, but not today."

"Why ever not?" she asked incredulously.

"Because…" *Because I need a drink.* Silas gestured out the open door at the darkening sky. "The calculations take time, and it's getting late. You should be getting home. I'll walk you. It's not fit for man nor beast out, and some rough types loiter along the waterfront. I'll do the calculations tonight and bring you the results in the morning."

"Um, yes, OK." Abigail stood and wrinkled her nose at the pouring rain out the door. "Oh, fiddlesticks! I lost my umbrella."

"You can wear this." Silas pulled his slicker out of the wet locker and a sou'wester as well. "It'll keep your book drier than an umbrella."

"But you–"

"I'm fine." He helped her into the oversized slicker and hat, then banked the stove and guided her out on deck. "Now let me help you up onto the quay. Falling in the river might not end the world, but it'll end your life right enough."

"You have a way of stating things in matter-of-fact terms, Silas. Thank you." She didn't quibble about rough handling or his hands on her waist when he lifted her up onto the quay as some women would have. "And call me Abigail, please."

"All right, Abigail. Now, let's get a wiggle on before the really rough types come out of their holes." The slashing rain soaked his shirt as he guided her down River Street, but he found the chill strangely comforting after the stuffy cabin and disconcerting prophecy.

CHAPTER 2
The Miskatonic River

The iron back door of the Golden Plaice clanged closed behind Silas, and the blustery nor'easter slapped him in the face. After his encounter with Abigail Foreman, he'd needed a stiff drink, and two whiskeys had reinforced his long-practiced denial of such hokum. Nightmares, sure, everyone had nightmares, but the notion that some moldy four hundred year-old tome could predict the end of the world down to the second was rubbish. The illustrations' resemblance to his nightmares had to be simple coincidence. Myths of sea monsters were as common as barnacles on boats, and this was undoubtedly just another sea story. He'd transform Abigail's humbug prophecy into ten clams hard cash, load up Old Man McIntire's lobster pots, and get back to his life.

My life... He hunched his shoulders against the wind and strode down the narrow alley toward River Street, welcoming the chill rain that soaked him to the skin. Abigail had wanted to give him back his coat and hat, but he'd told her to wear them until she could get another umbrella. He'd pick them up from her tomorrow when he gave her the location of her prophetic

Armageddon. *Nightmares and monsters and the end of the world…*
What a crock of bilgewater!

And yet the chill down his spine wasn't entirely due to the
rain trickling down his back. Deny as he might, something about
this whole thing wasn't quite right. It felt like an itch he couldn't
scratch. The illustrations had been too familiar. He must have seen
them somewhere before, and whatever subtle insanity plagued the
Marsh clan had latched onto them. Abigail had said the legend had
been copied from an even older scroll. Others may have copied
that scroll over the centuries, and those copies could have ended
up in museums all over the world. He'd certainly seen a lot of
strange things in his travels, and that would explain everything.

Emerging from the narrow alley onto River Street, Silas glanced
back the way he'd come with the practiced vigilance of a world
traveler. He hadn't been exaggerating when he told Abigail that
the waterfront spawned some rough characters, and he'd learned
the hard way to watch his back after being shanghaied once in
Montevideo. Silas was a big man, his arms and chest well-muscled
with years of labor, and although he'd had a couple of drinks, he
was far from drunk. If someone jumped him, they'd better be
toting iron or they'd be in for a surprise.

Back in the alley, the gleam of light on something silvery
caught his eye. A car clattered by on the street, and the light of its
headlamps swept into the alley for a moment. A hunch-shouldered
figure stood there, its large eyes and a wide mouth illuminated for
an instant. Silas blinked, shaking off a shiver of familiarity, and
moved on. *Probably just some rum-soaked old sot.* But he hadn't
noticed anyone there when he'd left the speakeasy.

Silas crossed River Street, striding east along the quay. He cast
another covert glance over his shoulder. The stooped figure stood

at the mouth of the alley he'd just left, cloaked in a slicker and hat, collar turned up against the rain, face in shadow. *Following me?* But the man just stood there as if waiting... or watching.

Silas wasn't sure whether his uneasiness was due to his encounter with Abigail, or his usual discomfort with dry land under his boots. He knew well how to cure that uneasiness, however, and shake off any ne'er-do-well trying to stalk him at the same time.

Silas stepped aboard *Sea Change*, slipped her stern line, then ducked into the cabin and stowed his sodden shirt in the wet locker. Feeling better already with the motion of the river under his boots and cool air against his skin, he knelt, opened the engine room hatch, primed the carburetor, and hauled on the crank start. The engine sputtered to life. He closed the hatch and reached over to feel the belly of the stove. It was warm, but not hot, and he'd want coffee. A wad of newspaper, a few sticks of dry kindling, and a match quickly resurrected the flame. While the stove and the engine warmed up, he filled the percolator and secured the pot in the fiddles on the stove, then shoved a few more sticks of wood into the fire.

Ready to go.

Striding up to the pilot house, Silas jammed the shifter into forward and revved the engine up just enough to take the tension off the bow line. He flipped the switch that ignited the boat's electric running lights and stepped out of the pilothouse door. Shielding his eye from the rain, he scanned the river for traffic and found it clear; apparently no one else was crazy enough to be on the water on such a foul night. Glancing up and down the quay, he saw no one. Either his stalker had given up, or he'd been imagining it. A flick unwound the bow line from the piling and he stepped back into the pilothouse. Silas freed up the wheel, eased her to port, and pulled *Sea Change* out into the turbulent waters of the Miskatonic, pointing her bow downriver. Glancing back at the quay again, he saw a few bargemen or longshoremen hurrying this way and that, bent against the rain, but no one watching him. *Just my imagination.*

Silas squinted through the rain-streaked windows into the storm, silently cursing his lost eye. Navigating the Miskatonic in the dark was challenging enough, adding a nor'easter elevated the risk, and doing so without decent depth perception made it even worse. The tide should have slacked by now, but it was still ebbing hard.

Sea Change shot under the Peabody Avenue Bridge like a bullet from a gun. As the lights of Arkham passed astern, his vision improved. Once he cleared the Rivertown bend, and trees lined the shore instead of houses, Silas turned the boat up current and eased her over to the northern shore into a familiar anchorage.

Silas kicked *Sea Change* out of gear and strode up to the bow. The boat immediately drifted downriver, but the release of the brake on the windlass sent seventy pounds of anchor and thirty feet of heavy chain plunging to the bottom. He paid out another couple hundred feet of anchor rode, then secured it. The line came taut and the boat lurched around into the flow.

Silas stood there in the rain awhile, watching the shore to make sure the anchor held. Rain trickled through his hair, down his shoulders and back, washing away his unease, the comforting roll of the deck beneath his boots massaging his soul. The Miskatonic wasn't the sea, but at least he was on the water.

Content that the anchor was set, Silas ducked back into the cabin to the intoxicating scent of percolating coffee. He toweled off, cleaned up the wet floor, lit a kerosene anchor lamp, and shut off the boat's running lights. The engine wheezed to silence as he shut it down, and the blustery howl of the nor'easter settled in. Kicking off his sodden boots and soaked pants, he hung them to drip in the wet locker, wrapped the towel around his waist, and poured himself a cup of java. From the cupboard beneath the table, he liberated a bottle labeled "Medicinal Spiritus Frumenti" and topped off his cup. The scent of Canadian whiskey mingled with that of coffee. The first sip of the heady brew set his teeth on edge, just the tonic he needed to sharpen his mind for the task at hand.

Sitting at the chart table, Silas pulled out his own tomes – *The American Ephemeris and Nautical Almanac for 1926* and the current volume of declination tables. The almanac contained the positions of the sun, moon, planets, and certain stars for every hour of every day of the year, and tables for calculating adjustments down to the second. The declination tables gave him the ability to convert the angles of these sightings, with some laborious calculations, into angular distances from the celestial equator, and thence into latitude and longitude. Each fix had two sightings, which added accuracy by simple triangulation.

For the author of Abigail's prophecy in 1540 to give the stellar data for a position on Earth four hundred years in the future would have been impossible, which was why he didn't expect the calculations to yield anything but gibberish. Silas copied Abigail's data onto a sheet of paper and began the meticulous process that would transform the numbers into latitude and longitude. He was no mathematician, but long practice had made these calculations so familiar that he had little trouble. Still, they were involved, and he found his unease dwindling even further with the occupation of his mind.

Silas's brow furrowed as he finished the first fix. The result actually gave a meaningful location, and somewhere in the northwest Atlantic at that. Well, the accompanying stellar fix would certainly tell the tale. He ran through the calculations and stopped cold. For a moment, he thought he'd run the same fix twice, but when he rechecked, he found that wasn't the case.

Someone's pulling a fast one, he thought, for the two locations he'd calculated weren't just close, they were identical. Nobody took fixes that accurately, even in perfect conditions with modern equipment. This had to be some well-planned hoax. *Well, we'll see just how deep this hoax goes.*

Silas started on the second set of data. The time of the sighting was two days nearer than the first, and the third set was a day closer than that one. He smirked as he ran the numbers. It sure seemed like someone was trying to scare Abigail.

The numbers resolved and again he stared in disbelief. "Well, blow me down." The position denoted was exactly the same as the first two, right down to the minute and second of longitude and latitude. He gritted his teeth and ran the next fix, knowing what he'd find. Sure enough, it came up the same.

Now for the ones I watched her copy from the book.

He ran the numbers meticulously, forcing himself to be careful. When they both came up exactly the same as the others, he sat back with a snort of disgust. "Impossible. It's got to be a trick." But why would anyone try to pull such a trick on a librarian?

The position was somewhere near New England, north of Boston. Working up all the numbers from different times and sightings would have been a monumental task, and if someone were really trying to scare her, the location would have been someplace she knew, like her apartment or the library. He remembered her mentioning an astronomer at the university, but couldn't think of any reason why someone like that would want to scare a librarian.

There was only one more thing to do: find that location on a chart.

Downing his whiskey-spiked coffee and putting the cup aside, Silas rifled through his store of charts beneath the table's hinged top. He chose two, one that displayed the coast from Boston to Cape Ann, and another from the Cape to the Merrimack River. Laying them flat and checking the latitude of his calculation, he knew instantly the spot would be north of Cape Ann. He picked a pair of dividers and parallel rulers from the rack of tools.

"Forty-two, forty-two, point oh three..." He walked off the latitude on the chart's sidebar and drew a line with his ruler. "Zero seven zero, forty-five, point nine." Another line marked the longitude, and they crossed just east of the mouth of Plum Island Sound and the town of Innsmouth.

Silas dropped his pencil, coffee roiling in his stomach. "Devil Reef."

He knew those waters well, having fished them in his youth. They were some of the best fishing grounds north of Cape Ann, and the main Marsh family did not suffer outsiders plying those waters. He'd heard stories aplenty about that reef, from ghost ships wrecked there in centuries past, to more recent reports during the war of strange lights beneath the water, and even figures dancing on the exposed reef at low tide when the moon was new.

Sailors were a superstitious lot, and Silas had heard tales of ghosts and haunts from Singapore to Maine, but the locals of Innsmouth believed the tales about Devil Reef. He had always considered the stories nothing but superstitious drivel contrived to keep strangers away, but all the same, he took heed. Silas fished his old logbook from under the table and started flipping pages, looking for his notes on Devil Reef.

But why would someone concoct such an elaborate hoax to fool a librarian into thinking the end of the world was going to take place there?

Something thumped hard against the hull, and *Sea Change* lurched on her anchor, snapping Silas out of his musing. He was up in a heartbeat, dropping his logbook and reaching for his powerful electric lamp. *The last thing I need is a floating stump to foul the anchor line or damage the rudder.* Pulling on his sodden pants, he turned down the cabin lamp so the light wouldn't ruin his view outside, and stepped out into the storm.

Silas shone his light over each side and the stern but saw only turbid brown water. He went forward through the cabin and out the pilothouse door, checked the anchor line, and found it tight. Shielding his eye from the slashing rain and peering into the gloom, he noted that the few lights on the far shore weren't changing position. *At least the anchor's not dragging.* He relaxed a little. *Sea Change* wagged back and forth as the wind and current fought for control over the small boat, but the impact of something heavy hitting the hull had been unmistakable. Flotsam floated past: tree limbs, trash, even an old boot, but nothing large enough to cause that kind of lurch.

Must have been a log or something, he resolved, squinting into the distance looking for larger floating debris. Something silvery flashed beneath the surface, a roil of water, then nothing. *Sea Change* lurched again, swinging hard on her anchor, but this time there was no thump against the hull.

Just the current and wind playing hay with her now, he concluded, but something had hit the boat before. "Anchoring out in the river in a nor'easter, Silas? You're lucky you weren't hit by a barge broken loose." The tide still seemed to be ebbing harder than it should. With this rain, the river would continue to run, but the shift of tide should have eased the flow by now. He had no option but to ride it out, as motoring back upriver to town and docking in the dark would be more dangerous than staying put. He scanned the dark river once again but saw nothing.

Ducking back through the pilothouse to the main cabin, thinking of another whiskey-laced coffee, Silas reached up for the overhead lamp but then froze. His chart, logbook, the papers with his calculations, and the notes from Abigail were gone, and there was water all over the table.

"Who the hell…" He whirled to shine his light down into the fo'c'sle, but there was nobody there. He'd just come through the pilothouse, and there was no place to hide there either. He turned back to direct the light out the aft door onto the deck. The cabin floor was wet. He'd walked through from the aft deck, and his wet footprints were clear, but there was a second set beside his that went to the chart table, then forward to the engine compartment hatch.

Somebody came aboard, but there's no other boat out here. Silas would have seen one when he was on the bow. *How could anyone have gotten aboard?* Then he realized the more pressing question: *And are they still aboard?*

Silas stepped to the cabinet opposite the wet locker and pulled out the heavy knife he kept there, pausing to consider grabbing the double-barreled Remington secured to the bulkhead inside. *Best not*, he thought. He had to explore below and needed one hand to carry the lantern. Besides, firing a shotgun aboard a boat below the waterline was a great way to blow a hole in the hull. No, for the engine compartment and the fo'c'sle, the knife was better.

Working his way forward, shining his light on the deck, he saw that the wet footprints were larger than his own and splayed wide at the toe. They stopped at the engine compartment hatch, but he couldn't tell if they went back out the aft door. Someone standing there could see through the pilothouse windows to the foredeck, and they might have stood here watching him. Suppressing the urge to call out in an attempt to scare the intruder off, he slipped the knife through his belt and bent to grip the handle of the engine room hatch. Taking a deep breath, he jerked the hatch open and shone his light down into the compartment.

Nothing but a wave of heat and a greasy old engine greeted him. A quick visual check revealed no intruder, no wet footprints, and nothing obviously tampered with, so he closed the compartment and continued his search. There were no more wet footprints forward except his own, but he checked the pilothouse and the fo'c'sle as well. Finding nothing out of place, and no more signs anyone had been there, he returned to the main cabin. The water on the table and missing papers confirmed that this wasn't some hallucination induced by bad hooch, but who would steal a bunch of papers?

"And how the hell did you get aboard?"

Silas went back over his departure from the Arkham quay in his mind. Could someone have gotten aboard and hidden someplace while he started the engine? It was possible someone could have leapt from the quay to the cabin roof, although he would have heard the thump or felt the boat lurch. He looked up, as if he could see through the cabin roof. Could they have climbed back up there?

Now's the time for some firepower. He traded his knife for the

Remington, checked the loads, and worked out how to hold both the gun and the lamp. He shone the light across the aft deck from the door, saw nothing, then readied the shotgun and backed out with the twin barrels aimed up at the roof. The powerful lamp shone over the edge of the roof, but there was nothing up there but the stays securing the mast, the overhead boom, the stove's smokestack trailing a streamer of wood smoke, and sheets of slashing rain. Lastly, he checked the fish hold, but that, too, was empty. He scanned the river once again. Even if the intruder had stowed away somehow, they couldn't have gotten away. He would have heard another boat, even with the howling wind. That left only one possibility: someone had slipped over the side to *swim* away, fighting the current, the rain, and the storm.

"Crazy…"

Back inside the cabin, Silas wiped the Remington down with an oilcloth, secured it, and bolted the aft cabin door. He secured the pilothouse door as well, then turned up the cabin lamp and put away his electric light. After toweling dry, he wiped up the water on the cabin sole and table as well, stowing his books and tools. Lastly, he checked the anchor lamp to make sure it had enough kerosene, then took his lantern and the heavy knife forward to the fo'c'sle and lay down in his bunk. Turning down the lamp, he settled in, listening to the howling wind and the burble of water flowing past the hull. The haft of the heavy knife in his hand felt solid and comforting.

No more bumps or unusual lurches rocked *Sea Change*, just the roll of the boat swaying on her anchor, and the mournful moan of the strengthening nor'easter overhead. For Silas, this was as soothing as any lullaby, and he soon found his tension easing and his eyes drooping closed.

As sleep took him, however, nightmare faces loomed out of the darkness, bulbous eyes and wide mouths grinning with needle teeth, but he didn't know if he was dreaming or being plagued by visions of the illustrations in Abigail Foreman's book.

CHAPTER 3
The Orne Library

Silas stepped up onto the Arkham quay feeling a strange sense of deja vu; the nor'easter still roared, the river still ran like a millrace, *Sea Change* was docked in exactly the same spot, and he was again going to talk with Abigail Foreman. If not for the fact that his chart, logbook, and Abigail's notes were still missing, he might have convinced himself that he'd dreamed yesterday's odd events.

He crossed River Street and started for the university, splashing through the rain-soaked streets. One block up, he turned onto Main Street and started west. There weren't many people out, and those who were shot him curious looks from under umbrellas or hunkered in raincoats. The damp didn't bother him, long used to working days at sea soaked to the bone, but city folk probably thought he was daft.

Abigail had told him to ask for her at the main information desk of Orne Library. Silas had been to the library only once before and didn't relish visiting again. The librarians hadn't been very friendly. Maybe they'd be less prickly this time since he was just there to see Abigail, not touch any of their priceless treasures. What would

Abigail's reaction be when he told her someone had stolen his charts, pages of calculations, logbook, and her notes? Would she even believe him? Regardless, she would positively flip her lid when he told her all three sets of celestial fixes had pointed to the same spot.

Turning up Garrison Street, he headed south until he reached the university, then crossed and hurried along Church Street. Orne Library hove out of the sheets of rain like a pillared steamship out of a winter squall. Silas crossed the street and dashed up the stone library stairs. When he hauled on the lofty door, it creaked abominably. He wondered if he should tell them to oil the hinges, but decided they probably wouldn't appreciate the advice of a sailor.

The wind grabbed the door when he released it, slamming it shut hard enough to echo through the entry hall and draw a few shocked looks from the patrons in view. Silas shrugged, stomped the water from his boots, shook it from his hair, and promptly sneezed. The air in here felt stuffy and smelled of old paper.

"Shhhh." A skinny fellow in a black jacket and bowtie glared at him.

"Sorry." Silas wiped his face with his sleeve and asked, "Can you point me to the information desk?"

The man wrinkled his nose and pointed to the centrally located pair of double doors. "It is the desk with the sign that reads 'Information,'" he said in a hushed voice.

"Thank you." Silas ignored the man's snide look, wondering why people whispered the same in churches and libraries.

The huge, vaulted room beyond the doors sported three different desks, each with its own polished brass placard: Reference, Lending, and Information. *Probably could have figured that out yourself, Silas,* he thought, altering course to approach the information desk.

Eyes followed his progress across the marble floor. Those of the patrons ranged from curious to surprised, while the librarians looked mildly horrified. The woman at the information desk paled as he approached, stiffened, and licked her lips. Silas tried to smile amiably, but a near-sleepless night filled with nightmares and thoughts of intruders hadn't put him in a pleasant frame of mind.

"Can I help you?" the librarian asked when he was still several steps away.

"I hope so. I'm here to see Abigail Foreman."

"She works in the restricted section." The librarian's eyes traversed him head to foot. "You are *soaking* wet, sir."

Silas bit back a surly comment. *More flies with honey…* "Yes, I know. I forgot my coat and it's raining out. Could you point me to the restricted section, please?"

"No." She didn't elaborate.

He blinked at her. "Um… why not?"

"Because, sir, it is *restricted*. That means only university faculty and library staff may enter."

"Oh, well, that makes sense, I suppose." Silas reinforced his effort to be civil in the face of rudeness, knowing belligerence would get him nowhere. A legitimate explanation for his presence might serve better. "Could you please have someone fetch Miss Foreman for me, then? She asked me to work out some celestial navigation problems for her, and I have."

"Celestial navigation problems?" she asked dubiously.

"Yes. Sailors use the stars to navigate, you see, and she asked me to—"

"I *know* what celestial navigation is." she huffed.

"Oh, well, good. Miss Foreman said the astronomy professor was too busy to help her, so you understand why she needed a *sailor* to help her with the calculations." Silas waited for a count of ten, but she just stared at him as if unable to make sense from his words. "So, if you could *please* send someone to fetch Miss Foreman for me, I'll talk to her and stop dripping on your nice, polished floor."

She pursed her lips so hard they blanched white. "Very well. Stay here."

She reached under her desk and the high-pitched chime of a bell rang through the chamber. A harried-looking young man in a white shirt and pleated pants emerged from behind the lofty shelves of books.

"Yes, ma'am?"

"Go to the restricted section and tell Miss Foreman that a... man is–"

"Silas Marsh, ma'am," Silas offered.

The librarian flashed him a cold glance. "That a *man* is here to see her."

"Yes, ma'am." The young man hurried off.

Silas kept his face neutral. He understood the librarian's animosity – an unwashed oaf had invaded the halls of higher learning and might damage their priceless works of literature – but that didn't mean he had to like it. Of course, he'd seen enough prejudice against landlubbers from sailors, so such things were a two-way street. He folded his arms and stood there dripping on their floor while he waited.

Finally, Abigail bustled into the room, her short quail steps click-clicking on the floor. Again, she held the tome close to her chest, and her face was alight with something that might have been eagerness mixed with fear. Silas knew that feeling well.

Abigail glanced at the librarian behind the information desk. "Thank you, Evelyn."

"See that your… associate does not damage anything, Abigail. He is *dripping* wet."

Silas opened his mouth to say something, but Abigail beat him to it.

"Mister Marsh is a *sailor*, Evelyn, not a barbarian. He knows the value of books."

The librarian looked skeptical but didn't respond.

"Please, Mister Marsh, let's find someplace quiet to compare our findings."

Any quieter and you could hear a pin drop, he thought, following her as she tap-tapped down an aisle between two towering shelves and through an archway into a smaller chamber. Here, several reading tables and chairs were arranged amid more shelves of books.

"They've changed again," she hissed in a library whisper as she put her book down on the nearest table. Flipping to the correct page, she pointed to the celestial notations. "Compare them to the ones I gave you."

"I can't. I don't have them anymore." He leaned near the book and noted that the date and time, at least, were different than those she'd given him the night before. Someone must have changed them again.

"You don't *have* them?" She blinked up at him as if he'd slapped her. "Whatever happened to them?"

"They were stolen off my boat last night while I was anchored out in the river. I don't know who could have done it, or why, but someone stowed away aboard, took your notes, my calculations, logbook, *and* my chart, and *swam* away."

"What?" Her eyes widened and her cheeks paled. "They *swam* the river? Who on earth would do that?"

"I don't know, but I'll bet you double or nothing on that ten clams you owe me that if I ran the same calculations on *those* numbers," he stabbed a finger at her book, "I'd get the–" Silas stopped cold, staring at the date and time noted in plain block script on the tome's pages. They weren't the same ones he'd seen only moments before. "Abigail..." His finger shook as he pointed to the new numbers.

"What?" She looked and caught her breath, stumbling back a step. She fumbled frantically for her notebook and opened the page, her eyes darting back and forth between the two. "Again! They've changed again!"

"They did! Just this moment." The chill in his spine turned to ice. Silas had seen a lot of strange things, but never a book that changed letters and numbers by itself. "What in the name of heaven and hell *is* that thing, some kind of hocus pocus?"

"I *told* you they changed. Didn't you *believe* me?" The last came out accusingly.

"I believe you now, sister, and I don't want any part of it." Silas turned away, intending to walk right out of the library, Arkham, and maybe right down to Boston to sign on with the first foreign-bound ship to set sail.

"Wait," Abigail grasped his arm, her small fingers barely getting a grip on his tense bicep. "You *can't* just leave."

"The *hell* I can't." He wrapped his much larger hand around her wrist and pulled her grasping fingers free with little effort. "I'm a sailor, not some kind of magician. I'll have no truck with nonsense like this."

He turned to go, but she dodged in front of him, her face livid. "You *can't* just go, Silas. You haven't told me what you found. What these numbers mean."

He stopped and considered shoving past her, but he *had* promised to tell her what he found out. "Fine. All three sets of numbers you gave me pointed to the exact same location. A spot just east of Innsmouth called Devil Reef."

"Innsmouth…" Abigail glanced past him at the book open on the table, blinked, and bit her lip. She trembled, and blood welled from between her teeth.

"Abigail." He grasped her arms as tears filled her eyes. "Abigail, stop!"

She drew a ragged breath and her eyes flicked up to his. "Silas… please… look at the numbers again now and tell me I'm not insane."

He let go of her and whirled around to stare down at the tome. Yet again the date, time, and celestial data were different from what they'd been only seconds before. Cold fingers closed around his heart. "Jesus, oh Jesus…"

"It *knows*," Abigail whispered, stepping around him to stare down at the book. "It changes every time I get closer to an answer. First, when I spoke with Professor Withers, then when I spoke with you. It happened again this morning just before you arrived, and now again when you told me the location. Every time I get closer, the answer changes!"

"The time changes, but not the place." Silas gritted his teeth against the urge to flee, to run away from this intangible threat. "And if you're insane, then so am I, but how can a *book* know anything? How can it *change* anything?"

"I don't know, Silas, but it's the only answer."

"Well, the *book* didn't swim out to the middle of the river last night and climb aboard my boat to steal my chart," he countered. "Someone left wet footprints across the cabin. Who would ... no, who *could* do that? Nobody could swim the Miskatonic the way it's flowing now and survive."

"No one?" She blinked up at him, then tapped the margin of the tome where fish-like faces stared up from the page with lurid eyes. "No one *human*, you mean."

"No!" Silas stepped back, denial rising like an inexorable tide from his gut. "Those are just pictures, Abigail. They aren't real. They *can't* be ..." Silas swallowed hard as his nightmares surged up from his memory, the voices calling him to the sea ... *Can there really be a connection to my nightmares?* "Why me, Abigail? Why did you come to *me*?"

"I ... I didn't. Well, not you in particular. I was just looking for someone who knew how to navigate using the stars. The other men I spoke with thought I was crazy. Then you seemed to understand." She shook her head. "I thought you believed me."

"I believe you, Abigail. How can I not when I saw it change with my own eyes? But what do you want me to *do* about it?"

"I thought ..." She bit her lip again and winced, licking away the blood. Flipping to the page beyond the prophecy, she pointed to a full-page illustration. "I thought you would help me try to stop this. It's Armageddon, Silas. The end of the world."

Silas's eyes fell on a scene straight out of his nightmares. A vast city beneath the sea loomed up from the page. A huge beast, its wingspan blotting out the sky, rose above masses of shapes. Some were human; others half-fish, half-man; others unnamable horrors; and all were devouring and being devoured in grisly detail.

No one would call Silas Marsh a coward. He'd stared down the throat of a hurricane at sea, sailed the iceberg-strewn Southern

Ocean, stood against pirates and cutthroats the world over, but this… The illustration was too much like his visions to be a coincidence.

"Bloody mother of…" Silas clenched his gnarled hands into fists and closed his eye tight, but the half-fish, half-man faces waited there in the darkness for him, calling him home. *Why… Why me? Why do my nightmares and some ancient book foretell the same thing?*

"Silas?"

He snapped his eye open and whirled to face Abigail, gritting his teeth so tightly he thought they might shatter. "Fine. I'll *help* you, but there's not a whole hell of a lot we can do as far as I can see."

"What do you mean?" She still looked scared but wasn't trembling quite so much.

Though loath to touch the vile tome, he flipped back a page and jabbed his finger at the recently transformed entry. "I'll run the calculations on those numbers for you, but if they point to Devil Reef like the others, there's nothing we can do." He tapped a finger on the date and time. "That's only three days away, and this nor'easter's not going to let up before then. I can't take *Sea Change* around Cape Ann in this weather."

"Then they'll win, Silas." Her voice came out as lifeless and cold as a corpse, defeated. "Whatever *they* are, they know we've discovered their plans, and they've changed them to beat us. There's *got* to be an intelligence behind this."

"*They*…" Silas furrowed his brow. *These things can't be real. They have to just be nightmares.* Half-man, half-fish – twisted limbs, voices calling to him, calling him home. *Home…* He glared at the margin of the tome and thought of his childhood home, of Innsmouth. *Maybe… maybe the old stories about Devil*

Reef aren't just stories. And maybe there is a way to get out there and stop this... thing from happening.

"Maybe..." Silas turned to Abigail and gripped her gently by the shoulders. "Do you have a car?"

"No," she said, but her eyes brightened. "But I can borrow one. Where are we going?"

"We're going to Innsmouth, Abigail." Silas dragged the musty air of Orne Library into his lungs and let it out slowly. Try as he might to avoid the place, the town of his birth seemed to be inexorably drawing him back. "From there, the waters out to Devil Reef are protected from the storm. Someone there might have a boat we can use."

CHAPTER 4
Innsmouth

The old rattletrap Abigail borrowed had nearly pounded Silas's backside to jelly by the time they crossed the last bridge to Innsmouth. The road from Arkham to Bolton, rough in the best of conditions, had been reduced to a mire of puddles and potholes strewn with debris by the storm. Twice they'd had to stop for Silas to move downed tree limbs from their path. Thankfully, Abigail drove. Silas could pilot a ship through the eye of a needle, but he was all thumbs when it came to cars. Once on the highway, they made better time, although the old flivver could barely make twenty miles an hour on the best of roads. They stopped in Ipswich for a quick bowl of chowder and a sandwich, and rolled into Innsmouth early that afternoon.

The dilapidated town of Silas's birth greeted them like a stranger in a speakeasy. Pale faces watched from behind rain-streaked windows, and passersby scowled from under broad sou'wester hats. Many buildings had been boarded shut, left vacant after the plague some eighty years ago. Their windows glared like eyes stitched closed, the paint on their clapboard siding peeling with neglect. That nobody ever moved into those empty houses from other towns seemed normal to Silas when he was growing up here. Now, he wondered why.

"Looks like the place has seen better days," Abigail said as they clattered up Eliot Street and rounded the old statue in the square. Turning onto State Street, they paralleled the roaring Manuxet River until, finally, he caught a glimpse of the ocean ahead.

"It has." Silas struggled to keep his voice even. There had been little cheer for a young boy to find in a town like this, and the only time he'd regretted leaving had been when he received news that his parents had died. "Good-sized ships used to run cargo in and out of here back in the day, but storms silted in the harbor. There was talk of dredging, but the only folks in town who had the money to do it were the Marshes, and they refused to pay. Now only fishing boats come and go, and the old Marsh family has the corner on that market."

"Marsh? Relatives of yours?"

"Yes." Silas didn't elaborate. He hadn't told Abigail his connection with Innsmouth or anything about the old family of Marshes. He'd also kept his nightmares to himself. She'd think him stark raving mad if he told her his dreams were mirrored by the illustrations in her book. But insanity might be a kinder fate than discovering any truth to the tome's prophecy. "I grew up here."

"Well, that's ducky. I mean, your relatives will help us, right?" She stopped at the corner of Water Street and looked at him when he didn't answer. "Right?"

Silas stared out the windshield. From here he could see beyond the spit of land that protected the harbor, beyond the lighthouse flashing across the stormy sky, out the channel with its dented red and green buoys bobbing in the buffeting winds and chop, to the sea. The waves crashing on the rocks called to him, as they always had, but now, instead of the freedom of the sea in their roar, a more sinister susurration urged him. *Come home…* The yearning to heed that call plagued him like a toothache, impossible to ignore.

"Silas?"

Silas tore his gaze from the sea. "Maybe. We'll just have to see." He tamped down the nagging, pleading call echoing with the pounding waves, and pointed left. "Cross the bridge and find a spot on the shore side to park this jalopy. We'll see who we can find to talk to."

"OK."

Along the shore, the town had fallen into even deeper disrepair. The old shipping warehouses stood like emaciated scarecrows, weathered down to their bones by years of neglect. Roofs sagged and boards had been stolen from some, while others had completely fallen in, victims of fire, salvagers, or simple vandalism. At the north end of the bay, a dozen or so fishing boats bobbed on moorings near the one remaining fish plant in town, Marsh Seafood.

That, Silas resolved, *will be the last place we'll ask for help.* With any luck, they could find a weathered-in fisherman willing to earn a few bucks and keep his mouth shut. They'd get no help from the main family of Marshes.

The sheltered harbor wasn't much better off than the rundown buildings lining the shore, with half-sunk vessels dotting the once-bustling waterway. The silting had made the harbor unnavigable to all but shallow-draft boats about the size of *Sea Change*. He scanned the water, looking for anything they might rent or borrow. An old ferry sat at one pier, unable to move, stripped of what little brightwork or gear that could be sold. Other large vessels lay scattered about like tombstones in an ill-kept graveyard. There were several relics of the war waiting to be scrapped, and one old cod schooner now down at the stern, her once proud masts denuded and warped. The shipyard itself had fallen into ruin and rust, the jitneys streaked with the hue of dried blood, and powerful cranes thrust up like the bones of a skeleton's rotting fingers reaching from the grave. Smoke streamed away from only one of the old furnace's stacks, the one that the Marshes used for whatever ironwork they still did.

This place, that unforgiving shore, the familiar desolation and ruin, drove the siren song of the waves home within him. *Come to us… come to us… come home…* He felt guilty, that was all. Silas had fled Innsmouth barely out of boyhood, unwilling to be pulled down into decay and neglect with the rest of his relatives. Only his mother had pleaded with him to stay, but he'd refused, thinking a life on the sea would fulfill something in him that Innsmouth never could. He'd always longed for the sea, swimming and fishing as a boy, watching the ships ply the waves. The sea meant freedom, and he'd had that freedom for more than two decades.

And now I'm back… Funny how time makes liars of everyone.

"Where?" Abigail asked, dredging him out of his hypnosis.

"There." Silas pointed to a barn-like structure with an old flatbed truck parked out front. Smoke whipped away from the building's single metal stovepipe, so he knew someone was working. "That's a net loft. There'll be someone there we can talk to." The real question was, would they listen?

"Sure." Abigail pulled over, set the brake, killed the engine, and reached for her newly purchased umbrella.

"It's probably best to let me do the talking here, Abigail." Silas gave her an imploring look. "Folks around here are standoffish. If we start telling them about books that change and prophecies of the end of the world, we won't get anything but blank stares."

"All right." She didn't look happy about it but nodded. "What *are* you going to tell them?"

"I've been working on that." He shrugged and reached for the door handle. "Just follow my lead."

"OK by me." She opened her door and stepped out under her umbrella.

A quick splash through the rain, and Silas stepped inside the open loft door. Rain drummed on the roof, echoing hollowly within. The air hung thick with pipe smoke, the faint reek of fish, and the acrid tang of burnt coffee. Mounded nets, crates, buoys, coils of line, and various fishing gear littered the loft's periphery so thickly one could barely see the walls. In the center of the cluttered space, wide-mesh gillnets hung from block and tackle overhead. Four men sat on crates there, net needles darting in and out of the mesh, wielded deftly in their thick, calloused hands.

"Afternoon." Silas's greeting drew disinterested glances from three of the men, grizzled old faces beaten into lines of gray by lifetimes on the sea. The fourth, younger, with a wide, pallid face and sloping brow beneath his stocking cap, inspected first Silas, then Abigail with large watery eyes.

Definitely a Marsh. Silas considered turning on his heel and trying to find someone else to talk to, but stood his ground.

"Not the day for an outing to the shore." The young man turned back to his work, his short, spindly fingers handling the mesh with precision.

"That's the truth," Silas admitted, knowing that he and Abigail made an odd pair. He'd worked out a story during the bone-jarring drive that he hoped would sound tempting. "We drove up from Arkham. The lady here works for the university and needs to do some research out on the reef." *True enough, after a fashion.*

"The reef?" The younger man looked up at them again. "What reef?"

"Devil Reef. I'd take her myself, but my boat's in Kingsport, and I can't round Cape Ann in this blow. I'd hoped to rent a boat here."

The man stood and picked up an empty tin coffee cup. "What do you know of Devil Reef?" He strode to the stove and poured liquid as black as tar from the pot.

"I've fished there many times," Silas said with a casual shrug. "I grew up here. My name's Silas Marsh."

The coffee pot clanked down hard on the stove. All four men looked at him, the youngest with his sloped brow furrowed.

"Silas *Marsh*?" one of the older fellows asked around his pipe. "Knew yer father. You left some years back to go a sailin', didn't you?"

"That's right. Saw a good part of the world and put enough aside to buy my own boat. I'm working out of Kingsport now."

"Why the rush to go out?" the young one asked, taking his tin cup back to his crate. "The reef's not going anywhere. Why not wait until this storm blows over?"

"We can't." Abigail stepped up beside Silas, clutching her umbrella in both hands. "There's no time."

"Her project's got a deadline," Silas added, trying to sound casual. "All we need is a boat for a few hours. It's all protected waters from here to the reef."

"I'll pay," Abigail offered. "Ten dollars."

That raised some eyebrows. Ten dollars was more than a day's earnings for the average fisherman.

"*Tch!*" With a scornful look, the young man sat back down and picked up his net needle. "Ten dollars won't buy a new boat. It's too risky. Come back when the weather's laid down."

Silas opened his mouth, but Abigail stepped forward. "We *can't* wait. The time will be passed by then. We have to go *now*."

"Nobody's goin' out to Devil Reef today, missy."

The gravelly voice from the back of the loft caught Silas by surprise. He peered through the clutter of nets, buoys, rope, and rigging to see two figures, a stooped old woman and a taller man behind her, picking their way forward. There was a small room in the corner, buried in junk, that he hadn't noticed before. The voice had been the old woman's, her stringy gray hair and bent posture telling her years. A gnarled stick in her hand, its wood so black it looked like polished obsidian, thumped the floor with each step. Large, rheumy eyes regarded Silas from under a sloped brow, and her wide, thick lips stretched in a disagreeable frown. Her broad-shouldered companion loomed over her protectively, a man so similar to her in features that they had to be kin. Silas knew that look all too well.

"You're a Marsh," he said, a statement, not a question. "One of the main family."

"I am," she said, rapping her stick on the wooden floor as she tottered up to him. "And nobody goes out to Devil Reef without the approval of Old Man Marsh, which you haven't got."

The three older men continued their work without looking up, but the younger now stood as well. The two Marsh men had rigging knives at their belts, and their intimidating glares might have given a lesser man pause, but Silas remained unimpressed. They wouldn't resort to violence, not against him. However, the old woman's gnarled walking stick – *black coral, not wood,* he noted – made his skin crawl. It seemed to change shape under her knobby knuckles even as he watched.

"And how do we get his approval?" Abigail asked, as dauntless – or clueless – as ever.

The old woman's bulging eyes turned to Abigail, thick lids flicking in a reptilian blink. "You *don't*, missy." She looked to Silas and rapped her stick again, and a chill seeped up through the soles of his boots into his bones. "*He* may be a Marsh, by name if little else, but *you're* not."

"What's going to happen out there?" Abigail blurted. "*Something* is going to happen."

"Go back to your books, child. There's *nothing* for you here." The old woman rapped the floor twice more with her stick, and her thick lips parted to reveal rows of jagged teeth.

Abigail drew a sharp breath and stepped back unsteadily.

Silas grasped her arm. "Come on, Abigail. Let's go." He clenched his jaw to keep his voice steady and faced down the old woman's smile with the last sour dregs of his courage. "There's no help for us here."

Abigail let him usher her back to the car. She forgot to open her umbrella, and the rain drenched her before he settled her in her seat and closed the door. He cranked the car over and got in the passenger side to find her gripping the wheel in white-knuckled fists.

"What in the name of–" Abigail's voice quavered like a loose shutter in the wind.

"Just drive." Silas glanced back at the open door to the sail loft. The old woman stood there staring at them, the two Marsh men looming at her shoulders. "Just turn around and drive."

"Yes." Abigail ground gears and wrenched the wheel hard to the left. They lurched around with astonishing speed, as if the car itself longed to be out of this place.

Silas couldn't disagree. He glanced back to see the Marshes still staring at them from the net loft door, watery eyes, pallid faces, wide mouths... *What was I thinking to come back here?*

"Now tell me what the... heck just happened?"

"I'll explain." He pointed straight as they rumbled over the bridge "Drive straight along Water Street until we're out of town, then find a place to pull off. You can see Devil Reef from the beach."

"Fine."

They bounced along the shore road for a quarter mile. To their left, the raging nor'easter broke hard on the rocks until finally the riprap gave way to a wide, sandy beach. Silas gestured to a turnout, and Abigail pulled the jalopy over.

Setting the brake, she turned to face him. "Now what–"

"The old Marsh family's jealous of their fishing grounds. They don't like strangers out there." Silas opened his door and stepped out into the rain, breathing the salty mist in greedy gulps as he stared out over the beach. Breakers curled onto the sloped sand here, their beauty, grace, and power the embodiment of the sea.

"It has *got* to be more than that," Abigail joined him, gripping her umbrella fiercely against the greedy wind. "That woman... her *face.*"

"That's the Marsh family look. The main family, anyway." Silas clenched his hands and let the cool rain wash away his anxiety. "There are stories... about them, and about Devil Reef. I don't know how much of it is true and how much is just made up to run off strangers. I'm third cousin to the main family. They run the only fish processing plant in town, and pretty much call the shots. They came into real money somehow, more than just from fishing, and they own damn near every going concern in town. They've been known to run off other fishermen who set nets or longlines along the coast hereabouts. That old woman's one of the main family." Silas strode down the rocky incline to the beach, the crunch-squeak of the sand beneath his boots stirring memories from his childhood.

"But she…" Abigail teetered after him in her impractical shoes. "She seemed to *know* why we're here. And why is she so protective of Devil Reef?"

"That's it." Silas pointed across the waves, through the mist-laden air to a thick line of white just below the horizon. "That's Devil Reef, about two miles out. It protects the approach to Innsmouth from the ocean swells, so there's no danger taking a boat out from town. But no sensible captain would round Cape Ann in this weather, and she knows it. All she had to do was say no boat would leave the harbor, and we were done here. No Innsmouth fisherman will flout the Marshes, not if they ever want to sell their catch again."

"But… how… why…"

Silas let the roar of the surf drown out Abigail's questions. It didn't matter any longer, but she wouldn't listen to reason. The crashing waves thrummed up through his legs, their rhythm syncopating with the beat of his heart.

"I swam here as a boy."

Come home…

Silas breathed in the mist like a tonic, taking in the tremulous roar like music, letting it infuse him. "I would swim for hours, just to feel the water."

Come…

"They're my best memories… being in the sea… feeling the waves."

Abigail's voice yammered on behind him, but it was of no more import than the squawking of seabirds.

Be with us… your time is nigh…

Sand squeaked beneath his boots. *Yes… Now… Finally…*

A gull screeched – or was it a voice? – but Silas ignored it. Coolness enveloped his feet, his legs, refreshing… welcoming.

Come home…

Something tugged at his arm, tearing at his shirt, but he pulled away. *The sea… it's all that matters… it's the only thing that will endure… forever.*

Pain lanced through his back as something sharp poked him.

Silas whirled, flinging out a hand to fend off the attack. He snatched the tip of Abigail's umbrella and stared at her in shock.

"Silas!" Her eyes widened and focused past his shoulder. She released her umbrella, turned and ran as well as she could, slogging through knee-deep surf in her sodden dress.

"What the hell?" Silas looked down. He stood thigh deep in the ocean, with no recollection of having waded in. A bone-jarring roar rose behind him.

Silas ducked into the massive curling wave, but the power of the sea was not to be so easily thwarted. It flung him down like a rag doll, smashing him into the hard sand. He went limp, knowing better than to fight that power.

Come to us! The call tore through him with the cool embrace of the sea, a vision of welcoming arms, webbed hands…

He came up sputtering spray and sand. The wave receded, its greedy grasp dragging him back into the sea, but he crawled forward, lurching up to stumble onto the shore, the siren song fading from his mind.

"Silas!" Abigail was there, gripping his arm, shaking him, terror honing her voice like a knife. "What in the *hell* were you doing?"

He coughed and dragged in a breath, glancing back over his shoulder at the sea. *Come to us...*

"No! Don't you dare." Pain lanced through his shoulder as her nails latched on hard. "Don't you *dare* do that again."

"What..." Silas turned, rubbing his sore shoulder, then his aching back. She'd attacked him, but... Then he remembered the call, the yearning, his nightmares, the tome, and Devil Reef, and he knew there was a connection. But what connection other than utter madness, he couldn't fathom. "God in heaven." His knees folded and hit the hard sand.

"What *happened* to you?" Abigail's hysteria seemed tempered now. "Were you intending to *swim* out to Devil Reef?"

"No... I just... lost myself for a second." She'd never believe him if he told her of his nightmares and the siren song pulling him in. She'd think him stark raving mad. "I remembered swimming here as a boy, and just..."

"Come on." She tugged at his arm. "You're *soaked*, and you owe me another umbrella."

"I..." Silas glanced again over his shoulder at the sea. Its call still pulled at him, but he could resist it now. He staggered with her back to the car and hurled himself into his seat. The door thumped closed, dulling the siren song of the surf. "I'm sorry. I don't know what came over me."

"Well, never mind." Abigail jammed the shifter in gear and wheeled the car around. "We've got to figure out some other way to get out to Devil Reef. Something's happening around here, and you deciding to take a *swim* in the middle of a storm corroborates my theory that it's affecting us *both*."

"Yes." He couldn't disagree but had little more to add. They couldn't get a boat in Innsmouth, and couldn't take *Sea Change* around the cape in this weather. They were done. There was nothing to do but go home.

They drove in silence, Silas's thoughts running in circles. What would have happened if Abigail hadn't broken his trance? Would he have drowned in the surf, unable to help himself? Why did he feel that the answer to the connection between his nightmares and the tome's prophecy was to be found out on Devil Reef?

"What next?" Abigail asked as Arkham hove into view.

"Next?" He barked a laugh and wiped the gritty salt from his face with the sleeve of his sodden shirt. "I have no idea, Abigail."

"Well, the end of the whole world is looming, and we know where it's going to start, Silas Marsh. We have to do *something*. We can't just run away from this." Abigail's old determination was back, and it infected him like a fever.

No more running… "We need to think."

"Yes, we do."

"And I need a drink."

"If you mean something stronger than coffee, I'm with you."

He looked at her with surprise. "Really?"

"Yes." Abigail swallowed hard and nodded. "The end of the works of *mankind*, Silas. *Hell*, yes."

He pointed to a diner as they neared the edge of town. "Join me, then. Maybe we'll come up with an idea."

CHAPTER 5
Hibb's Roadhouse

"Lordy, you two are soaked right through," the waitress said as she sauntered over. "Need a little something to warm you up?"

"Yes." Silas knew this place and knew what to order. "Two sweet iced teas with lemon."

The waitress blinked at them, but then winked and nodded. "Comin' right up, sugar."

"Sweet iced tea?" Abigail made a face. "I thought you said–"

"Trust me."

Ordering sweet iced tea with lemon wouldn't have raised an eyebrow south of the Mason-Dixon Line, but no New Englander would ever request it. Prohibition put the kibosh on the legal sale of alcohol, but that didn't mean it couldn't be gotten. Speakeasies like this one often used subtle codes to order spirited libation. In this case, "sweet iced tea with lemon" would get you Canadian whiskey on the rocks, and nobody would know the difference.

The waitress returned in moments holding two tall glasses with lemon wedges perched on the rim. "Enjoy," she said with another wink as she put the glasses on the table and sashayed off.

"Drink up." Silas lifted his glass and took a swallow. The cold Canadian whiskey burned a track of icy fire down his throat.

Abigail sniffed her glass and her eyes widened. "Sweet tea, huh?" She sipped and stifled a cough. "Jesus, Mary, and Joseph, that's more like it." She took another sip and then a deep breath. "Are you feeling any better?"

"Some." Silas stared at his drink. *She must think I'm loony, walking into the sea…* But he could still feel that call, that yearning, and the rap of the old woman's stick on the floor of the net loft reverberating through his bones.

"Those people, the Marshes… the main family…" Abigail paused as if unsure how to proceed. "Do they all have that… look?"

"Most." Silas took another big swallow and felt the whiskey start to dull his nerves, ease the pounding in his head. "It supposedly started generations back with Old Obed Marsh. Old Obed went to sea and came back with a new wife and… some strange notions. That wasn't long before a plague wiped out nearly a third of the town. Since then, the Marshes tend to keep to themselves, mostly marrying within the extended family."

"Innsmouth…" Abigail drank and hiccupped. "God above, Silas, what's happening in that town?"

"I don't know." He shook his head in honest befuddlement. "I grew up there, but I never did learn the truth. Nobody talks about it and asking questions will only get you trouble."

"And what happened to you on that beach?"

"I… don't really know." Abigail's eyes showed only concern. She'd saved him back there and deserved an honest answer. If she called him crazy, well, he wouldn't call her a liar. "The sea calls to me, Abigail. It always has, but lately it's been… hard to ignore.

Until now, I've been able to resist. Being on my boat, on the water, helps, but there on that beach, I just…"

"*Calls* to you?" Her brow furrowed.

"I know. It sounds crazy." He drank more whiskey and sighed. "It *is* crazy."

"No crazier than a book that changes and speaks of the end of the world." She gripped his arm hard. "What do we *do*? I'm *scared*, Silas."

"You'd be a fool or crazy *not* to be scared. Hell, I think I *am* crazy, and I'm *still* scared."

"You're not crazy, and neither am I." Abigail gulped from her glass and gasped a deep breath. "Look, I thought a lot on the way back. That… woman in Innsmouth didn't even flinch when I asked her what was going to happen out on Devil Reef. She *knew*."

"Maybe, but so what?"

"Don't you see? She refused to let us borrow a boat. She stopped us from going out there." Abigail leaned over the table. "That means we're onto something here. They're afraid we *can* do something to stop this. Just like the date in the book changing – it's changing because it *knows* we're onto it. It wouldn't be trying to stop us if we weren't a threat."

"It?" Silas didn't like the sound of that. "Before you said 'they' knew we were onto them and were changing the date to foil us. You think my damned relatives have something to do with this, and now you're saying '*it*'. What do you mean?"

"I don't know, but something or someone's behind this, Silas. I don't know what *it* or *they* are, but something's out there on Devil Reef. It's involved with those *freaks* in Innsmouth, and it damn near dragged you into the sea this afternoon." She gripped his arm again, her nails biting in hard. "And it intends to end the world of man."

"But how can we stop something we don't understand?"

"I don't know that either, but if we *couldn't* stop it, would it be working so hard to try to stop *us*?" Abigail sipped her whiskey and let go of his arm. "Why fight us if we had no chance?"

That made a terrifying type of sense. Maybe they could stop it. Silas downed the rest of his whiskey and decided not to argue with her use of 'we'. He was in this now, and he knew as surely as he knew he would have swum right out to Devil Reef this afternoon if Abigail hadn't jabbed him in the back with her umbrella, that if he didn't put an end to this, he would finally succumb to that call. But if he could stop it, maybe… maybe his nightmares would end.

"Fine. We can stop this, but how?"

"We've got to get out to that reef and find out what's there, but without a boat, how can we?"

"Whoever stole my chart must have been trying to keep us from…" Every plot pricked the chart at exactly the same spot. "The location I plotted wasn't on the reef, but *behind* it. There's a slough that runs right up behind the reef. That's deep water."

"So, now we need to look *underwater*?" Abigail's nose wrinkled in disbelief. "How in the name of–"

"Abigail, that's it! That's why whatever's behind this is worried. When I'm not fishing, I work deep-sea salvage, recovering lost fishing gear or sunken boats. I've got a diving rig in Kingsport, but I can't get *Sea Change* around the cape."

Abigail's eyes widened. "Wait! What about the canal?"

"Canal?"

"Yes, Blynman Canal, from Gloucester to Annisquam. I've seen it on maps in the library. You said you couldn't take your boat *around* Cape Ann, but the canal cuts *behind* the cape. Can't you take your boat through there?"

"Sonofa…" Silas bit off the curse. "I've never used it. The channel's narrow and shoaled, and the drawbridge is more apt to be *stuck* than working properly. I can't get *Sea Change* under it without lowering the entire mast rig, which takes hours, so I've always gone around the cape."

"But you *can* lower it, right?"

"I *suppose*, but…" Silas preferred open sea to a stinking ditch, but now, with the storm ravaging Cape Ann, it made sense. "You're right. We can do this, but we've got to hurry to get out of the Annisquam bar before the wind backs to the north. Drink up. We've got work to do." He pushed her glass toward her. "We need to pick up that book from the library in case the date changes again, then lower the mast and get down to Kingsport before dark. You can help me run the diving rig."

"Um…" Abigail took another gulp from her glass and put it down. "OK, but you'll have to show me what to do. I've never been on a boat in my life. I can't even *swim*."

He blinked at her. "You can't *swim*, and you waded into the surf after me?"

Her cheeks flushed pink. "That was entirely different."

He didn't want to argue that it really wasn't different; she'd saved his life, after all. "Well, come on." Silas dropped four bits on the table and bustled her out into the storm. "If we hurry, we can be through the Annisquam end of the canal before the tide starts to ebb."

CHAPTER 6
Devil Reef

Light slashed through the rain as they rounded the last bend in Blynman Canal, and Silas breathed a sigh of relief. The wind only kicked up wavelets in the narrow waterway, and the tide was still flowing in, instead of out, but that was about to change. He'd been surprised to find the tide at Blynman Bridge dead low when it should have been flooding, but that had been to their advantage. The laborious process of lowering the mast and boom had been worth it. They'd slipped under the bridge with feet to spare. The light swept like a scythe over them again, a great cyclopean eye questing through the night.

"That's Wigwam Point Light." Silas pointed. "The bar's just beyond. If the wind's backed too far to the north, it could be breaking, but we'll see. The tide seems to be flooding still, but it *should* be on the ebb. That's good for us. The storm must be causing a surge."

"I didn't understand a word you just said." Abigail gripped the pilothouse console as if hanging on for dear life, even though the boat barely rocked. She'd changed into flat shoes, trousers, flannel

450

shirt, and a raincoat buttoned up to her neck, hardly the prim librarian any longer. She'd asked him about life preservers, but he didn't have any. The bulky things were more likely to kill you than save you on a working fishing boat.

"That lighthouse marks the opening of the canal to the sea," Silas gestured. "If the wind's blowing from the north, the waves will be big across the mouth of the channel where it shallows. The tide's still coming in, which it *shouldn't* be doing, but that'll help. If the waves are breaking, we won't be able to pass."

"Oh." She swallowed hard. "OK."

"Just hang on. It'll get bumpy, but *Sea Change* can take it."

She nodded and gripped harder, bracing her back against the aft bulkhead.

The run from Kingsport to Gloucester had been rough, but not dangerous. Despite her terror, Abigail had been only mildly ill. The Annisquam bar, however, would be the telling tale. The winds of a nor'easter backed from east to northeast to north as the storm progressed up the coast. If the wind had already shifted to the north, the seas would race right into the mouth of the canal, and they'd be in for a real trouncing. Passing the bar in daylight with this weather would have been dangerous enough. Silas didn't tell Abigail that doing it in the dark bordered on suicidal.

Silas squinted into the gloom as the lighthouse beam swept the sea. The swells rose across the bar in dark lines of shadow through the rain-streaked windows. They were large, but they weren't breaking. *Good timing or dumb luck, I'll take it.* He eased the throttle forward and *Sea Change* picked up speed.

The bow lifted as they mounted the first real swell, then tilted down into the trough. The next was steeper and the next even higher as they passed Wigwam Light. Silas flicked his gaze constantly between the compass and the sea. When the lighthouse beam swept past from astern, he glimpsed one of the channel buoys and altered course.

"What's that light?" Abigail's voice trembled as she pointed ahead.

"The sea buoy. It's a good reference, but the one we need to find is red number four. That one's not lit, but it marks the western shoal. Once that's behind us, we can make our turn."

Abigail bit back a squeak of terror as *Sea Change* pitched violently over a sharp swell.

"Don't worry. The waves aren't breaking." *Thank God…* "We can make it."

"OK." She didn't sound convinced.

"Just help me look for a red buoy. Doing this with only one eye isn't easy."

"Sure." She pressed her face closer to the rain-streaked glass.

Silas leaned out the pilothouse door and squinted into the rain as the beam of light swept the sea once more. *Nothing…* He couldn't see when they were in the trough between waves. He had to get a look when they were atop one. *Sea Change* climbed over another swell, but the light didn't sweep in time. *Come on…* Silas throttled back a bit, trying to time his progress with the light and the next wave.

A wave loomed, and the light swept the sea. Silas leaned out again and shielded his eye from the slashing rain.

"There!" Red number four shone clearly for an instant only fifty yards off their port bow.

"I see it!" Abigail sounded both panicked and triumphant.

"That buoy is our mark to turn. We're right where we need to be." He flashed her a grin, realizing that the tension and the motion of the sea had him feeling better than he had in weeks. "We're good. We're going to make it."

"Oh, *good.*"

They passed the buoy, and Silas watched the swells. He'd have to time his turn just right. "Hang on, now. We'll take at least one hard roll before we get pointed in the right direction."

"I *am* hanging on."

Silas counted the swells, waiting for the peak seventh in the set. They climbed over the peak swell, and he wrenched the wheel hard to port. *Sea Change* answered as they raced down the back side of the swell. The next was not so high, but it caught them on the beam, rolling the boat so far that her gunnels dipped. Something crashed across the cabin behind him – the coffee pot maybe – but he didn't have time to look. Another swell rolled them hard before her bow came around. The next they took on the quarter, lessening the roll but making steering more difficult. He fought the wheel to keep the bow down the wave and watched white water roar past.

"We're making good time now." He grinned at Abigail, but her eyes were squeezed tightly shut. "Abigail! We're clear. We're headed for Devil Reef. Just a few miles. It's going to be roily, but in half an hour we'll be in protected waters." He steered by feel as another wave picked up their stern and they raced down a wave, keeping his eye on the compass.

"It's pitch black out. How do you know where we are?" Abigail still didn't sound convinced that they weren't in mortal danger.

"See that light?" Silas pointed to the sweeping beam far off the port bow. "That's the Innsmouth lighthouse."

"OK."

"And that smaller light over there," he pointed to starboard, "is the Essex Bay sea buoy. We'll see the Plum Island Channel sea buoy before long and that'll mark our turn inshore. I know the compass headings through the channel by heart." He wasn't about to tell her the danger of miscalculating his approach and actually hitting one of the reefs. There was no reason to worry her any further when the careening corkscrew motion of the boat already had her terrified.

After half an hour of enduring that millrace run downwind, white water roaring down the sides of the boat at every roll, Silas pointed out the Plum Island buoy and lined up his approach. Glancing behind them at the lighted buoy, the lighthouse, and the compass, he made his turn. The seas were now on the port stern quarter, which made the steering tricky. If he took one wrong, they could broach and roll. Without a chart or his logbook, he was going from memory, but when the sweep of the Innsmouth lighthouse illuminated a ghostly white line of breakers on the reefs to starboard, he knew he was in the right spot. In ten minutes, the seas calmed, and he turned north.

"We're behind the reefs." Silas eased his grip on the wheel and flexed his hands to relieve cramped muscles.

"Thank heavens." Abigail rubbed her eyes and blinked, peering into the darkness. "I still can't see a thing."

"I know where we are, and I know the approach to Devil Reef from inshore. It's tricky, but I've done it dozens of times." He left out the part about not having his chart.

"I thought you said the Marshes don't let anyone fish there."

"They don't." He grinned at her. "But they can't watch all the time. You can't see the reef from town unless you climb the lighthouse or drive out to the beach."

She peered out the window, then up at the sky. "What about our lights? Won't they see them?"

"Oh, hell. Thanks." Silas flipped the switch that killed their running lights. "I forgot. I never run at night without lights."

"Nice to know I'm good for something."

"I couldn't do this without you, Abigail. This is *your* mystery, remember?"

"I wish I could forget."

When Innsmouth light shone at the right bearing, Silas turned north and slipped between the shoals behind Devil Reef. Again, without his chart, he was going by memory. Then the light swept past to illuminate the roaring white line of the breakers on the reef.

Come to us…

So focused upon piloting through the storm, the shoals and reefs, Silas had forgotten the siren song that he felt on the beach. Now it sang along his every nerve. He gritted his teeth against that call, that yearning, and throttled back, approaching slowly. He no longer needed a chart to tell him where to go.

Almost home… yes… come to us…

"We're close." He pulled the throttle back to an idle. "I can *feel* it."

"You can?" Abigail looked at him askance.

"Yes." They slowed until the boat came to a dead stop against the howling wind. "Steer her straight into the wind for a moment while I drop anchor."

"OK." Abigail took the wheel tentatively.

Silas strode out onto the bow and released the anchor. It plunged down into inky blackness, running free for sixty feet before it struck bottom. He resisted the urge to dive in after it, and let out another two hundred feet before tying it off.

"We're here," he announced as he stepped back into the pilothouse and kicked the engine out of gear.

"Finally!" Abigail hurried aft to the chart table and pulled her tome from her satchel.

He joined her to peer at the page under a shuttered lantern. "Anything new?"

"Yes." She looked up at him. "The time's changed again, Silas."

"When is it now?"

"Tomorrow night, just past midnight." She jotted down a new set of numbers in her notebook and turned to show him. "It's skipped up a whole day."

"Damn it!" An uncharacteristic surge of anger welled up as if he'd just seen the second ace of hearts in a deck of cards. "Ever feel like we're being flimflammed?"

"What, like this is just an elaborate trick or something?" Abigail blinked and shook her head. "No. You saw the numbers in the book change. That's no trick."

"I know, but what if…" His anger evolved into a cold dread in his gut. "Twelve hours ago, I walked into the surf because this place was calling to me. Now here I am, ready to get in the water. Maybe that's exactly what it *wants* me to do."

"What it *wants* you to do?" Confusion furrowed her brow.

"Yes. I can *still* feel it calling me, Abigail." Silas clenched his scarred hands into fists. "Maybe we're not *preventing* anything. Maybe that book's lying to us, or whatever *is* going to bring about this end of the world needs *me* to do it. Maybe *it* sent you to me."

"Silas, I… You don't think that I'm trying to–"

"No! No, Abigail, not you. You saved me on that beach, but that book," he stabbed a finger at the tome, "could just be a… a tool or a piece of something bigger that wants me to go down there."

"But if you don't go, and we *can* prevent this…"

"Or that's what it wants, and I help bring an end to the world."

She shook her head. "I don't believe it. A four hundred year-old prophecy just to lure *you* into the water?"

"Unless it needs me to fulfill that prophecy." Silas gritted his teeth against the call of the sea that sang through his bones. "Damned if I do, and damned if I don't." He closed his eyes and saw the grinning teeth of the old woman in Innsmouth. "I feel like if I go down there, I'll never come back."

"Silas, *I* was the one who discovered this passage, not you." Abigail thumped a finger to the text, and Silas would have sworn the figures in the margin writhed. "I asked you to help me, but I also asked about a dozen others. Everyone else thought I was crazy, and *you* believed me. That's not a trick. That's being human: a real, honest-to-God human being willing to lay down his life for someone he only met two days ago. That's why you're here – not because of some curse."

He opened his mouth but didn't have anything to say. Her trust in him, her faith in his humanity, cut through his fear like a knife.

"Besides," she continued, "if that *revolting* old woman in Innsmouth tried to stop us from coming out here, we *have* to be on the right track."

Silas swallowed and nodded. She had a point. "All right." He flexed his big hands, looked down at his scarred palms, and took a breath. "All right, then, come on. I need to get the mast and boom back in place, and show you how to work the compressor and lift."

Opening the engine compartment, he threw the lever that diverted power from the gearbox to the winch. An hour of dangerous labor later, the mast and boom were once again up, their cables cinched down tight. Finally, he stepped out on deck to show Abigail how to work the controls.

"It's just like a car. Pull the clutch and shift up or down to spool the line in or out. If there's tension on the line, and you pull the clutch, it'll spool out, just like a car coasting downhill."

"OK."

"The compressor's simple." He jerked the pull start and it sputtered to life. "Keep gas in the tank there and it'll run forever. Just don't kink the air hose."

"Right."

"There's also a telephone setup so we can talk." He pointed to the simple box propped against the side of the cabin out of the rain. "You can tell me if anything goes wrong, and I can tell you what I'm seeing."

"Well, *that's* a help." She experimented with the phone as he shrugged into the heavy breastplate and massive boots.

Silas clomped back inside the cabin and opened the locker, grabbed his heavy knife and clipped it to the belt of his dive suit. The light from Innsmouth lighthouse swept over the boat to glint on cold blue metal in the back of the locker.

Better safe than sorry. Silas pulled the Remington from its bracket and a box of shells from the shelf. "You know how to use this?"

Abigail looked at the shotgun dubiously. "In theory, but why would I need a firearm?"

Silas nodded to the lighthouse as he broke open the breech and checked the loads. "Someone might see us from the lighthouse. If they do, and Old Man Marsh hears that there's someone out here, they might send a boat out to run us off." He propped the Remington in the corner just inside the cabin door. "If you have to use it, just remember to hold it tight against your shoulder and don't aim below our waterline. Double-aught buckshot'll put a hole right through her hull, and then we'll be in a real pickle. Now, help me with the helmet."

Abigail bit her lip and nodded. "Sure."

They muscled the heavy helmet over his head and sealed it to the suit, but Silas left the faceplate open for now. He picked up the powerful dive lantern and briefly flipped the switch to check the battery while Abigail hooked the lift line to the eye bolt on the top of the helmet. He shuffled to the rail and sat down. With weights, boots, and helmet, the rig weighed about two hundred pounds, so he couldn't go anywhere fast. Once in the water, he'd be able to move easier.

"Check the telephone."

"Right." Abigail cranked the handle and spoke into the microphone. "Can you hear me?"

Her voice crackled in his ear. "Yes, I hear you fine." His own crackly voice came out of the telephone speaker. "OK, we're in about sixty feet of water, and there's two hundred feet of hose coiled on deck. I'll have to search around, so if I come near the end, just let me know."

"Right." She pointed to his nose and smiled weakly. "Don't forget the faceplate."

"I'd be in for a shock if I did." He closed the plate and dogged it down tight. The outside world vanished from his senses. No howling wind, slashing rain, lapping water, only the echo of his fear and the siren call pulling him into the depths. *Just do it, Silas.* He adjusted the air flow, and said, "OK, I'm ready. Lift me up. I can't climb over the rail in this rig."

"OK." She worked the lever that engaged the lift, and he felt the weight leave his shoulders. The straps of the suit pulled him up, and he braced a foot against the rail to keep from swinging.

The familiar tasks of getting everything ready had settled his nerves, but now that it came to actually descending into that inky blackness, terror rose up like bile from his gut.

"Be careful," Abigail's voice crackled.

"Careful?" Silas barked a nervous laugh, marshaled his flagging courage, and pushed off the railing. With nothing beneath him but water, he said, "Down."

"Down," came her reply.

Silas descended into blackness.

He flipped on the light, but the beam vanished into the hazy distance no matter which way he directed it. He turned his head inside the helmet, but with only one eye he couldn't see out the back left porthole. There was also no way to look straight down with the tension of the line keeping him upright. Cold crept up his legs as the suit pressed in on him like a chill embrace. He adjusted the air flow, yawning to pop his ears, and the chill receded.

"Forty... fifty... sixty..." Abigail's crackly voice called off the marks on the winch line, his only link to the world of air and light.

His boots hit something, and he staggered as the weight of the helmet came down on his shoulders, less than it was on the surface, but still heavy. "Stop. I'm on the bottom." He shone the light around. Silt billowed up around his legs in an obscuring cloud. A few sleepy fish and one lobster skittered among the algae-covered rocks. Nothing unusual. "I can see only about twenty feet. The water's all churned up from the storm. I'm going to start walking a big circle, so give me some slack."

"How much?" He could barely hear her over the roar of the surf on the reef and his pounding heart.

"Twenty feet at a time." Silas began trudging forward. "I'll walk out until it comes taut then do a circle." His shuffling steps stirred up even more silt, obscuring his view. "If I don't find anything, you give me twenty more and I do it again."

"Right."

Silas shuffled along until the lift line pulled him up short. He shone the light around, twisting back and forth in the cumbersome suit for a better view. With only one eye, he had to turn his whole body to look to his left. The inky blackness yielded nothing but indistinct shapes that flicked at the limit of his vision. *Just fish attracted to the light.* He swallowed the lump in his throat, turned to his left, and continued along, all but blind.

Come to us…

"What?" Silas stopped and rapped his helmet. "What did you say?"

"I didn't say anything," came Abigail's reply.

"I thought–" He jerked to a stop as his light reflected off something silvery, snapped his head around inside the helmet to look, but it was gone. His heart hammered in his ears, his mouth suddenly dry. Silas swung the light around frantically. Nothing. "Talk to me, Abigail. I… need to hear a voice."

"Oh, OK. You're between the boat and the reef. You didn't walk in a circle. You walked straight toward the reef."

"I did?" He turned left to walk a circle.

No… come to us… come home.

He stopped. The voice wasn't Abigail, and turning his back on it felt like pressing a knife into his own flesh. His legs refused to take a step. He turned back and shone the light, but still there was nothing there.

"Give me some more slack, Abigail. I can… feel it. It's calling me."

"Silas? You sound strange!"

He shook his head sharply. Sweat dripped off his nose. "I'm OK." He wasn't OK, not by a long shot. "Talk to me. Hearing your voice helps. Just give me slack."

"OK."

The line slackened and Silas trudged forward, sweeping the light back and forth. *Nothing…*

Abigail's voice crackled, "Ninety feet… one hundred…"

When she reached one hundred and fifty, a dark wall of riveted iron loomed out of the blackness.

Silas stopped. "I found something." He shone his light up the wall to illuminate a porthole and a railing high above, bending his back to look up through the helmet's portholes. "A shipwreck. A freighter, maybe." He started toward it, but the line jerked him to a stop. "Slack."

"OK, slack." The tension eased. "Be careful, Silas."

Careful… right. Silas gritted his teeth to keep them from chattering and shuffled forward. The light illuminated a jagged hole in the side of the ship, the thick iron bent inward. Something glittered within, a flick of motion, silvery, then nothing. "There's a hole in the hull. She must have struck a mine during the war."

The air hose yanked him back hard, nearly toppling him backward.

"Slack on the hose! Is the boat drifting?"

"I *am* giving slack, and no, I don't think we've moved at all. You're taking more air hose than rope. I don't…" Her voice crackled and started to break up.

"Abigail?" It didn't make sense that he was taking more hose than rope unless the hose had gotten hooked on a rock or something. He grabbed the hose and pulled, struggling toward the ship.

Yes… come home…

Abigail's voice crackled. "…don't know… something… with the…"

"Bad connection. You're breaking up! Crank the phone again."

The hose went slack, and he nearly fell with the release. He lunged forward in the cumbersome suit, the dark hole yawning in his light like a toothed maw. Another flicker of silver within.

"Something's pulling... end of the... to do!"

"What?" Silas tugged on the hose, lurching forward.

Yes... come... come home...

"Just a bit more." Two more steps and he reached the gaping hole.

Grasping the edge, Silas leaned in and raised his lamp to shine inside. The light scattered a school of small fish. Larger shapes filled the space beyond, a mass of pale bodies vague through the hazy water. They rolled and roiled in a confusing swarm.

Come... Come to us... Come home.

A shape darted forth into the light, and Silas's breath caught in his throat. Bulging eyes and pointed translucent teeth, human hands with webbed fingers and claws. He panned the light, illuminating hundreds of the grotesque faces, all staring at him.

Come to us!

The call reverberated through his skull, drowning his panic, grasping his very soul, pulling him in, impossible to resist.

Carefully grasping the edge of jagged metal, Silas hauled himself up onto the edge. A piercing, crackling scream sang in his ears, but he ignored it. He scrabbled over the edge into the wreck, finally answering the siren call.

Come home... Home.

Something jerked Silas backward so hard he cracked his forehead on the helmet. As he fell backward through the jagged hole, the beam of his light swept up into the rusty iron frames of the wreck's hold. Something larger loomed there, something inconceivable, huge and writhing, eyes as big as platters, tentacles with clawed tips. At the center of the nightmare, a maelstrom of darkness within darkness swallowed his light like a hungry maw.

Then he was lying on his back, a full ten feet from the opening. Before he could even try to get up, he was dragged back over the rough rocks then jerked upright toward the surface. A scream crackled from the telephone. *Abigail?* She was hauling in the lift line. Something must have happened.

Silas surged from the water and into the air, his helmet clanging against the boom pulley as he jerked to a stop. A deafening boom split the air with a flash like lightning.

Dangling like a side of beef in a butcher shop, unable to get down, Silas played his light over the deck. Abigail sat against the cabin bulkhead, the smoking Remington in her lap. Some feet away, a shape lay sprawled on the deck. Abigail stared wide-eyed at the thing, trembling, her finger still tight on the triggers of the shotgun.

"Abigail!" he yelled, but either the phone line was out, or she couldn't hear it. He considered cutting the lift line, but with the boom out over the water, that would send him plunging back down into the depths. Instead, he worked the dogs of his faceplate and swung the tiny window open. "Abigail!"

She jerked and looked up at him as if stunned that he'd somehow levitated into the air. Realization dawned on her face, and she scrambled up. Her hands shook as she put aside the smoking shotgun and worked the crank to swing the lift boom inboard. As she eased the clutch and lowered Silas gently to the deck, he noticed that the engine wasn't running. The sudden stop of the lift must have killed it.

"Silas!" Abigail helped him with the helmet, her face pale and dripping in the rain. "Silas, what *is* that? It climbed up your air hose! It tried to… to *grab* me."

Finally, the helmet came off and he could see. One of the creatures he'd seen inside the wreck lay splayed on the deck, a smoking hole as big as Silas's fist in its chest. Once free of the cumbersome suit, he crossed the deck and knelt by the dead creature.

"I don't know what it is, Abigail, but…"

Half-fish, half-human, it reminded him of the illustrations in Abigail's tome. *My nightmares…* Its thick lips, wide mouth, bulging eyes, and sloped forehead bore an unsettling resemblance to the old woman in Innsmouth. *The main Marsh family…* Silas poked the cold, scaly flesh with a finger and shuddered. He couldn't deny what he'd seen in the wreck now, not with the proof lying before him. He wasn't crazy. *The family curse isn't madness, it's this!*

"It tried to *grab* me, Silas!" Abigail whirled and snatched up the Remington, snapping open the breech and loading two more shells from her pocket. "It climbed up your air hose."

"There are *more* of them down there, Abigail." Silas gritted his teeth against the call echoing in his mind, the memory of those writhing shapes. He strode into the cabin, pulled the bottle of spiritus frumenti from the cupboard, and wrenched the cork free. The whiskey burned a line down his throat. "Here." He traded the bottle for the shotgun.

Abigail drank down two swallows, coughed, and said, "*More* of them?" The bottle quaked in her hand as she handed it back. "How many more?"

"I didn't *count* them. A *lot* more." *Enough to drag us down there.* He handed her the Remington and took the bottle back, the memory of what else he'd seen screaming through his mind. *Got to get the hell out of here.* Replacing the bottle in the cupboard, he went back on deck and started hauling in the air hose. "And something else. Something bigger and... darker. I don't know. I only got a glimpse."

"Bigger?" Abigail stood in the doorway out of the rain, the shotgun steadier now in her grasp.

"Yes, a *lot* bigger! And some kind of... maelstrom, or something." When he had the air hose hauled in, Silas killed the compressor and glared down at the slimy corpse on the deck. Loath to touch it, he pulled on a pair of thick gloves and heaved the disgusting thing over the side. The rain would wash the vile creature's blood and slime away by the time they got back. He threw his gloves overboard and stepped past Abigail into the cabin. "Keep an eye out while I get the engine started and haul anchor. We'll be out of here in ten minutes!"

"What? Where are we going?"

"Home, Arkham, anywhere! As far the *hell* away from here as possible!" Silas heaved open the engine room hatch, flipped the transfer coupling back to the drive shaft, and cranked the engine to life.

"Wait!"

"For what, one of those monsters to come up here and drag us down to Davey Jones' Locker?" He slammed the hatch and started forward.

"Listen to me," she followed him to the pilothouse, still holding the shotgun. "Nothing's *changed*, Silas. We still have to stop this,"

"Stop it?" He whirled on her. "There's no *way*, Abigail. Those things are huge. We've got to get away!"

"Away where? Don't you remember the passage? All the works of man will be cast down. Everything! You *can't* run away from that." She wasn't exactly pointing the Remington at him, but at the deck between them. Her finger rested very near the triggers.

This is crazy. She's crazy. Silas's nightmares had become real. There were monsters beneath them right now, a seething mass of horrors that called to him even as they argued, and she wanted him to dive down there and take them all on with nothing but a belt knife. Terror pounded through his veins, drowning out the siren call. If he moved quickly, he might get the gun away from her before she blasted a hole through the deck and maybe even the hull, but what then?

The end of the world of man… Armageddon. No place to hide.

"*How*, Abigail? How do we stop this? I *can't* go down there again."

"What? Why not?"

"*Because*, damn it. You remember the beach. Remember me walking into the damnable ocean? They called to me when I was down there, Abigail, and I couldn't resist. If you hadn't pulled me up, I'd have walked right into the whole swarming mass of them."

She stumbled back half a step, her face white as a sheet. "Then the world's doomed, Silas. I can't do this without your help, and you won't help. You're dooming millions by doing nothing."

"There's nothing *to* do."

"Isn't there?" She stepped forward. "You're telling me there's no way to blow that wreck to hell? Gasoline? Dynamite? Anything?"

"We don't *have* anything like that." He needed to make her see reason. She hadn't seen what he'd seen. "And even if we did, we don't know if it'll work. If I go back down there, I'll *die*."

"We *do* know. We *must* be able to stop this, or they wouldn't be trying so hard to stop us! If we don't destroy that evil place, we *both* die. All of *mankind* dies. Don't you see?"

Silas gritted his teeth. *The end of the world of man…* He whirled away from her and leaned on the boat's wheel, gazing out into the howling darkness, trying to think through his terror.

Light swept over them from the Innsmouth lighthouse, drawing his eye out of habit. *Innsmouth…* Could they get something there, barrels of gasoline, maybe, and some way to get them down to the wreck and set them off? No, gasoline would float. Barrels of it would be too hard to weigh down. *We'd need a bomb, a case of TNT, or…* Memories of Innsmouth and the ships they'd seen in the harbor popped into his head, the derelict relics of the war waiting to be scrapped, and the gaping hole in the wreck beneath them.

"Sonofa–"

"What?"

Silas turned to face Abigail. "I know where we can get something that should do the job."

"Where? What do you mean?"

"Innsmouth," he pointed to the gleaming lighthouse. "We've got to go back to Innsmouth."

Abigail looked out the window at the lighthouse and swallowed hard. "All right. Tell me what to do."

"I can't navigate the channel until dawn, but I'd just as soon haul anchor now before more of those things climb aboard." He pointed to the Remington in her hands. "Put that away, but don't unload it. My relatives are *not* going to be happy to see us."

CHAPTER 7
Innsmouth Harbor

Silas guided *Sea Change* deftly through the treacherous channel into Innsmouth Harbor with the first torpid light of dawn. The nor'easter still howled, but the wind had backed to the north in the last few hours. The storm was passing.

Innsmouth had not miraculously transformed since yesterday. The dismal, dilapidated buildings glared at them as if murderous intent lurked in their windows. It might, for all Silas knew.

"You're sure about this?" Abigail asked, biting her lip.

"No, but we should be in and out of here before anyone even knows we've arrived." Silas throttled back and turned *Sea Change* toward a derelict minelayer left over from the war. Eighty feet of rust-streaked iron, she lay with her keel buried in silt, her hull slowly rotting away. "That's the one we want. I remember hearing that she had her last load aboard when she grounded here. The war was nearly over, and the Navy was too busy to care about one old, converted fishing trawler. The Marsh family claimed her as salvage, of course."

"And you think the mines are still aboard?"

"Probably. Thousands of mines were deployed in New England waters during the war. The government defused and buried the ones they never deployed. They're not worth much, dangerous to scrap, since they're packed with TNT, and the Marsh family didn't need the money. They salvaged what they wanted from the ship, and left it to rust."

"But will they still work after so long?" Abigail sounded dubious.

"As long as water didn't get inside them, they should."

"But if they see us out here fiddling with it…" Abigail cast a nervous look toward shore.

"They'll try to stop us." Silas pulled alongside and brought them to a stop. "That's what the shotgun's for."

He stepped out of the cabin and tied them to the derelict so he could cast off quickly if they had visitors.

"We'll need the lift." Silas opened the engine room and worked the power transfer lever, but left the hatch open. "As soon as we get the mine aboard, I'll shift her back, and we'll get out of here."

"Good." Abigail propped the Remington just inside the cabin door. "I'd rather we didn't have to kill anyone."

"Me too, but if they pick a fight, I'll not back down." After facing the horrors of Devil Reef, a confrontation with his monstrous relatives seemed less daunting. This was something he *could* fight, unlike what he'd seen in that sunken ship. Silas cranked the winch until the boom hung over the deck of the rusty ship. "Give a yell if you see anyone coming and be ready on the winch."

Silas grabbed a crowbar and the weighted clip on the end of the lift rope, and clambered aboard the derelict ship. She'd been a steam-powered fishing trawler before the war, taken by the military to lay mines around New England. The hatch to the main hold looked intact, which was both good and bad. The ship's cargo had been kept out of the weather, but he'd have to break in.

The lock on the hatch was as big as his palm and caked with rust, but no match for a crowbar and the expertly applied force of a desperate sailor. The pieces clanked to the deck, and Silas hooked the lift rope to the hatch cover.

"Up on the lift, Abigail. I've got to get the hatch cover off."

"Right." She engaged the winch, and the heavy rope came taut.

Rusty iron hinges screeched, but the hatch cover lifted free. When it was almost vertical, he yelled "Stop", then pushed it past the tipping point and waved for her to lower it. He unclipped the line and took it to the hatch.

The muted predawn light barely illuminated the depths of the hold, but as his vision adjusted, he discerned six black, bulbous shapes resting in a wooden frame. *Like eggs in a basket.*

"Slack the lift!" Silas called, and lowered the hook into the hold until it neared the bottom. "Stop!" Silas climbed up onto the hatch coaming, wrapped a leg around the lift line, and stepped off into the open hatch. The heavy rope bit into his calloused palms as he lowered himself into the hold's dark confines.

Eerily quiet after the howling winds above, the hold felt close and smelled of mold. *Not good…* Mold meant moisture, which meant corrosion. In fact, rust streaked the edge of the hatch, and water had dripped right down onto two of the mines. A quick inspection told him they were ruined, the threaded holes that had held the fuses were full of water and rust. The next two were dry, but when Silas swiped a finger down into one of the fuse holes, it came back with flakes of grime and rust.

"Damn!"

The last two he could barely see in the dim light. His finger probed the fuse holes and came back dry and reasonably clean. The trouble now was that the other mines were in the way. If he hooked the lift to the one he wanted, it would bowl the others out of their cradles when he lifted it. The mines *shouldn't* explode without fuses, but hundreds of pounds of iron-bound explosives rolling around the inside of a ship's hold wasn't healthy. The only option was to lift the other mines out of the way first.

"Nothing for it." Silas hooked the lift cable to the first mine and climbed up hand over hand, swinging easily over the hatch coaming. "Abigail! I've got to move some cargo out of the way. Listen for my instructions." *Best not to tell her what kind of cargo...*

"Hurry. I see some people on one of the docks looking at us."

Silas squinted to the north. Several figures clustered on the Marsh Fish Products pier. *Not good...* "OK, up on the lift."

Abigail threw the lever, and the rope came taut. The motor lugged with the effort, but the first mine lifted out of the cradle and swung free. Silas pushed the rope to keep it from slamming into the bulkhead, but it was like trying to hold back a falling tree. Iron boomed with the impact, and he cringed. *Well, if it explodes, I won't have to go back down to that cursed wreck anyway.*

"Down."

Abigail complied, and iron boomed again as the mine dropped against the hull.

"Hold there." Silas climbed down, switched the cable to the next mine in the way, and climbed back up. "OK, up."

The lift line came tight against the hatch coaming, the stout rope riding over the sharp lower edge and peeling away flakes of rust. The mine came free of the cradle and swung, hitting the forward bulkhead hard enough to dent it.

"What are you *doing*?" Abigail called.

"Moving cargo, just like I said." He glanced back at the fishing pier. Six figures were climbing down onto a boat. Silas yelled, "No time to be gentle! Down!"

The mine boomed to the deck below, and Silas slid down the line. He unclipped the hook and pulled it aft. "Slack!" Clicking the hook onto the lift ring, he looked up to where the rope would ride over the edge of the hatch coaming. Rusty iron offered a dangerously sharp edge. If it broke the lift line, they were sunk.

Need something… Silas cast about the hold, looking for an old jacket or piece of canvas, anything he could put between the line and the coaming to keep it from chafing.

"Silas. They're coming!"

No time for this. Silas tore off his shirt and wedged it between the lift line and the sharp corner of the hatch coaming. "Up!"

The line snapped taut, straining to pull the mine out of the wooden cradle. Four hundred pounds of iron and TNT cracked free and swung forward. Silas scrambled out of the way and cringed as the thing crashed against the forward bulkhead. At the noise, Abigail stopped lifting.

Silas scrambled up the rope, leapt to the deck, and waved to her. "Up!" Beyond *Sea Change*, a boat left the Marsh pier.

Abigail flipped the lever, and the mine rose. Silas guided it out of the hatch and then leapt down to *Sea Change*'s deck. "Hold on there. We've got to move the boom over, but we can't let it swing. I'll work the boom crank. As soon as it's clear of the rail, lower it to the deck."

"OK." Abigail glanced over her shoulder, her face white. "Are you sure it won't explode?"

"No, but it hasn't yet, and we bashed it around pretty hard."

Silas worked the crank and watched the deadly weight swing

out over *Sea Change*. If something broke, the mine would plunge right through the deck and maybe even the hull. Abigail slipped the clutch, and the mass of iron came down hard, but not catastrophically, to rest against the port side rail. Silas unclipped the lift line, secured it, and cast off.

"Get on the wheel, Abigail." Silas lunged for the engine room and slammed the power transfer over to power the propeller shaft.

"The *wheel*? I can't–"

"Just steer out the way we came in." Silas slammed the engine room hatch closed and flung the gear shift into forward. "I've got to deal with my blasted *relatives*." He grabbed the Remington, pocketed a handful of shells, and stepped out onto the deck as *Sea Change* screeched alongside the old hulk into open water. Abigail turned before they'd cleared the wreck, and the port aft rail slewed around to splinter against the ship's hull.

"Sorry! I told you I couldn't steer a boat," came Abigail's cry.

"Don't worry about it. Just drive it like a car. The red lever's the gas pedal."

"Oh. Well, I can do *that*." The engine revved up, and she roared for the channel under full power.

Silas cringed at the engine's high-pitched howl. "Don't fail me now, girl."

As they came on course for the channel, the approaching boat charged after them. Six people crowded the aft deck, and at least one stood in the wheelhouse. Several had the unmistakable wide mouth and bulging eyes of the main Marsh family.

As the pursuit narrowed, a broad-shouldered man stepped onto the foredeck of the boat, pointed to the minelayer, and shouted, "That's private property, you thieving bastard."

"It belongs to the Marsh family, and I'm a Marsh." Silas raised the shotgun to show them he meant business. "I'm not taking anything that's worth anything to you, so bear off."

"You're a thief. Now heave to or we'll board you and take back what's ours." The boat closed at a steep angle.

"You try, and you'll have a talk with Mister Remington." Silas aimed the shotgun just off their bow and fired one barrel.

The man on the bow cursed and ducked into the pilothouse. Silas reloaded the spent round, but his warning shot proved no deterrent, for the boat full of his relatives bore on.

Silas leveled the Remington at the pilothouse. "Bear off or I swear I'll blow you to hell."

The boat continued on a collision course.

Put up or shut up, Silas. "I warned you." He aimed at the pilothouse windows and pulled both triggers.

Buckshot ripped through wood and shattered glass, but the pilot had ducked behind the console and popped up unharmed. On they came.

Silas fumbled to reload but knew he wouldn't get another round off before they hit. "Hang on, Abigail! Steer to port."

"Port? What port?"

"Left!" Silas grabbed a guywire as the two boats collided.

The deck lurched with the impact, and Abigail screeched a word he'd never thought a librarian would utter. They veered hard to port, and Silas heard a deep rumble from behind. He whirled in time to see the mine rolling across the canted deck at him. His reflex was to leap out of the way, but a deeper dread gripped his heart at the thought of so much weight crashing into the bulwarks. If the mine broke through, it would plunge to the bottom of the harbor. Their entire plan would go straight to hell, and the world of man with it.

Silas dropped the Remington and braced his feet against the bulwark, flinging out both hands to slow the massive sphere of iron. *Idiot,* he thought just before the mine slammed him backward, pinning him against the bulwark. Something cracked, and pain lanced up his leg, a hoarse scream escaping his clenched teeth. Then *Sea Change* leveled out, and the weight of the mine eased enough for him to roll it off his leg. That hurt even more than the initial impact, and he crumpled to the deck.

"Silas! They're coming back."

"Steer for the red buoy," he bellowed, sitting up to peer over the splintered gunnel.

His relatives were charging at them on a collision course again, but not at such a steep angle as before. They held billy clubs and net hooks. They were going to board *Sea Change*, and from their expressions, they weren't interested in negotiating.

Scrabbling for the shotgun, he slammed two shells into the breech and cracked it closed. At the rate they were closing, he would only get one shot. Silas leveled the Remington over the gunnel and took aim. At such a short range he could easily kill two of them, but that would only ensure his fate. The others would swarm aboard, and with a broken leg, Silas couldn't stop them.

Or can I?

Silas lowered his aim and fired both barrels at the waterline of the approaching boat, blasting a hole in the hull bigger than his two clenched fists. Seawater rushed into the small boat, and she lurched, but momentum brought her crashing into *Sea Change*.

Silas staggered up onto his one good leg and flipped the Remington around, gripping the twin barrels like a club. The Marsh boat heeled with the inrushing water and the men on her deck staggered, uncertainty clear in their eyes. The big man who had shouted from the bow brandished a net hook and lunged across the gap, but Silas swung the Remington like Babe Ruth aiming for the center field wall and connected with his assailant's thick jaw. The man spun like a top, blood and teeth spraying, and started to fall between the boats. Three of his companions grabbed for him, one even sinking a net hook into his arm to keep him from falling. The others fell back, less enthused now about leaping aboard *Sea Change*.

Suddenly a horrendous screech tore from the belly of the Marshes' boat, and steam billowed briefly from the exhaust stack. The engine died, and the boat fell immediately behind, listing badly. The incoming water had evidently reached the engine's air intake.

Silas took a step before remembering his injury. His leg felt like someone was twisting a knife in it, but it supported his weight. *Maybe it's not so bad…*

Using the Remington as a crutch, he hobbled into the cabin and yelled, "Throttle back a bit. We're clear."

"Thank the Lord." Abigail glanced back at him, her knuckles white on the wheel. "I don't know where I'm going."

Silas limped up beside her and peered out the pilothouse window through the rain. They were close to the channel, but not close enough. "Steer right about ten degrees. See the compass there. We put that red buoy on our left but pass it close. There's a shoal to the right that's not marked. Then …" He hissed in a breath as a wave rocked the boat and his leg twisted. He grabbed the edge of the console to keep from falling.

"What happened?" Abigail altered course as he'd directed, glancing down at his leg.

"That damn heavy mine rolled and pinned my leg to the bulwark.

I think something's broken." He pointed to the next mark. "That green can. Put it to our right, then turn northeast by the compass. We'll get the anchor down and I'll have a look at my leg."

"But..." Abigail bit her lip and nodded. "Right. First things first..."

"Exactly." Silas pointed to the northeast as they rounded the green can. "We'll anchor well away from the reef until we're ready. I don't want to be close to those things until we have to be."

"I can't argue with that."

"Then we have to talk," Silas continued. "I can't walk. We'll have to figure out some way for you to manage the dive suit."

"What?" She gaped at him. "You can't be serious. I know nothing about it – the suit's too heavy – it won't fit me!"

"Then we're in trouble." Silas's head spun and his leg throbbed in time with his heart. "Just about a quarter mile more, and we'll... put the... anchor down."

"Are you OK?"

"No. That's what I've been telling you." Silas peered down at his leg and cringed. His pants were tight from the knee down. "If I don't get my leg up soon, I'm afraid... I'm going to... pass out."

CHAPTER 8
Devil Reef

They anchored in shallow water behind a shoal east of Devil Reef with little difficulty. This put them far enough from Innsmouth that the sheets of slashing rain hid them from view, but near enough to the reef that they could still see the line of breakers. Unless someone climbed the lighthouse or drove out to the beach, the Marshes should think they were long gone. Silas sat down with his leg on the chart table, and Abigail split his pant leg with a pair of shears. She hissed an indrawn breath. From knee to ankle his leg was hugely swollen.

"Well, the fibula is certainly broken, but you were able to stand on it, so I think the tibia is intact."

"What?" Silas took a pull from the bottle of spiritus frumenti and grimaced as she pulled off his boot.

"Basic anatomy," she smiled thinly. "I read a lot. Part of being a librarian, I guess."

"Oh."

"You've two bones in your leg here, and the smaller one's broken. Fortunately, the larger is the one that supports most of the weight. If we splint it so it doesn't twist, you should be able to walk." She looked around. "I need some slats of wood and cloth to bind it up."

"The locker there's got a couple of swabs... er... mops. You can use the handles. And there's bed sheets in the fo'c'sle." He took another pull from the bottle.

"OK, but not too much more of that." Abigail pointed at the bottle of whiskey. "You need your wits about you."

"Wits..." He shook his head. "I've already *lost* my wits just considering this madness."

Abigail ignored him and bustled about, tearing a sheet into strips and breaking two swab handles into shorter lengths for splints. As she wrapped his leg tight, Silas bit back all the curses he'd learned in two decades at sea and marveled at her.

"How do you know how to split a leg?"

"I read a lot, remember?" She cinched a knot and started wrapping another strip.

"Good. Maybe you can figure out a way to set that mine off, then." He pointed the neck of the whiskey bottle to the massive sphere of iron on the deck.

"What do you mean?" Abigail continued to work but looked at him worriedly. "I thought we just dropped it over the side and... boom."

So, librarians don't know everything, after all. "No. Mines have fuses." He winced as she drew the wrappings tight. "Prongs that stick out so when a ship hits them, it sets off the mine."

"How do they work, these fuses?"

"No idea, but they're soft, made of lead. I worked on a cargo steamer during the war that transported hundreds of mines to England. They showed us they were safe as long as they didn't have fuses. The inside of the hole they screw into looks like the inside of a flashlight, two metal terminals, so I think when the fuse is bent it makes an electrical connection that sets off a charge inside."

"That can't be." She pointed out to the rain-soaked deck. "Water conducts electricity. If that's all it took, the mine would have already exploded."

"Huh... that's right."

"So maybe it needs a current to set it off, like a demolitionist's blasting cap."

Maybe..." Silas considered. "Maybe once the mine's placed I could use my lantern battery and some wire to set it off." Of course, he'd have to be right next to the mine when he did that. *Death by explosion, Armageddon, or answer the siren call of those things... not much of a choice, Silas.*

"Placed? What do you mean?"

"The mine needs to be placed *inside* the wreck."

"Why?"

"A blast outside might not do the job. The ship's hull is thick iron. Also, *unlike* the wreck, *Sea Change* is wood. If that mine blows up under her, it'll rupture the hull."

"Oh." Abigail bit her lip and cinched the final knot. "Well, then we'll just have to figure out a way to set it off from up here after you come back up, won't we?"

"That won't work. Even if we had enough wire to reach the boat, there's not enough current in that light to overcome that much resistance. I'll have to trigger it from down there."

"And blow yourself up?" She grimaced and reached for his boot. "There's *got* to be a better way, Silas."

"What *else* will work?" He was sick of arguing with her.

His boot wouldn't fit over his swollen foot, but when he stood and put careful pressure on his leg, it held his weight, although it hurt like blazes.

"Wait…" Abigail looked around. "How does the telephone work when you're down that far, then?"

"The phone box has magnetos that generate alternating current." She looked at him blankly.

"You read a lot and you don't know about *electricity*?"

Her face reddened. "I read about ancient history, natural history, and advances in medicine, Silas. Nobody can read *everything*!"

"Sorry. The batteries in my light provide direct current, which weakens over a long wire run. Alternating current, like the lights in your house, overcomes resistance better–" He stopped cold and stared at Abigail wide-eyed. "That's *it*! The telephone! We can rig wire from the telephone box! Abigail, you're a genius!"

"I thought you said we didn't have enough wire to reach."

"We don't, and we'll need the telephone. Damn!"

"Why do we need the telephone?"

"So I can tell you how to maneuver the boat. There's no way we can anchor in exactly the right spot, so you'll have to steer *Sea Change* at anchor when I'm down there. But maybe…" Silas looked around the cabin. He had some spare wire – not enough – but there *was* more wire aboard. "We can scavenge it! If we rip out the running lights and cabin lights, we should have enough!"

"But we have no way to make sure it'll work." Abigail looked at the black iron sphere resting against the splintered rail. "Do we?"

"Not short of blowing ourselves up, no." He shrugged helplessly. "But at least we've got a chance now." *A chance to survive, and maybe to be free of this damn thing in my head…* For even now the siren call of Devil Reef cried out to him.

But would he be able to resist that call when he descended into the wreck? *If I can't, Abigail will detonate the mine, and that'll be the end of it.*

"Come on. We've got a lot of work to do, and I can't crawl around in the bilges scavenging wire."

Recovering enough wire took hours. They ate the last of a stale loaf of bread slathered with salted butter and pots of double-strength coffee to keep going. Neither had slept in more than a day, and fatigue dragged at them. Abigail was covered in filth and dead on her feet when they finally had enough wire, but the work still wasn't done. They spliced the ends of the short lengths together, dipping the splices in hot decking tar and wrapping them with tape. Silas checked the connections by hooking the wire to the telephone and touching the wires together while Abigail cranked the box. A bright blue spark arced between the wires. Connecting the wires to the mine and filling the fuse orifice with tar swallowed more precious time. Silas worked with his injured leg up as much as possible, but the pain wore on him like a beast gnawing at his gut.

All the while, they both cast glances at the rain-shrouded tower of Innsmouth lighthouse. The Marshes either thought they'd fled or had some other reason not to come after them. What that reason might be, he didn't care to speculate, but he kept the Remington handy. By the time they had all the wiring rigged, the rain had eased off and the clouds had thinned. The gray light of day was fading to evening, their remaining time dwindling fast, when another problem rose up like one of the fish-faced monsters from the depths.

"The lift." Silas sat down hard and lifted his leg onto the table. "Damn."

"What about it?" Abigail tried to wipe a gob of tar from her cheek and left a black smear.

"We've got one lift, and two things to lift. Me and the mine."

"Um…" She squinted up at the winch. "Can't it lift both simultaneously?"

"I don't know. The dive suit's about two hundred pounds, I'm another two hundred, and the mine's probably four hundred. *Sea Change* wasn't designed to haul anything so heavy. Eight hundred pounds is almost double what that winch is *supposed* to lift. Once I'm in the water, it'll be fine, but lifting both off the deck…"

"All we can do is try."

Silas squinted at the sky. "We better move *Sea Change* before it gets dark. We'll try it once we get anchored."

"We anchored in the dark before," she argued.

"I know, Abigail, but this time we need to be as close to the wreck as we can manage without dropping our anchor right on it." Silas tried to bite back his temper, but fear, pain, and fatigue swirled in his skull like a hurricane. "Once I'm down there with the mine, I don't want to have to walk too far with my leg."

"Oh." She nodded. "I just… imagine those things coming up while we're getting ready."

"So do I." He imagined a lot worse, tentacled horrors big enough to drag *Sea Change* down to whatever hell lurked within that maelstrom of darkness inside the wreck.

Silas started the engine and laboriously hauled anchor, working the windlass crank with his injured leg propped up on the bow gunnel while Abigail kept them on station. When the anchor cleared the surface, Silas maneuvered close to Devil Reef, using the siren call hammering in his head as much as dead reckoning to gauge their position.

"This is as good as I can guess," he said, handing over the controls to Abigail. "Keep her idling into the wind. When I signal you, shift into neutral."

"Right." Abigail glanced over her shoulder through the cabin to the deck as if suspecting swarms of fish-faced monsters any moment.

Silas lowered the anchor slowly, trying to minimize the noise. The roar of surf on the reef would probably douse the thrum of the engine, but metallic clanks and clatters traveled far underwater. When he felt the tension on the anchor ease, he signaled Abigail and she shifted the boat into neutral. They drifted downwind, and Silas paid out rode. When the yearning call in his head rose to a crescendo, he tied it off. *Sea Change* jerked as the anchor set and their bow came into the wind.

"The sky's starting to clear." Abigail pointed west as he hobbled back into the pilothouse.

"Good. It'll give you some light. The moon should be up soon." He limped aft. "Now, help me with the dive gear."

With his injury, struggling into the dive suit was challenging, slow, painful, and nerve-racking. When they came to the last piece, Silas ran one of his heaviest dock lines through the helmet's lift ring, and then the lift eye on the mine.

"I can cut it free when it's in position and clip the lift line to my helmet."

"And then I winch you up, right?"

"Right." Once inside the wreck, however, Silas doubted he would ever come out again. *Abigail will do the right thing...* "I'll tell you to stop lowering when the mine's just above the seabed. Then you'll have to shift the power transfer lever, and idle *Sea Change* to the left until I'm inside. Then you can just slip the clutch on the lift to drop the mine. You'll have to disconnect the telephone wires and hook up the mine wires to detonate the mine. Just turn the crank hard, like you're making a call, and it should do the job."

"OK, but …" Abigail glanced between the winch, the pilothouse, and the open engine room hatch. "Too bad we don't have help."

"Well, we can't ask anyone now. You can do it, just one thing at a time."

"Yes, but… I'll have to flip the power transfer lever again to pull you up, and the boat will drift back on the anchor. Won't it pull the wires out or break one of our connections?"

"Damn, you're right." Fatigue, pain, and alcohol were wreaking havoc on his concentration. The answer came easily: idle *Sea Change* into position, lower him and the mine into the wreck, and detonate the mine, but Abigail would never agree to that. When it came to his life or Armageddon, he knew she'd choose the lesser of two evils, but she wouldn't accept a plan to kill him. He thought furiously for some answer she would agree with. *Make something up!* "When the mine's placed, I can drop my weight belt. That'll let me climb the lift line up."

"But without the lift, I won't be able to get you aboard."

Damn it, quit making perfectly sensible arguments. "No, but I can hang onto the air hose while you set off the mine. That'll free the lift line, then I'll tie it around my chest and you lift me up."

"Sounds dangerous."

He barked a laugh. It sounded impossible. "This whole *thing's* dangerous, but–"

Abigail's eyes focused beyond his shoulder and she stabbed a finger to the east. "Silas! Look!"

For a moment Silas feared some monster had risen from Devil Reef, but when he turned, it was only the moon shining from between scudding clouds. But something wasn't right about it. As a sailor, he knew the phases of the moon innately, for the moon governed the tides. It should have been waxing gibbous, but it shone full. *The tides in the canal… they were wrong, too. What the hell?* Then something else caught his eye: the full moon.

"Something's *eating* the moon!"

CHAPTER 9
The Deep Gate

"It's an eclipse. It's a lunar eclipse, Silas."

"Impossible! It's not supposed to happen for another week."

"Another week…" Abigail dashed into the cabin. At the table, she rifled through the tome. "Here! 'When Father Sun and Mother Moon join with the Earth in blood, Father Dagon and Mother Hydra will join in the deep to usher the third of their triune into the world of man.' The moon turns *red* in the shadow of the Earth."

"Joined in blood…" Silas swallowed hard. "Why didn't you tell me this before?"

"I didn't know what it meant. I didn't think it mattered."

"It matters! The Marshes of Innsmouth formed a… society a long time ago. The Esoteric Order of *Dagon*."

"I'm sorry, I… just thought it was nonsense."

"But the moon's not *supposed* to be full at all." Silas hobbled to the table and snatched up his nautical almanac. He flipped to the date and pointed to the entry. "Full in one week."

"Which was the original date of the event in the tome, Silas. They changed the moon to change the date of the event."

"Changed the *moon*?" He blinked at her. "That's insane."

She pointed to the moon. "Then explain that."

Silas cursed and shook his head. "We're out of time, Abigail. Help me with the helmet."

They muscled the helmet on and dogged down the seals, then Silas hobbled over to sit on the gunnel next to the mine. "Get the hook!" Abigail retrieved the lift hook and he clipped it to the center of the line connecting his helmet to the mine. "Good, now rev up the engine a bit and engage the lift. I'll close the face plate when I'm up."

"Right!" Abigail complied, but when she engaged the lift, the engine lugged dangerously with the weight before his feet left the deck.

"Stop!" Silas gritted his teeth. "Rev it up some more and put some slack in the line before you try again.

"OK." She revved up the engine just short of full throttle, ran out some line, and threw the lever again.

The engine screamed, then lugged and died.

"Damn it!" Silas untied the line from the helmet to the mine.

"What do we do?" Desperation edged Abigail's voice like a razor.

"You'll have to lower me first, then the mine. I'll push it into the wreck, then drop my belt and climb the rope. It'll just take longer." He unclipped the line. "Can you get the engine started?"

"I think so." Abigail hurried forward, climbed down into the engine room, and grunted with the effort of hauling the crank.

To Silas's relief, the engine coughed to life. "Now, if we haven't burned out the clutch…" He checked his light and the big knife at his belt and nodded to Abigail. "Do it. I'll tell you when I'm on the bottom." He closed the face plate.

The lift labored, but he rose into the air. Abigail cranked the boom over the sea and lowered him. The ink black water enveloped him in a chill embrace, feet, legs, hips, chest, and finally his head. One last glimpse of the half-eaten moon, and he was under.

"Can you hear me?" Abigail's voice crackled in his ear.

"Yes." Silas flipped on the dive light and shone it around. Nothing but blackness surrounded him. The descent seemed to be taking much longer than the first time, until a sudden jolt of pain up his leg as he hit the bottom wrenched a yelp from his throat. "I'm down." He teetered there for a moment, fighting for balance, then unclipped the line from his helmet. "The line's free. Take it up and attach it to the mine. Be careful not to tangle the wires."

"I've got it."

Silas waited. Two eternities passed while he imagined the moon slowly being devoured in shadow. He pointed the light straight up, not daring to pan it around for fear of arousing the nest of monsters in the wreck. The yearning hammered at his mind like an echo inside his dive helmet, pulling him, pleading with him to join them. *Come to us. Come home. Join us...* Pain lanced up his leg, snapping his hypnosis, and he realized he'd taken a step toward the wreck, toward oblivion.

"Thank God," he muttered. "Never thought breaking my leg would save my life."

"What's that?" Abigail asked over the phone.

"Nothing. Just talking to myself. How's it going?"

"It's on the way down."

Silas arched his back to look up. The mine descended out of the murk. When it neared the height of his head, he yelled, "Stop!" into the phone.

The mine stopped at the height of his chest, bobbing up and down with the waves jostling *Sea Change* above. He pushed against it, but it barely moved, and his leg stabbed him with the effort.

"OK, Abigail, the depth is perfect. Now disengage the power transfer lever, and idle the boat hard over to port, that's *left*. In this wind, she'll swing on the anchor without making any forward headway." Silas didn't even have to look to know what direction the wreck lay in. The call pulled him, pleading with him to join them. He gritted his teeth against the urge. *Oh, I'll join you... I'll send you all straight to hell.*

"OK. Yell when you're in position. I can barely hear you from forward."

"OK." Silas waited, and the mine started to drift away. He limped after it, a slow shuffling gait that minimized the strain on his leg. The pain jolted him back toward sanity with every step.

The wreck loomed out of the dark ahead of them, the gaping hole in her side like the maw of some leviathan waiting to swallow him. His calculations had been good: the mine was arcing right toward the gaping hole. In the glare of his light, shapes flicked around inside the ship, dark within dark accented by flecks of silver, luminous eyes reflecting the beam.

The yearning pulled him, and he answered now. *Yes, I'm coming... I've got a present for you.*

A clawed hand reached over the jagged metal edge, followed by a face. Bulging fish eyes stared at him, the lipless maw opening to reveal rows of needle teeth. Silas's stomach lurched, and he swallowed to keep from vomiting into his helmet. He pointed his powerful light straight into those disconcerting eyes, and the face jerked back out of sight.

They don't like the light... Maybe he could keep them at bay long enough to get the mine placed. "Almost there. Tie off the wheel and get on the lift, Abigail."

After a short delay, her reply crackled, "OK. I'm on the lift."

Lurching closer, he strained to shove the mine over the edge, trying to ignore the movement roiling within the deeper darkness, the unblinking eyes, the impossible shapes above, and the deafening call in his skull. The lift rope met with the upper edge of the hole, and the mine swung in. *Thank God the metal's bent inward…*

"Now! Down!" Silas screamed into the phone, but Abigail's reactions weren't so swift this time. *Sea Change* continued to drift, the line lifting the mine up. The iron sphere clanged against the edge of the jagged hole, the trailing wires dangerously close to being snagged and severed. Silas couldn't reach the wires, but he could reach the mine and braced his one good leg to push it in as Abigail released the clutch.

As he heaved the mine forward, the light dangled from a lanyard tied to his wrist, sweeping the interior of the wreck. The man-sized creatures shied from the light, but as the mine lowered, the light struck the edge of the jagged hole and shone up overhead. The massive shapes he'd only glimpsed before now became clear: huge ropy arms with clawed tips, pulsing flesh, and plate-sized eyes. As the beam touched one of those huge orbs, the pupil contracted and focused upon him.

Terror unlike anything he'd ever felt lanced through him. A low wail of woe echoed within his helmet, his own voice. Then another voice reverberated through his head, hammering at his skull.

Join us, Silas Marsh. Your only future lies with us. The voice washed away his fear, his confusion, and his will.

Yes… Silas started to crawl over the jagged edge, but a four hundred-pound sphere of iron clanged against his helmet, ringing even louder than the yearning call. Sanity... solidity... and the stabbing pain of his leg vied against the compulsion. He slammed his shoulder into the massive iron sphere, driving it into the hole as the lift line paid out. But as the mine screeched against the bent teeth of the ruined hull to settle down in its final grave, clawed hands reached around it to grasp him. One caught the wire, and it came dangerously taut.

"NO!" Silas shone his light in their faces, reaching for the heavy knife at his belt. The fishy figures reeled back, cringing away, but others swam forth, claws reaching for him.

"What?" Abigail cried. "What's happening?"

"They're all over the damned place. They're on me!" He slashed at the scrabbling hands, the gnashing teeth. Black blood darkened the water, but there were too many. Claws raked the heavy canvas of his suit, unable to penetrate, but dragging him in while the yearning call hammered at his fragile will. There was only one answer, one refuge where they couldn't reach him. "Trigger the mine! Do it, Abigail, before it's too late."

"No!" her voice crackled, edged with panic. "Unclip your weights and climb. I won't kill you."

"Blow it, Abigail, or you'll kill *everyone*." A lurid face lunged at his faceplate, jaws gaping, but Silas filled that maw with his knife, driving the tip deep. The teeth came down on his wrist, and pinholes of wetness dampened his forearm. Hands grasped, pulling him over the ragged edge of the hole. His leg struck something, and he screamed.

"Silas! Your weight belt. Don't make me do this. I can't!"

He slashed madly, releasing the light and scrabbling desperately to his feet. The agony of his leg stabbed his every movement, jerking him back to reality, away from the irresistible call. The creatures had released him but swam in a mass just out of reach. The knife had taught them fear, and they hated the light. Thankfully, they seemed to be ignoring the mine. *Maybe... maybe I've got a chance.*

But as Silas reached for the clip holding his weight belt, another light filled the wreck's hold. A sickly yellow illumination shone from the depths of the maelstrom of darkness swirling above him. At its core, a space yawned open, widening like a mouth that would swallow the world. Within, beyond that pit of blackness, a city, a world, and a monstrosity that defied sanity swelled into view. The city from his nightmares, impossible structures, improbable angles, and hundreds... no, *thousands* of hellish shapes skittering about like maggots and beetles and flies swarming a rotting corpse. And above it loomed an unimaginable shape, writhing tentacles amid a bulbous head, wings that spanned the sky like the coming of night, clawed hands that could crush ships.

The deep gate... The prophecy of Abigail's tome, the end of the world of man, reached forth.

Silas's numb fingers found the clip to his weight belt and pulled. His feet left the twisted tangle of steel and he rose up, but his nightmares would not let him go so easily. The fishy shapes swarmed in on him, scrabbling and biting, dragging and clawing. One caught the lantern and pulled so hard the lanyard snapped. The light spun away. He screamed and slashed, fumbling through the mass of shapes to find the lift line, knowing he couldn't, knowing he would fail. Abigail wouldn't trigger the mine, and that impossibility of madness would claw through the hole in creation to consume the Earth.

"Do it, Abigail." Amid the writhing and gnashing of scaled flesh,

Silas's free hand found a taut rope. He clenched it and pulled, catching a glimpse of open water outside the ship.

"No! Climb, Silas. You can do it. The moon's not red yet. You have time."

"They're on me! I can't fight and climb." His light flickered among the writhing shapes.

"Silas! Cut the…" Her words ended in static.

"What?" He slashed and stabbed blindly, trying to climb one-handed. He couldn't drop the knife with so many of them on him. They'd drag him back inside.

"I said… the air… bubbles will… and climb."

Bubbles? Of course. Silas stabbed over his shoulder with the heavy knife and felt for the air hose. One slash opened it, blasting compressed air into the wrecked ship and enveloping him in a cloud of bubbles. The valve that kept the sea from rushing in through the severed hose clacked closed, and the grasping hands and gnashing teeth fell away.

Free… I'm free. With the voices of a thousand monsters yammering in his mind, Silas Marsh renounced his life, his family, and the siren call. *Survive. I can survive this.* He dropped his knife and climbed madly for the surface.

"I'm free, Abigail! I'm climbing."

But he received no answer, nothing but static.

Probably cut the phone line with the air hose. He dragged himself up hand over hand, going by feel in the faint light of the waning moon gleaming down through the water.

Abigail would be frantically changing the phone wires to the detonation circuit, her hand hovering over the crank that would send a jolt of electricity down the cables to blast the wreck, the monsters, and that vile hole in reality straight to hell.

Do it! Do it now, before it's too late. No mine, no explosive or bomb made by mankind could harm that monstrosity beyond the portal. If it gained purchase in this world, it would end mankind as a man might end a colony of ants.

Silas... come back... come home...

His ears popped as pressure eased, then pain lanced through his leg and his grip slid back on the rope. Silas twisted and looked down through the side port of his helmet and wished he hadn't. Through the cloud of bubbles, the light from inside the wreck illuminated a mass of fishy shapes boiling from the jagged hole. They swam up to grasp him, to drag him down. One had hold of his broken leg, its grip sending lightning bolts of pain through him. Teeth clamped on his thigh, moisture seeping in through the holes in the heavy canvas. Water trickled down his leg, filling his boot and weighing him down. He clubbed the thing with a fist, gouging at its bulbous eyes. It released him, and he got a few more precious handholds before the next one reached him.

Claws scratched at the canvas of his suit, scrabbling up his back, trying to pull him off the rope. A lurid face peered at him through the side port of his helmet, webbed fingers scrabbling at the wing nuts that held the glass in place. Bronze squeaked as one of the nuts began to turn.

No, no, no! Not now. Not when I've got a chance...

Silas freed one hand and grasped the fishy throat. With the grip of a sailor fortified by panic, Silas squeezed. The toothy mouth gaped, clawed hands grasping at his wrist as fragile bones crunched under his fingers. A hoarse scream reached his ears as the grip on his wrist weakened. The scream, he realized, was his.

Releasing his grasp, he climbed frantically. The fading light of the moon overhead shifted from silvery to the hue of dried blood.

It was time. A subsonic thrum of energy began to sing along his bones. The deep gate was opening, and Silas envisioned the great clawed hand reaching through from beyond. The surface loomed just overhead, but even as he broke through the undulating mirror, another clawed hand closed on his broken leg.

Silas… come back to us…

Agony shot through him in torrents as the ends of fractured bone grated through tortured muscle. His grip on the rope slipped, but he fought upward, reaching through to the world of air, the world of man. He caught a glimpse of Abigail at the rail of *Sea Change* grasping the phone box in one arm, her hand on the crank, eyes impossibly wide, and her face pale with panic. A sanguineous moon shone down from the sky, Father Sun, Mother Moon, and the Earth joined in blood.

A webbed hand reached over Silas's shoulder, claws grating against his faceplate. Gold glinted on one of the digits, a ring grown over by the membranous webbing, three familiar braided strands of tarnished gold.

Silas, my boy… come home… The call beat on his mind like a hammer on fragile glass.

Oh, God, no… not that… please no… Silas reached up and grasped the rope higher, pulling with his last ounce of strength.

"*Do it!*" he screamed, praying to God that Abigail would hear him.

Between the clawed fingers obscuring his view, past the glint of the ring, Silas saw Abigail crank the handle. He wrapped an arm around the suddenly slack lift line in one last desperate grasp for survival.

A pressure wave slammed into Silas like a runaway train, wrenching muscles and cracking joints. His head slammed against the back of his helmet, shooting stars through his brain. The creature's grip on him loosed as he was thrown. Then something slapped him in the chest, and his forehead clanged against the faceplate.

Silas wondered, as darkness closed over him, why the moon tasted like blood.

EPILOGUE
At Sea

Silas woke to the familiar thrum of *Sea Change*'s engine vibrating through his head and the taste of blood in his mouth. There was pain, too, and plenty of it, but he was breathing, and therefore alive. *Death wouldn't hurt like this.*

He blinked his one good eye open and wondered if he was blind for a moment, but then moonlight, silvery and clear, swept into view. The roll of the deck and the pitch of the engine told him *Sea Change* was underway, and at sea. He was lying on his back on deck, still in his dive gear except for the helmet.

He worked his tongue around in his mouth and found a split lip, a newly chipped tooth, and a good bit of blood. He reached up to touch his pounding forehead and felt a lump there the size of a goose egg. He had a similar one on the back of his head, and his neck ached. *Rattled around inside the dive helmet like a bean in a cup...* He closed his eye and saw again the three braided strands of gold, his mother's wedding ring on the webbed hand of that monster.

He closed his eye and prayed. *They're dead. Please, God, let them be dead.* He dragged in a breath, the faint siren call still ringing in his mind. His prayer, it seemed, would not be answered.

Silas tried to sit up and failed, but he managed to roll over. His leg stabbed him, but it seemed still attached, which was more than he'd expected. He forced himself up to hands and knees and felt every muscle protest.

"You're alive."

"Sort of." Silas glanced up through the cabin to the pilothouse to see Abigail at the wheel.

She grinned at him. "You may want to come up here and steer if you can manage it. I have no idea where we are."

He glanced around and caught a glimpse of the Innsmouth light about a mile behind them. Still on all fours, he leaned over the gunnel and peered forward. They topped a swell, and he caught a glimpse of the Plum Island Sound sea buoy.

"Steer ten more degrees to port. We should be clear of the shoals already."

"OK." She turned the wheel and *Sea Change* answered. "How do you feel?"

"Like I've been chewed up and spat out, then stomped on for good measure." Talking hurt his head. He looked around the deck and spotted the dive helmet. The lift line was looped under his arms and tied in an incomprehensible knot. "How did you get me aboard?"

"You were just floating there, so I hooked the lift line with that pole thingamabob and tied a knot. Easy as pie." She seemed positively ebullient. "I didn't want to just sit there over the wreck, but I couldn't hoist the anchor, so I cut it loose. Sorry."

"Don't be." Silas didn't want to be anywhere near Devil Reef either.

Gritting bloody teeth, he managed to push himself up on one good leg, discovering dozens of new aches and pains. He sat on the dormant air compressor, and worked at the suit's seals, finally freeing himself of its clammy embrace. The air felt good against his skin again. He hobbled into the cabin and retrieved the bottle from the cupboard. There were perhaps two good swallows left. He limped forward and stepped into the pilothouse.

"Breakfast?" He held out the bottle to Abigail.

"On an empty stomach?" she grimaced. "No, thanks. I'd be sick."

"Coffee then?" He pulled the cork and upended the last of the bottle, swallowing twice. The alcohol stung his cut lip, but the taste of blood vanished in the burning glory of Canadian whiskey.

"I'd love a cup, and maybe something to eat if there is anything."

"Coffee and crackers is the best I can do." He turned back to the cabin.

"Sorry I nearly killed you, by the way," she called over her shoulder.

"What?" Silas blinked back at her in shock. "You're the only reason I'm still breathing, Abigail. You should have blown it earlier. Those things could have pulled the wires from the mine at any moment."

"Yes, well, I couldn't, and they didn't." She sounded a little hurt, and he realized how ungrateful he was being.

"But thank you for risking the entire world to save my life."

"You're welcome." She flashed him a smile and turned back to the wheel.

As he started making coffee, the siren song hummed in the back of his mind. The power of that call seemed lesser now, although it was still there. He didn't have to ask Abigail what had happened to the creature that had been trying to drag him down at that last moment. The persistent, familiar call to come home told him she had survived. He hobbled forward again, grabbing a box of crackers on the way, and tossed them on the console.

"I'd say it feels good to be alive, but I hurt all over." He leaned back with a wince.

"We *are* alive." Abigail took a cracker and nibbled it. "We *beat* them, Silas. We outfoxed those hideous people in Innsmouth, we stopped this… *thing* from happening, and we even saved ourselves in the process."

"Well, we sure as hell won a battle, but…" Silas looked over his shoulder. Devil Reef was far behind them now, out of sight, but the yearning remained.

"But what?" She looked at him sidelong. "You don't seem very happy."

"Oh, I'm happy to be alive, but…" He looked over his shoulder again. *I'll be doing that for the rest of my life, I suppose.* "I… saw things down there, Abigail. Things that shouldn't be, but are. Things that… *can't* exist, but do."

"But we blew them up. That blast…" She shook her head. "Well, you should have *seen* it. I wonder how you survived, really. Nothing down there could have survived that."

Silas wondered if she was right, prayed so, but honestly didn't know if things like what he'd seen through that portal *could* be killed. And if they couldn't, they would try again, another time, another place; when and where, there was no way to know. "Maybe… I don't know whether you *can* win against things like that."

"Take the wheel. I want to show you something."

"All right." Silas edged past her, embarrassed for the first time about his condition, bloody, pants soaked, one boot, shirt torn. "Grab a clean shirt from the fo'c'sle, too, please."

"Sure."

Abigail went below for a bit, and Silas adjusted course minutely out of habit. They'd be in Annisquam before sunup, so he throttled back some. *Better to take the channel in daylight on a rising tide.*

"Here." Abigail held out a flannel shirt as she stepped back up into the pilothouse. Under her arm, she held the old tome that had set them on this crazy adventure to begin with.

"Thanks." Silas struggled into the clean shirt, the muscles of his back and shoulders protesting with every move.

"So, look here, Mister *Can't Win.*" She flipped to the familiar page with the coordinates of Devil Reef, and pointed to the passage. "Look."

Silas peered down in the wavering lamplight and gaped. The celestial fixes, and the date and time of the event were gone. There was a gap in the text. The rest of the page remained, the lurid illustrations in the margins, but the details were blank.

"And here." She turned to the page with the impossible city he'd seen both in his nightmares and through the portal within the wreck.

The entire page was blank.

"Well, I'll be damned." A weight lifted off Silas's aching shoulders.

"You see? We really did win." She closed the book and put it on the console. "As improbable as it sounds, we saved the world. Cheer up, sourpuss."

"Sorry." He smiled at her, but it felt forced and his lip hurt. "I hit my head pretty hard. I guess I'm still not thinking straight."

"Oh, you really should sit and put your leg up." She nodded to the wheel. "I can steer. I'm getting pretty good at it. You've made a sailor out of a librarian, Silas."

That brought a more genuine smile. "OK, Able Seaman Foreman, steer about ten degrees to port of the lighthouse until you see the Annisquam sea buoy, then give me a yell."

"Aye, aye, captain." She sketched a snappy salute and slipped past him to take the wheel. "And I would take a cup of that coffee, if you can manage it."

"Be a few minutes." Silas limped back into the cabin, sat at the chart table and put his leg up. The swelling had increased again with all the walking. He watched the pot on the stove, willing it to boil.

"So, what do you plan to do now?" Abigail asked over her shoulder.

"Do?" He frowned and considered the question seriously. Could he go back to just fishing, running lobster pots, doing salvage and deliveries to the islands? Yes, fishing and running his boat... that he could do, but he'd probably sell his dive gear. "Get *Sea Change* fixed up, buy a new anchor, and keep doing what I've always done, I guess."

"You don't think your family will press charges for stealing the mine and damaging their boat?"

"Oh, the Marsh family doesn't go in much for calling the coppers, and I'll never set foot in Innsmouth again. If they come looking for me in Kingsport, well..." He shrugged and rubbed his eye, wondering if time would make him a liar. "What about you, Abigail? You're going back to the library, right?"

"Oh, of course."

"No more magical tomes or adventures?"

"Ha! Not on your *life*, Silas Marsh." She grinned back at him. "I think I'll stick to reading novels from now on, go see a picture show now and then, or maybe a play. There's a new production in town, you know. *The King in Yellow*. It's supposed to be quite scandalous. Maybe when you get out of the hospital, you'd go see it with me?"

Surprised at her forward question, he thought about it, about Abigail. *A sailor and a university librarian?* Silas shook his head with a smile; he admired Abigail's spunk, but they were too different. Their lives would mix like oil and water. "Sorry, but picture shows and plays aren't really my cup of java."

"Suit yourself." She turned back to the wheel. "There's more to life than fishing and boats, you know."

"Perhaps, but…" Silas looked out over the turbulent ocean. His mother's call echoed faintly in his mind, and he knew he couldn't resist it forever. "I belong to the sea. It's in my blood."

ABOUT THE AUTHORS

Erstwhile teacher, editor, and game designer, DAVE GROSS is the author of *Forgotten Realms*, *Iron Kingdoms*, and *Pathfinder Tales* novels. His stories appear in anthologies including *Shotguns vs Cthulhu*, *Shattered Shields*, and *Champions of Aetaltis*. He lives with his wife and their critters near the North Saskatchewan River.

frabjousdave.com

GRAEME DAVIS discovered the Cthulhu Mythos in 1982 after picking up an imported first edition of Chaosium's *Call of Cthulhu* RPG. He helped develop *Warhammer Fantasy Roleplay* and *Vampire: The Masquerade*, and he has written Cthulhu Mythos gaming material for several publishers. He is also the author of a *Dungeons & Dragons* novel and several published short stories.

graemedavis.wordpress.com
twitter.com/graemejdavis

RICHARD LEE BYERS is the author of fifty horror and fantasy books including *This Sword for Hire* and *Blind God's Bluff*, novels for Marvel's *Legends of Asgard*, *Forgotten Realms*, and the Impostor series. He's also written scores of short stories, some collected in *The Things That Crawl* and *The Hep Cats of Ulthar*, scripted a graphic novel, and contributed content on tabletop and electronic games. A resident of the Tampa Bay area, he's an RPG enthusiast and a frequent program participant at Florida conventions, Dragon Con, and Gen Con.

twitter.com/rleebyers

CHRIS A JACKSON has been a sailor, writer, reader and gamer, and is the Scribe Award-winning author of over thirty novels including nautical fantasy novels and tie-in fiction for *Pathfinder Tales*, *Iron Kingdoms*, *Shadowrun*, *Arkham Horror*, *Legendary Planets* and *Traveller*. His most recent work is in the Dragons of Boston urban fantasy series, the new nautical fantasy series Blood Sea Tales, and in the new Five-Fold Universe novel, *Pacifica*.

jaxbooks.com
twitter.com/chrisajackson1

Arkham Horror™

Riveting pulp adventure as unknowable
horrors threaten to tear our reality apart.

Something monstrous has risen from the depths beneath
Arkham, Miskatonic University is plagued with missing
students and maddening litanies, and a charismatic
surrealist's art opens doorways to unspeakable places.

A movie director captures unnameable horrors while
making his masterpiece, and an international thief
stumbles onto a necrophagic conspiracy.

ARKHAM HORROR™

Fresh eldritch terrors coming soon...

Deep in the Amazon jungle, the boundaries between intrepid adventurers, dreamers, and deranged fanatics blur inside a web of terror.

A daring actress and a barnstorming pilot team up to investigate a disappearance, but must instead save the world from supernatural disaster.

WORLD EXPANDING FICTION
Do you have them all?

ARKHAM HORROR
- ☐ *Wrath of N'kai* by Josh Reynolds
- ☐ *The Last Ritual* by S A Sidor
- ☐ *Mask of Silver* by Rosemary Jones
- ☐ *Litany of Dreams* by Ari Marmell
- ☐ *The Devourer Below* edited by
  Charlotte Llewelyn-Wells
- ☑ *Dark Origins, The Collected Novellas Vol 1*
- ☐ *Cult of the Spider Queen* by S A Sidor
  (coming soon)

DESCENT
- ☐ *The Doom of Fallowhearth* by Robbie
  MacNiven
- ☐ *The Shield of Daqan* by David Guymer
- ☐ *The Gates of Thelgrim* by Robbie MacNiven

KEYFORGE
- ☐ *Tales from the Crucible* edited by
  Charlotte Llewelyn-Wells
- ☐ *The Qubit Zirconium* by M Darusha Wehm

LEGEND OF THE FIVE RINGS
- ☐ *Curse of Honor* by David Annandale
- ☐ *Poison River* by Josh Reynolds
- ☐ *The Night Parade of 100 Demons*
  by Marie Brennan
- ☐ *Death's Kiss* by Josh Reynolds
- ☐ *The Great Clans of Rokugan, The Collected
  Novellas Vol 1 (coming soon)*

PANDEMIC
- ☐ *Patient Zero* by Amanda Bridgeman

TWILIGHT IMPERIUM
- ☐ *The Fractured Void* by Tim Pratt
- ☐ *The Necropolis Empire* by Tim Pratt

ZOMBICIDE
- ☐ *Last Resort* by Josh Reynolds

**EXPLORE OUR WORLD
EXPANDING FICTION**

ACONYTE

ACONYTEBOOKS.COM
@ACONYTEBOOKS
ACONYTEBOOKS.COM/NEWSLETTER